D1527060

II

The Sphere of the Winds

By

Rachel Neumeier

Copyright © 2021 Rachel Neumeier
Cover art and layout © Ivan Zanchetta &
Bookcoversart.com
All rights reserved.

DEDICATION

To every reader who told me they loved The Floating Islands and wished there were a sequel. Thank you all, and I hope you enjoy this story.

CONTENTS

ACKNOWLEDGMENTS

As always, I owe a debt to my proofreaders. Allan Shampine, Hanneke Nieuwenhuijzen, and particularly my mother, Dolores Neumeier, did a great job catching many, many typos. Thank you all!

1

Araenè opened a door at random and glanced through it at the bare room thus revealed, maybe fifteen paces or so across, unfurnished except for a single chair and gauzy draperies blowing in the warm breeze. The room's windows were narrow and numerous, so there was a lot of gauze. *Pink* gauze. The chair, carved with ornate swirls and ripples, had been painted pale violet. Its cushions were a deeper purple. The walls were a sky blue. The combination of colors in the small space was a little ... well, it was a little ...

Ceirfei, peering with interest over Araenè's shoulder, murmured, "Sugar cakes."

Araenè had to laugh. That was exactly right. The room was exactly like a plate of cakes rolled in pastel sugars, the sort given out to children too young to have any subtlety. She shut the door, gently, and looked up and down the wide white marble stairway upon which they'd found themselves. "This wasn't exactly what I had in mind," she admitted, glancing sideways at her companion, "when I said I'd show you the hidden school."

"Well, we certainly are seeing some new parts of it," Ceirfei said, in a very serious tone that was like a smile.

He wasn't nervous. He didn't mind being lost. Araenè was relieved. If Ceirfei wasn't nervous, she didn't have to be, either. Embarrassed at her inability to find her way to places she knew, maybe. But not nervous.

She opened the door again. The room was still filled with pink gauze and blue-painted walls and that ridiculous violet chair.

"Up?" asked Ceirfei. "Or down?"

They'd already explored a series of chilly, windowless rooms far underground: one with long shelves stacked with delicate porcelain plates and platters and bowls, far fancier than the ones anybody actually used; and one with all sorts of fancy scented candles shaped like animals and birds and fish and flowers; and one with, prosaically, about a hundred sacks of rice and bundles of noodles. Araenè had hoped that last one would lead them back to the familiar kitchens, but instead they'd found themselves entering a long, hot gallery with dozens of high windows that let in the rich afternoon light and the sharp briny scent of the sea. Finally they had come out of that gallery upon this wide spiral stairway. The gallery seemed to have let them out right in the middle of the stairway, because from this landing, it coiled endlessly up and down a perfectly smooth shaft of white marble, with nothing visible above or below but more loops of wide, shallow stairs and the occasional landing. Looking down made Araenè dizzy and looking up made her tired, but the pastel-sugar room didn't seem to hold much promise. And going back along the gallery would be boring.

Araenè had meant to show Ceirfei some of her favorite places within the hidden school: not just the kitchens, but also the aviary where the little birds flitted among potted trees and flowers, and the room of glass, and the hall of spheres and mirrors. But today she couldn't seem to find any door that would cooperate at all. Not even the 'friendly door', Akhan Bhotounn, which was nearly always accommodating. Araenè might have called out to Master Tnegun for help, but if she did that, she would have to admit, not only to Ceirfei but also to her master, that she couldn't find her own way back to familiar places. She didn't want to do that. She was already slow to learn things the other apprentices all seemed to absorb as naturally as bread absorbs melted butter.

Besides, she wasn't really nervous, yet. And Ceirfei didn't seem impatient. That made sense, actually. He was never very eager to return to his family's home, though the Feneirè apartment in the palace was beautiful and filled with every luxury, with servants to do all the work and bring you things.

Araenè never commented on the way Ceirfei preferred to visit her at the hidden school rather than ask her to come to the palace. She knew *all about* needing to get away from your home and family, so you could be yourself instead of the person everybody else wanted you to be. And no one worried much about chaperones or propriety, so long as they stayed in the hidden school—Master Tnegun and the other mages being presumably capable of keeping track of one young apprentice and her visitor. Even if her visitor was a Feneirè and the son of Calaspara Naterensei herself.

Araenè glanced at Ceirfei again. He still had that particularly sober expression that meant he was actually thoroughly amused. If he wasn't worried about his parents' fretting, she didn't see why *she* should be. Really, Ceirfei was lucky in his parents. Mostly. In some ways. Anyway, he was lucky just to have a home and a family to go back to. Not that she would ever say so.

Besides, if it got too late, so that Ceirfei's mother might miss him or Master Tnegun might miss her, or if they stumbled across anything frightening, she could call out *then*.

"Up," she decided, because she knew Ceirfei would prefer it. He was a kajurai, and kajuraihi always preferred heights to any kind of secret subterranean chambers. "Up would be better?"

Ceirfei looked at her, knowing exactly what she was thinking. The corners of his eyes crinkled. "Definitely up," he said gravely.

Araenè couldn't suppress a laugh. Embarrassing to be lost? Maybe; but if she had to be lost and wandering through unknown parts of the mage's hidden school, well, there was surely no one better to be lost with than Ceirfei. "Definitely up!" she agreed, and ran ahead of him, taking the shallow steps two at a time.

Steps and steps, white marble underfoot and white marble walls, with a cool breeze blowing down from above.

At first, the spiral stair didn't seem to lead anywhere at all. There were no landings for the first four or five turns of the stairway. Araenè dropped back to a more sedate pace, breathless and starting to feel the strain in her calves. She might have suggested they go down, but no, she'd selflessly offered to go up ... Ceirfei caught up to her, gave her an amused sidelong look, and took her hand in his.

He wouldn't have done that if there had been anybody else nearby. Araenè, suddenly breathless for a reason that had nothing to do with running up stairs, decided that getting lost had actually been a clever idea. Then she wondered whether Ceirfei thought she'd gotten them lost on purpose. Then she wondered whether maybe she *had* gotten them lost on purpose, without even realizing it.

Surely not. Anyway, too much thinking was definitely not good. She pointed ahead, to the upward curve before them. "There's another door!" She wasn't sure whether she was relieved to see it, or not. She wanted to get them back to the familiar parts of the school ... or she mostly wanted that.

"That's fancy," Ceirfei said, looking the door up and down. "Shall I open it? Or do you want to?" He didn't sound confused or uncertain or breathless. He just sounded interested in finding out what lay on the other side of that door. But he didn't let go of her hand, either.

"I'd better ..." You never knew what you might find, opening doors in the hidden school. Araenè touched the latch carefully. It was made of crystal, to match the door, which was all ebony and crystal and very fancy indeed. The kind of door that looked as though it really should open to something more interesting than sacks of rice. But the latch didn't feel hot or cold, or shower her fingers with sparks, or do anything but click down.

Araenè opened the door carefully, ready to slam it again if she found a basilisk or a coiled serpent or a roaring fire surging toward her or anything else alarming.

But the room on the other side didn't match the fancy door at all. It was a tiny square room, which contained nothing but layers of dust and a single unstrung harp resting on a stool in the middle of the floor. Dust had poofed up as the door skimmed across the floor, and now settled again slowly. The air smelled of age and solitude, and somehow of darkness and silence.

"Hmm," murmured Ceirfei, peering over Araenè's shoulder.

The harp, framed in the bar of light that fell in through the open door, was extremely elegant, carved of some dark red wood with ebony inlay. There was no dust on the harp at all. Araenè suspected that it might actually be strung with the winds, or with musical notes that played without strings, or maybe with the voices of the forgotten dead. It looked like that sort of harp, somehow.

She closed the door again and said out loud, in her firmest tone, but without a great deal of hope, "You know, the *kitchens* would be *better*." But when she opened the door a second time, she found exactly the same dusty room and exactly the same stool. Only, disconcertingly, this time the stool was occupied not by a mysterious stringless harp, but by a little dragon, perched perfectly still, its silvery-dark wings half open and its fine-boned head turned toward the door, its yellow eyes glittering.

Ceirfei, hearing Araenè's indrawn breath of surprise and alarm, drew her swiftly back and stepped in front of her. Araenè was too startled to protest, but then she blinked and saw that the dragon wasn't real after all. It was made of polished hematite, its glittering eyes of a striated brass-yellow mineral that, after senneri in the hidden school, Araenè identified automatically, even from a distance, as chalcopyrite.

The dragon's long serpentine tail was twined all through the legs of the stool, its body curled upright on the seat. Its wings fell in graceful curves to either side. Its claws and quills and the margins of each of its carved feathers had been painted with gold and sprinkled lightly with powdered pearl, like sugar on an elegant pastry.

"You and dragons!" Ceirfei said. "That's ... it's quite a good carving, isn't it?"

"Too good," Araenè said, not quite shakily. She was *sure* it was just carved hematite, but on the other hand, if this little dragon turned its head, she decided, she wouldn't scream or run away. She would very quietly and sensibly close the door, and very calmly call Master Tnegun. She'd have every justification, if the dragon moved. You were *supposed* to call your master if you got into trouble. There was a rule about that. Along with the one about not speaking to dragons.

On the other hand, it was stupid to be afraid of a statue carved out of hematite, no matter how real it looked. She half wanted to go into the dusty little room and lay a hand on the curve of the dragon's neck, to convince herself and maybe a little bit to show off for Ceirfei. But she hesitated, and Ceirfei reached past her and gently closed the door before she could make up her mind. "Up?" he suggested. "This was worth seeing, but it's not ... I mean, this stairway must be *leading* somewhere, right?"

"In this school, who knows?" But Araenè was willing enough to turn her back on the ebony door and run up the steps, one long curving spiral turn and then another. She was no longer tired or stiff. She could hear Ceirfei behind her, matching her steps.

There were other doors set into the stairway, but as though ruled by some unspoken mutual agreement, Araenè and Ceirfei passed each one by without opening it. The stairway spiraled endlessly upward, but it couldn't *actually* be endless, and Araenè could tell that Ceirfei was as determined as she to find that end.

At last, unexpectedly, they turned around one final curve. The ceiling arched overhead, a low, flat dome of white marble, and below that, the stairway ended abruptly. There was a door there on the final landing, an ornate door of glass panels framed by silver scrollwork. The door must have once been really beautiful, though now the glass was pitted with age and the silver tarnished.

Araenè found she liked this door and at the same time felt sorry for it. It seemed a shame everybody had neglected a beautiful door like this one. At the same time, thinking of stringless harps and carved dragons, she was a little afraid to open it. Nevertheless, she put out a hand to its knob. This was a lacy confection of silver filigree that looked too fragile to bear even a gentle touch, but it felt strong and cold under her fingers. "Ready?" she asked, but turned it without waiting for an answer.

The door swung open easily and soundlessly, to show one of those common mysteries of the hidden school: though they had gone up and up and up, they nevertheless found, stretching out before them, a huge and brilliantly lit chamber that had been carved out of stone so far underground that the carvers had come right out the underside of the Island. There was no floor, exactly. Wide tiles of red stone, not spaced evenly but arranged in a complicated pattern that crossed and re-crossed itself, each floated right out in the open air. There was plenty of space between the tiles for light and a warm sea breeze to come up into the chamber. Araenè could glimpse the sea far below, with ripples of white-edged foam making lacework of its azure surface. Gulls flew, crying plaintively, through the empty air below the floating tiles of the floor.

Despite the height, the sense of light and warmth and space was so welcome, and the thought of going back down the long, long stairwell so daunting, that Araenè stepped through the glass door without hesitation, before she even turned to look questioningly at Ceirfei. But of course he loved heights, and followed her without hesitation, looking somehow relaxed and pleased even though he hadn't seemed particularly tense or worried before. "Beautiful," he said, looking around. "All this space! Do you know what this place is? Or what it's for?"

Araenè shook her head, turning to gaze again out over the floating tiles. The tiles were each easily big enough to sit on, even to stretch out on if somebody were bold enough to nap on a stone tile floating hundreds of feet above the sea.

Araenè doubted she would ever be that bold, though now that they'd stopped, she was tired. And her feet hurt. She wanted a nice comfortable couch and a steaming cup of tea with honey. She thought again of calling for Master Tnegun.

But Ceirfei looked happy. If she called her master, she'd be admitting the day was over and Ceirfei would have to go home. She could see he didn't want to. And she could see from the light coming up between the tiles that it wasn't really late. Not *really* late. Not yet.

If this had been a new tangle of Third City alleyways she'd just found—if she'd been dressed as a boy and free to explore just as she liked—Araenè wouldn't have hesitated. It was stupid to feel adventurous and daring only when she was pretending to be a boy. She tried to feel adventurous and daring right at this moment, but couldn't quite manage that.

It was a long way across this … place, but she was almost sure she could see another door on the other side. At least one. She was sure that was the door they really needed, because arranging things that way would be *just* like the hidden school. She tried to see if there was a way they might follow the complicated interlocking pattern of the tiles all the way over to the other side of the chamber. One line of tiles led out into the chamber from where they were standing, then another turned and led away to the right, and then the pathway branched, but she thought it led farther toward the opposite side from there. She wasn't sure. The tiles practically formed a maze … and with that thought, she realized at last where she was. "It's the labyrinth!" she exclaimed. The labyrinth had been carved into the deepest level of the hidden school, where she had never come. When the other apprentices had told her about the labyrinth, she'd envisioned a series of narrow passageways buried in cold stone. But, of course, the *deepest* levels of any Floating Island really were likely to come out just like this: with a fine view of the open sea.

"A labyrinth?" said Ceirfei, interested and pleased. "Aren't you supposed to find your way to the center of any labyrinth? That must be the center, way out there: that set of eight or so tiles, all together in a square. Where that plinth is standing, do you see, with that glittering thing on it? What do you suppose that is?"

Almost despite herself, Araenè was starting to share his enthusiasm. The tiles were wide enough. A child could walk safely along them. Certainly any Island child could. She'd never been afraid of floating bridges in her life, and wasn't this exactly the same? "Aren't you supposed to turn right on the way into a labyrinth, and left on the way out?"

"We can try it and see." Ceirfei stepped out onto the first tile in the nearest row and held out his hand in invitation for Araenè to join him. She didn't hesitate. Even if those tiles had been narrow and widely spaced, she knew he would never let her fall.

"This isn't working at *all*," Araenè said, exasperated, after they'd turned right eleven times in a row. They were farther from the center than ever, way out along one side of the labyrinth, faced with two obvious dead ends and a third path that would only take them back toward the wall where they'd come in. She turned in a full circle, trying to visualize the maze from above. "If you had your wings ..."

"That would be cheating." Ceirfei sounded altogether too cheerful.

He was enjoying himself. Probably he very seldom had a chance to get lost in a magical floating labyrinth. Probably his mother wouldn't approve. Araenè gave him a jaundiced look. "I'd be happy to cheat! Anyway, cheating is just a way of winning when nobody's looking."

"That's one perspective, certainly."

Araenè ignored his amused tone. She turned slowly in a circle once more, examining the rows of tiles. Something about the pattern of tiles looked wrong. She frowned, concentrating. They'd started over *there*, and come *that* way, and turned right, so they'd gone *that* way ... only that was wrong, because they'd come immediately to a left turn, which

9

of course they'd skipped, and after that to a three-way intersection, and of course they'd turned right, but she could see perfectly plainly that if they'd turned right there, they'd have immediately come to a dead end. Which they hadn't.

"They've *moved!*" she said, outraged. "The tiles have been rearranging themselves when we aren't looking! Talk about *cheating!*"

"Are you sure?"

"Yes!" Araenè stabbed a finger at the intersection that gave it away. "That's all wrong! We came that way, but it wasn't like that! Those tiles are all different. And look, those over there, see that spiral that goes off in that squiggle? That wasn't there before, either!"

Ceirfei put a hand on her shoulder, a calm-down gesture that at the moment Araenè found infuriating. She thought she had a perfect right to be angry at this stupid labyrinth, where it looked like you could win but then tiles moved so you would lose. Araenè stepped away from Ceirfei and called, in a good, clear voice, "Master! Master Tnegun! Help! I'm lost!"

Then she waited. Ceirfei took her hand again. This time Araenè didn't move away. Far below, the gulls cried. The wind had died, so the sea lay flat and featureless. The lowering sun gilded the water and sent light reflecting up past the tiles to strike glittering notes from tiny crystals in the stone of the ceiling and walls.

Nothing else happened. Master Tnegun did not come, and Araenè and Ceirfei remained exactly where they were, standing way out in the labyrinth, with nothing but air and ocean underneath their feet, and the sun sinking toward evening. Araenè tried to imagine finding the way through this labyrinth in the dark. Then she tried not to imagine it.

"Master!" she called again. Her voice scaled up, embarrassingly childish, and she bit the word off. She couldn't believe he hadn't answered. The masters were *supposed* to help if you got into trouble. That was the *rule*. She shouted one more time, "Master Tnegun!"

But there was still no answer, and the sun was sinking into the western sea, the water below turning slowly from gold to blue and then to azure before shading off into pewter-gray. The white gulls were gone. A black one flew past beneath, its voice sharper and somehow colder than the voices of the ordinary gulls.

Araenè knew they should sit down exactly where they were and wait for rescue. No one would notice if *she* missed supper, they would only think she'd decided to eat in the kitchens or in her room. Master Tnegun would only guess something was wrong when she missed their tutorial in the morning. But very soon, someone would miss Ceirfei. He was always supposed to be somewhere, doing proper things, being a good example. He was always representing his family. It was very tiresome for him, especially since he just wanted to be a kajurai, but it did mean someone would miss him *soon*. His mother would make inquiries, and then Master Tnegun or one of the other masters would come find them. It wouldn't be long.

And then everybody would know she'd gotten lost in the hidden school and hadn't been able to find her way back. That she'd failed to summon any useful door. That she'd been too stupid and stubborn to call for help—or worse, they'd all find out she hadn't even been able to make her own master hear her when she called.

She wanted to stamp her foot. If she'd been by herself, she would have stamped and screamed and thrown things, if she'd had anything to throw. But Ceirfei was watching her, a humorous quirk to his eyebrows, not really worried even yet. "Better to get out of this ourselves," he observed. "How can we do that? If I had wings, I could fly up and look at the labyrinth from above. What can we do instead?"

Being expected to think of something clever somehow made it easier to stay calm. Nodding, Araenè tried to think of something clever. Ceirfei was right: if they could see the tiles from above, the way a bird or kajurai might, they should be able to run through the labyrinth really fast before the tiles could move around again. They could be to the center and out again and right through the far door before the light failed. If they could only see the right path—she stopped, blinking. "Vision," she said out loud. "Flying high isn't the only way to see things from above, you know!"

"And you have a gift for vision, don't you?" Ceirfei agreed encouragingly. "But don't you need a glass sphere?"

"I'll get one." Araenè knelt down on the red stone of the tile, concentrating. She'd summoned things before: chalk, a feather, a book ... on one memorable occasion, a glazed pot full of custard. Cesei, youngest of the apprentices, had deserved it, too. Even Master Kopapei had agreed with that, although he'd still forbidden her to have any sweets for a whole senneri, since she thought so little of them she dumped them on other students. She still blushed to remember his tone.

But a custard-filled pot was certainly at least as heavy as ... she closed her eyes, put out her hands, and caught a glass sphere as large as both her fists. It fell right into her hands, but not only was it heavier than she'd expected, it felt as though it had fallen from a considerable height. She snatched after it with stinging fingers, but her wild grab only sent it flying. She said, vehemently, a word girls weren't supposed to know, much less say out loud.

Araenè thought the sphere would come down on the tile and shatter, but it didn't break after all, only struck the red stone with a ringing sound, and rolled. She stared, horrified, knowing it was going to roll right off the edge of the tile and fall. She wasn't at all sure where to find another sphere of glass already primed with the proper spells for vision—she didn't want to use obsidian, not with night coming—

Ceirfei flung himself after the sphere, catching it right at the edge of the tile. For one appalling moment, Araenè thought he might skid right off the edge and fall, kajurai or not, but he caught himself in the sharp breeze that suddenly swept up and around the tile, and wound up kneeling at the very edge of the tile, holding the sphere smugly up for her to see, apparently completely oblivious of the empty air waiting for a misstep.

Araenè gritted her teeth and didn't say anything at all. She thought that after all this, she was really *due* a cup of steaming chocolate to sooth her nerves, and maybe a buttery pastry filled with toasted nuts and honey. But after one moment to sit and feel sorry for herself, she held up her hands, mutely, for Ceirfei to give her the sphere. He sat down to watch, even after all this looking perfectly relaxed and comfortable, as she prepared to release the spell for vision it held. She held up the sphere in both hands and stared down into the smooth glass, cool and heavy and transparent as water.

An affinity for vision. That was what Master Tnegun said she had. An affinity for doors and fire and vision. Spells for vision were always best stored in glass or crystal or obsidian. Only crystal took a lot of work because it was so heavy it sort of pushed vision off sideways, so it was hard to see what you wanted to see. And obsidian tended to give you dark visions, especially at night. So glass was the best for straightforward scrying. Anybody could work with glass. This sphere held plenty of magic. It tingled with ginger and pepper. The ginger was sweet and hot and very prominent, so Araenè knew that the sphere held all kinds of spells for vision. The pepper might be a spell for light—a sharp burst of brilliant light, she thought; not very useful when she would really prefer a soft and steady glow that would last for a while.

She released only the very easiest and most obvious spell, the one closest to the surface: the one for plain, ordinary vision. Because she knew exactly what she wanted to see, she could immediately make sense of what the sphere showed her. What it showed her was the labyrinth, of course: from above, the way a kajurai might see it. She could see rows of tiles going left and right, intersecting and separating, forming square-cornered spirals and crooked paths that started off one way and then went a completely different direction. The labyrinth looked even bigger and more complicated from above than it did when you stared out across it from the side. She could see that the center was actually sixteen tiles, twice as big as Ceirfei had guessed, and that the plinth rising up from its exact middle was taller than she was and square-sided, though she still couldn't see the object on the plinth well enough to know anything about it except that it glittered.

She could see herself, too, and Ceirfei, which was an odd feeling. They looked surprisingly small in the middle of the complicated geometry of pathways.

And she could see how, behind them, a scattering of tiles suddenly dropped away sideways and down, slid underneath other tiles, and rose again, clicking that whole section of the maze into a different pattern. She glowered into the sphere. "That's not *fair!*"

Ceirfei laughed, and after a moment Araenè smiled, too, though unwillingly. "We'll cheat right back," she said. "It moves: fine! Let it! Looking down from above, we'll *still* see which way to go. Look, we should go that way, don't you think? And then the first left, and then over here, we should go this way." She traced the path she saw with the tip of her finger, looking up to see if Ceirfei agreed.

"We'd better hurry," he said mildly, rose, and offered her his hand.

Araenè took his hand and let him lift her to her feet. He was right about needing to hurry. A moment ago, it had still been light. But now, though a grayed-lavender glow still rose past the floating tiles, reflected from the distant sea, each tile looked dusky red-violet at the edges and nearly black at the center. Araenè could still see the edges perfectly well, but it was abundantly clear that this would change as the light failed.

"They'll be missing you soon ..."

Ceirfei shrugged. "I won't—" he began, and stopped.

Won't let them blame you, he'd meant to say. Araenè knew he'd pretend exploring the labyrinth had been all his idea and not an accident. He wouldn't say a word about her getting them lost. His mother would think Ceirfei—would think she—everyone would think the two of them—Araenè clenched her teeth. Without a word, she shut her eyes and released the light trapped in the sphere she held.

A sharp burst of brilliant light, she had thought. She had been right. Her eyes watered with the intensity of light, even though they were closed, and she heard Ceirfei swear, which ordinarily he didn't. The light burned hot, too: not fire-hot, but with a forceful warmth she suspected would leave her with tender skin on her face and hands and arms. Slitting her eyes open, she shielded her face with her hand. The light burned high up under the rough-carved stone of the ceiling, hard and white and far too bright to look at directly, casting a harsh radiance across the whole of the labyrinth.

"A *warning*, next time!" said Ceirfei, blinking and rubbing his eyes. "Now I can hardly see!"

"Sorry," Araenè said, embarrassed because of course she should have warned him, annoyed because she was embarrassed. She took a step forward. Then another. Then she glanced down at the miniature maze she held in her hands, contained in the glass sphere. The right path was fairly easy to make out. She could see how this whole corner of the maze linked into the part nearer the center. She could find her way, if she was patient and didn't try to rush forward too quickly. She took Ceirfei's hand and led him forward, with the sphere held up in her other hand so she could look into it as she went.

Turn and turn and turn. She had the idea that there *was* a pattern to it, but she couldn't quite recognize what it was. Left and then left again while the light faded, and then right, three times; and then there was a short right that seemed to be a dead end, only it really bent around to the left, and then the light hovering above them began to flicker like a candle blowing in a breeze just as the sound of their hurrying footsteps took on a different, duller sound and they came at last out from the complicated pathways into the center of the labyrinth.

The hard white light had become a dim yellow in just these few moments. Yet even though she knew they dared not linger, Araenè couldn't resist a glance up at the plinth as they passed it. She didn't mean to stop. But she hesitated, and Ceirfei dragged her to a full stop, and they both stood for a long moment, staring.

On the plinth was a crystalline sculpture in the shape of a dragon, stylized but clearly recognizable. Yes, there was the fine head, and that glittering fall of delicate needles represented the quills, and that curved bit, shimmering in the light, was undoubtedly a half-opened wing. Supported by the dragon's claws and the tip of its coiled tail was a small sphere that, at first glance, closely resembled the one she held in her hand.

"*Another* dragon!" Ceirfei sounded amused and pleased. "Araenè, is there any dragon in the hidden school you *haven't* found? And this one's a proper dragon, isn't it, a dragon of sky and wind. Look, you can see right through it. I wonder who sculpted this? This is no casual afternoon's work: I've never seen anything to match it even in the palace."

Araenè stretched up on her toes to study the dragon's sphere. It might have been glass, or perhaps quartz, or barite. It didn't seem as heavy as quartz, and barite was usually striated. But she didn't think it was glass, either. It looked fragile as a soap bubble. It was so perfectly flawless that it would have been invisible if the fading yellow light had not glimmered off it.

She somehow had the idea this sphere might be hollow, but it couldn't be, because spheres made to hold spellwork never were and she could tell immediately that this sphere was stuffed full of spells. It was practically a *confection* of spells, tingling with cardamom and palm sugar and rosewater and vanilla and jasmine and a tiny bit of pepper, everything perfectly balanced. Only behind all the bright sweetness something else glittered, something she didn't recognize, something fierce and wild, with an unusual bitter edge.

It wasn't perilla, although, like perilla, it was minty and musky. It definitely wasn't anise, though it was also like anise. She almost thought she didn't like it, though she wasn't sure. She thought perhaps the whole balance of the sphere might have been thrown off somehow, if that difficult flavor hadn't been behind the rest. She reached up to touch the sphere, curious and fascinated, and the dimming light of the spell ebbed suddenly and then failed completely.

Araenè's legs folded under her and she sat down where she stood. She didn't want to think of what it would have been like if they had been racing through the other side of the labyrinth and then the light had suddenly flickered out like that. She swallowed hard.

"A little too much like being in a play," Ceirfei commented above her. "A farce, I imagine, rather than a tragedy ... are you all right? Can you make more light?" He must have crouched down by her, because his hand pressed hers in the dark.

"I can't. That was the only spell for light in this sphere," Araenè said stiffly. "They'll have missed you by now, I expect." She ought to apologize for that, too. She was sure Ceirfei's mother would never permit him to visit the hidden school again. If he even wanted to, after this.

"I might have decided to have supper with Master Kopapei and the other mages." Ceirfei said, wry and resigned. "Not with you, of course. That would be inappropriate."

He sounded so prim that Araenè had to laugh. She opened her eyes on the darkness of the labyrinth. It was not utterly, completely dark, which was some comfort. A little, a very little light glimmered faintly up between the floating tiles, starlight reflected off the distant sea, but that wasn't the only source of light. After a moment, she tipped her head back to gaze up through the shadows toward the top of the plinth.

The fragile sphere glimmered with light. This was nothing like the harsh brilliance of the light she had released from her ordinary sphere. This was like moonlight: soft and silvery, cool against the face, casting velvety shadows across the dark tiles. The glimmer wasn't nearly as bright as even the quarter moon, but it was *light* and it was right there.

Araenè got to her feet, reached up, and touched the sphere very gently indeed with the tip of one finger. It didn't pop like a soap bubble. It felt cool and smooth and somehow alive. Cardamom and pepper tingled across her fingers and tickled her hand and the back of her throat. The fragrance of roses seemed to fill the whole labyrinth. The other flavor behind the rest seemed gone, now. Or, no. She could tell that flavor was still there, musky perilla-and-anise. But whatever magic that was had sort of turned sideways and out of sight, tucking itself away far behind the other spells. She had no idea what it might be.

But she knew how to delicately tickle the pepper until the soft glow increased and intensified: bright as a quarter moon and then a half and then a full moon, until her shadow and the shadow of the plinth lay out black and sharp-edged behind her. Holding her breath, she lifted the fragile sphere, as carefully as she could, from its resting place on the plinth and held it in the palm of her hand. It seemed almost as weightless as air, as a feather. It truly didn't seem like glass, but she couldn't imagine what else it might have been made of. Solidified moonlight? She could almost believe it.

"Clever," Ceirfei said. "Beautiful. I knew you'd think of something."

He sounded as though he meant it, though Araenè knew she didn't deserve any compliments. She said absently, "I didn't put it in there. I mean, it was already there. There's a lot of spellwork in this." Vision, she thought. Vision, or something like vision, and something else like luck, all wrapped around with something else a lot less familiar.

She held the dragon sphere up and gazed into it, finding that not only could she bring a vision of the labyrinth into it, but also that the sphere's own pale light bent through the vision and somehow tangled around some of the pathways at a sharper angle than around others. She could see at once which path was the right one. She could, for the first time, see *exactly* what turnings to take to get out of the labyrinth. And she could glimpse, beyond the labyrinth, the waiting doors, three of them, all the same, only the light bent around just one of those, too.

One of the spells hidden inside this sphere must be a spell of finding your way. She could hardly believe she could be so fortunate. Although, after this whole wretched afternoon and evening, the hidden school *owed* her a little good fortune.

But was it really all right to just take this special sphere out of the labyrinth? Nobody had ever said *anything* about a sphere in the labyrinth. She was a little afraid she would break it, though of course it couldn't actually be anything like as fragile as it looked or it couldn't hold all those spells. Anyway, if Master Tnegun hadn't wanted her using any random spheres she happened to find, he might have come to find her when she called him. Besides, if the masters wanted this sphere on that plinth, they could perfectly well put it back.

But it seemed somehow wrong to leave the stand on top of the plinth just empty. Araenè impulsively picked up the ordinary glass sphere she'd summoned and put it carefully in the crystal-dragon stand. She stepped back and looked at it. It looked very solid and coarse after the other sphere, but not actually wrong. It looked better than an empty stand. She thought it would be all right, for a few minutes or a few hours or overnight. "All right," she said. "All right." She glanced at Ceirfei. "Can you see? Is this all right?"

"It's perfect."

Araenè returned his smile. Then, holding her new sphere in both her hands and putting her feet down carefully, she led him from the center of the labyrinth and set her foot on the first step that would take them both through the sharp-angled and changeable pathways to the far side of the labyrinth.

2

Trei flew above layers of air as lucent as crystal. He could see a cool, dense wind arriving from the north, shoving the warm southern air upward. He could see the swift rushing wind that skirled out as the winds mingled, carrying streamers of cloud that formed and coiled and stretched out and dissolved again. He flew above all that activity, so high that the air seemed as still and pure as glass and he barely needed to shift a feather to hold his position. He flew so high even Milendri looked small. The white towers of Canpra glinted like tiny chips of white marble at the eastern edge of the Island, and the pastures stretched away from the city in a featureless blur of green. A scattering of other Floating Islands were just visible in the distance, Kotipa nearest, the rest half lost against the unbroken sapphire haze of the endless sea.

Trei had never before flown so high. That had been the assignment: to climb above all the winds that touched the earth. All the novices had immediately wagered hours of tedious featherwork on who could fly highest. Trei thought he might have won, but it was hard to be sure. Away to the east he could make out the dark fleck of another novice suspended in the crystalline sky, but it was impossible to tell which of them was higher.

That speck was probably Genrai, but it might be Kojran. Kojran was sometimes annoyingly vain, but Trei had to admit that none of the other boys was as good at bending the winds as he was. Kojran might have coaxed a dense lower wind to follow him all the way up the column of the sky to support his climb. But Genrai was the strongest flier, and he wasn't bad with windworking either. Trei wouldn't mind losing the wager to Genrai, but if Kojran won, Tokabii would be jealous– he always ran after Kojran and tried to beat him, like a little brother after an elder. And Rekei would be angry if either of the younger Third City boys won. Rekei always wanted the Second City boys to do best at everything, and that meant him or Trei. It would be all right if Genrai won because he was so much older, but Trei wasn't sure his rival was Genrai.

If Ceirfei had been allowed to fly today, *he* would have won. Ceirfei was always the best at everything. Nobody would mind Ceirfei winning. But Ceirfei's family wouldn't let him try anything that seemed dangerous. Obviously falling from the very vaults of the heavens was no more deadly than simply falling into the sea off the balcony of a First City tower, but people who couldn't fly never thought of that. It was too bad. Everything was better when Ceirfei was allowed to join the rest of them. And every time his family refused, everyone had to wonder whether they were going to ground him permanently. Trei didn't like to think about it.

Probably that other novice was Genrai. Trei tilted his wings a minute degree, spreading the feathers of his left wingtip, sliding through the sky toward the other boy. He was beginning to think that other novice *was* above him. If he was, and if it was Genrai, Trei though he would just concede. He could go down, back to the novitiate. He could strip off his wings and have a hot bath and something hot to drink, everyday comforts after the grandeur of the heights. His wrists and arms were tired and his back ached all down his spine. And the other novice was close, now. Almost close enough … yes. It *was* Genrai. Trei recognized the older boy's angular, bony build, so different from stocky Rekei or little Tokabii.

Then he looked again, staring through the layered winds with his crystalline kajurai eyes, and saw he had been wrong after all. The other novice was not Genrai at all. It was Nescana.

Nescana, Genrai's sister, was the very first girl novice ever. She was fifteen—three months older than Trei. She'd been supposed to get married. Genrai had actually put off his own audition for *years* so she would be old enough to get married. But it turned out she hadn't actually wanted to get married at all. She'd put it off and put it off and then the kajuraihi had announced the special audition for girls, so she hadn't had to after all. There was a lesson in that, though not the kind adults wanted you to notice.

Nescana said she'd walked all the way from Third City the day before the special audition and then sat outside all night waiting. Trei understood that perfectly, but then he wasn't from the Islands. Kojran and Rekei were offended by the whole idea of girl novices and annoyed to have a whole third of the novice hall blocked off for a *girl*—not that they'd say so where Genrai could hear, of course. Trei thought that was ridiculous. Obviously anybody, girl or not, might be sky-mad, so why not let girls audition if they wanted to?

Master Anerii had been the one to make the kajuraihi audition girls, after Trei had pointed out how ridiculous it was to refuse girls the chance. "If the dragons approved a half-blood Tolounnese boy, I expect they'll approve full-blooded Islander girls," he'd pointed out. "Why not? Everyone says we need more novices. Well, then, don't you think the dragons would know better than you whether girls would make good kajuraihi?"

Master Anerii had been gruff and sarcastic and impatient, but then he had argued Wingmaster Taimenai into allowing the special audition after all. Nescana hadn't been the only girl to audition. There had been three. But one out of three wasn't bad. Usually only about one out of five boys succeeded.

"The only girl novice, and she *would* have to be my own sister!" Genrai had complained. "What use is that? I ask you!" But he had been proud when his sister had woken up after her audition with crystalline eyes that could see the wind. Trei had been surprised to find himself jealous of Genrai because *his* sister was a kajurai novice—because *his* sister was here. Alive. Obviously it only made sense to let girls be novices, but he had discovered he hated even looking at Nescana at first, because she made him think of Marrè.

But of course that wasn't fair. Nescana was nothing like Marrè. Nothing at all. So he had made himself be nice. He would have wanted the boys to be nice to his sister, if it had been Marrè.

And Nescana did work very hard to catch up with the boys who had auditioned at the beginning of the summer.

That was the problem. Because Nescana was not supposed to be in the sky today. That was partly because she wasn't supposed to try the advanced exercises yet, but mostly because she was grounded. Nescana wasn't always good at following rules, at least not the ones that kept her from flying, and she *really* wanted to catch up to the boys, so she'd slipped out six nights in a row to practice. Everybody did it, but not everybody made it *six nights* before they got caught. Nescana had been grounded for a whole senneri.

But here she was anyway. She was even a little higher than Trei. He could see the warmer air she'd coaxed to rise with her. She had a real gift for pulling the winds, but he wondered whether she really understood how long and exhausting the flight down would be. She wouldn't know the tricks for resting on the wing. She might be in a *lot* of trouble, and not know it yet. Trei arched his wings just a little, turning in a slow, climbing spiral to catch Nescana's column of warmer air. She wasn't stupid. Probably he could get her to listen to him.

And besides, he wanted to get above her because it wouldn't be fair at all if she won the exercise when she hadn't even been supposed to fly today at all.

She'd seen him, though, and was laboring to climb. Trei was so close now he could see the strain in her tight wrists and the way she caught short, gasping breaths of the thin air.

Nescana really looked a *lot* like her brother. She and Genrai weren't twins, she was three years the younger, but they looked almost like they might be twins. Even though she was a girl, Nescana was actually a little taller than Trei was, which wasn't fair. That was probably another reason she'd gotten so high: she was really tall and strong for a girl. Where Genrai was thin, Nescana was gawky, all knees and elbows, with hands that looked too big for her narrow wrists. She was much too bony to be pretty. Besides, her eyes were too wide-set, her nose too large, her mouth too wide, her chin too strong. Trei thought she would have made a far more convincing boy than his cousin Araenè had ever managed. Not that he would ever have said so to either girl.

But she wasn't clumsy in the air. For a girl who'd just started flying, she was really good. Not that Trei was jealous, that would be stupid. But he wasn't going to let her win, either. He gritted his teeth and put a little more arch into his wings.

Nescana ducked her head, looking for him. When she saw how close he was, she swore, her voice thin and breathless.

"You'd better go down!" Trei shouted up at her. His own voice was thin, too, at this height. "You're going to be in so much trouble!"

"Less, if I win!" gasped Nescana. "I can *do* it! I said I could and I *can!*"

"Down will be harder than you think!" Trei called. He closed up the last of the distance between them, his wingtip almost overlapping hers. He held the arch in his wings … and held it … and closed up the spread feathers of his wingtips … and he was above Nescana at last. She swore again, her language pure Third-City. Trei might have laughed at her except he didn't have enough breath to laugh.

"You should let me win!" Nescana called up to him. "That would be polite!"

"I won't! Don't be stupid! Give up, and we can both go down!"

"I won't!"

Trei didn't think it mattered, actually. He thought they were both going to run into the limits of the thin air, and it wouldn't matter how good either of them was at rising in place or coaxing the winds to help them. But he could show her the techniques she would need to get down safely. She'd be all right. He was sure she would be. He let himself slip back down, or he let her catch up, until their wingtips once more nearly overlapped and he could talk to her without shouting. "Let's go down!" he called. "I'll say you got just as high as I did!" It was almost true. If they stayed high, she might make it true. She wasn't going to stop.

"I can get higher!" Nescana's jaw tightened as she tried, but Trei could see how her narrow wrists trembled and how the muscles of her neck and back clenched with effort.

"You *really* don't know how much strength going down will take!" Nescana was so new to flying, she probably thought down was as easy as falling. "You're going to overfly your strength! We need to go down!"

"You wouldn't say that to Genrai!" said Nescana. "We *can* get higher! At least, *I* can!"

"*Genrai* has more sense than to overfly his strength!" Trei snapped. "You overfly your strength and fall into the sea, you'll drown! It's *really hard* to get out of the water once you're in! You haven't learned anything about that yet! You don't want to find it out the hard way!"

Nescana was too stubborn for a girl. Changing tack, he called, "I'll show you a trick! A way to rest in the air!" Then he tucked one wing and turned the other and swung neatly over on his back, instantly taking the strain off his arms. He meant to rest just for a moment, surrounded by thin air and brilliant light. He meant to make sure Nescana tried this trick, too. Then he would talk her into dropping back toward the sea. He would stay close to her all the way down, in case she got herself into trouble. More trouble.

Instead, turning, Trei found himself staring into a twisting, layered complexity of barely-visible shape and movement, terrifyingly huge and close, so close he could have almost put out a hand to touch it.

He couldn't breathe. He spilled air and dropped and barely caught himself. Beside him and now a little above him, Nescana cried out.

The dragon was transparent as ice, glittering with opalescent blues and golds around the edges. Its long body coiled and uncoiled, rippling in several directions at once until the whole sky seemed streaked with half visible movement and Trei was dizzy from trying to focus on it. The dragon's great wings spanned the sky from east to west; the sunlight slanting across the feathers turned the quills and barbs to crystal and spun glass. Its head was as fine-boned and delicate as a bird's, but crystalline teeth longer than a man's hand glinted within its narrow jaw. The deep-set chatoyant eye that gazed at Trei was larger than his whole head.

In that first instant, shock almost made Trei feel he might fall, just as though he was an ordinary earthbound boy. He was breathless with terror and awe and only dimly aware of Nescana, hovering beside him, her wings shivering as she caught the wind, and lost it, and caught it again.

The dragon spoke. Its voice was like the ringing of chimes or the scattering of harp notes, like the voice of the wind itself, yet Trei understood it. It said, "Kajurai. You ride upon the winds, yet you stand also upon the earth."

Trei stared at it, speechless. The dragon's long coils twisted and looped all around him, light scattering from its translucent feathers.

"Kajurai," said the dragon. Its tone had become, not sharper, but more intense. "You have held fire in your hands. Fire attends the birth of glass." It turned its head to fix him with one great luminescent eye. "The winds answer your call. Call the winds. Summon the living winds and bind them with fire to the earth."

Trei had no idea what it meant.

The dragon's vast wings tilted, its feathers fraying into pearl-and-opal winds until even with his kajurai eyes Trei could not tell what was dragon and what was sky. The wind flickered and gusted, thin and powerless at this height, scattering music like harp notes as it tangled in the feathers of the dragon's wings. The dragon said, to him or to Nescana or to both of them, "Fire attends the birth of glass. Fire burns at the heart of glass."

"Glass?" said Nescana. "I don't understand!"

"Call the winds," said the dragon. "Kajuraihi. Summon fire. When time turns and the sky rises, set the sea alight with the living winds." Then the dragon lifted away, rising smoothly into layers of the heights where no kajurai could hope to follow it. Trei found himself both vastly relieved and yet stricken with grief to see it go. He looked for it, for diamond etchings of feathers against the sky, but the vaults of the heavens arched empty, infinitely far above.

"Let's go down," Nescana said, her voice almost too quiet for him to hear.

It was a long, long way down from the great heights to the novitiate's balcony. It was like falling out of a dream back into the waking world. Trei didn't know if Nescana felt that, the unreality of what had happened. When he stole a glance at her face, she looked blank with weariness. She had stopped pretending to know everything about a third of the way down. Trei was really glad he'd been there to show her the tricks that made flying easier when you were tired. He was pretty sure neither of them had actually been in danger of falling. Much danger.

Canpra gained detail as they drew nearer the Island, the shining white towers of the First City built proudly out to the very edge of the Island. There were few lingering signs of damage from Tolounn's attempted conquest earlier in the year. Trei was glad of that. That sight had roused too many difficult memories. Inland of the shining towers lay the orderly red brick homes and graceful tree-lined avenues of Second City where Trei had so briefly lived—he didn't like to think of that, either—and beyond those the cluttered alleyways and narrow shops of Third City, which Araenè loved so much. The great cemetery at the northern edge of the city was green now, no longer bare red soil, but Trei still flinched from looking at it and tipped his descending spiral out over the sea instead. Nescana followed closely. Trei thought she was too tired to care which angle of descent he chose. He smoothed and flattened his flight path, leading her in toward the novice's balcony at the easiest possible angle.

The kajuraihi lived in Canpra's First City, in three white towers and various associated underground chambers and galleries. The towers were not crowded, for the numbers of the kajuraihi had dwindled in recent decades. Kajuraihi of rank occupied large airy apartments high in the towers, with chambers that opened out directly into the air, and each kajurai kept his personal wings in his own apartment.

The novitiate, however, lay largely underground, carved down into the red stone. Novices slept in one long hall and ate in another and shared common bathing chambers and one flight balcony, and common wings in various sizes to suit novices who might range in age from twelve to nineteen. It was the common duty of all the novices to keep their chambers tidy and their wings in good repair. Trei had no idea how many broken feathers he had personally removed from wings and replaced with new, nor how many hours he had spent at this painstaking labor, but it was a lot.

He had mostly recovered, he thought, from seeing the dragon. Every kajurai saw the sky dragons clearly, but never so close. Never to *speak* to. He almost wondered if he and Nescana truly *had* come so close to a wind dragon that either one of them might almost have touched it with their hands. Whether it had really spoken to them, saying things about fire and earth and glass. It all seemed wholly impossible. Truly like a dream, or a vision. Until he saw the novice-master waiting for them on the balcony, scowling. Then it seemed all too possible.

Novice-master Anerii Pencara was a powerful, stocky man with iron-gray hair and a lined face and a stern set to his mouth. He was standing now with his arms folded over his chest, scowling. Trei had been scared of him at first. Novices

28

were *supposed* to be afraid of him. But then had come the Tolounnese invasion, and everything that had followed. And one small but welcome result of all that was that Trei wasn't afraid of Master Anerii anymore. Not even when he frowned so thunderously.

Trei glanced over his shoulder to check on Nescana one final time. She looked all right. She was just three lengths behind him and squarely in the proper approach path, and he could see the winds thickening in front of her as she prepared to cushion her landing.

Then his own landing was suddenly in urgent need of attention and he forgot her. He came in fast, backwinged hard to stall, tucked his chin down, and landed almost exactly right. He took half a dozen quick steps, straining to hold up the suddenly massive weight of his wings. He was exhausted. He wanted nothing but to collapse right here on the stone floor, but he was used to that, too, now, and managed to keep his feet.

Nescana came in too hard. The novice-master scowled, catching her with a hard thrust of wind, and she took two staggering steps forward and fell to her knees. She held her arms high, straining to keep her wings from raking the stone. She was starting to sag, though, her arms trembling—she wouldn't be able to hold them up more than a moment longer –

Master Anerii, with an exclamation of annoyance, strode forward to help Nescana with her wings before they could be too badly damaged. Trei fumbled to get his own wings off, pretending not to notice the novice-master's grim expression.

Then the master stepped back and set his fists on his hips, glowering. "What was that up there?" he demanded. "Approaching a dragon! You know better, novice!" He pointed a stubby finger at Trei. "*You*, at least, know better!" He glared at Nescana, switching his accusing finger to her. "I couldn't begin to guess whether *you* know anything at all! Flying while grounded, taking part in an exercise when you were *expressly* forbidden—"

"I flew higher than anybody!" Nescana declared. Trei suspected she'd meant to sound stubborn and defiant, but her voice came out smaller than she'd probably intended.

"She got just as high as I did," Trei said, to be fair.

"Genrai got higher than either of you. If it matters! You!" He glowered at Nescana. "If you'd got highest of all, was that supposed to excuse your behavior?" Master Anerii lifted heavy eyebrows at Nescana. "Well?"

Nescana opened her mouth, closed it again, and said in a meek tone, "I thought it might help, sir."

"Defying my order!" growled the novice-master. He switched his glower to Trei as though too disgusted by Nescana's behavior to even address it, or her, a moment longer. "And you both flew right up to that dragon!"

Trei stood up straight, with his shoulders properly back, and looked Master Anerii in the eye. "Yes, sir, I do know better. I didn't approach the dragon. It approached me! Us."

"It was above you *long* before either of you climbed high enough to steal its feathers!"

"But we weren't looking up, sir," Trei said reasonably. "We didn't know that. It must have known we were below it and rising, Novice-master, and it didn't move out of the way—"

"It's not a dragon's duty to avoid clumsy novices!"

"No, sir," said Trei.

The Novice-master's glower did not lighten. "Did it speak to you? Well?"

"Yes, sir." Trei tried to remember exactly what the dragon had said. It all seemed somehow very long ago and indistinct, as though he tried to recall a dream. He said uncertainly, "It said ... something about fire. And glass."

"It said, 'You ride on the winds but stand on the earth,'" Nescana said rapidly. "It said fire makes and destroys glass and burns at the heart of glass. Or something like that. It said we should hold fire and stand on the earth and bind the winds. Or ... something like that."

Trei tried to remember if the dragon had said those things. He thought Nascana hadn't gotten all that exactly right. But it was hard to remember. "It said to call the winds. I remember that. I think. I think it said to summon fire. It said, 'Set the sea alight.'" He turned to Nescana. "Didn't it say that?"

It was the girl's turn to look uncertain. "I *think* so ..."

Novice-Master Anerii snorted. He tucked his hands in his belt and gave them both a look of heavy disapproval. "I'll report this to Wingmaster Taimenai. He'll want to hear about every word that dragon said, and he'll want to hear something better than *I'm not sure*, so I suggest you give this matter some thought, both of you. Unless you had a deep philosophical debate with the dragon, you should be able to recall your conversation adequately. Is that clear?"

Trei traded a look with Nescana. "Yes, sir," he said. He knew the dragon had only actually said a few words. It ought to have been easier to remember those words. It would have been, probably, if anything it said had made sense. He wanted very much to lie down somewhere flat and soft and remember every detail of that astonishing encounter. He looked expectantly at Master Anerii.

"For approaching a dragon—you're grounded," the novice-master growled. Then he added, still growling, "For two days."

Trei nodded, keeping his expression carefully sober. Two days was like not being punished at all, so he knew Master Anerii really agreed he couldn't have avoided the dragon and wasn't at fault. Or maybe that he'd been right to leave his position and help Nescana. Trei had to pretend not to realize that, of course.

"And you ..." the novice-master turned toward Nescana.

The girl swallowed and braced herself.

Trei said quickly, without thinking about it, "She's been grounded enough. How's she supposed to learn to fly if she's never allowed in the air?"

Master Anerii glared at him, then transferred the glare to Nescana. "If you followed the *rules*, novice ..."

She said, almost managing to sound repentant, "Yes, sir. I'll try to do better."

"You'll *try*, will you?"

"If I'm allowed to fly, sir!"

"You don't have to *ground* her, you know," Trei put in.

"I can hardly whip a girl!"

Trei was genuinely astonished. "You can't? Why not? That's not fair, sir! Any novice would rather be whipped than grounded!"

For a moment, the novice-master stared at him. He said under his breath, "Tolounnese!" But then he looked at Nescana and said, "Well, and is that right, novice?"

Nescana swallowed, raised her chin, and met his eyes. "Yes, sir."

"Out!" snapped the novice-master, speaking to Trei. "Back to the novitiate, and stay there!" He flicked a broad hand in curt dismissal. "You—" he crooked a finger at Nescana. "Come with me, novice."

Trei got out, moving fast.

3

There were actually three identical doors on the far side of the labyrinth, all of pale wood inlaid here and there with tiny chips of smoky quartz and pink tourmaline, but the dragon sphere outlined only one of them with starlight. Ordinarily Araenè might have been curious about where each door might lead, but at the moment she was tired and embarrassed at getting lost and, all right, yes, maybe a little bit frightened, so when she finally stepped off the last tile of the labyrinth, she ignored the two unlit doors, let go of Ceirfei's hand, and shoved open the one that glowed with pale reflected light.

It opened directly to her apartment: a set of three pleasant rooms with dark wooden furniture and plaster walls painted the restful blue of the spring sky. The window was open, so that a warm evening breeze fragrant with herbs and damp earth wandered in from her small private garden.

Araenè found tears prickling behind her eyes. She said fiercely, "That's better! And not before time!" But she said this only after prudently stepping through the door and making sure Ceirfei had come through after her and they both really were in her own apartment, surrounded by her own familiar things. The tension of the interminable afternoon poured out of her, and she dropped gratefully onto her nicest and softest couch, leaned her head back against the cushions, and let her breath out in a long, slow sigh.

"Ah ..." said Ceirfei, who was forbidden to visit her in her personal apartment.

"I know!" Araenè set the dragon's sphere carefully on a holder meant to hold spheres, to one side, on an end table. Then she jumped to her feet, and opened her door again, this time with a confident flourish. She was sure the door would

33

cooperate now, and it did, opening to show a familiar white marble hallway that wasn't, she knew, part of the hidden school at all, but of the palace. Windows on the other side of the hall showed a sweeping view down across the city, white towers with lamplight glimmering in windows right out to the edge of the Island, and then moonlight shining across the wide, dark sea. She said, "Of course, now that the school's made us run all over and find our way through the labyrinth and everything—*now* it cooperates." But though she made sure she sounded confident and a little derisive, she was actually a little bit relieved. "It's not *too* late—is it?"

"It's fine." Ceirfei took her hand in his and looked into her eyes, his mouth crooked with wicked humor. "My mother will be happy I'm spending time courting you and not with the kajuraihi. She likes you, you know! As much as she likes anyone. She just hasn't made up her mind ..."

"Where your best advantage lies?" Araenè asked tartly. "She might try working a little less for your advantage and a little more for ..." but it was her turn to hesitate, uncomfortable with the direction of this sentence.

Ceirfei let it go. "You'll be well enough?"

"Me?" Araenè was genuinely surprised. "Of course! Why not?"

"You've no intention of finding any more dragons tonight, then? Good, that might be best. Let me know what Master Tnegun says of the ones we found today; I'll be curious. Sky dragons and dragons of iron to go with your dragon of fire: it's not what one expects in the hidden school! Or is it? You may tell your master I'm intrigued. But—" he glanced over his shoulder at the open door—"I really *must* go, Araenè. I'll visit you in a few days—or you can visit me—"

"Or we can both visit Trei!" suggested Araenè.

"An excellent notion! Yes, we'll arrange that. Be careful, at least a *little* careful, until then, Araenè!"

Whether she was supposed to be careful of getting lost, or of labyrinths, or of finding too many odd dragons made of hematite or crystal or other minerals, Araenè couldn't guess.

Maybe all three. Ceirfei didn't say. He only stepped backward, through the door and into the palace, sketched the merest suggestion of a farewell bow, and gently shut the door between them.

Araenè sank back down on her couch. Unfortunately, she realized almost at once, she couldn't actually just go to sleep sitting right here. She was starving. And very thirsty. There was an earthenware jug of water on a table in her bedroom, sweating in the evening cool. That was wonderful. She poured a cup, and then another, but supper ... she wasn't sure what to do about supper. It was probably not too late to have her supper with everyone else in the dining hall. But somehow she just didn't want to face all the other apprentices. Not now. Not tonight. Not after having spent the whole afternoon with Ceirfei, who actually *liked* her.

She wanted to visit Trei right now, just open a door and step through right this minute. Her cousin had no doubt had his supper already, and would probably now be joking with the other kajurai novices as they all tied feathers into the frameworks of wings. Trei said that was terribly boring and everyone worked on it together so they could talk. Araenè had been a little jealous when he told her that, though she hadn't let her cousin see. *Trei* had friends. Especially now, after the special audition. He'd told her about that, too, and it certainly seemed like a good idea, this new kajurai notion about auditions for girls. But in the hidden school, the apprentices worked by themselves, mostly, and none of them was exactly Araenè's friend anyway. Not anymore.

Which was *fine*. She didn't need them anyway. Except she would have liked to talk to Trei. Only you had to arrange visits to the kajurai novitiate through the kajurai novice master, which was all very tedious and formal, but her cousin would get in trouble if anyone found out she'd dropped by without permission.

Araenè sighed. She found herself longing for her old, *ordinary* life where you never stumbled across stringless harps that changed into dragons or strange spheres that looked like glass but weren't. But her old life was gone, locked unreachably in the past. Memories of that old life, of her parents and home, rose up forcefully. Araenè blinked hard and, to distract herself, picked up the mysterious sphere.

It still glowed, very faintly. It definitely wasn't made of ordinary glass. It had now taken on a milky appearance, and its opaque surface seemed to swirl, very gently. And it seemed smaller than at first. But heavier. Spheres never changed like that. But this one did. She felt uneasily that maybe she shouldn't have taken it out of the labyrinth ... but no one had *ever* said anything about any special sphere in the labyrinth; they should have *said* something if it was important. She would give it to Master Tnegun in the morning, and if she'd done anything wrong, he would fix things. Tonight ... she was just too tired to worry about it, tonight. Tonight ... she wanted ordinary things, an ordinary night, a memory of ordinary life.

And thinking of that, she knew at last exactly what she wanted. Setting the sphere aside, she shuffled rapidly through her small wardrobe for a boy's shirt and trousers and floppy hat, counted out a handful of coins from her small store, and then stepped up onto her windowsill and down into her private garden. The brick wall was high, and the gate made of close-set loops of wrought iron too small to even get a hand through, but it swung open smoothly as soon as Araenè touched it. She stepped out of her quiet garden and left the hidden school behind, walking away into the narrow alleys and freedom of the Third City.

She relaxed immediately. She'd thought she was almost too tired to move, but now that she was out in Third City, she felt much better. She walked fast, with a boy's long stride, she looked boldly at people in the streets the way a boy might. She turned right at the end of the alley and right again at the end of the next alley, and then left—she recognized all these narrow streets, with their overhanging balconies that shut out the sky. Cheap paper lanterns hung beneath almost every balcony, because Third City never really slept. You could buy a lamb pastry or a cream cake at any hour, if you knew where the vendors had their carts. Araenè *did* know. She could go anywhere. No one would notice her. When they saw her, they would only see the boy she pretended to be. Only Arei, and not Araenè at all. She strode past a woman carrying a heavy basket and a knot of men throwing dice and rods against a wall, and headed down a slightly wider alley, walking fast.

Even far down the street, the fragrance of baking bread and roasting mutton, of caramelized sugar and toasted cumin and hot oil emanated from Cesera's. The scent of hot sugar tickled at the back of Araenè's tongue and across her finger-tips with an intimation of power, though she could not decide what kind of power it suggested. She had never noticed this before—the way the fragrant spices here tickled at the edges of her magical sensibility. But then, she had not come back to Cesera's since ... well, not since the summer. So much had happened, and at first she had not wanted to come here, and then she had not dared.

Araenè longed to stop thinking about anything to do with magic. She rubbed her hands down the seams of her boy's trousers and stepped into Cesera's, firmly leaving everything complicated behind.

The place was busy, of course. Cesera's was always busy at least until midnight, with students getting out of late lectures at the University. At least half the tavern's patrons were students, for the owner famously allowed University students to try their skill in his kitchens. Araenè shoved her way through the crowds. Students clustered around tables in the huge common room, laughing and arguing and waving narrow mugs in the air to emphasize a joke or a point of debate. The smells of ale, hard cider and sour wine competed with those of roasted meat and baking bread. She was swept by a painful longing for her old life. Which was gone. Irrecoverable. Because of things that had happened and things she had done ... she didn't want to think about any of that.

Near the door, a group of young men were drawing on a table with sticks of soft charcoal and the points of daggers, arguing some point so fiercely they all seemed to have forgotten the platters of cakes that occupied the other side of their table. Farther away, a pair of intense boys were studying a set of revolting anatomical drawings. They had pinned their drawings up on a kind of triangular frame, which made them all too visible to the whole room. Physician's apprentices never had any sense of decency. Araenè looked the other way, toward the kitchens, where three stern-looking older men sat at a small table, more intent on evaluating and taking down notes about their meal than on eating it. Two of them in turn took a bite of some dish and solemnly wrote down a note about it. Those were masters from the University, Araenè knew. Everyone knew masters came to Cesera's to evaluate student efforts, which was why students cooked here without pay. They competed with one another to make the flakiest pastries and most interesting sauces, all hoping a master would offer them a place. Once, she had hoped that might happen to her. Though she could never have taken up any master's offer, of course. And less now than ... well, than before.

But so long as she was dressed like a boy, she had as much right to try her skill in the kitchens as anyone. By the time the real crowd had begun to build, Araenè was deeply involved in making tea-cloud eggs. She experimentally added star anise as well as salt to the strong tea and then lowered in the whole cooked eggs, their shells delicately cracked all over, to gain both flavor and decoration from the tea as they simmered. Turning to a second station in the wide kitchens, she carved small pieces of fresh coconut into the shapes of flowers, set them into place on little tarts filled with orange- and vanilla-scented coconut cream, and grated moist shavings of ginger over everything.

The scent of the ginger tugged at another part of her mind, the part that worked magic, but she paid no attention. When she glimpsed flickering, indistinct shapes in the shiny side of a copper-sheathed pot, she immediately looked away. Even so, as she shelled the finished tea eggs, the lacey patterns imprinted on them by the seasoned tea seemed to swim in her vision, flowing into images of clouds and dragons. Araenè lowered her head to breathe in the tea's anise-scented fragrance, and the visions faded.

"You're Arei, aren't you?" asked a student, pausing by Araenè's station. "I haven't seen you here in a long time!" Then, peering over her shoulder, he was immediately distracted. "Oh, that's interesting, you put anise in the tea?"

Happy to be distracted herself, Araenè nodded. "They're to go with the rice and broth Torei's making. Torei said we needed to make something that would use up a lot of eggs and all the students are going to order his broth—" Because rice and broth with a tea egg would be the cheapest supper offered, she meant.

The other student nodded understanding. "Everyone will ask for those tarts, too, they're so beautiful. May I?" He ate one, closing his eyes in concentration. "Oh, nice. Did you use coconut cream along with butter in the pastry? That was clever." He glanced at her face and away again, oddly shy. "I know you don't need any suggestions from me, but maybe you might simmer a few cardamom pods in the cream next time? Here, let me—don't worry, I'll give credit where it's due—" he loaded a tray with the little pastries and went up the stairs to the main floor.

It seemed strange to Araenè that once she might have worried about the other student trying to claim credit for her tarts. Now it simply didn't seem to matter. She bit into a tea-cloud egg, frowning, but the frown eased as the savory flavors developed across her tongue: the anise balanced beautifully against the tea and salt.

A familiar and, she realized, half-expected voice broke into her concentration. "Arei! I thought I recognized your inimitable style in those pastries! Unable to endure the dull life available elsewhere, you return at last to Cesera's! Or was it my scintillating company you missed?"

Araenè turned, her heart simultaneously leaping up and sinking like a stone in the sea. But she managed to say in an almost normal voice, "Well, 'Naiki, who let you in here? Did I forget to warn everyone you'll curdle the expensive cream?"

"I only ever tried to add lemon juice to cream once!" Hanaiki protested. He was a few years older than Araenè; tall and vain, with a quick tongue and a casual confidence she had always envied. "I was a mere infant, far less experienced then than I am now! But—" he hesitated, then said in a much more serious tone, "But how is it *you're* here? After so long?" His gaze searched her face. He was thinner, Araenè saw. He had always been sharp-featured, but now his cheekbones could have been used to slice bread. And there was something in his eyes that hadn't been there before: not a loss of confidence, but maybe an awareness that he was not immune to grief. "This past summer was unspeakable," he said in a low voice. "I feared for you. When you disappeared, I was afraid—" he stopped.

Araenè had not thought of this. She should have. She had been afraid he would know—that he would have heard of Milendri's first girl mage, that he would have guessed that she must be that mage, that she was therefore a girl, and that she had been lying to him for years.

She had not realized that of course Hanaiki was too used to her as a boy to think for a moment that she might be the famous girl mage. Of course his first guess would be so much more obvious. She was suddenly deeply ashamed that she had left him to worry. She said awkwardly, "No. I mean, yes, in a way. My parents ..."

Hanaiki touched her shoulder. "I am sorry to hear of it. Your father was far too hard on you, you know I thought so, but I wouldn't have wished for such tragedy. May the earth lie light on his bones! But are you—surely you are not wholly alone? Do you need—" he gestured, at once expansive and uncertain. "Money? A house? Anything?"

"A friend," Araenè whispered, looking down so Hanaiki wouldn't see her blinking. "I need a friend." Which was stupid; she had Trei, didn't she? Sometimes, at least. And she had Ceirfei. Sometimes. But that was ... that was different. Ceirfei courted her, but she knew that was mostly to make sure her reputation didn't suffer, now that everyone knew she was a girl. Ceirfei always wanted to put her on display. She was *his* girl mage, symbol of the changing customs of the Floating Islands. Which was *fine*, she understood about that, but he always made her feel like she was changing into somebody else.

Hanaiki wasn't like that. Hanaiki was from *before*. He made her feel ... he made her feel like herself, like the self she recognized. The self she'd almost forgotten.

She understood suddenly that she'd come to Cesera's to look for Hanaiki, though she hadn't admitted this to herself until this moment, when it became unavoidably clear. She had not dared look for him. Not since everything had happened. But then tonight, she had come straight here. She knew she needed to tell him the truth. Only she didn't know how, and hardly dared look at him for fear he would see it in her face, in her eyes, in her smooth girl's throat.

Hanaiki gripped her shoulder, giving her a little shake. "You should have come to me much earlier, then. My father—if you need a place to stay—"

"I don't," Araenè said. "Truly." She rubbed a hand quickly and casually across her eyes and said, much more briskly, "But you could help me carve this coconut; you've always had steady hands."

Hanaiki picked up a piece of the white flesh and rapidly turned it into an amazingly true replica of a flower. But he barely looked at what his hands were doing: he looked mainly at Araenè. "I *am* your friend," he said, frowning. "If you are in need, Arei, you know you've only to tell me."

41

Of course he knew something was wrong. He wasn't stupid. Blinded by what he thought he knew about her, but not stupid. Araenè bit her lip hard. She wanted to cling to Hanaiki and weep against his chest, but of course that was impossible. She needed to tell him ... she couldn't tell him. She picked up a knife of her own, but then just looked at it and at the piece of coconut she held. "I should go."

"Arei—"

"Arei!" another voice broke in from above. "Is Arei still here? Oh, there you are! Master Terii wants to see you!"

"Oh, ho! I'm not the only one who recognized those pastries! You know, Arei, you don't need to turn Master Terii down if he makes you an offer. I'm sorry about your father, truly, but if he's no longer forcing you toward a ministry post, well, you must know Terii's last apprentice runs Prince Imrei's kitchens! You could step right from Terii's patronage to a royal kitchen, be running it yourself before you're thirty. Nothing holds you back now ... Arei?"

Araenè shook her head. She felt ... fragile. As though she had already been stretched too thin, and the invitation—really more a command—from Master Chef Terii threatened to shatter her hard-held pretense of calm. "I should go—"

But Hanaiki caught her by the wrist and dragged her up the stairs, refusing to listen to her protests. "You can at least listen to Terii's offer!" he said over his shoulder. "Hush! You're far too clever in the kitchens to immure yourself in any ministry, no matter what your father wanted!"

Master Terii was seated at a table off to one side, where other patrons wouldn't crowd into his privacy. He was a big man with plenty of extra flesh, but muscle under it: his arms were three times as thick as Araenè's, and his hands half again as wide. He studied her from eyes set deep under heavy brows in his broad, moon-round face.

Though the physician's students across the room were arguing over some point of anatomy or diagnostics, a hush had fallen around Master Terii's table. That was on Araenè's account, of course. Everyone was watching. But she couldn't think of any graceful way to get out of it, now. She said, "This is a mistake, master, truly." She crossed her arms over her chest, uncrossed them, couldn't decide what to do with her hands, and crossed her arms again.

"It certainly is not," Hanaiki said strongly. "At least listen, Arei!"

The master said, "Your friend gives you good advice, boy." He had two of Araenè's pastries before him on the table. He nudged one with a thick finger. "Orange and vanilla. What gave you the idea?"

"Nothing, exactly," Araenè answered. She blinked, realizing that in fact the balance she'd perceived between those flavors was something she'd gotten from her new sense of magical balance, not something purely based on her knowledge of flavors. She said, hesitantly because this insight had startled her, "I—I just thought they would go well together."

Master Terii nodded thoughtfully. "You hadn't heard that Master Lai tried something similar earlier this season?"

Araenè shook her head.

"Lai didn't use coconut, however. Nor did he grate ginger over. That's unusual—the use of ginger with vanilla. Most people would have used cardamom syrup instead. The ginger sparks up the orange, doesn't it? Is that what you had in mind?"

Araenè nodded. "I did think about using cardamom. But I wanted something with a little bite to it. To contrast with the smoothness of the coconut and the floral notes of the vanilla."

Master Terii inclined his head. He began to speak, but a new voice, sharp and disapproving, cut through the hush. "Araenè!"

Araenè flinched, jerked horribly off balance as the two parts of her life abruptly collided.

"What are you *doing* here?" demanded the newcomer, shouldering his way through the crowd with a complete disregard for Master Terii's rank and reputation. It was

Tichorei, Master Camatii's apprentice—oldest of the apprentices, several years older than Araenè, an apprentice who would soon, everyone knew, be made officially a mage.

Tall, bony, and serious, Tichorei had been kind to Araenè when she'd first come to the hidden school, before anybody had found out she was really a girl. Then *everybody* had found out. When the truth had come out, the easy friendship he'd offered her so casually had turned into something else. Araenè didn't think Tichorei actually hated her. Or resented her the way half the other apprentices resented her. He was too far ahead of the rest of them to resent any new apprentice, girl or not. But he had become stiff and reserved and hard to talk to about even the simplest things. Araenè hated it, because she'd liked and respected Tichorei, and now he would barely even look at her.

He said now, still with that grim tone of disapproval, "Don't you know everyone's been looking for you all afternoon? Master Tnegun and everybody? We were starting to think you'd stumbled across a basilisk, got yourself turned to stone or something, except we ought to have been able to find you even then. And then at last I glimpsed you—and all the time you've just been here? At a common tavern?" He glanced around disdainfully.

Everyone was staring at her. *Hanaiki* was staring at her. Araenè wanted to sink into the floor, right through the red stone of the Island, and just fall straight into the sea. She wanted to scream. She wanted to slap Tichorei. She said furiously, "You have the manners of a pig, Tichorei! Except a pig is cleverer. I have *not* been here all afternoon. I was *lost*. I *called* Master Tnegun; he didn't answer. You *know* the hidden school has whims. Who do you think you are, blaming me for not guessing anybody had missed me? You never have before!"

Tichorei, who had clearly been prepared to yell at her some more, paused.

Araenè turned her shoulder to him. She didn't want to look around, she didn't want to see anybody's expression, not

Master Terii's or anybody's. She especially didn't want to look at Hanaiki. But of course she didn't have any choice.

Hanaiki was staring at her. His gaze dropped to her chest, but jerked up again at once. He was blushing, Araenè saw. Hanaiki never blushed. He was sometimes outrageous, but never embarrassed. But he was obviously embarrassed now.

He'd heard of the girl mage, clearly. He'd put everything together fast. Of course he had. Everyone knew about her. Ceirfei had made sure of that, because he said it was time for her to stop hiding—that it was impossible for her to hide any longer, and a good thing, too, he said. Because the Floating Islands needed her. Because she set the right kind of precedent, he said. She knew he was right, but she had not wanted to give this up irrevocably. This other part of her life. This part where she was free to tell the truth about herself, as long as she told just one lie.

Only then the lies had multiplied. She should never have come back here. Araenè met Hanaiki's eyes, but flinched from the astonishment she saw in them. "You were my first real friend, you know," she whispered.

"Was I?" Hanaiki said. His normally expressive voice had become quite unreadable.

"Hanaiki—"

He reached out, not too fast, and took the floppy-brimmed boy's hat off her head. Her hair, only carelessly pinned up, tumbled down her neck to her shoulders.

No one made a sound. Even the physician's students had been drawn in at last.

"My father always warned me against getting tangled up with girls. If he'd only known." Hanaiki started to say something else, but stopped and shook his head.

Tichorei said, "Araenè—"

Araenè ignored him. She tried to explain, "I always wanted to be a chef. Only I couldn't, of course. And then the mage-gift came ... came up in me. And that was impossible, too. Everything was impossible. And then last summer my

45

parents ... so I went to the hidden school after all. And they ... they found out. Only they said maybe a girl could be a mage after all. So ...”

“I see.” Hanaiki was still staring at her. Araenè could see herself change in his eyes, into somebody he didn't know. Somebody she didn't even know herself. He said, “I—it's not right. What you're doing. What you've done. You—I—you made me think you were a boy!”

“Hanaiki ...”

Hanaiki shook his head. He looked shocked more than angry. He didn't step back. But it was as though he had. It was as though he was changing from someone who had been her friend to someone she didn't know at all.

“I'm sorry,” Araenè whispered. It hadn't been like this when Ceirfei had found out she was a girl. But he'd realized she was a girl at once. Of course it was different, when there were days and senneri and years of pretense between you ...

“Are you?”

“Araenè,” said Tichorei. “I'm sorry. I wasn't thinking. But things are happening. It's important you come back to the hidden school.”

Araenè didn't look at him. She wished she had never come back to Cesera's. Of course this had been a mistake. She longed to step back into the past. But of course she couldn't. You could never go back. She wondered for the first time if she hadn't been a little in love with clever, sardonic Hanaiki. She wondered how outraged he would be, if he guessed. Not that it mattered, now.

“Araenè—” said Tichorei.

Still not looking at him, Araenè put out a hand and opened a door that hadn't stood there a moment ago; the heavy, carved Akhan Bhotounn—‘the friendly one’. *Now* it cooperated, of course, now when it didn't even matter. Through it, she glimpsed the small, warm confines of her master's personal library, with books piled on the small tables and on the floor and Master Tnegun himself turning swiftly to meet her eyes across all the disconnected space that lay between them. "Araenè," he said. His deep, quiet voice echoed in the silence that filled, not only of his own library, but also Cesera's common room.

"I'm sorry," Araenè said, to Hanaiki, as though the two of them were alone. "I never meant—" only of course she *had* meant to lie to him. To everyone. She'd done it for years. It had hardly been an accident, or an impulse. She shook her head and stepped through the open door she had brought into Cesera's. She didn't hold the door for Tichorei, though she knew perfectly well he didn't have her gift for doors. She didn't care how, or even whether, Tichorei made it back to the hidden school.

"Araenè," said Master Tnegun, very quietly as the door swung shut behind her. "Forgive Tichorei. He was upset. When we lost you this afternoon ... you will forgive us, I hope, if we could not help but recall your tendency to find yourself at the center of events."

"I was lost," Araenè said sharply. "I *tried* to call you, but you didn't hear me. It wasn't my fault!"

"Hush. I know. At least, I am not surprised to learn of it." Master Tnegun sank into the library's one chair, motioning for Araenè to join him. All around the room, candles flickered to life, tall white tapers that burned with clean pale flames.

Her Yngulin master wore plain black robes rather than the jewel-toned fabrics of the Islands. He was tall and lean, with severe hawk features and a stern set to his mouth even when he was pleased, which he was not, right now, though she could see he wasn't angry at *her*. Which was good, because that wouldn't have been fair at all.

A long-tailed green lizard with topaz eyes clung to Master Tnegun's shoulder. In the palm of his dark-skinned hand, he held the sphere Araenè had taken from the center of the labyrinth. It tasted of cardamom and palm sugar and rosewater and vanilla and jasmine and pepper and the strange, cool minty bitterness that was almost like perilla, only not really. And now, she thought, also of cumin and fenugreek.

Although that might have been the taste of some other magic clinging to Master Tnegun.

"I was concerned," he said quietly, his voice as dark and smoky as magic. The sphere glowed like a small, pale moon in the palm of his hand. "This is a most remarkable sphere. Indeed, it is unique. Kanora Ireinamei made it—yes, I thought you would find that an interesting detail. Kanora Ireinamei made it, as I say; and then it was lost."

Araenè stared at her master. Kanora Ireinamei had been a lady mage, long ago. She had been a student of the legendary Cassameirin, back when the Floating Islands had first torn themselves free of earth and sea and risen into the sky. She knew that. But that was almost all she knew, though she'd read everything she could find about the long-dead lady mage. No one knew much about her. Araenè no longer felt angry, exactly. She felt—she wasn't sure. Uncertain. Nervous. Cesera's seemed very far away, truly part of a different life. Someone else's life.

Kanora Ireinamei had made this sphere? And *she* had found it?

"It was lost?" she said. "You *lost* it?"

"Well, not lost, precisely. It was, I believe, where it needed to be. But we did not know where it was. And now it has fallen into your hands. Where did you find it?"

"In the labyrinth," Araenè said uncertainly. "All these floating tiles. That was the labyrinth, wasn't it? And they *moved* when you weren't looking. Nobody told me ... and nobody told me Kanora made a special sphere!" She glared at her master. "*You* never told me about Kanora Ireinamei making any special spheres!"

"Araenè," Master Tnegun said, his tone mild. "Think, please. I had no reason to mention a sphere that had fallen out of our ken. And though I gather you did indeed find Kanora's sphere in the labyrinth, it wasn't there the last time I happened to go there. You are quite right that the hidden school has whims." He looked at her, a speculative, considering look. "This is, as I say, an interesting sphere." He held it out to her, but did not let her touch it when she reached for it. "Tell me, what does it seem to you to be made of?"

Araenè frowned. "Well, not glass. Not quartz. I thought ..." she hesitated. "I almost think it might be hollow. I know spheres aren't made that way, but this one—only it's *not* glass, but I don't know how you'd make a hollow sphere except by blowing glass."

Master Tnegun turned the sphere over in his long fingers. "It is not glass. No one living knows precisely what it is. We know, however, that it contains a great deal of dragon magic. And a great deal of ordinary human spellwork as well. Here, take it."

Araenè lifted it from her master's hand, a little nervously. The sphere didn't *feel* like glass. It felt alive. Cold. Densely magical. She couldn't imagine what it was made of. How strange. How impossible ... how could any ordinary mage, no matter how gifted, put dragon magic in a sphere? It didn't make sense, it wasn't *reasonable*.

In her hands, the sphere brightened and expanded and lost its opacity, until it was again as transparent as glass. Within it, images flickered. Fire burned through the sky and ran across the sea and then into a roiling darkness, lightning-shot, towering—a great storm, she saw at last; dense and powerful, a dry storm that was all driving wind and black grit, but no rain. Ships rode before that storm, slashing elegantly through the winds. Araenè leaned closer to the sphere, peering at the tiny ships, puzzled by something she couldn't quite pin down, but the vision was only there for one brief moment, and then gone, lost behind milky swirls that told her nothing.

Master Tnegun reached out and plucked Kanora's sphere out of Araenè's hand once more, holding it up thoughtfully so that the candlelight shone through it. If he had glimpsed her brief vision, he showed no sign of it. "A sphere containing dragon magic," he said thoughtfully. "Lost, and now found. By you."

"I didn't find it on purpose!"

"No, indeed. I suspect that your earlier exposure to dragonfire and dragon magic led you into a particular ..." he hesitated. "Sensitivity, perhaps," he said at last. "In any case, I believe you may have come to possess a rare ability to stand on the boundary between dragon magic and ordinary human magecraft. Wherever this sphere has been, whatever the use to which it has been put, I strongly suspect it was not any human intention that set it directly into *your* hands."

"Not as directly as all that," Araenè muttered. "You don't think the dragon ... ?" She knew *all about* the dragon at the heart of the hidden school. But surely her master couldn't mean to imply that the *dragon* had put Kanora Ireinamei's sphere in her way and made her find it?

Master Tnegun gave her an ironic look. But before he could speak, if he had meant to say anything, a new door opened suddenly, and they both turned in surprise to see who might have opened it.

4

When Trei at last got back to the novitiate, everyone else was already there. It was fairly late, he realized—later than he'd thought; he and Nescana had been the last down, but he hadn't realized until he saw the other novices, gathered impatiently around the dining hall table, how late it really was.

Genrai was in his place at the head of the table, with dark-skinned cheerful Kojran on one side and thin, intense Rekei on the other, all three of them with feathers and thread and bits of wing frameworks in front of them. You got so used to working with feathers and thread that it felt strange to sit around and talk with your hands empty. But everybody put the feathers and thread aside as soon as Trei came in. Kojran jumped up and said, "Trei! What was it like?" and at the same time, Tokabii said enviously, "Did it talk to you? Was it splendid? I bet it was splendid. Why do *you* have all the luck? And Nescana! That's not even *fair*!"

Of course all the boys knew about the dragon: exciting news like that rushed through the novitiate like a fast wind.

Genrai shoved a chair out with his foot. "Of course Tokabii's right—you *would* be the one to fly right into a dragon. That'll teach you to look where you're going."

Trei dropped gratefully into the offered chair. "It wasn't *my* fault. I wasn't expecting to run into anything at all way up there!"

"Of course not," muttered Rekei, not quite under his breath.

Trei knew that Rekei, who was from a ministerial family, thought he should really be senior in the novitiate. Everyone had been glad to defer to Ceirfei, but now that Ceirfei was gone, Genrai was senior, and of course Rekei pushed him, nip, nip, nip, just as far as he could get away with. But Genrai was years older than Rekei, and the younger Third City boys listened to him much better than to Rekei. Which was fine, in Trei's opinion. He liked Genrai. If Ceirfei couldn't be senior, Genrai should be. And it was better for Nescana that way, too, of course.

Tokabii, youngest and most annoying of the novices, didn't have any feathers to hand—he was too impatient to do featherwork right and usually wound up having to do it over, so no one let him work on anything but practice frames. He complained, "I didn't even get to see it. You flew close enough to *touch* it, and I didn't even get to *see* it!" He sounded like Trei's failure to share the excitement was a serious and deliberate bit of selfishness, like grabbing after the last pastry at supper.

Kojran, ignoring Tokabii, pushed piles of feathers and spools of thread away and demanded, "Did the dragon notice you at all? Did it *say* anything? Kajuraihi are supposed to be able to understand what they say. So did it?"

"How'd you get so high, anyway?" Tokabii put in. "You can't pull winds like Kojran and me, so how come you got up so high? It should have been me! Or Kojran, anyway."

Rekei snapped, "*Quiet*, brat, and let Trei tell it!"

At the same time, Genrai said sternly, "Someone's always going to fly faster and higher, and if you start thinking you're the best at everything, you'll quit trying and then you'll be the worst."

"He is already," said Rekei, but the look he got from Genrai at that was so fierce he looked away and pretended he hadn't said anything. And Tokabii intercepted another of Genrai's looks and *he* pretended he hadn't heard. So then there was a moment of quiet.

"It spoke," said Trei, quickly, while the peace held. "And if you're all quiet and let me remember, I'll tell you what it said. *After* I've had a chance to think." The memory of the dragon was already vague, even though at the same time it seemed one of the most vivid and powerful memories of his whole life. He said, forestalling the protest he could see everyone, even Genrai, was going to make, "It's like trying to remember your audition. It said things about fire and earth and summoning the winds, but I don't ... I need time to think about it, all right?"

Genrai leaned back in his chair, frowning. Rekei, who had been obviously prepared for a sharp response, closed his mouth. Tokabii started to say something, but Genrai put up a hand and the younger boy shut his mouth, too.

"And I'm grounded for two days."

"Two days!" said Kojran. And, after a pause, "What about Nescana?" Genrai turned his sternest look on Kojran, but the dark boy didn't look abashed.

"It's all right," Trei told them both. "I think she's not going to be grounded. Any longer than she was already, at least. Maybe only for a couple of days, like me."

"That's all right, then. Fine." Kojran's tone was hard to read. He could be jealous sometimes—and everyone must know that Nescana had gotten up as high as Trei, in an exercise that was supposed to have been too advanced for her. But he didn't sound jealous, exactly. Trei wasn't sure what he *did* sound like.

Genrai's frown deepened and he thumped one hand lightly on the table several times, though he wasn't usually given to nervous gestures. But he said only, "Well, a few days stuck in the novitiate, that's not so bad. You can help Nescana with her navigation."

Trei suppressed a sigh. It was true that Nescana needed help with her navigation. No one taught girls math, on the Islands. "I guess. My arms are going to be stiff, though."

"Oh, well, your *arms* are tired," Tokabii said. "As long as there isn't anything wrong with your *fingers*, you don't do math with your *elbows*, now do you?"

"*You* might as well be using your elbows," Genrai said drily. "You could use the practice, too, brat."

"Not me!" Tokabii jumped up and scooted away into the sleeping hall.

Trei grinned, shoved feathers out of his way, and collected instead a sheet of paper and a writing quill. Rekei put a bottle of ink where he could reach it, and he nodded absently, remembering the chill, thin air of the heights. Around him, everyone was silent, letting him fall into memory.

Really, the dragon had said only a few words. It had not called him by name. It had called him only *kajurai*. The memory was vague, but he knew that was true. Maybe dragons didn't have names. Nobody knew. It was amazing how little the Islanders knew about the dragons of sky and wind, even after living so close to sky dragons for hundreds of years. They still didn't know *anything*.

You have held fire in your hands. The dragon had said that. Trei was almost sure those were the exact words. He held onto the fragile memory. He scribbled quickly, trying not to think too much. Then he read over what he'd written, frowning.

> *You ride upon the winds but also stand on the earth.*
> ~~*You hold fire.*~~ *You have held fire.*
> *Call the winds. Summon the fire and the earth.*
> *Set the sea on fire.*

"That's not everything," Nescana said behind him. She had come in without him noticing and stood now looking over his shoulder and frowning. Taking the quill out of his hand, she wrote quickly, then turned the paper around to show Trei.

> *Fire attends the birth of glass, fire is the heart of glass.*
> *You hold fire in your hands. Call fire.*
> *The winds answer your call. Call the winds and ~~burn the sea~~ set the sea on fire.*

Her writing was nothing like as neat as his. Just as nobody taught Island girls math, no one taught Third City girls to write. Ceirfei had been teaching Genrai, before he'd had to leave, and now one of the older kajuraihi was, but Trei himself had been teaching Nescana, since no one else seemed inclined to. Which meant he was used to her clumsy letters, at least.

"You missed the part about the glass," Nescana pointed out.

Trei nodded. He remembered that now. He didn't understand how he'd forgotten it. He said, "But you forgot the part about the earth. Is there anything we both forgot?"

Nescana, frowning, bent forward. They both peered carefully at the papers, she and Trei together. Trei didn't think they'd left out anything—but he hadn't remembered about the glass until he saw it written down in Nescana's careful, clumsy writing.

"But what's it say?" Tokabii demanded, snatching the paper and peering at it. Bored and curious, he had come back to the table, but of course he couldn't read much at all, which was his own fault for being too bratty and lazy to let anyone teach him. Rekei reached for the paper, but Tokabii skittered backward, keeping out of reach.

"Tokabii," Genrai said sharply, and held out his hand. The little boy hesitated, then reluctantly handed it over—then stuck out his tongue at Rekei and dodged away when Rekei cuffed at him.

Nescana caught Trei's eyes, rolled hers expressively, and grinned.

"Well," Genrai said, carefully working his way through the lines, "Any kajurai can summon the winds, but you're the only one who's held fire, aren't you?" He glanced up at Trei, a sharp, considering look.

"What's it *say*?" demanded Tokabii. He snatched after the paper again.

Genrai held it up out of the little boy's reach, gave him a quelling stare, and handed the paper to Rekei instead. "Read it out loud."

Rekei obeyed, stumbling a little over Nescana's clumsy writing. Then he looked at Trei. It was not an entirely friendly look. "Anyway, the dragon spoke to Nescana as well as you."

"*I* never held fire," Nescana objected promptly.

"Maybe it's all figurative," said Trei. "Maybe we're not supposed to think of it so literally. Anyway, there's all that about glass, I never did anything with fire and glass. I don't even know what that means. And how could anybody set the sea on fire? That doesn't even make sense." He hesitated. "Wingmaster Taimenai will figure it out, I guess. But it's not ... I mean, don't look at *me*."

Turning Nescana's paper around, he began to make a clean copy of everything both of them remembered. Then another, since he wanted to keep a copy himself. He didn't try to figure it out, but just wrote it all down.

Probably the wingmaster would take this account to the mages. They might know more about dragons, since they had one, Araenè said, in their school. A fire dragon. The young one, the offspring of the one who had given her fire to carry, sort of. And then Araenè had given the fire to him. Sort of. It had never occurred to him that the dragons would remember that, or care, or that it might still *matter*. Trei didn't even want to *think* about fire dragons, about the way they lived and swam in fire and only came out into the air when a mountain roared with fire and the earth broke open and all its molten insides poured out ... he clenched his teeth against memory.

Behind him, a quiet, familiar voice said, "Trei."

"Ceirfei!" said Trei, turning, surprised and pleased. But then, looking more closely, he asked, "Ceirfei, are you all right?"

Prince Ceirfei was only a few years older than Trei, but somehow seemed a lot more adult. It wasn't just that he was tall, though he was; or that he wore court white, with a ribbon of royal sapphire blue threaded through his dark hair and a thin gold ring on one thumb. It was his air of assurance, of always knowing the proper thing to do and always being prepared to do it. That was part of being a prince, of course.

Ceirfei had only been a kajurai for a few months, but that royal manner was as much a part of him as his own skin.

Only now Trei could see that something had shaken that assurance. Ceirfei looked ... tired, but more than tired. His eyes looked bruised. Trei asked again, with trepidation, "Ceirfei?"

The prince took one hard breath. Then he said, "I grieve to be the one to inform you that my uncle Terinai Naterensei has just this evening been taken up into the hands of the Gods. My cousin Imrei will be king, as soon as the mourning period is over." He stopped, painfully, as though he simply could not think of anything else to say.

"Oh!" Trei said stupidly. "Oh—I'm so sorry. That's ... I'm sorry, Ceirfei. That's awful. That's *terrible.*"

It was, and for more than one reason. Just last year, four cousins and two brothers had stood between Ceirfei and the throne of the Floating Islands. That was why Ceirfei had been allowed to participate in the kajurai audition even though his mother was Calaspara Naterensei, the king's own sister. His mother had let him audition because he was safely distant from the throne and because there were plenty of other princes in line to inherit.

But then had come the terrible summer just past. So now, with the king's death, Prince Imrei would have to be king. And, until Imrei got a son of his own—and he wasn't even married, yet—Ceirfei would have to be his heir. In all the Islands, maybe only Trei and the other kajurai novices really knew how much he hated that.

Trei traded a glance with Nescana. Everybody had known the king wasn't well. But no one, Trei thought, had expected Terinai Naterensei to actually *die.* Not now. Not yet.

"Yes," Ceirfei said quietly, reading Trei's expression without effort. "It can't be helped."

Trei nodded. "Your mother ..." he began.

"Yes. She would have preferred I remain within the royal precincts. I came ... I said I wished to inform Wingmaster Taimenai personally."

Trei nodded uncertainly. That made perfect sense, but then why did Ceirfei put it that way, as though he'd said that only because it was a plausible excuse?

"I hear you encountered a dragon this morning?" Ceirfei looked at Trei, one eyebrow rising in a wordless comment on that event. He was smiling, too ... it was almost like a real smile, if you didn't know him. The prince could hardly say, like little Tokaii, *It should have been me! It's not fair!* But of course he wanted to.

Trei hardly blamed him. He said, "*You'd* have been the one to find the dragon right above you, if you'd been there."

"I doubt it." Ceirfei's tone was dry. "You do have a way of finding yourself in the middle of things, Trei. And I doubt I've had enough practice to get so high." Only the faintest flattening of his tone revealed his longing for the living winds, for enough practice time to outfly any other kajurai in the sky, for the chance to climb so high his wings would brush the arch of the heavens.

"That's not really fair," Trei objected. "Nescana was there, too. She got just as high as I did."

"Indeed? Good for you!" Ceirfei said warmly to Nescana. "Wingmaster Taimenai didn't mention that to me— but we barely discussed the details. Well done, Nescana!"

"Don't tell her that!" Genrai said. "She's too impatient already—and she breaks too many rules! Every time you turn around, there she goes, right out where she's not supposed to be." He glowered at his sister. "She'll get expelled before she's even been here a year!"

Trei thought Nescana would yell back at her brother, but the girl only blushed, hesitated, glanced at Ceirfei and away again, and said at last, "Oh, well ... it was really too high for me. Trei had to help me get down. And Genrai got higher, Master Anerii said."

"Well done, nonetheless!" Ceirfei didn't seem to notice her nervousness. He tapped the table gently with the knuckles of one closed fist, and went on, "Even if you weren't the highest, you and Trei, the dragon came to you. The two of you."

"Yes. But ..." said Trei. "I should have ... I didn't ... I should have at least *asked* if it meant *I* should summon fire and earth and everything. If I'd *told* it I didn't understand—"

"I'm sure the encounter was not so very orderly."

Trei made an impolite sound. "It would have been for *you. You'd* have asked how one goes about summoning wind and fire and earth, and the dragon would have told you *just* what to do. I expect the Little Emperor would be really surprised if we summoned dragons of fire and earth to destroy his steam engines."

Those engines were a real and serious threat, and figuring out what to do about them, and the power they gave Tolounnese mages, was a real and serious priority. None of that was Trei's problem, for which he was very grateful. He'd been far too involved in destroying the last ones.

Ceirfei grinned. "I doubt your dragon had anything so useful in mind. I imagine it wants something important to dragons and has no idea about our concerns." He was silent for a moment, considering.

"*Your* dragon—" Trei began, but then hesitated.

Ceirfei's smile twisted. "*My* dragon. Yes. We do indeed owe the dragons what service they demand. *I* owe them that. I have not forgotten. I do think it's possible *your* dragon means to call in that debt."

"I don't know," Trei said. But he held out the written account, in case Ceirfei should see something in the dragon's vague words that he himself had missed.

Ceirfei took it, glanced over Trei's neat, small writing, and glanced up again. "Very good. Very useful. Trei, I'm afraid I need you to take me over to the hidden school, if you would be so kind."

"Of course," Trei said, surprised. Now it was clear, at least, why Ceirfei had made up an excuse to come the kajurai precincts, and then slipped down to the novitiate. He said, "Of course I'll take you."

"If you can open a door that will take us straight to Master Tnegun, that would be perfect. That door over there, perhaps—"

Trei shook his head. "I can take you to Araenè, that's all. Any door I open, it only leads to Araenè." He guessed anew at Ceirfei's distress because normally the prince wouldn't forget something like that.

"Of course," said Ceirfei. "Of course. Well, if you can take me to Araenè, then *she* can take me to Master Tnegun. It's not venturing," he added suddenly, and that wasn't like him either, to forget things and then have to scramble to catch them up. "I told Wingmaster Taimenai I would ask you, so you have leave. Indeed," he added in a lower tone, "I have told the wingmaster everything. Now I must speak with Master Tnegun ..."

"It's no trouble," Trei said hastily, and went across the dining hall to the nearest door, to give Ceirfei time to collect himself.

That door ordinarily led to the bathing room. But, of course, when Trei took out his crystal pendant, laid his hand on the door, whispered his cousin's name, and shoved it open, it opened to show, not the novices' bath, but the quiet dimness of Master Tnegun's private library. Araenè turned to look at them, and beyond her, Master Tnegun himself was dimly visible, the pale candlelight gleaming off his ebony skin.

"I'll never get used to that," commented Genrai, not quite loudly enough to carry to the mage.

"I wish *I* had a crystal like that," said Rekei, and Kojran nodded. Trei was a little surprised to find he had no idea to what, or whom, each of the two boys wished they could open a door. But he didn't have time to wonder about that, not right then, because Ceirfei, at his shoulder, said, "Perfect!" and gave Trei a little nod, meaning *Go on*. Trei rubbed his crystal, pressed a hand firmly against the doorframe, and stepped through the door, out of the novitiate and into the hidden school.

Master Tnegun's library was a small, richly appointed room. Right now it occupied a place high up in a square Second City tower, though Trei had been in it before and thought it hadn't always been so situated. Every wall was lined with shelves of books and racks of scrolls. A single chair occupied the center of the room, upholstered in dark cloth. Master Tnegun sat in this chair, a small milk-white sphere held in one dark hand, framed by his long, elegant fingers. Araenè stood before him, an odd tension in her face. She looked up quickly when Trei opened the door, and her expression lightened immediately. Then she saw Ceirfei, and first smiled but then frowned.

One of Master Tnegun's eyebrows tilted upward when he saw Ceirfei, and he rose to his feet, a small green lizard running up his sleeve and darting across the back of the chair, where it posed, its yellow eyes glinting like jewels. Master Tnegun ignored it. Standing, he was very tall and, Trei always thought, rather intimidating.

Trei was sure his cousin's master could not be mistaken for any other man in all the Floating Islands. In the novitiate, Kojran never tired of reminding people of his Yngulin grandfather, who had in his day been an important emissary to the Islands. Kojran showed his mixed blood not only in his smooth, dark skin, but also in his tall, lithe build and in the exotic cast to his face, all high cheekbones and narrow chin and wide-set oblique eyes.

But Master Tnegun was pure Yngulin, without a drop of Tolounnese or Island blood. His skin was nearly true black, his features hawk-sharp and fierce, his narrow mouth sardonic. Rather than the jewel-toned clothing native Islanders preferred, he wore a plain robe even blacker than his skin. Trei was a little afraid of him—had always been a little afraid of him—but it was easy to believe that the Yngulin mage would listen to everything Ceirfei told him and immediately propose a clever solution to all their problems.

The mage said now, in a tone of faint surprise, "Prince Ceirfei. You have heard, then?"

Ceirfei's eyebrows rose. "I thought *I* had news for *you*. Perhaps we had better trade."

"Ah." Master Tnegun also stood very still, and Trei saw that it was the kind of stillness that braced against an expected blow—that they both stood that way, the mage and the prince. Master Tnegun said, "Tell me your what word you bring, Prince Ceirfei."

Ceirfei inclined his head. "I grieve to be the first to inform you that my uncle has passed into the hands of the Gods."

"Oh, Ceirfei!" exclaimed Araenè. "That's *terrible!*" She crossed the room to put a hand on his arm, looking anxiously into his face. Ceirfei touched the back of her hand with the tips of two fingers, but of course he couldn't do anything so undignified as put an arm around her, not with Master Tnegun in the room.

Master Tnegun said formally, "I am sorry for your loss, Prince Ceirfei. The sea is made of salt tears, and the waves of the griefs of men, but I am sorry those waves should rise so high for you. I pray the earth will rest lightly over his bones."

"Yes," said Ceirfei, his tone tightly controlled. "There is worse. Or at least, there is more. A fleet has put out from Tolounn. Ships of war, not fat-bellied merchant ships."

Master Tnegun did not move. "We had suspected the Tolounnese must be building more of their new engines to feed power to their mages. I gather this must have occurred. Perhaps Cen Periven—"

"I fear we can expect no aid from that direction. We have had word from our emissary. Cen Periven," Ceirfei said deliberately, "has declared formally that it is unable to assist the Floating Islands."

"Ah." Master Tnegun didn't look surprised. "Regrettable, but perhaps not astonishing. Cen Periven has always depended on distance as its great defense, as the Islands have depended on height. Then we have no hope, unless we immediately find and destroy the Tolounnese steam engines that are feeding power to their mages."

"Our kajuraihi will delay those Tolounnese ships as they can. However ... my cousin Imrei—" Ceirfei paused.

Master Tnegun said, "One supposes that Prince Imrei may perhaps prove a trifle hesitant to choose one action over another, so that in the end he may choose inaction by default. Perhaps Lord Manasi Tierdana might encourage your cousin to some active course?"

"Perhaps," said Ceirfei. "In fact, my mother met with Lord Manasi this very evening. In fact ..." he hesitated and then finished even more quietly, "In fact, he requested a meeting with her."

Master Tnegun looked enlightened. "Ah."

"He doesn't care to deal with my mother. Nor is he pleased that I am Imrei's heir. However, we find he has been active on my uncle's behalf. Those engines on the coast were, we now know, merely decoys. We find now that Lord Manasi has discovered where the Tolounnese built others: roughly a hundred miles upriver from Gaicana. Four engines."

"How very clever of Lord Manasi," said Master Tnegun, his tone absolutely neutral.

"As it turns out," said Ceirfei, "Yes."

Araenè looked at Trei. Her raised eyebrows asked: *Do you know what they're so carefully not saying?* Trei shook his head, a minimal gesture because he didn't want to interrupt. It was fascinating watching Ceirfei with Master Tnegun, neither of them quite saying anything plainly, yet clearly understanding each other. But, at the same time, alarming. He wished *he* understood, too.

"If we know where the engines are, then our powder-bombs—" began the mage.

Powder-bombs were wooden disks filled with an explosive powder, meant to be cast down from a height by kajuraihi. Trei had practiced with that kind of disk, but he wasn't very good at pulling the winds to guide the bombs toward their targets. But at least he understood now some of what Ceirfei and Master Tnegun were talking about.

"I fear they will not avail us as they did against the decoys. If Tolounnese warships have already set sail, then we will assuredly find that at least one of those engines is already working, and our kajuraihi will find the entire area already protected beneath a region of dead air. Kajuraihi cannot, of course, fly into such a region—and I do not know how we may destroy the engines if the kajuraihi cannot reach them." Ceirfei paused. Then he said, "I have already discussed the matter with Wingmaster Taimenai. Now, of course, I come to you, in the hope that the mages may have some useful advice."

Master Tnegun nodded in understanding. He held up the little sphere. "We had wondered why this was put in our way just at this moment. The precise function for which this sphere was made is a matter of some debate. But I do believe it may function as a means of drawing the dragon winds into the region above the Tolounnese engines, despite the best efforts of their mages." He turned the sphere in his fingers. It was small, hardly bigger than a man's fist, and white as pearl. Or as cloud, Trei thought. He almost fancied he could see its surface swirl, as cloud might swirl through the sky when a strong wind came.

Master Tnegun was watching him, his expression ironic. "Your cousin found it," he said, a little drily. "We may well surmise that Araenè stumbled across it for a reason, as apprentices seldom find themselves encountering such items in the ordinary course of events. That is hardly coincidence— or so I surmise." The mage held the sphere out to Ceirfei with a slight flourish.

"It's a thing of dragon magic, of course," said Ceirfei.

"It contains dragon magic, certainly. A great deal of dragon magic, we believe."

Trei leaned forward to look at it more closely. He could see at once that Ceirfei was right. He said, "But if *Araenè* found it—I mean, you know, this morning—"

"Yes," said Ceirfei. And said to Master Tnegun and to Araenè, "A dragon descended this morning, far enough to speak to high-flying kajuraihi. In fact, it spoke to Trei."

"Trei!" exclaimed Araenè. "Are you all right?"

It was nice to have someone understand that having a dragon come down to talk to you wasn't necessarily a pleasure. Trei nodded reassuringly. "It was strange, but beautiful. I didn't really understand it. But it didn't—I mean, you don't expect to understand a dragon, after all."

"Indeed," murmured Master Tnegun. He took the sphere back into his dark hand, where it looked smaller and denser and whiter than ever. He held it up so that they could all stare at it. "This is very old. I suspect no mage living is quite certain what it will prove to do, or be, or become, if the magic it contains is released. However ... the act of releasing the magic it holds would certainly draw down from the heights a powerful and living wind. Of this I think we may be quite confident."

"I see," said Ceirfei. "Yes, I see."

"This sphere contains ordinary spells for light, for summoning, for finding your way, for weightlessness, for confusing your enemy, for drawing structure out of confusion, for silence, and for breath when there is no breath. Also for turning air into glass, which may possibly offer a hint as to how it was made. Nine spells, which is three threes and lends them all greater stability and power. These spells are ordinary in one sense, as they have been fashioned of ordinary human magic," added the mage. "But they are surprisingly subtle and complex examples of human magecraft." He glanced over at Araenè, smiling faintly at last. "Araenè does seem to have a tendency to find—or be given—interesting and unusual items."

"If the living winds were brought down upon the Tolounnese engines," Ceirfei said, "I gather that nothing would then prevent our kajuraihi from following those winds and throwing down any number of powder-bombs."

The mage inclined his head. "Prince Ceirfei, I hope that such a tactic would very likely prove efficacious. What else might be freed if this sphere were used in such a manner is, however, more difficult to guess."

Araenè said uneasily, glancing from her master to Ceirfei and back again, "I don't think ... that is ... I'm not *so* sure you should plan on releasing the magic in Kanora's sphere."

"No?" Master Tnegun's looked at her, one eyebrow rising.

"I just don't like the idea," Araenè said apologetically. "I don't know why. I mean ... I do think it would *work*. I mean ... I think there's quite a lot of dragon magic in that sphere. But I ... I just don't like the idea of letting it out like that. I just don't."

"Such a tactic could indeed be dangerous," said the mage, more to Ceirfei than to Araenè. "It's unclear to me whether it might be better to free these other spells, the ordinary ones, before freeing the winds contained in the sphere itself. It's also unclear what the effects of releasing the dragon magic held within this sphere will be."

Ceirfei turned to Trei. "Your dragon must have had a *reason* to approach a kajurai, Trei. This seems like it might be a very good reason. I doubt the dragons have forgotten the events of last summer any more than we have. Don't you think it might have intended precisely this?"

"No!" Araenè said at once, but then looked flustered when everyone turned to her. She said, "*I* don't know! I don't think *anybody* should do anything to my sphere—I mean, *Kanora's* sphere—*anyway*, I don't think anybody should do anything to it that will ruin it, or use it up, or whatever! I'm sure that's not what the dragon meant!" She glared at both Master Tnegun and Ceirfei, her shoulders straight and her chin raised, waiting, Trei could see, for one or the other of them to tell her she was behaving like a foolish girl.

"I think ..." Master Tnegun said slowly, speaking to her but again mostly to Ceirfei, "That we should respect Araenè's perception in this matter. Or else agree that it is mere happenstance that led her to find Kanora Ireinamei's sphere." His tone made it clear he thought this was not very likely.

Ceirfei gave the mage a minimal nod and turned to Araenè. "I'm sorry. I don't doubt you. Only, when other options fall through our fingers like sand down the glass ..."

Araenè nodded unhappily, not protesting again, although Trei could see she wanted to.

Master Tnegun said to Trei, "What precisely did the dragon say to you? If I may ask?"

Ceirfei gave him Trei's report.

"Well," said the mage after a moment, thoughtfully, "certainly none but the kajuraihi ride the winds as well as standing upon the earth. This about fire and glass, I do not understand, but again it is kajuraihi who may summon the living winds. There is certainly fire within the Tolounnese engines, and I suppose we might be said to have summoned fire, last summer." He glanced up from the paper. "I should consult with Master Kopapei, and perhaps Master Akhai. But if we must send our kajuraihi to destroy these Tolounnese engines, I think we must send with them this sphere of dragon magic."

"You shall have at least a brief time to consult," agreed Ceirfei. "I think I must inform my mother and Lord Manasi of what you suggest. And my cousin, as well, of course," he added as an afterthought.

Master Tnegun bowed his dark head. "Prince Ceirfei ... I am your servant."

Though the mage put no special emphasis on the pronoun in that statement, Trei thought the *your* stood out. There was a brief, tense pause. Trei certainly didn't dare break the fraught stillness. He hardly dared breathe. Araenè shifted to stand closer to him, looking nervous and young and uncertain. Trei wondered whether she, too, had caught the implication that her master had not quite put into direct words.

Then Ceirfei, frowning, moved one hand in a small gesture as though he were sweeping something away and out of sight. "I don't doubt you, Master Tnegun."

"I hope you do not. You need not," said the mage. "I am grateful that you permit me to advise you. I know well that you—"

"Don't say it," Ceirfei warned him.

"And if someone must, at some fast-approaching moment?"

"Not you, and not now."

Master Tnegun inclined his head.

There was another pause, this one longer but not quite so fraught. Ceirfei broke it, by asking at last, "I shall, as I say, bring these matters before my cousin."

"Of course, Prince Ceirfei."

"I am aware we might all prefer to consider at leisure what we might do," Ceirfei said. He rose to his feet and went on, his tone now very formal. "However, I fear that time has run out. If we have even now a Tolounnese war fleet riding a magewind across the sea toward the Islands, we must act decisively. And effectively."

The mage inclined his head in acknowledgement. "An inarguable point, Prince Ceirfei; and I assure you I do not argue it. If you call upon me, I will assuredly hear you. And in the meantime ..." he held the cloud-white sphere out to Ceirfei.

Ceirfei reached out to take it, but before his fingertips touched it, Araenè snatched it out of Master Tnegun's hand. Her eyes wide and startled, as though she had astonished even herself, she took three quick steps to the side and back and vanished neatly through a door that, an instant before, hadn't been there.

5

When she fled, Araenè had no idea where she was going. She had an aptitude for doors—well, let it work for her, then! The hidden school, or maybe one or another of its hidden dragons, wanted to push her out of familiar places, wanted to show her or give her things—fine. Let the school itself, or the dragon at the school's heart, take her someplace useful or show her something she could use. She was furious, and not even sure whether she was angry with Master Tnegun or with Ceirfei, or maybe with herself. She was frightened, maybe just of Master Tnegun catching up with her, but maybe of something else, something she didn't recognize. She was so tired she was stumbling, and she *didn't care* what anybody said or thought, she wasn't giving Kanora Ireinamei's special dragon sphere to anybody, not if they were going to destroy it.

The door she had ducked through instantly spun away into nothing, leaving her alone, somewhere she didn't recognize, somewhere far outside the ordinary precincts of the hidden school. She found herself out of doors, somewhere high up. Araenè blinked, dizzied by the sudden sense of space and height. To her right, the dark bulk of mountains rose jagged against the star-lit sky, and to her left the wide sweep of empty space fell away to the shimmering great blackness of the sea far below. Brilliant moonlight poured over sea and stone and across the tangle of branches of a nearby tree, and across a pool of water at the foot of the tree. The stone and branches were a hard-edged black in the moonlight, but the pool was silver. The shadows of the branches were stark across the water, but when she moved a step closer to the pool, she found the light of moon and stars was not enough to make her own reflection visible. She saw only the shadows of the branches, and an ocean of reflected stars.

She was so tired. This day had gone on forever already, and she felt that the night would go on forever, too. She had been so angry, angry at everyone, but the anger seemed to have burned out. Or perhaps it had drained away into the sky and the sea ... she knelt down upon the smooth, round pebbles that bordered the pool, white as pearls in the moonlight, and reached out a hand to touch the water. Though the night was warm, the water was cold. The ripples spread out from her fingertips, rippling against the pebbles with a low music. The air was fragrant with a scent she didn't recognize, a cold, wild fragrance, like mint, but not mint. Maybe it was the fragrance of starlight. She drew back her hand, drops of water spiraling around her fingers and scattering, silver and sparkling, back into the pool.

When she held out Kanora's sphere, she found it had condensed, so that it was now hardly the size of an egg. It seemed heavier, too, and yet it felt oddly tenuous in her fingers, as though it was made of clouds and air and magic. It had taken on a pearly sheen, though that might have been the moonlight that poured across it like water. Within the sphere, light bloomed; a strange gray-lavender, like sunlight filtered through fierce storm clouds ... she blinked and bent over the sphere, peering more closely.

Clouds towered within the sphere, an ominous dark purple-black, flickering with lightning. Brutal winds whipped the pewter-dark sea into a frenzy below those clouds. But ships surged across the violent waves, striking up the crest of one and plunging down again, over and over, yellowish froth flinging upward from their sharp prows. Lots of ships. Eight, twelve ... fifteen ... more than that, as the vision contained within the sphere widened, and widened again. Narrow-prowed warships, gray-gold sails ... she said out loud, frustrated and beginning to be angry again, "But what does it *mean*? And what am I supposed to *do*?"

There was no answer, not from sky or wind or dragon. Of course not. That would make things too easy. But anger seemed too much effort. It seemed to her that the wind blew it away, like the morning mist. She sat back on her heels, sighing.

A door of iron and crystal and white wood opened against the air, a door that stood hard against the edge of the cliffs, and Master Tnegun stepped through. He closed the door gently behind him. Unlike her door, his didn't disappear. It waited until he, or someone else, should want to open it again. Doors Araenè called up seldom cooperated like that. If she were a *real* mage, she could make doors cooperate all the time too, and then she wouldn't have such problems.

Master Tnegun stood for some time, considering her. She stared back at him, the sphere heavy and cool in her hand, and wondered what he was thinking. What *would* a master mage think or say or do, faced with a still new and suddenly defiant apprentice? Moonlight slid across her master's eyes so that, for a moment, he looked blind. The edges of his cloak rippled in the wind, cool at this height. It was black as night, that cloak; he was all black against the darkness, cloak and face and hands alike. He looked like something made of the midnight dark and of magic. He looked ageless as the mountains and the sky.

Then he moved, stepping forward to crouch at the edge of the pool beside Araenè, and became familiar once more. Araenè let out a breath she hadn't realized she was holding.

"You were upset," Master Tnegun said, his tone prosaic.

Araenè didn't dignify this with an answer. She felt thoroughly childish. She stared down at the little ripples the wind sent out across the surface of the pool. Wavelets ran gently and repetitively against the rim of stones.

"But it wasn't any ordinary fit of temper that brought you all the way from the hidden school to these heights," Master Tnegun added. "I'm sorry for it. I *am* sorry for it," he added, at her swift, surprised look. "Because having considered the matter carefully, I remain unable to think of any weapon we have readily to hand that will enable us to face down the Tolounnese mages. They and their engines, and the Tolounnese warships approaching us now, and the ten thousand Tolounnese soldiers those ships carry ...”

"You can think of something else," Araenè said, hearing her own voice small and uncertain in the moonlit darkness.

"Events rush down upon us," Master Tnegun said gently. "I don't think we shall have the leisure to consider many other options."

Araenè didn't say anything.

"I shall certainly discuss the matter with Kopapei and Akhai," her master added, still gently. "But if we are to act at all, we must do so very soon. We do not have days in which to consider. We may not even have a bell. Of all possible paths forward from this moment, the one paved with delay and hesitation is surely the most unwise. I need not remind you of what so nearly happened last summer ...”

Araenè shook her head.

"And it is hard to see why this sphere of all spheres should fall so neatly into our hands just now, unless we are to use it."

"Not for this," Araenè whispered. "Not to destroy it."

"Whatever difficulties arise from its use, we will handle them one way or another. But, Araenè, we do not have leisure to try one thing and another and then yet another, while Tolounnese soldiers rush upon us, protected and abetted by Tolounnese mages, whom *we cannot match*, Araenè, as you assuredly recall." Master Tnegun held out one long hand. "I am sorry for it, Araenè, but you must give me the sphere."

Araenè lifted it in a hand that seemed barely to belong to her. The sphere seemed to weigh on her more and more heavily as she reluctantly began to offer it to her master— and, without thought, with hardly an intention, she suddenly tossed it away instead. It arced through the moonlight without a sound, glimmering like a great pearl, and fell neatly, with a sound almost like a bell being struck, into the pool. It vanished instantly in the black water. Ripples ran gently out from the place it had struck the water.

"Araenè!" snapped Master Tnegun. He was on his feet, though she hadn't seen him rise. If he hadn't been angry before, he was *now*. Angry and shocked. "You threw a sphere containing *dragon magic* into a pool *brimming over* with dragon magic? Into *Kotipa's* pool, shaded by the shadows of the dragon's mountains?"

Araenè stared at him, mute. She hadn't even known where they were, she realized, until that moment. But it made sense. Of course it did. Kanora's dragon sphere, brought to the Islands of Dragons ... dragon magic must be all through this mountain, and now she had brought a different kind of dragon magic here, too. She should have recognized it, she thought, even in the dark, because of course she had been here once before, though ordinarily no one but kajuraihi ever came here.

Master Tnegun took a step toward the pool, knelt, and reached a hand toward the water—but hesitated before the tips of his fingers touched the water. The dragon sphere had vanished into the pool and was completely invisible. In the dark, the pool's surface was opaque. It might have been any depth. Perhaps it was no deeper than a man's hand could reach. But in the dark, she could imagine that the pool sank away through unseen crevices in the stone, so deep its waters might eventually trickle out, chilled and heavy from its journey through stone, drop by slow drop, and fall into the sea far below.

And, Araenè realized slowly, her master hesitated for another reason. He hesitated because this was Kotipa, and the waters of Kotipa's pool were not for a mage.

He drew back his hand, and straightened, and said, in a biting tone, without quite looking at her, "I shall have to bring a kajurai to fetch it out. And we had all best hope it has not been harmed or changed or had its magic released untimely by what you have done."

Araenè said nothing at all.

It was Ceirfei whom Master Tnegun brought to fetch the dragon sphere out of Kotipa's pool. Araenè should have expected that. Of course it would be Ceirfei. He told her he was sorry. Ceirfei said that, very gently, as though he spoke to a child. Araenè knew she had flushed. She wanted to shout at him for treating her like a baby. She wanted to beg him not to give Master Tnegun her sphere—no, *Kanora Ireinamei's* sphere, of course, not hers at all. But she couldn't. Because what could she say? That she hated the idea of using the sphere the way Master Tnegun had suggested? They all knew that already. Only she had no way to explain, even to herself, why she hated that idea—and they couldn't think of anything else to do—and they all knew how desperately they needed to do *something*. Even she knew that.

So she didn't argue. She stood back, her arms folded over her chest, trying not to look sulky, and watched as Ceirfei listened to Master Tnegun's terse explanation of just where the sphere had struck the surface of the pool, nodded, stepped forward, bent, and thrust his hand and arm into the cold water. And straightened again, almost at once. He held the sphere. He had found it just that easily. Kajurai magic, dragon magic—of course he had reached directly down to touch it. Of course the pool had only been deep enough to wet his arm to the elbow. Araenè might as well not have bothered even trying. She clenched her teeth, but didn't know if she was trying to hold back anger or tears.

The sphere had changed, though. It had been small, only about the size of an egg, and white as the summer clouds. Now it was much bigger, so big that Ceirfei had to use both hands to hold it up. And it had become transparent as the purest crystal, as clear as the water of the pool, as pure as the dragon's living winds. It glimmered with reflected light, until it seemed that the moonlight and starlight collected within it and then radiated out once more, coldly brilliant. The taste of dragon magic, so reminiscent of perilla and mint and yet so different, tingled sharp and vivid across Araenè's tongue and the palms of her hands. She gasped, and the air itself seemed cold and sharp.

"It's changed," Ceirfei said, unnecessarily. "It didn't look like this even when we first found it." Turning, he tried to offer it to Master Tnegun, who took a quick step back and held up a forbidding hand.

"It's not for a mage," Master Tnegun said, with considerable force. "It's too much a thing of dragon magic, now. I can barely perceive the ordinary human spellwork it holds. Better for a kajurai to keep it. Which is as well, as it must go with a kajurai anyway."

"It can still be used as you proposed?" Ceirfei said, his tone sharp, not even glancing at Araenè. She couldn't even blame him, because of course Ceirfei would ignore what she wanted, or what he himself wanted, if he thought he had to. Of course he would. He had to. He was even right, and how could he know that Araenè was right, too? *If* she was. She didn't even know she *was* right, and she did know that everything Master Tnegun had said was true, about the Tolounnese mages and ships. So she couldn't even be angry.

She was frightened instead. It wasn't an improvement.

"I should think," Master Tnegun said, gazing at the sphere, and squinting a little as though it dazzled him, "that if the dragon winds that sphere contains are freed, those winds will assuredly tear through any possible barrier any number of Tolounnese mages might put in its way. I cannot imagine any human spellwork, powered by adjuvants or by steam engines or by anything at all, that could possibly prevent those winds from going where they chose, if they were freed."

"Well, then," Ceirfei said, rather drily, "that should suffice."

Master Tnegun sent her back to her apartment. To her room, like a sulky child. Araenè didn't care. She felt like a sulky child. She wanted to go back to her room anyway. She didn't want to see anybody or talk to anybody or argue with anybody. Not even Ceirfei. Definitely not Ceirfei. She would have liked to talk to Trei, maybe. She felt she couldn't bear anybody else's company, but she would have liked Trei ... . But her cousin must have gone back to the kajurai novitiate. Where he belonged. At least he really did belong there. She couldn't help but doubt whether she belonged in this apartment in the mage's hidden school. She wondered what Master Tnegun thought of her now. She wasn't even very good at learning the kinds of things apprentices were supposed to learn, math and everything, and now ... this. She wondered whether her master would find time, despite everything else, to talk to Master Kopapei about her. She liked Master Kopapei. She thought he liked her—the senior mage seemed to like everyone. But she couldn't imagine him keeping her in the hidden school, if her own master didn't want her.

She didn't even know if she *wanted* to stay in the hidden school.

She was homesick. She realized that at last. She wanted her old life back. Constrained as it had been, she wanted it back.

Well, not the boredom, having to stay in unless she could sneak out. Not the ignorance, which she hadn't even noticed at the time because she hadn't cared about math or minerals. Not the absence of magic ... she wouldn't want to go back to the time before the mage-gift had risen in her like a tide. She didn't want to give up her new life. Only she didn't know if she could keep it.

And she missed her mother.

She wanted her parents back. Grief, which had, over the long summer, mostly settled to the back of her mind and her heart, rose unexpectedly into her throat. Her eyes prickled. She didn't *really* want to go back and live with her parents in their house on the Avenue of Flameberry Trees in the Fourth Quarter of the Second City. But she wanted to know they were *there*, alive and happy and going on with their lives. She wanted to be able to go back and find them there and have them say they were glad she had found the mage-gift in herself, that they were proud of her. She blinked hard, her eyes prickling.

There was a quiet rap on her door.

At first Araenè thought it must be her cousin Trei. She was halfway to the door before she realized that no, it was probably Master Tnegun. Then she almost ran back into her bedroom and jumped into the bed and pretended to be asleep. Only that would be childish, and anyway, he would only come back in the morning.

She crossed the room slowly and opened the door.

It was Tichorei. Araenè couldn't imagine what he was doing knocking on her door in what must be, by now, the middle of the night. "What?" she said, both the surprise and, she suspected, the wariness clear in her voice.

With his free hand, Tichorei shoved dark hair back from his high forehead, a restless, nervous gesture, though he was seldom nervous. His eyes were shadowed, and his mouth pressed to a thin line. He didn't look like he was very pleased to see Araenè. But he'd come out of his way to knock on her door. She stared at him, waiting to hear what he would say.

He said, "I was looking for you. I wanted—I need to apologize."

Araenè blinked, taken utterly by surprise.

"For giving you away to, well, everyone," Tichorei said uncomfortably. A dark flush spread up his throat to his cheekbones. "In that tavern. I saw you were dressed up as a boy. But I didn't think. I was—I didn't—anyway, I'm sorry."

Araenè started to say, *That's all right, it doesn't matter.* Only it *wasn't* all right, and it *did* matter. She said stiffly, "I can't ever go back there again, now. I had *friends* there, Tichorei!"

The older apprentice started to say something, stopped, hesitated, and said at last, "I know. I mean ... I know. I really am sorry, Araenè."

That was three times he'd apologized. Refusing to accept his apology now would be, well, Araenè could just imagine what her mother would say. Except she really could, she realized, and flinched from a renewed stab of grief. She said, her tone still stiff and not very gracious, "It doesn't matter, I guess. I would have ... I needed to tell Hanaiki anyway. I didn't think he ... but I had to tell him, and I was scared to. So I guess it's just as well you made me tell him right then."

Tichorei gave her a searching look. "You should go back. I mean, you should go back there as yourself. I mean, later, when ... after everything is over. I'd go with you. If you want."

Araenè stared at him. He'd go with her. To Cesera's. In her head, the two parts of her life collided, soundlessly but with a shocking impact. She said at last, not very kindly, "I wouldn't want you to put yourself to any trouble."

Tichorei winced slightly. "I don't blame you for being ... for thinking ... I know the rest of us haven't been very nice to you since ... well, Kanii, of course, but Kanii gets along with everyone." He tried to smile. It wasn't a very successful effort. "Look, I heard about you finding that sphere of dragon magic. Kanora Ireinamei's sphere. And, well, everything, I guess."

She was sure he had. Everyone would have heard about the dragon sphere and what Master Tnegun had thought of to do with it and that she'd tried to hide it by throwing it into the pool on Kotipa. All the really interesting news seeming to fly through the hidden school by some unknown but very efficient magic of its own. Araenè wasn't so sure she liked the idea that everyone must be talking about her. She could just imagine what they were all saying. At least, Kanii would be nice about it, and little Cesei would probably just want to try to get his hands on Kanora's sphere and see if he could make one like it, but the others ... she knew they would be jealous and angry, and they'd think she was so stupid. Such a *girl*. So unfair *she* should find one dragon after another. *Last summer and again now?* they'd say. And she couldn't even exactly blame them. She glared at Tichorei.

He frowned back at her, but his expression was more searching than angry. He said, "And Kanora Ireinamei was a lady mage, after all. Even if that sounds ... a little strange.

We'll—I'll get used to it." Araenè started to say something sarcastic, but before she could, Tichorei added, "And if we can, they can. Those people at that tavern, I mean. Anyway, they've no business saying whether you can be a mage or not. That's our business, not theirs—"

"Is that supposed to be an improvement?"

Tichorei winced again. "Well," he said, "I hope it is. Or will be. I was thinking. About, well, you know our masters are all involved with finding ways to slow down those Tolounnese ships. And the adjuvants are helping them, of course, *they're* important. We ... I thought we might practice the sorts of things we can do to help. Catching overextended mages, I can show everybody that, that's going to be important later, probably."

Araenè nodded, a little unwillingly, because probably he was right. "But—" she began.

"That's too advanced for some of you," Tichorei admitted. "But there are other things you—we might be able to do. Little things. Dropping basilisk eggs on those ships, that's something you could do, Araenè, because you've got gifts for vision and summoning doors. Cesei could find the eggs for you. Floating a brilliant light in front of a ship so its crew can't see, Taobai could do that—he's got a gift for light, you know. Everyone's in the workroom. I thought you might come down there, too. If you wanted. Kanii's there already. And ... I mean, I will be, too. I can keep Kepai and Kebei and Jeneki and everyone from, well ..."

"All right," Araenè said abruptly. "All right. If you want." She wasn't afraid, at least, that Tichorei might be setting her up for some kind of mean joke. Kepai or Kebei, yes, the twins might pretend to be nice just so they could be mean later. But Tichorei? She couldn't even imagine cool, serious Tichorei playing that kind of trick on anybody. No. He was so much older. He was almost a mage himself.

Almost a mage. Tichorei was almost a mage. He knew so much more than she did. He knew almost everything. Caught by an unexpected thought, Araenè stood still, gazing at Tichorei.

He straightened uneasily under her stare. "What? Araenè?"

"You know how to make a sphere," Araenè said slowly. "Don't you." It wasn't a question. "You know how to make spheres of metals and minerals and glass and wood and everything. Don't you. And how to put spells into them. You know all those things."

"That's *far* too advanced for you!" Tichorei declared, alarmed. "Making spheres—"

"It's something master mages do, I know! And then they draw on an adjuvant's power and make spells and invest them in the sphere, and then anybody can use them later. Only *you* don't need an adjuvant, do you? Because you're not old enough to have started losing your power yet. So you can make a sphere *and* invest it with spells, can't you?"

Tichorei looked unsettled. "Maybe," he admitted warily. "Why?"

Araenè smiled at him. "I know just what kind of sphere I want you to make for me." She was so exhausted she was dizzy, and thoughts scattered in her mind before she could really catch them, and maybe that was why she'd thought of it in the first place and why it seemed like such a good idea now. But she thought it might work. It was the first thing she'd thought might work since ... well, since Master Tnegun had first suggested using up the magic in Kanora's dragon sphere to break the power of the Tolounnese mages. She said, "I want you to make me a sphere that will let me—or anyone—catch dragon magic."

The older apprentice did not actually retreat in terror; he had too much dignity for that, but Araenè could tell he wanted to. He said, "Araenè—"

"Not *all* the dragon magic," Araenè said hastily. "I mean, there's too much! I know that! But a little, you can make a sphere to capture just a little bit of dragon magic, can't you, Tichorei? So that when Kanora's sphere is broken and the dragon winds come out, just a little bit of the winds can be caught again? That way, we can use Kanora's sphere, but not all of it, not all the way, isn't that right?" She saw Tichorei was going to refuse, and said urgently, "I promise it will make up for you giving me away to everyone at Cesera's. I promise it will. I'll never ask you for anything again—"

Tichorei held up a hand to stop her. Then he came a step farther into her apartment and shut the door behind him, as though afraid some whisper of her idea would float out through halls of the hidden school if they weren't careful. He rubbed his face with his other hand, looking, Araenè realized, almost as tired as she felt. He said at last, not exactly asking but just getting it straight in his mind, "You want to catch some of the dragon magic in Kanora's sphere, after the kajuraihi use it to break the dead air over their engines. You want me to make a sphere that can hold dragon magic? Araenè, I don't know how to work with dragon magic! Dragon magic is for kajuraihi, not for us!"

"Kanora did it," Araenè pointed out. This seemed to her to be an unanswerable argument. "If she did it, you can do it!"

"Araenè—"

"Or at least you can try! Or show me how!" Araenè took an urgent step toward him. "I can do it, I'm sure I can, if you show me! What harm could it do? Just a little bit of dragon magic, there will be plenty left to break the dead air of the Tolounnese mages, just as it's supposed to. Glass or quartz or barite or something, you know Kanora's sphere looked like it was made of something like glass—" she didn't let herself think that it hadn't, really.

"How," said Tichorei, in the tone of someone glad to point out an insurmountable obstacle so that he could stop arguing without actually refusing, "How do you expect to get this special sphere, even if I could make one, to Tolounn anyway? You can't expect a kajurai to volunteer to carry it for you!"

"That's my problem," Araenè said firmly. "You can let me worry about that. All I want is for you to make me a sphere. Or show me how!"

Tichorei threw up his hands. "Making a sphere is far too advanced for you!"

"I know! That's why I need you to do it!"

Tichorei glared at her. "Girls!" he said. "Every single thing's the most important thing ever!"

Araenè laughed. She couldn't help it.

Tichorei didn't give up glaring, but he laughed, too. "All right!" he said. "I'll make your sphere. But I warn you, I'm going to tell Master Tnegun—well, Master Kopapei, anyway—so he can stop you if you've got some mad notion that would ruin everything."

Araenè could see protesting would do no good at all. "All right," she conceded. "I don't care! Tell anybody you like. The masters will *agree* with me, I know they will!" She tried to sound confident of this, which wasn't easy. "Just make the sphere," she added. "A sphere to capture freed dragon magic—"

"I know!" said Tichorei. "At least, I know what you want. I don't know that I can do it." He rubbed his forehead. "It might be a little like a spell for weather working. The dragon winds really are a lot like any other winds, aren't they? A kajurai would be helpful ... no, never mind, I didn't mean you should trouble your cousin! Kajurai don't know anything about magework. Here, do you have any blanks? A chunk of quartz or something? There aren't many minerals harder than quartz ..."

In the end, Tichorei decided to use a piece of quartz he'd been holding onto for years: smoky quartz the color of storm clouds, with a thread of white stone along one edge. "It's never felt right for anything else," he said. "It might work for this."

They were both kneeling on the ground in Araenè's garden, since Tichorei thought it might help to work out of

82

doors, under the wide sky, where the winds could come and go freely. He had spent some time sketching patterns and writing equations in the sand around Araenè's pool, and chewing on the end of the twig he was using as a stylus, and muttering to himself.

"It's a strange kind of spell," he told Araenè. "I'm not trying to do anything to the living winds, you know; I'm just trying to set it up so a spell will wrap a thread of itself around the freed winds, so they'll sort of circle around, you see, and thus be held."

Araenè nodded as though this made sense. She had entered some state past exhaustion, where everything—Tichorei and the garden and her apprehension, everything—seemed sharp and clear and very far away. She watched with wide eyes and a heightened awareness of magic as Tichorei wove his spell inside and around and through the uncarved chunk of quartz, smoothing it into a sphere and investing it with magic at the same time. It was like watching a flower bloom, except that Tichorei was unfolding every petal himself. What Tichorei did looked extraordinarily delicate and impossibly complex. Araenè tried to follow the unfurling spell, but there were so many pieces and so many of them seemed to change shape just when she thought she'd grasped the pattern.

Then she blinked, because suddenly the structure of the spell glittered entire and complete and beautiful in her mind. It tasted of ... pine and ice, she decided. With obscure and slightly disturbing hints of cinnamon, that didn't really go with the pine.

"There!" said Tichorei, looked pleased with himself. He scrubbed a hand across his face and gave the sphere he'd made a close look, squinting as though he'd developed a sharp headache. "I think it will work," he decided. "There's a little bit of that white stone along one face, but I don't think that's a flaw, exactly. It might even help magic get into it, and out of it, too, later. I think it will work, *if* you find someone to carry it into free dragon winds. I suppose you're thinking of your cousin."

"I think he'll do it," Araenè admitted. She considered the older apprentice warily. "I was right last summer," she pointed out. "Mostly." She didn't want to think about what that *mostly* had almost cost Trei, last time. She said instead, "I'm right this time, too. And it should be easy, shouldn't it? Trei can just go through a door into Tolounn. He can just carry my sphere—I mean, your sphere—through the living winds and then come right back, and ..." she hesitated, looking at the glittering structure within the quartz sphere. "And everything will be fine," she finished, in her firmest tone.

Tichorei didn't look impressed, and he didn't give Araenè the quartz sphere. "I'll ask Master Kopapei. If he says it's all right, then you can have this sphere and try to get your cousin to do what you want. But if Master Kopapei doesn't approve ..." he shrugged.

Araenè had to admit that this stipulation made sense. "Or Master Tnegun," she said reluctantly. "I would have asked him, only ..." only he was most likely pretty angry with her, and she hadn't been able to bring herself to try to find him, which she probably couldn't have, anyway, if he was busy and didn't choose to be found. Master Kopapei ... she'd never been afraid of him. No one could be afraid of him. She said, "I'm sure he'll think it's a good idea. Catching back a little of the dragon magic. I'm sure he will."

"Probably he will," said Tichorei, possibly because he was eager to show off the sphere he'd made to the senior mage.

But though Tichorei led the way confidently back into the hidden school from Araenè's garden, the door he'd summoned didn't take them to Master Kopapei's study, or anywhere Tichorei had intended. Instead, with a dizzying swoop and an odd sideways judder, the door took them straight to the center of the labyrinth—straight to the sixteen squares that held the plinth.

Araenè clutched Tichorei's sleeve and blinked dizzily.

"There's someone here," Tichorei said sharply.

Araenè jumped. The older apprentice was right. On the other side of the sixteen-tile square, on the other side of the plinth topped with its crystal-dragon stand and the ordinary glass sphere she had put there, someone moved. At first she thought it might be Master Tnegun, but almost at once she saw it wasn't. He was as tall a man, but much larger and sort of shapeless and untidy, with tangled hair falling over his shoulders and a round, forgettable face, and a tall mug almost lost in one broad hand.

She knew him immediately, of course. She would have known him even if she'd been blind, just for the scent that wafted around him: the wild, green, herbal fragrance of magic and a completely prosaic smell of ale. After the first startled instant, she wasn't even exactly surprised. She hissed, in case Tichorei didn't realize, "It's Master Cassameirin." She was, she realized, both glad and sorry to see the old mage. Cassameirin had lived nearly forever, which meant he had hardly any power left at all, but he must know *everything* about magery. That part was good. But new as Araenè was to the hidden school, she already knew that Cassameirin had a way of showing up when some huge problem was about to break and come crashing down like a wave. That part was unsettling.

Master Cassameirin glanced up from the glass sphere and across to where they stood, his muddy green-brown eyes vague, as though he might not recognize either of them. Lifting the mug in a distracted salute, he said absently, "It's a problem, yes, but not the greatest problem. That's the problem."

"What?" said Tichorei, his eyebrows rising. He looked at Araenè, his expression speaking for him.

Araenè had forgotten how vague Master Cassameirin could be. She was seized with a completely unsuitable desire to laugh. Embarrassing little giggles wanted to sputter out of her. She tried swallowing, and then holding her breath, and finally coughed.

"Come look," Cassameirin said, gesturing to them both with his mug. "See here?"

A storm roared silently through the glass sphere: black and bruised-purple, shot through with lightning, with a violent sea lashed to yellow foam beneath. It was a vision Araenè recognized, but she wasn't sure if it was Cassameirin's or hers; or whether, if it was a real storm, it was striking across the Islands or the coast of Tolounn or somewhere else entirely. She squinted at the sphere and then stared expectantly at Master Cassameirin.

"It's a problem," Cassameirin muttered, his tone vague. "I'll do what I can to delay it, but mind you do your part, girl, or it'll all come to nothing in the end. You have Kanora's sphere?"

"I ... I ... the kajuraihi have it," Araenè stammered. "Master Tnegun gave it to the kajuraihi ..."

"Good, good. That should do," muttered Cassameirin. "The kajuraihi, good. You'll need to match it, you know, girl. Kajurai and mage, air to balance stone, and each filled with fire. That young cousin of yours, Tolounnese balanced with Islander, he'd do well, I imagine. Yes. Get him to help you."

"Yes, all right," said Araenè, startled at this vindication of her idea. "But what—"

"But that storm won't wait long! You had better get on at once," said Cassameirin. He gave Tichorei an absent look and nodded toward the quartz sphere the tall apprentice held. "That's a decent job there, boy." Then he frowned at Araenè. "Only you remember, girl, it's glass that's allied to both fire and stone! Glass is *made* out of fire and stone." He put a powerful hand on Tichorei's shoulder, and another on Araenè's, and shoved them both inexorably back toward the door still standing open behind them.

"But *Kanora's* sphere—" Araenè said, refusing to be diverted. But either she had stepped backward without realizing it or else the door slid forward to meet her, because then she staggered and stepped sideways to catch her balance, and found herself in the middle of the dining hall of the kajurai novitiate, with Trei and his friends all scrambling to their feet in amazement, exclaiming.

"He said it was a decent job," Tichorei said to Araenè, sounding rather stunned. "That was Master Cassameirin. *Master Cassameirin* said I did a decent job." He held up his quartz sphere and stared at it, as though it had changed dramatically when the legendary mage had praised it.

"You see!" said Araenè, not certain herself whether she felt more frightened or relieved. "He said it was worth a try! I told you! *And* he said Trei was a good choice!"

"A good choice for what?" Trei wanted to know, understandably wary.

Araenè gave her cousin her best earnest look. "It's not like last time," she promised. "I'll be watching all the time! We both will—I mean, Tichorei too! So it will be *perfectly safe.*"

6

How, Trei wondered, did his cousin always manage to talk him into her mad schemes to save the Islands?

Well, no. That wasn't actually fair. Last time, *he'd* been the one to be sure that the adults were making a mistake that might cost them everything. He'd been the one who'd gone to Araenè, that time. She hadn't said she thought he was mad. She'd found a way to help. It was only later that everything had gone wrong and there had been all that desperate scramble to get things to work out.

That kind of terrible problem wasn't going to happen this time. Araenè was sure about that. His part would be easy. It really did *sound* like it should be easy. Trei only had to be present when that special dragon sphere of hers was broken. He wouldn't have to actually *do* anything. This new sphere she and Tichorei had made would just automatically capture a little bit of the freed dragon magic.

"It's important," Araenè said anxiously. "I can't explain exactly, but I'm sure it's really important, Trei, and it'll be perfectly safe. I'll get a door to take you straight to Tolounn, I'm sure I can open a door that will take you straight to Kanora's sphere, you see? And then you can come straight back afterwards. And that's all! I honestly can't think of any way it could go wrong."

"Those kajuraihi will see me," Trei pointed out. He meant the team of adult kajuraihi that would be sent to destroy the Tolounnese engines. "They'll tell Wingmaster Taimenai and Novice-master Anerii and everybody. You know they will. I'll get grounded for a senneri. Or worse. You know the rule about venturing!"

Araenè did know, but she said, "Ceirfei won't let them expel you, you know. Please, Trei? I'll get my door to bring you in really, really high; so high the other kajuraihi won't notice you at all. They'll be concentrating on the steam engines, you know they will, so they won't have any reason to look up so high! It'll work! And you'll just be there a minute, isn't that right? Because we already know when the kajuraihi will arrive, don't we?"

They did. Everyone did. The news had raced through the novitiate and across the whole city as though the winds themselves had carried it. A dawn raid against the Tolounnese engines, that was what everybody said, with the adult mages doing for the kajurai team exactly what Araenè proposed to do for Trei: open a wide door that would carry them straight into the sky above the engines.

"I can do it," Araenè insisted. "And if I can, *you* can! Just out through the door and back again. Tichorei will help me, so there's no reason at all to worry."

Trei thought of the other time, when he'd gone to Araenè to ask for help. How could he say no?

Genrai, listening to all this, frowned. "Trei, we ought to run this past the wingmaster. If this is so easy and safe and important, he'll say yes—or he'll assign someone in the raiding party to do it, not one of us. Araenè ought to ask her master, too."

"I should, and I would, but I can't!" Araenè told him. "The mages are all out of reach. They're so busy, they're not answering us. Tichorei, tell him!"

Tichorei didn't look any happier about any of this than Genrai, but he shrugged. "That's actually true. Everyone's involved in dealing with those engines. But, the thing is, *Master Cassameirin* said this sphere is the right kind and *Master Cassameirin* said Trei was the right person to use it."

Tichorei plainly thought this settled everything right there. And he was almost a mage, after all. Trei said to Genrai, "Master Cassameirin is this very important mage who knows all kinds of things about magic. If he said this was the right thing to do, it has to be true—and you know the wingmaster won't agree without checking with the other mages and arguing through the idea with the ministers and who knows who else. We can put through a request to talk to the wingmaster, but you know he's not going to have time to bother with us. If we have to set this up before dawn, there's not a lot of time."

Genrai, obviously torn, looked at Tichorei, who raised his chin and stared back. "If Master Cassameirin said we need to do this, then we do," he said firmly.

Obviously more willing to be swayed by someone Tichorei's age, Genrai said reluctantly, "I suppose. Maybe."

"It will be *perfectly safe,*" Araenè promised again. "I wouldn't want Trei to do it otherwise, Genrai, you know that!"

"It does sound pretty safe," Trei said. "Honestly, Genrai."

It really *did* sound like it should work. And Araenè was *so* sure.

And so, just past dawn, Trei wasn't at all surprised to find himself trying to sidle through a door that was almost too narrow even when he tried to fold his wings up as small as possible. Everyone else stood around anxiously, watching, which didn't make it easier. He finally threw himself awkwardly sideways through the door, away from the novitiate balcony, and fell into the empty sky far, far above the Tolounnese mainland. Then he finally had room to spread his wings and catch the air.

Trei hadn't realized, until he found himself soaring far above the Tolounnese countryside, how accustomed he'd become to the omnipresent sea: the sound of it below and the sharp scent of it in the air. The air was different here, even so high above the ground: warmer and softer, the scents all damp earth and crushed leaves, woodsmoke and the occasional whiff of cows or cut hay from an unseen farm. It was still dark, but the sky had taken on a dove-gray glow in the east. Trei couldn't help but worry over what he might see as the sun rose. Black smoke already rising from destroyed Tolounnese engines, maybe. More likely, the team of adult kajuraihi sent to destroy those engines, flying in formation below him. Araenè was probably right that they wouldn't look up, and Trei thought he could probably explain to Wingmaster Taimenai if he had to. Even so, he couldn't quite decide whether he'd been brave to agree to Araenè's plan, or very, very stupid.

The air over these hills was good for flying: warm and buoyant. The river wandered around the curve of one low hill, a glimmering silver ribbon in the dawn light, visible while the hills and fields themselves were still all one great featureless black. The river looped around one way and then another and finally spilled away south and west. Trei tilted his wings and swung around in a broad loop, echoing the curve of the river. The edge of the sun came up above the horizon at last, tinting all the sky rose and peach, gilding the surface of the river, revealing the wide flat fields cradled within the curve of the river and, standing four-square within those muddy fields, the squat heavy shapes of the Tolounnese steam engines, each with its own rolling column of thick black smoke from burning coal, and its own plume of white steam, too. The bad air surrounding those engines was unmistakable: a huge area of heavy stillness above and around those bulky shapes, an area that somehow seemed dim despite the brightening day. The black smoke and the white steam rose straight up, neither dissipating until they rose at last past the limits of the unnaturally still air.

The engines looked hardly the size of bricks from this height, but he knew *exactly* how big they really were. The countryside sprang into its proper size, Trei suddenly perceiving the immensity of hills and fields, the breadth of the river, the immensity of the area of dead air. Those little squared-off boats docked all along the curve of the river must be coal-barges, and wagons tiny as children's toys were already trundling forward in this first light, to bring the coal to the hungry engines. They had been set at the four corners of an imaginary square, those engines, each as far from the others as possible. Blowing one up, he guessed, might very well not destroy the others. He worried about that, though destroying the engines wasn't *his* problem.

The power from those engines would be fed to the distant Tolounnese mages, unless the engines could be destroyed. Using engines that way had been the brilliant idea of some Tolounnese mage or artificer: to use the steam pressure from those engines not to lift a piston or turn a wheel, but to create power for magecraft. Thus Tolounnese mages gained the power they needed to push aside the dragon magic of the Floating Islands, and the mages of the Floating Islands had no possible way to stop them.

So the kajuraihi would stop them instead.

The kajuraihi were visible, too: not so far below Trei as he'd really hoped. Of course they dared not descend so far as to risk coming into the dead air. The kajuraihi flew like eagles, but with wings of fire. Trei saw not only the crimson of Milendri, but also the gold of Candara and one hot blaze of orange from Bodonè.

The men hauling the coal had seen the kajurai, too, by this time. They pointed and ran in every direction. They must be shouting, but Trei couldn't hear them. Their voices were muted by more than distance; the dead air smothered sound as well as stilling the winds and dulling light. There would be a mage down there somewhere. At least one. With luck, though, the kajuraihi were all far too high above for any spell to affect them, especially as any mages would have to concentrate on keeping the living winds pushed back and away from those engines.

One of the kajurai, a man with wings of Candaran gold, tucked his wings back and in and began a downward plunge.

There was a trick to flying and yet finding the chance to snatch something from your flying harness and throw it down. You had to let your wings take care of themselves for just a second. You couldn't let your wings close up or bend, of course, not even for just that second, or you'd wind up tumbling and out of control, and that was dangerous as well as embarrassing. No, you locked the elbow and wrist joints of your wings, and then you had a *very limited* ability to move your hands and arms without slipping air. And if you needed to maneuver, you had better be able to pull the winds good and hard, because you sure couldn't do any clever flying until you finished your throw and took back active control of your wings.

Trei wasn't very good at this. But naturally all the kajuraihi who'd been sent on this mission must be good at it. The Candaran kajurai plunged down and down and down, and then curved around again, and up, just before he would have entered the region of bad air, rising in a smooth arc back toward the heights. Trei saw Araenè's sphere fall away toward the earth. It seemed to glow with its own light in that dim heavy air, sparkling like a fallen star, clearly visible even at this great and growing distance. It glittered coldly as it fell, beautiful as the crystalline wind, but with a sharp density all its own. Trei found himself holding his breath. The sphere he himself carried swung heavily in its net, seeming somehow to weigh more now than it had before. He dropped into a steep dive without even thinking, feeling somehow that he should be closer when the special dragon sphere shattered.

Only the dragon sphere didn't exact *shatter*. Trei saw it happen, but he didn't understand what he saw. It was as though the sphere blew up and expanded and roared in like the tide, all at once. Trei had never dreamed anybody could have fit more than a little wisp of the living wind in such a small sphere. He'd almost expected the winds, released, to be quickly smothered by the dead air. But this wasn't like that at all. Instead, the living winds became a huge, brilliant, rushing hurricane that flung itself outward and around and up; a storm of cold, sparkling wind tearing through the still air, of translucent sharp-edged glittering magic that shredded the heavy smothering stillness imposed by the Tolounnese mages.

The kajuraihi, lower than Trei, cast their powder bombs down, meaning to guide the bombs through the new living winds toward the engines. But the freed winds were far more violent than they'd expected—they hadn't been prepared—

Trei had just time to watch in shocked horror as first the bombs and then the kajuraihi were all flung out and away.

Then the hurricane caught him as well, and after that he caught only fragmented glimpses of the other kajuraihi, spinning in the distance above him and below him, all of them helpless as leaves in a storm, tumbling through the immensity of the sky. He couldn't see what happened with the powder-bombs or with the engines or with anything. He could do nothing but tuck his wings in tight to his body, protecting both the wings and his arms from tearing in the violent storm. He thought he glimpsed the Tolounnese engines, seeming solidly unaffected by the furious crystalline winds—only he thought he also saw the river fountaining upward and the black soil whipping into the air, carts driven into tumbling disorder, so he couldn't imagine even the great engines could survive the upheaval of the earth.

He couldn't open his wings—he tried to spread just the feathers of one wingtip and instantly spun into a ragged forward roll so violent he thought all the feathers must be torn from his wings. He thought he cried out, but heard nothing but the roar of the wind.

Dazed by the rushing winds, he struggled to understand his own orientation in the sky, and turning, glimpsed the ground—close, amazingly close, *horrifyingly* close, he was going to smash into the ground in half a heartbeat—he snapped his wings open and cried out again as the winds flung him violently aside and upward, wrenching his arms so hard he thought both his shoulders must be broken. Hot pain drove through his back, like knives had been shoved under his shoulder blades. He didn't slam into the ground, but the wind surged beneath him, impossible to ride or control. The air roared, a great concussive thunder that might have been the explosions of the powder bombs or of the engines themselves, of just the thunder of the winds, Trei couldn't tell.

Trei shut his eyes tight and thought of the Islands. Of Milendri in the distance, hanging motionless in the morning haze above the sea. Of the gulls flying below the Island, white wings flashing vivid against the red rock and the blue sky and the bluer sea. White gulls and the larger black ones that Araenè said sometimes laid basilisk eggs ... Quei riding the updrafts above Canpra. You could hear the Quei even before you saw them, their voices higher and wilder than the voices of the gulls ... He longed to be in the air above Milendri, to be dropping down along a long easy curving path through the sky, the wind gliding sweetly through the feathers of his wings, the white towers of Canpra coming closer and closer ...

And then the last of the freed winds poured up past him, rushing up to the far heights, and the air around him flattened out and went dead, and Trei realized, as he fell like a stone, that at least one engine must still be just fine, and that the Tolounnese mage must not have been killed after all.

He fell. His wings were utterly useless. He might as well have strapped himself into carved wooden wings and tried to fly. He screamed, and knew he was screaming, but he couldn't stop. He tried to stretch out his wings, forgetting pain, but nothing he did made the slightest difference. Only then a door flashed into place below him, open wide, facing him, pivoting around to stay beneath him as he tumbled. He didn't gasp his cousin's name, there wasn't time and he had no breath anyway.

The door wasn't wide enough to accommodate a kajurai's wings. Of course it wasn't. He'd had to sidle through sideways to get through it the first time; how was it nobody had thought about the impossibility of getting back through it from the air? He couldn't have done it even if he'd been able to fly, and he couldn't, he couldn't, it was impossible. With an enormous effort, Trei wrenched one wing straight up and stabbed the other straight down, and tucked his legs tight up against his body—and saw, with a cold thrill of terror, that he was going to miss the doorway—and then the door leaped up and sideways, right into place below him—and one of the other kajurai fell past him, plunging down with all the dull clumsy weight of an ordinary earthbound man who has never known the living wind. Trei cried out, but there was nothing he could do. For just an instant his eyes met those of the other man, and then Trei fell straight through his cousin's doorway as though he was threading a needle with his own body, straight into the sky above Milendri.

7

Araenè flinched back and covered her eyes at the last instant. She couldn't help it. She was terrified Trei would miss her door, or smash into its heavy frame. She heard sharp gasps and muffled exclamations, and she couldn't bear it and peeked through her fingers. But it was too late, whatever had happened had happened, the only thing she could see from the novice's balcony was the empty sky. Tichorei was gripping her shoulders hard, and she shook him off, taking a step forward—she couldn't see Trei anywhere and was sure he'd missed her door, desperately hauled into place below him—she was sure he'd plunged past, just like those other kajuraihi, her cousin had fallen right out of the sky, and it was *all her fault.*

And then all the novices pointed, shouting, all at once, and Araenè knew that Trei must have managed to fall through her door after all, from one sky to another. The door had answered her after all, Akhan Bhotounn, 'the friendly one,' the heavy door of carved oak and ebony, the one she always called in great need. It had answered her again. She was certain there could be no better gift than one for doors. She whispered shakily, "Thank you. Akhan Bhotounn."

There was no answer of course, but far away, way up in the sky, she spotted her door spinning slowly in the empty air. She couldn't see Trei right away, even though she tried to look just where all the novices were looking. All she could see was the black speck of her door before it spun once more and vanished. There were dragons flying way up high. She couldn't really see them, not properly, but she somehow glimpsed the glittering sweep of an immense wing out of the corner of her eye, and the sunlight came down slantwise across a shimmer of feathers. There were certainly dragons ... but where was Trei?

Then she saw him.

He was still falling. He was not exactly flying: he was staggering sideways and down in a horrifying lurching motion that was going to end with him falling into the sea. But he hadn't fallen *yet*. He was still in the air *now*.

Araenè took another step toward the balcony's edge. Tichorei caught her shoulders again and she didn't shake him off, comforted by his hold against the empty space that plunged away from the balcony and down to the sea below. All the novices were shouting, a meaningless clamor until Genrai's deeper voice commanded, "Pull the winds up around him! Tokabii, help us get some dense air under his wings, can't you? Kojran, leave the minor straps, just get the wings on!"

Araenè held her breath, not believing anyone could reach her cousin in time. But Genrai told her, his voice harsh and strained, "We'll get him, we'll catch him, don't worry, we've got him, we won't let him fall—"

Looking again, Araenè saw this was true. Nescana and Genrai and Rekei and even that brat Tokabii all stood right at the edge of the balcony with the ordinary kajurai disregard of heights, but they weren't just watching helplessly the way she and Tichorei were. The kajurai novices were doing something. Pulling the winds, Araenè realized. That, whatever it meant, was something *real* that they could actually *do*. That was why Trei was falling so ... so ... he wasn't *really* falling. He was plunging jerkily sideways in a series of skewed, awkward dips. It looked horrible, but he was actually approaching Milendri faster than he was falling.

"His wings are a wreck," Genrai muttered. "The right one's just *shredded*, that's why he keeps going sideways like that—Tokabii, can you get a stronger wind coming up under him from the right?"

"Trying!" Tokabii snapped. "Let me alone!"

Genrai didn't shout back. Both boys were working too hard to spare breath for arguing, Araenè understood, and didn't know whether she should find that reassuring or frightening.

Kojran strode purposefully past the row of novices and flung himself into the air, wings snapping open instantly. Why Kojran, Araenè wondered, but trusted Genrai would have had some reason to pick him. He seemed fast and sure in the air, at least. And somehow Trei seemed steadier as soon as Kojran took a place below him and to his right. Maybe the other novice was somehow helping him compensate for his battered wing?

Araenè had never before wished for kajurai eyes that could see the wind. She stood still, leaning tensely forward, her left hand clenched and her right pressed against the wall for balance, straining to see whether the angle of Trei's descent had smoothed out and flattened enough that he might make it all the way back to the novitiate balcony. Could he swim? Hardly any Island children learned to swim; was it different where he'd grown up in Tolounn? She couldn't see any fishing boats that might pick him up ...

"He'll make it," Genrai said in a gritty, strained mutter. "We've got him. He'll make it."

He was speaking to her, Araenè realized. Even at this moment Genrai remembered that she couldn't see the wind, and spared enough attention from whatever the novices were doing to tell her, and Tichorei, what the rest of them saw. She hadn't ever paid much attention to Genrai before, but she felt a rush of gratitude now, that he was here, that he knew what to do.

"Here they come!" Tokabii shouted, and Rekei said in a strained tone a lot like Genrai's, "Got him, got him—watch it! Gods wept, watch it, Nescana, you're piling the wind up too densely against Milendri, you'll create a backflow!"

Nescana flinched, and Genrai flung out his hands, a sharp gesture—Araenè wondered for a flashing instant what the winds actually looked like, to those who could see them—

and Trei, Kojran beside him, hurtled suddenly directly at the balcony, stunningly close and fast. Araenè pressed herself against the wall, and her cousin swept by her so close he might have knocked her down if she hadn't ducked, and Trei twisted in the air, slammed into the balcony floor with appalling force, and sprawled in a tangle of limbs and feathers. Araenè, too shocked to move, prayed to the Gods that only the feathers were broken.

"Tokabii, help Kojran with his wings," Genrai said sharply. "Nescana, help me with Trei—Rekei, run up and get Master Anerii, or if you can't find him, then Kisai or somebody."

The best Araenè could do was stay out of the way while Genrai and his sister Nescana helped get the broken wings off her cousin. The right wing really *was* shredded; if there was a single unbroken feather, she couldn't see it. And she thought the frame was broken in two places, and was afraid his arm might be broken, too. She guessed that Trei must have actually raked that wing against the door when he fell through it. She couldn't understand how her cousin had managed to stay in the air. Dragon magic, she supposed—and the Quei feathers.

Trei was moving, vaguely, to help the other novices get his wings off. That seemed reassuring. He managed to sort of kneel up awkwardly, but when he tried to lift his arms, he stopped, gasping in pain. That wasn't so reassuring, but there were no bones sticking out that Araenè could see. She said nervously, "Isn't there some kind of healer or anything here? No, wait—" Araenè, remembering suddenly whose apprentice Tichorei was, gave the older boy a half-hopeful, half-commanding look. "Tichorei—"

"Yes," said Tichorei, sounding reassuringly confident. His own master, Master Camatii, was a self-effacing, quiet man who was nevertheless Milendri's best healer. Tichorei was already stepping forward, kneeling to run a quick, confident hand through the air above Trei's arm. "Broken," he reported. "Wrist and arm both. And two fingers, but those hardly matter. The wrist is bad ..."

"You can fix it!" Araenè said, not knowing herself whether she was pleading or demanding. "Do you need a sphere—can I get you anything?" She was ready to leap to her feet and fetch anything the older apprentice needed, but Tichorei only shook his head.

"No, bones want to be whole. It's not a matter of ..." his voice trailed off, and he stared intently into the air. Then he tapped the air above Trei's arm, sharply. Trei yelped, and then stopped, looking surprised.

"That's got it," Tichorei said absently. "That's the hard part, getting the pieces lined up. Lots of little pieces, in that wrist ..."

Araenè nodded, leaning forward, almost able, she thought, to see what the other apprentice saw. The glittering structure of magic unfolding around Tichorei's hands and Trei's wrist and arm was ... well, it was ... it wasn't exactly like anything Master Tnegun had ever shown her; she knew that. But then, her master wasn't a healer like Master Camatii. The spellwork Tichorei was doing sent little shocks of unfamiliar icy lemon and coriander tingling across Araenè's tongue, and the palms of her hands. The lemon was almost painfully sharp—of course, Tichorei was still young enough his power hadn't even started to fade, yet. Araenè was grateful for that.

"I'm all right," Trei said in a faint, hoarse voice. "I'm all right."

"You are now," Tichorei agreed sitting back and letting out his breath. "I think you are! Can you lift your arms?"

"Almost—sort of." Trei lifted one arm about waist high, and then the other, grimacing. "Thanks. Thank you, Tichorei. Araenè—Gods, did you *see* –?" Her cousin looked at her with helpless horror, and Araenè remembered for the first time that of course there had been those other kajuraihi in the sky with him. Men who had fallen, whom she hadn't caught. She'd forgotten them instantly when she saw Trei fall. That was ... that was terrible. And besides that ... how awful ... it wasn't the *first* time her cousin had been the only one to survive a disaster. She flinched from the realization. She wanted to say something, but had no idea what she could possibly say.

"It—I—" Trei stopped and took a hard breath. Then he said, "The sphere?"

For just a moment, Araenè thought he meant Kanora's dragon sphere. Then she realized that of course her cousin was asking about Tichorei's quartz sphere, the one he'd taken with him to Tolounn—Gods, she'd forgotten all about it! She was suddenly terrified Trei might have dropped it, that everything he'd risked and suffered might have been for nothing.

But then Genrai's sister Nescana silently held up the net bag, Tichorei's sphere dangling safe and secure inside.

"I thank the Gods!" Araenè said fervently. She took the bag, peering at the sphere within. It tasted of wild, astringent dragon magic, without any kind of ordinary human magic blurring the astringency.

"That's very ... that's very odd," Tichorei said, peering at the sphere uneasily. "That's very ... odd."

Araenè had to agree. It really was. She tipped the sphere out into her hand. Somehow it seemed to weigh a lot more now than it had an hour ago, as though the magic it contained was some dense, tangible thing. Her hand dipped under its weight. And the sphere was so cold now that it burned her hand.

"Put it down!" Tichorei said sharply, coming abruptly to his feet. "Araenè, I don't think—look, I think we'd better get rid of it—"

"Get *rid* of it?" one of the novices protested indignantly, "After we went to all that trouble to get it in the first place, and now you want to get *rid* of it?"

Tokabii, that was; of course it would be Tokabii. He was a brat, but Araenè thought he was right. She cradled the quartz sphere in both hands, setting her teeth against the aching cold. "Anyway," she said, not very coherently, "get rid of it how?"

"Let me have it—" Tichorei reached for the sphere.

Araenè jerked back, and there was a short, sharp, confusing moment where Tichorei tried to get the sphere and she tried to keep it, and then her numb fingers lost their hold, and she snatched after it and missed, and everyone else grabbed, too, Trei and Genrai as well as Tichorei, and Tokabii shouted, and the sphere hit the stone floor of the balcony with a sound like a struck bell, and rolled. The astringent taste flashed and brightened, and Tichorei exclaimed wordlessly and dove after the sphere, Kojran and Nescana leaping out of his way, and the quartz sphere rolled off the novice's balcony into the empty air, and shattered or dissolved or thawed or something. The freed dragon wind, savage and cold, whipped across the balcony, so that Araenè actually took a step back with the force of it. All around her, the novices were staggering and crying out. Somewhere a Quei cried, too, a sharp wild sound, like the winds given voice.

Around them, the Island shuddered.

At first Araenè thought she'd imagined it. But then she saw Trei's expression—and then Milendri trembled again. The Island didn't fall, though for a sickening instant as it stuttered sideways beneath them, Araenè was sure it was going to. She dropped to the floor before the unsteadiness of the Island could knock her off her feet, and tucked herself against her cousin, clinging to him, too afraid to even cry out.

It was horribly like last summer, only this time there weren't any Tolounnese ships waiting at anchor, which wasn't so very reassuring because at least they'd known the Tolounnese mages hadn't wanted to drown the Islands. This time they had no idea what was happening. But the Island didn't fall, though it shivered uneasily beneath them. Around them, stone creaked and groaned. Red dust swirled in the breeze.

Genrai, already kneeling, braced himself against the nearest wall with one outflung hand and reached to steady Nescana with the other.

"It's not falling!" Trei said, but he didn't sound quite sure.

"It's not?" said Tichorei, grimly. "You sure? Araenè, that Gods-cursed sphere, *what* did it release into our sky?"

Araenè didn't know what to say.

"We're *not* falling—yet," said Genrai tersely, and raised his voice: "You boys, get away from the edge! Get the wings out—help each other with them—if the Island's going to fall out from under us, better if we're all in the air!"

"*There's* a really good idea," Kojran said, sounding shaken. He still wore his wings, and now Tokabii and Nescana hurried across the balcony to the frames where the wings hung waiting.

"Trei—" Genrai began, looking down at him. "*Can* you fly?"

"Of course!" said Trei, though he rubbed his recently-broken wrist and didn't look completely sure. "I'll be fine if I can just get in the air—"

"You will not!" Araenè cried. "Genrai!"

"Soaring's not hard," Genrai said, but then he added, "But a break's worse than overstrain, Trei, mended or not, and if you've torn ligaments, that's something else again. Tichorei—"

Tichorei held up his hands, defensively. "I just fixed the bones, the ligaments have to heal on their own, that's the way it is!"

Trei, who never shouted, raised his voice in something that came close. "I'll be fine if somebody will just *help me with my wings*—"

Kojran cried, "Look!" and everyone turned.

The dragons were leaving Kotipa. Even Araenè could see them as they rose away from the Island's jagged peaks: a glitter in the air where immense wings, transparent as ice, spread out in the sky, an opalescent sheen across the empty air. One dragon, and then another, and then several together, impossible for Araenè to count ... she thought she could make out their delicate, fine-boned heads and the pearl-white glimmer of their eyes. They called out in strange chiming voices. Their sinuous bodies rippled in the wind, seeming to move with leisurely grace and yet climbing fast ... they rose higher and higher, until she lost them entirely against the light and distance of the wide sky.

"Look!" Kojran said again, his voice tight and scared.

Araenè jerked her gaze back down and saw that Kotipa was breaking up. Huge jagged chunks of red stone broke away from the Island of Dragons, plunging downward, turning as they fell, tumbling end over end impossibly slowly until they struck the sea. Huge waves fountained up where they struck. The grinding shriek of breaking stone reached the novices, and the huge crashing as chunks of the broken mountains struck the water. It seemed to Araenè she could feel the noise in her bones, in a shuddering beneath her feet.

"Gods," she whispered. She felt numb. She felt as though, when the numbness wore off, she would shatter like glass. "Gods weeping. It's my fault ... releasing that dragon magic, letting it loose *here among the Islands* ..."

"It is not!" Trei snapped. "That doesn't even make sense: the Islands are filled with dragon magic anyway! Dragon winds blow around us *all the time*. Anyway," he continued, not very coherently, "how could you know? Anyway, you *told* them not to break Kanora's sphere! It's not *your* fault!"

Araenè couldn't look at her cousin. "It is," she said. "It really is. I took that sphere out of the labyrinth—"

"*Milendri* isn't going to break up like that, is it?" Tokabii interrupted her. His voice quivered.

"Wings," said Genrai, his voice flat and tense. "Everyone in the air. *Now*. If Milendri breaks up like that—Tichorei, Araenè, hadn't you better get back to the hidden school? Tell them—tell somebody—I don't know—"

"Yes," Tichorei said, grimly.

Araenè didn't say anything. She could think of absolutely nothing to say.

8

Trei flew with his eyes closed, mostly. In fact, *flying* was a generous term for what he was doing. He didn't ride the winds so much as just lie on them, passive as a leaf, letting the others pull the winds for him so that he hardly had to shift a single feather to follow a slow curving pathway out over the sea and back again. Even that was almost more than he could manage. The pain of stretched or torn ligaments radiated down his back from both his shoulders, and his right arm ached from wrist to elbow. Tichorei might have fixed the bone—Trei was sure, or almost sure, that he had—but when Trei tried to tilt or turn or bend that arm, the ache turned into knifing pain that almost made him think it was still broken. He longed to drop back out of the sky onto the novitiate balcony, but when he'd tried, once, to turn in that direction, Genrai had yelled at him and made him turn away again.

He knew why Genrai had shouted, of course. Genrai, like all of them, was afraid that Milendri might still break up and fall into the sea, and if it did, anybody who wasn't in the air would surely die. He knew, though, that if *all* the Islands fell into the sea, not even the kajuraihi who'd made it into the sky would be safe, because very few of them would have the strength to fly all the way to the Tolounnese coast without resting. Trei knew *he* couldn't.

Trei's thoughts tended darker and darker as he circled slowly out across the sea and back again toward Canpra's white towers. He wanted to cry out a protest to the Gods: hadn't there been *enough* death and loss and grief? But the Gods wouldn't answer, and besides, he knew the Islanders had done this to themselves. They had taken Araenè's sphere and shattered it and let all its magic loose. It *wasn't* Araenè's fault. But no matter whose fault it was, now all the Islands might fall, smashing into the sea, drowning all the proud white towers ...

"Trei!" Genrai shouted. "You all right?"

Trei, startled, flinched and opened his eyes. Genrai flew a wingspan to his right, in position to coax the winds around and up and thus help Trei balance himself in the air. Kojran and Nescana flew a similar distance in front of them to break the wind so that Trei wouldn't have to, and Tokabii rode the winds below them, helping buoy Trei up by increasing air density below him. None of them had left him, none of them had broken formation, and now Genrai called over to make sure Trei was still alert enough to stay with them and keep himself in the air. Trei experienced a sudden vivid rush of gratitude for them all that seemed somehow to help him rise in the air, almost like another kind of magic. He called back, "Fine!"

The novices flew in one slow circle, out and then back, riding the warm, light winds that took the least attention and effort. Other kajuraihi were in the air ... all of them, Trei thought. All of them that hadn't gone after the Tolounnese warships, or off on other missions. He could see thirty or more: a fabulous sight, under other circumstances, crimson wings vivid against the many-layered sky. He didn't see Wingmaster Taimenai's black wings, though he looked. He wished he could see the wingmaster—he felt, childishly, that Wingmaster Taimenai could protect them all and tell them all what to do, and knew it was childish, but he couldn't help it.

"Milendri's still in the air!" Tokabii shouted—the least patient of them, and the least willing to think ahead. "Can't we go back yet?"

No one answered immediately, partly because, Trei knew, they were all afraid that if they agreed, that then the Island would after all break apart and begin to tumble toward the waves. At least, that was how he felt. Even so, with the fiery pain of torn muscles and strained ligaments in his shoulders and back, Trei was willing to side with Tokabii. He shouted, "Let's go back!"

A single kajurai dropped suddenly toward them, and then another, spreading their wings to catch the wind, effortlessly sliding sideways into their formation. One was Rekei. He came in close on Trei's left, closing the tight bubble of dragon magic and dense air that the other novices had built around Trei. The other was Novice-master Anerii, back from Candara at last. Trei was surprised by the rush of relief he felt, the confidence that the novice-master would know exactly what to do and that he would find a way to save them all even if Milendri fell—which it *wouldn't*, it *hadn't*, Trei was sure if it was going to, it would have fallen already. But if it *did*, the novice-master would know what to do.

The novice-master's deep, gruff voice carried over the stiff rustle of wind through the feathers of their wings. "Genrai!"

"Sir!" Genrai answered, turning his head.

"Pay attention to your flight path, novice!" snapped the novice-master. "The sky's crowded, so watch where you're going!"

Genrai turned his attention forward once more. "Milendri hasn't fallen!" he shouted—a plea for reassurance.

"It's not going to!" Master Anerii declared.

The novice-master couldn't possibly be anything like so confident—but he had a way of sounding like the Gods themselves proclaiming a Truth for the ages, and at the moment that was exactly what Trei needed. It put heart into him and gave him strength. He was sure it did the same for the other novices.

"We're going to swing out and south, come down on Hei!" the novice-master told them. Hei was a tiny Island, immediately south of Milendri, It was hardly more than a floating pebble, barely big enough for the single temple that overlooked its one tiny village and its small, neat vineyards. Master Anerii seemed to think it might be safer than Milendri—and maybe it was.

Trei could make it to Hei. Probably. He was sure he could. He tried to tilt his wings in a smooth turn, flinched, and leveled out again, letting the other novices coax the winds around so that he wouldn't have to work for the turn.

"What's wrong with Trei?" demanded the novice-master, his voice harsh—he sounded like he was angry, but Trei knew he was actually worried.

"Shoulders!" said Genrai, briefly. "Bad landing!" Which was sort of true, and enough of an explanation for an experienced kajurai.

"Gods weeping! Trei, do you have any reach or pull at all?"

Trei tried to answer from somewhere that felt very distant, but he wasn't sure he made any sound. If he answered, he wasn't sure what he said.

"Gods weeping!" Master Anerii said again. "Genrai! If he starts to slip, give a shout!" The novice-master dropped lower in the air, his great wings stretching forward and back, the air piling up beneath and behind them until they all rushed forward. Below them, the sea ran in long blue ripples; to the west and north, clouds piled up in great shimmering towers. The sunlight poured around them, seeming as dense as the air ... Trei closed his eyes again.

It seemed they flew a long time, though in another way it seemed like only a moment before Master Anerii's voice broke into Trei's blank concentration once more. "You'll help him get down on the ground—you, Genrai, and you, Rekei! One per wing! You circle once more, Trei, with me. Tokabii, Kojran, help get the winds around to cushion him as he comes in! Nescana, stay out of the way! Clear?"

Trei was so glad to be able to come down that he didn't even flinch from the idea of the landing. But it was worse than even he had expected. He had to backwing, there was no other way to stall, and if he didn't stall he'd hit far too fast and hard—his shoulders screamed as he tried to catch the wind, and despite Tokabii's and Kojran's efforts, he *did* hit much too fast, and cried out as the weight came down on his wings. Genrai was there, and Rekei, already down, reaching to catch him, one on either side. Trei's vision whited out as

Rekei grabbed his arm too hard and in the wrong place. He might have made a sound, because Rekei flinched and let go again. Trei went to his knees on the rocky earth of the Island, sobbing for breath—not *really* sobbing, he thought—not quite, not yet –

Novice-master Anerii reached past Rekei and took the weight of Trei's wing with a light, sure grip, easing him down flat. "You're all right," he said gruffly. "You're all right, novice; catch your breath. Your arm, is it, as well as the shoulders? *What* did you do to yourself?"

Trei barely heard him and couldn't catch his breath to answer anyway. He was dimly aware of gentle, assured hands stripping his wings off, and hoped even more dimly that he hadn't damaged this set, too ... someone was speaking, he thought he heard his name, but it all seemed very far away ... he sank down into darkness as though into the sea, and was gone.

He woke in the dark, with the broad blank sky overhead, stars glowing against the vault of the heavens. The air was warm and still where he lay, but he could hear a sluggish wind stirring leaves not so far away. He could smell warm rock and earth, but also the musty scent of hot plaster. He thought he might be in a room, but a room that was open to the sky, which seemed strange and yet somehow neither surprising nor disturbing. He could smell, beyond and around everything else, the sharp tang of the sea. That was familiar.

For a long time, Trei just lay where he was, gazing up at the sky. The moon rose slowly into view, its pale radiance showing him glimmering white walls that seemed to ripple and shift when he looked at them. He felt heavy and slow, logy with weight as though he might be earthbound forever, as though he might even be sinking slowly into the earth, but somehow it was not an alarming feeling, but only sort of sad and peaceful. He was not in pain ... he couldn't remember why he should be in pain.

He could hear voices, dimly. One, low and brusque and familiar, which made him feel safe. Another, lighter, that might be Genrai. He blinked, slowly. It seemed to take a long time, so that he felt he did not so much blink as fall slowly into the dark and then rise again into the moonlight. The voices went on ... maybe he dreamed them. Maybe everything was a dream. He wanted everything to be a dream, but couldn't remember why ... *Dead air, and men falling. Fire above and below, and he was falling, falling*—He sat up with a jerk, his breath catching in his throat.

There was a low exclamation, not far away. The pale walls swirled like the wind and light bloomed, the soft steady glow of a paper lantern. Novice-master Anerii let fall the sheer curtains that Trei now saw he'd mistaken for walls, set the lantern down on the floor beside Trei, and bent to set a firm hand on his arm. He said firmly, "You're all right, boy. Take a deep breath. You're fine. How're your shoulders? Did a job on 'em, didn't you? Here I thought I'd taught you better than to use muscle and bone against a hard fall! That's what the winds are for! What were you thinking?"

Trei drew a shuddering breath, but this gruff reprimand was actually comforting, much more than sympathy—he knew he must truly be all right for Master Anerii to take that tone. He moved his arms cautiously. They felt heavy ... but there was no sharp pain, only a low residual ache down his back. And his right wrist ached a little.

"Let's see you lift your arms over your head. All right, not so bad, I guess. Put 'em down." The novice-master sat down on the floor, facing Trei. "You all the way awake, boy?" And, at Trei's uncertain nod, he went on brusquely, "All right, then. I've had the tale from Genrai. You fool boys, I swear to the Gods, I don't know what I did to deserve the lot of you as novices! No, don't say it—I know I wasn't there to ask! Well, let that go, for now. Listen, boy: Milendri's all right. So far as we know, the only Island that's fallen is Kotipa. Now I want the tale from you. Here, want some water? All right, then, start from the beginning and tell me what happened."

Despite his brusque tone, the novice-master was surprisingly easy to talk to. He listened quietly, grunting occasionally when Trei said something that surprised him, waving impatiently for Trei to go on when he hesitated, but asking only good questions that helped Trei understand what exactly had happened, or at least what might have happened.

"All right," the novice-master said at last, when Trei was done. "Genrai thinks, and I guess we all think, that you brought some of the magic in that Gods-cursed sphere your cousin found back to the Islands and let it go right here, and something about that made Kotipa fall. But Milendri's still floating, so it could be worse. Figuring out what really happened and what it means, that's not our problem, that's for the mages."

Something about that statement bothered Trei. Wasn't dragon magic a problem for the kajuraihi? But he said nothing.

"But checking on the rest of the Islands, that's for kajuraihi, right? And what with one thing or another, we're stretched far too thin. So you novices get your first real job to do, helping me check on the Islands to the south. It's clear enough you'd better stay under my eye! There's a little Island off Tisei," the novice-master went on. "Gohana, have you heard of it? No? It's a dragon Island, like Kotipa, so we're going to go check on it, see if it's still in the air. And then there's another Island of Dragons, a sharp-edged pebble called Fenaisa, way out at the tip of the Southern Chain; we're to go all the way out there and check on that one, too. That's a long flight, Trei, so if your shoulders aren't up to it, you'll wait here."

"I'm fine!" Trei protested. He thought it was true. The slow ache of his shoulders and back was nothing that would keep him from flying. Now that he wasn't so lost in his own exhaustion and pain, he was ashamed to think how much help he'd needed yesterday, and twice as ashamed because he knew Master Anerii was right. They should have waited to ask him, or Wingmaster Taimenai. But there *hadn't* been time—and Trei wasn't at all sure any of them, even Araenè, actually knew what had happened at all. But he didn't know how to say that. He only repeated instead, "I'm fine. I can fly—you can't leave me behind!"

Master Anerii grunted, unimpressed. "If you do have to wait, well, serve you right, boy." But his hand on Trei's shoulder was kinder than his words, and he added almost gently, "Get some rest, novice. Dawn's on its way, and we'll go up early. Then we'll see how your arms are once you're in the air."

Trei nodded, and lay back down obediently, but he didn't go to sleep. He couldn't. Telling everything to the novice-master had brought it back so vividly. Every time he closed his eyes, he saw the storm of winds rushing away into the heights and the kajuraihi falling through the dead air left behind, their wings trailing like dead things. They could not have survived. None of them could possibly have survived that fall. None of *them* had a cousin who was a mage, who had been watching over them, who could set a door into the empty air beneath them. Only Trei.

He hadn't even known those men. And still he wanted to cry like a child. He put an arm over his eyes, blocking out the moonlight and the glittering stars and the billowing white cloth of the curtains. His arm ached a little when he moved it. That was fine. It should hurt. No one should be untouched after a disaster like that, where good men *died* and there was *nothing you could do* to save them ... Trei's eyes stung. He could hear the novice-master or someone moving around, somewhere not far away. He lay perfectly still because he didn't want to make any sound that would disturb anyone. Especially not the other novices. He couldn't bear it if Rekei or Tokabii or someone saw him crying. Not that he was crying. Not that he would. He closed his eyes tight and tried to think of nothing, remember nothing. But terrible visions followed him back down into the dark of sleep, and his dreams were full of arrow-shot birds and falling men and a burning sky.

That lingering ache was still there in the morning, which found Trei far from rested. He sat up cautiously. There was a tightness across his shoulders and down his back, a hot feeling beneath his shoulder blades, an ache in his wrist and elbow. But it wasn't bad. He could ignore the discomfort if he wanted to.

He was sitting on a pallet in an airy room made of sheer curtains hanging from slender wooden rods, a room open to the sky ... he remembered that, dimly, from the night before. He got to his feet, finding himself only a little shaky, and tentatively put back the curtains.

Outside his room was a wide hall, a hall not closed off from the world by walls, but delineated instead by fluted pillars of white and red stone. High above, its vaulted roof swooped in a graceful series of arches to a single high dome ... a temple, Trei realized at last. A temple, of course.

The novices were all seated in a rough circle on the floor, sharing wheat rolls and the salted sheep's-milk cheese so popular on the Islands and some kind of small oval golden fruit that Trei didn't recognize.

"Trei!" said Rekei, gesturing toward him with a filled plate. "Just in time! We were going to eat yours."

"We were not!" Tokabii protested righteously. He propped himself up on one elbow, grinning at Trei. "Or maybe we were, but Genrai wouldn't let us."

"Genrai, nothing!" said Kojran. "Trei, you should know, those gluttons would have snatched every bite right out of your mouth. Genrai would've been perfectly happy to grab the last of the pastries. It was *me* who wouldn't let any of 'em touch it." With a proud flourish, he uncovered a plate holding a single small pastry.

Nescana rolled her eyes. "Don't pay any attention to those fools. You missed supper—not even my brother would steal your pastry!" She nudged Genrai, grinning. "Though he does love sweets, so I'm not *sure*—"

Genrai swatted his sister on the arm, and Nescana mimed brief agony. He said to Trei, "You did miss supper, so naturally you want real food before you fly, not sweets!" He gave Trei a careful, assessing look. "You *are* going to fly with us, right? Your shoulders are all right now? How's your arm?"

"We did save you real food," Kojran said earnestly. "Too." He uncovered a bowl of flaked fish and eggs and rice and put it down among the other plates and dishes, while everyone shuffled sideways to make room for Trei.

Trei could only stand and look at them all for a long moment. He knew that if he tried to say anything, his voice would shake.

"Come on, make room," Genrai said roughly, looking away and shoving at Rekei, even though the other boy had already moved. He said to Trei, but without looking at him, "Master Anerii's gone back to Milendri. He's supposed to be back soon, though. You know we're supposed to fly a sweep south, check on the little dragon Islands down that way?"

"A real mission!" cried Tokabii, bouncing up, irrepressible. "Do you *know* how far it is to Fenaisa? Way, way south! We're supposed to see if Fenaisa's still there, if there're still dragons there, and look at Gohana on the way, and find out from the kajuraihi along the Southern Chain what's been going on down that way—"

Trei could tell it had never occurred to the younger boy that anything terrible might have happened to Fenaisa or to any of the Islands of the southern chain. Even after watching Kotipa fall, Tokabii was sure everything was really just fine. Even after last summer, Tokabii felt that way. The younger boy made Trei feel old.

"Come eat," said Nescana, patting the floor by her side. "Before Genrai really does steal your pastry."

Trei blinked and looked at her. He could see she knew what he was thinking, and that surprised him ... but a girl at fifteen was almost a woman, after all, and he guessed a Third

City girl grew up fast. He came slowly to join her and take the proffered pastry. It was good—not as good as Araenè would have made, but good. Filled with rose-scented cream and a dab of some kind of fruit he didn't recognize.

"Your shoulders?" Genrai asked again, glancing over now that Trei had had a chance to collect himself.

"Much better," Trei said truthfully. He held up his right hand and flexed his wrist, rotating his hand one way and then the other, ignoring the flashes of discomfort that attended the movements. "Fine now. See?"

"Good," said Genrai. "Good." He stood up abruptly. "I'd better go check on the wings," He walked away without looking back.

"He was pretty scared," Nescana said quietly, glancing after her brother and then looking back at Trei. "I guess we all were. I never saw anybody come in like that. I thought you'd smash into the ground—and then I thought you'd made it down all right—and then you screamed—sorry, I didn't mean to remind you." She looked away, embarrassed, as Trei flinched.

Trei wanted to say something reassuring, but couldn't think of anything that wouldn't sound absolutely idiotic. He picked up the bowl of fish and rice. He was, actually, now that he noticed it, starving. "Thanks for saving this for me."

"Like we'd let you starve?" said Kojran, but he was smiling.

"Novices! On your feet!" snapped the gruff voice of the novice-master. "Are your wings ready? All of 'em? Well, why not? Not you, Trei, you sit down and finish that."

Master Anerii had strode into the temple and now paced impatiently around in a circle. "How're those shoulders of yours? Still feel up to a long flight? Good, good. Here, I'll take one of those rolls—it's been a long time since breakfast for me. We can't all sleep till mid-morning! You have time to finish that, though, and the pool's through there if you want a quick wash, which I expect you do. You remember what we're doing today?"

Trei nodded. "Tisai and Gohana, the Southern Chain and Fenaisa. Not all in one day, though—"

"Today and tomorrow and likely the day after that, too, but we'll cut straight across the open sea on the way back, shave a day off—as long as everyone's got the endurance for it by then. Don't look that way, boy, I'm thinking as much of Tokabii and Nescana as you." The novice-master lowered himself to the floor with a grunt and picked up another roll, tearing it in half with his big hands.

"Do they know?" Trei asked quietly. "I mean— Wingmaster Taimenai and everyone—have we figured out exactly what happened at the steam engines?"

The novice-master's eyebrows rose. "Exactly what happened? That's for mages to figure out. But I gather our kajuraihi destroyed at least one, maybe two, even as they fell."

Trei was silent, imagining this last desperate effort from men who knew they were only seconds from death.

"So now it's for the wingmaster and that bastard Manasi to sort out what to do about Tolounn—and Imrei, of course," he added, almost as an afterthought. "Glad I'm for the sky instead; I've no patience for arguments! But we do need to know what's happened in the south; that's dead true. And it's true we're stretched so thin we need everyone who can fly—and this should be safe enough for you children." He ate the roll in two bites and looked at the remnants of the food spread out on the floor. "Don't suppose there're any more of those pastries?"

"I don't think so, sir," Trei said, not admitting he'd eaten the last one. "Did you see Ceirfei?"

"No, but I didn't look for him, either. Don't worry, Trei," the novice-master added, more kindly. "The wingmaster will tell him you're all right. I'll give you leave to go see him when we're back—provided he's got time for you, and don't count on it, boy, he'll be busy doing—" he waved a broad, impatient hand—"prince things."

Trei nodded.

"You're finished, there? All right, then, up, and we'll hit the sky as soon as you're ready. Don't dawdle."

"No, sir," Trei assured him. He longed for the sky, for the clean simplicity of flight.

"All right—we don't know what's happened in the south," the novice-master told them all, once they were all properly harnessed into their wings and ready to leap off Hei into the wind. "We're going to go find out! This is a real mission, and you lot wouldn't be flying it if we didn't need you, though I expect the idea is it'll also keep you out of trouble. I promised Wingmaster Taimenai you could do this. Don't make me regret that promise, you hear me?"

"Yes, sir!" they all chorused.

Master Anerii glared at them. "You novices—you're sound enough on technique, so long as you don't try anything too complicated, but have you got good sense? Not much evidence of *that!* We'll be in the air a good long time, so don't tire yourselves out with fancy tricks. No showing off! Nothing clever! Understand me?"

"Yes, sir!" everyone shouted again.

"Good! Genrai, how's your navigation? Better than it was, I hope?"

"Yes, sir!" Genrai agreed firmly, refusing to flinch.

"We'll find out! You'll take the lead. Ready? Kojran and I will be behind you, then Nescana and Rekei, then Tokabii and Trei. I may or may not stay in the formation, so don't look to me to figure out where you should be. All right—up we go!"

Without a word, Genrai strode forward and leaped out into the air, spreading his wings to catch the wind. He swept around in a wide circle, waiting for everyone else to find their places—which they did with gratifying speed—and then tilted one wing and slid around in a long easy curve, until the mid-morning sun was off to his left. Everyone followed. Well, Tokabii let himself get a handspan out of position, but he recovered his place before the novice-master could do more than growl.

Nothing seemed wrong with the air. Nothing seemed wrong anywhere, if you didn't look around the curve of Milendri to see the empty sky where Kotipa ought to be. But Trei couldn't help glancing back.

"Pay attention to your flying, Trei," Master Anerii ordered, sliding through the air to come up on Trei's right. "All of you! If you were out in front, could you set our course? Is Genrai right in his direction?" Rekei started to call an answer, but the novice-master said, "Not you, Rekei! And not you, either, Trei. Kojran, *you* tell me, how's our direction?"

Trei didn't listen to Kojran sputter. He knew that they should really have turned a point east of south if they were heading for Tisei—maybe a point and a half. He didn't say anything. It wouldn't matter for a long time, and he was glad enough to have Master Anerii turn all this into a training exercise. If he didn't look back, he could almost believe that this *was* just a training flight and that nothing had ever gone wrong at all. And he couldn't look back, because Master Anerii wouldn't let any of them pay attention to anything but their flying.

Genrai took them higher, so they could dive to gain speed. Then they could just lock their wings and soar. Trei's shoulders ached, but only a little. His wrist felt all right. His elbow was fine, as long as his wings were locked. The winds were good, mostly from the north and west. Genrai finally realized he shouldn't be leading them due south, but overcorrected, Trei thought. But maybe not, maybe they did need to turn two points east of south, since they'd turned late.

They wouldn't reach Tisei by noon, but maybe by second bell. If they wanted to fly around the whole Southern Chain of Islands from there, they'd head straight east from Tisei, pass some Island he couldn't remember the name of, and look for Naransa, which was, depending on how you counted, at the top of the Southern Chain—at least it was the largest of the northernmost chain Islands.

From Naransa, the Southern Chain stretched around in a long uneven arc south and west until the last Islands in the chain were once again almost directly south of Tesei ... small Islands, all those, if he remembered his lessons. Pastures for sheep, fields for grain, gardens and vineyards and orchards. No cities, not even any big towns. Just little villages. Not much for any would-be conqueror to care about, no great wealth or important people. There was a reason Tolounn had gone straight for Milendri last summer, bypassing all the littler Islands.

It occurred to Trei that possibly Wingmaster Taimenai had sent his novices south to keep them safe and out of the way in case the Tolounnese ships arrived in Milendri—since he knew the Tolounnese still had at least one working steam engine left. Probably two. That the Islanders knew about. Trei knew, he was *certain*, that the Little Emperor wouldn't stop his fleet if he still had two working engines. Once he thought of it, it seemed very likely the wingmaster would want his novices out of the way.

Trei would have appreciated that more, except what about Araenè? He wanted to be back on Milendri just for his cousin's sake. He was suddenly desperately anxious about what *she* was doing this morning, whether she was in trouble for everything that had happened ... anything that had happened.

But no matter his sudden sense of urgency, it would still take till early afternoon to reach Tisei. Trei watched the crystalline winds rise and swirl together and descend, layers of density and pressure, warmer air and cooler. He used the sun and the time of year and their estimated speed to calculate their current position and figure out how they should correct their course so as not to overfly Tisei, and tried not to think of anything that mattered.

"Trei!" shouted Master Anerii. "Take the lead and correct our flight path!"

Trei flinched, blinked, tried to estimate how long they'd been flying, and realized he had lost track. He had absolutely no idea, and could already hear Master Anerii's acerbic response if he admitted it. He dropped out of his place in the formation, but shot Kojran a look as he moved forward. Kojran grinned—he was by far the best of them at estimating time—and showed Trei one finger, then one, then four.

So they'd been flying for about one and a quarter bells. It seemed longer. Trei glanced at the angle of the sun. He was almost sure that Genrai had overcorrected. And if that was so ... Trei made his best guess about their average speed and current position and tilted them half a point farther to the south. Master Anerii didn't say anything, which wasn't anything to go by; he wouldn't, until it was perfectly clear Trei had missed Tisei. After that, if Trei had got it wrong, he would probably say quite a lot.

It was hard not to push for speed, now, just to find out whether his navigation was right. That wouldn't impress Master Anerii at all. Trei concentrated on keeping a steady pace. If he'd applied the right correction, put them on the right flight path ... how much longer until they saw Tisei? Not long, he thought. One bell, a little more. His shoulders didn't really hurt anymore. Not really. He'd worked out the stiffness, or gotten used to it. Gulls flew by underneath them, crossing their flight path, narrow wings flashing white in the sunlight.

Had they missed Tisei? Shouldn't they see it by now? It was a big Island, not as big as Milendri but big enough, miles and miles across, big enough they ought to see it from a long way away. Trei, his heart sinking, began to suspect he might not have corrected far enough after all. Or maybe too far ...

Then sharp-eyed Tokabii shouted. Trei, following the direction of the younger boy's gaze, at last spotted the Island of Tisei hanging in the sky, off to the west of their flight path, visible from miles away. They could see not only the Island itself, but also the disturbance it created in the air as the winds broke around it and swirled into eddies in the lee of its bulk. Not even Tokabii could, of course, yet determine whether Gohana was still in its lee as well. But they could all see that they'd be soaring right over the Island in less than half a glass. Tisei was right where it should be, and Trei had found it after all.

9

Araenè followed Tichorei through half-familiar hallways of the hidden school and up a flight of four wide shallow steps. She didn't recognize the little stairway, but supposed he was taking some kind of shortcut to find Master Kopapei. She knew that was the one they had to see. And then, of course, Master Tnegun. She wasn't looking forward to either interview.

Kind as he was, she expected Master Kopapei to have a lot to say. True, no one had told her *not* to make a new sphere to try to catch some of the magic when Kanora's dragon sphere broke. The master mages had probably thought they didn't need a special rule for that, because no apprentice could possibly be stupid enough –

"Crystalizing the living winds is surely akin to turning air into glass! We know how to do that!" snapped Master Akhai's voice from the room in front of them, and Tichorei, who had been reaching to push the door wider, hesitated. She heard Master Kopapei answer with uncharacteristic heat, "Good! Then all's well! We can turn *air* into *glass*! Gods *weeping*, man! Even if we find a way to build such a sphere, there's no method *I* know by which to capture the high dragon winds!" And then her own master added, in a dry, acerbic tone she knew well, "We must learn, clearly, and hope our failures teach us enough we may quickly succeed."

"If *that's* our hope—" began Master Akhai.

Araenè looked at Tichorei, making a little *We could just slip away* motion with one hand.

"No help for it—come on," Tichorei murmured, rejecting this idea and evidently deciding the argument wasn't going to reach a lull. He shoved the door wide and caught her wrist to pull her forward. Araenè jerked herself free, ran her hands through her hair, took a quick breath, and stepped through the doorway.

Master Akhai turned quickly. Light glimmered around his hands as he moved, with a strong fragrance of coriander and pepper and orange—he had been working spells, but Araenè didn't recognize the combination. The handsome young mage was clearly angry, but there was somehow a vulnerability to his anger, and Araenè realized for the first time that he was really not much older than, say, Tichorei, and that he probably felt out of his depth and frightened.

Even Master Kopapei might feel a bit the same way. Master Kopapei was a big man, but always reassuringly rumpled and comfortable. But now he showed no sign of his ordinary good cheer. His eyebrows bristled with exasperation and impatience.

Araenè edged toward Master Tnegun. Her own master looked exactly as he always did: saturnine and reserved. He was frowning, but he often frowned. At least he didn't seem likely to actually start shouting.

Putting out one long, elegant hand, Master Tnegun drew Araenè forward. Suddenly she was the focus of everyone's attention, which was, under the circumstances, not very comfortable. She came reluctantly, trying to meet Master Kopapei's eyes and not just stare at the floor.

"Araenè," said Master Kopapei, and paused.

"*You* took that sphere out of the labyrinth," Master Akhai said, accusingly.

"Gently, if you please," murmured Master Tnugun. "She also was quite adamant that no one take it from the Islands or put it to any use that might harm it. It was *we* who thought ourselves compelled to such steps."

Master Akhai flushed angrily and looked away.

Master Tnegun continued, speaking now to Araenè, "Araenè, as you found Kanora's sphere, and as it now seems perhaps advisable to create another sphere, I—we—consider that it may be beneficial to examine that sphere through your memory and perception. May I enter your memory?"

If he did that, he'd also see what else she'd done—what she'd got Tichorei to do and Trei to help with. And everything. She bit her lip, knowing it was going to be awful once everyone knew everything. But she had to tell them anyway. Of course she had to. And maybe it was better to get it over all at once, as Master Tnegun wanted, rather than trying to fumble her way through explanations. After a moment, she managed to find the half-familiar trick of opening the outermost layers of her mind. She had only done this once or twice, and it was harder with Master Akhai glaring at her and the air swirling with the strong taste of oranges. What kind of magic *was* that, anyway? She *liked* oranges, usually, but this pepper-and-orange taste that tingled across her tongue and the palms of her hands was unsettling. She wanted to ask what Master Akhai had been doing, or trying to do, but didn't dare. She met Master Tnegun's hooded gaze instead, took a deep breath, and nodded.

His mind folded around hers, a cool intrusion that started off small and then opened out like a flower blooming. Only it was smoother and harder and colder and far less fragile than a flower, and it came too close to her inner self— past the outer layers of her mind and down into her memory. Her own mind rose into molten flames that both burned and flowed like water—an instinctive attempt at defense, which she flattened with an effort—she couldn't break her own defense, not completely, but her master caught her mind in his and her fiery defense settled, as though he had put his hand between her and a candle flame.

Good, he said, the word unfolding in her mind. Memories cascaded through her mind: the labyrinth and the sphere she'd found there, flawless and fragile, made of something like glass but not glass, resting in its stand of crystal rods. The tingle of cardamom and palm sugar, rosewater and vanilla, jasmine and pepper, prickling hot and sweet across her fingers and the back of her throat. And the dragon magic tucked out of sight behind all that bright sweetness, minty and musky and strange.

Araenè remembered how she'd felt when she found the sphere, the curiosity and the urgent pressure for light. The feel of it in her hands, cool and smooth, unmoving but somehow feeling like it contained the potential for movement. The reluctance with which she'd let Master Tnegun take it away, and the relief with which she'd given Tichorei's new-made quartz sphere to Trei, and the horror when he'd fallen ... and then the quartz sphere dissolving under the pressure of magic it had not been able to hold, and the violent dragon winds released into the skies above the Islands, and Kotipa shattering, falling ...

Master Tnegun drew himself back, a smooth motionless withdrawal that left Araenè gasping, herself again, alone in her mind, memory and terror alike subsiding. She blinked and put a hand up to her eyes, finding her balance suddenly uncertain. Master Tnegun steadied her with a hand on her arm, his expression unreadable. "You are certainly a constant source of astonishment," he said to her, and to the other two mages, "You saw that."

"A clever idea," Master Kopapei said. "And I must admit, I hadn't realized how far along young Tichorei has come in his skills." He gave Tichorei a nod.

"Clever!" exclaimed Master Akhai. "You saw what happened!"

Master Kopapei frowned at him. "We were *all* experimenting with magic we didn't understand—as it turns out. What did you make of Kanora Ireinamei's sphere, Akhai?"

"Very peculiar," muttered Master Akhai. He darted a hard look at Araenè, but added, reluctantly, "A harnessing of power, a binding of dragon magic to earth—*that's* what it was. I don't know how we missed it."

"We missed it because we weren't looking for anything of the kind," Master Tnegun said. "We needed a weapon. We weren't thinking of the sort of tool that might be used to bind dragons to earth."

Araenè stared at the mages. She could see perfectly well, now that he'd pointed it out, that the sphere might really have been used that way—to capture the essence of dragon magic and serve as the linchpin for a different magic, one that bound the dragons to the Islands. It had never occurred to her that the dragons might have been deliberately bound, the way a man might harness an ox. That they might not have been *driven* from the Islands by the destruction of Kanora's sphere, but *freed*. That was ... that was a very uncomfortable thought.

"Or not precisely a tool for binding, I think," murmured Master Tnegun, patting her shoulder as though he knew exactly how she felt. "But a tool for creating an affinity between earth and air, between the Islands and the dragons. Thus with the loss of that affinity, of course the Islands will gradually sink—"

"Oh, no!" exclaimed Araenè, then clapped a hand over her mouth.

Master Akhai glared at her. "Gradually, unless we *speed up* the process by our poorly considered attempts to release *all sorts* of dragon magic right *here*—"

"Gently, gently," Master Kopapei chided him. "Akhai, my friend. The Islands have always been surrounded by dragon magic—particularly the little dragon Islands such as Kotipa. Releasing a little more should not logically have produced such destructive effects. And you must admit that Cassameirin did not seem to object to the idea. Perhaps we should focus on what we must do now, rather than on the past? Whatever Kanora Ireinamei did, it's clear we won't manage precisely the same sort of working. But we had better manage *something*. What spells would *you* use to create such a binding? Or," with a nod to Master Tnegun, "such an affinity? If it's an affinity for dragon magic we want, it's not an apprentice we need, even one with a sensitivity to dragon magic. We need Cassameirin."

"Who is not here," Master Tnegun said quietly.

Master Akhai threw up his hands. "Really? No? I can't imagine how we could have mislaid him! But since Cassameirin is, astonishingly enough, not here, we will just have to find something to do on our own account! And since Kanora's sphere was clearly important and since we obviously did not understand its function, that may present something of a challenge! But any fool can well see that a binding would be substantially more straightforward than creating some sort of nebulous *affinity*!"

"Kanora's sphere—"

"*Kanora's* sphere—"

"That is enough," Master Kopapei said. The senior mage did not speak loudly, but there was a bite to his voice that made Master Akhai stop, looking ashamed. "Araenè, thank you. You may go," Master Kopapei said, still quietly. "Tichorei, if you will please stay."

Araenè cast Tichorei a quick look. His mouth was set. He looked tense, but not surprised. He didn't look at her at all.

But there was all too clearly nothing she could do to help Tichorei. Or the mages. Or anyone. She took a step toward the door. No one called her back. They were obviously waiting for her to go so they could question Tichorei or resume their argument or do whatever they needed to do to make things better. Araenè lowered her eyes and slipped out, because that was the best help she could offer—to get out of the way and let everyone else try to solve the disaster she'd created.

The next few days of staying quietly out of the way while Milendri slowly settled gently toward the sea nearly drove Araenè mad. None of the apprentices were speaking to her now. Well, not that she ever gave anybody the chance; she couldn't bear for anyone to see her, and stayed hidden in her apartment or—almost as safe—in the kitchens.

Ceirfei didn't come to see her—well, he must be so busy. She longed to go find him. She knew he must blame himself for letting her take Kanora's sphere out of the labyrinth, but he would have heard about the other sphere, too, the one she'd persuaded Tichorei to make. She was afraid of what he might think of her now. But of course he was too busy to come find her. Of course he was. And she didn't dare intrude into the palace.

None of the Islands was sinking fast; no more than a handspan a day, and Master Kopapei apparently thought they would find a new balancing point in the air before anybody was in danger of drowning. Maybe that was so and maybe it wasn't. Araenè tried not to think about that. Or about the Tolounnese ships, which so far the kajuraihi or maybe the mages were successfully delaying, somehow, or else maybe the ships had tacked away from the Islands to wait while Tolounnese artificers repaired the steam engines. But whatever had delayed those ships, how long could that last?

She tried not to think about what would happen when the Tolounnese fleet reached Milendri. But she could hardly think about anything else. She couldn't sleep at night, and she couldn't concentrate on anything, and the third time she let a pot of custard scald, the head chef, Horei, sent her away with a plate of cakes and a dish of honeyed fruit and firm instructions to *rest*. Which, of course, she couldn't. She put the cakes and fruit on the table in her apartment and stepped out of her low window and into her garden.

And found herself in a garden. But not, after all, *her* garden. This one was larger and far more overgrown, altogether wilder, with vines lacing together through quite large trees and shrubs with small silvery leaves tangled across the paths. Araenè turned in a quick circle, looking for the door she'd come through. She drew breath to call out to Master Tnegun.

"Hush!" said Cassameirin, absently but firmly. "Come look here."

He was kneeling on the damp earth, leaning over a pool—not her safe, tame little pool, but a bottomless one of black water, where old trees crowded close and drooping branches trailed long feathery leaves through the hidden depths. Fish moved in the pool, gold ones and white ones and splotched black ones, rising toward the tiny ripples where careless insects touched the surface of the water and then sinking back into the darkness. It wasn't at all the sort of pool which Araenè would have tried to use for vision: it was too dark, too filled with the darting distraction of living things. But she doubted Cassameirin was just inspecting the fish. She took a hesitant step forward.

"Everyone's looking for you," she said. It came out more accusingly than she'd expected, and she wasn't even sure it was true. "Well, everyone *would* be looking for you, if they thought you could be found! Why do you keep putting yourself in *my* way? Master Tnegun—or Master Kopapei—"

"I can't help *them*," Cassameirin said irritably. "They're not the ones who've held fire. Don't dither around over there; come look."

"If you—if Master Tnegun—you know I—" Unable to sort out what she wanted to say, Araenè stuttered to a halt. Cassameirin didn't even look around to see what was keeping her, and after a second she flung up her hands in surrender and came forward to kneel beside him. The scents of crushed herbs and damp earth and something like camphor filled the air—the camphor came from the vine's flowers, and the herbal scent was actually Cassameirin's magic. Beyond and behind and around those scents rose the fragrance of cardamom and oranges and black pepper, and of something else, the minty scent of dragon magic.

"The memory of magic," Cassameirin told her absently. "It lingers here. Dip some water up in your hands."

Araenè sat back on her heels instead and stared at the ancient mage. He didn't look even as old as Master Tnegun, but she knew he was a lot older than her master. Older than the Islands themselves. He'd been Kanora Ireinamei's master—he must know exactly what she had done when she'd made her sphere—probably he'd told her how to do it, or maybe even *why* to do it. She demanded, "Why did you let me take Kanora's sphere out of the labyrinth? You put it there, didn't you? Why didn't you put it someplace safer, someplace hidden—and you *told* me to give Tichorei's sphere to Trei—"

Master Cassameirin turned his round, plump face toward her, his bushy eyebrows rising, and she cut her protest off short.

"I did not put Kanora's sphere where you found it!" he told her. "Kanora made it as she saw fit, and disposed of it as she saw fit. And you found it, and picked it up—as you saw fit. Of course it wasn't wise to let the Tolounnese mages destroy it. But at least you did manage to capture a little of its magic and return it to the Islands—that was well done!"

Araenè stared at him. "It was? I mean ... it was?"

"What else do you think protected the great Islands from breaking up, after the dragon Islands fell? It won't suffice, of course. Too little, too late—and the tiny amount of magic you could trap in quartz would never have been sufficient to hold the dragons close to the earth anyway." Cassameirin turned impatiently back to his pool. "Now, stop chattering, girl. Cup water in your hands and look into it."

Araenè held her tongue, though she wanted to shout with frustration. She put out her hands, hesitated an instant, then dipped her fingers into the pool. The water was cool and clean. A white fish with a golden spot on its head rose up, nudged her fingers and sank back down, disappearing. The scent of oranges and cardamom filled the warm air around her, and a breeze stirred the vine's long leaves, sending camphor to mingle with the fragrances of magic.

Araenè drew her cupped hands out of the pool and looked into the water she held. It was crystal-clear. Sunlight slanted across its surface, shimmering brilliant and opaque as a mirror. She said uncertainly, "I don't see anything ..."

"You do," said Cassameirin. "What do you see?"

Araenè saw only her own reflection. Water dripped from her hands, running out between her fingers though she tried to hold it. She shook her head. "Nothing!"

"You found Kanora's sphere in your way for a reason," said Cassameirin. "And my harp as well. What was that reason?"

Araenè stared at him. "Your harp?" she repeated stupidly. "You mean the one that turned into the hematite dragon? I don't understand ..."

"You will," Cassameirin told her. He tapped her hands firmly, so that Araenè spilled the water she held. She stared at him in mute surprise. Then she said, hotly, "If you would *help*, and not just be all mysterious and confusing! If you know what I should do, what any of us should do, just *tell* me!"

"I don't have the least idea how to fix this. You'll know, when the time comes," the mage said, but now he sounded kind again. He patted her on the shoulder, a little clumsily. "You had better. It all has to do with establishing the proper balance, you know."

Araenè had no idea what he meant.

"You'll understand when you must." Cassameirin patted her again. Then he pointed firmly back to the pool. "Look!"

Bending over the water, Araenè stared into it. This time she didn't see rising fish or the reflections of leaves; and she didn't smell camphor at all, but only oranges and pepper and cardamom. She couldn't see anything in the water. Except ... maybe she did. She wasn't sure. She tilted her head and blinked and looked again, bending lower, until a loose strand of her hair trailed in the water. She brushed it impatiently out of the way ... it wasn't water she stared into, she realized suddenly. It was air. It was sky. It was wind. That slanting movement she half glimpsed was the trailing edge of a dragon's feathered wing.

"Too far away," Cassameirin said. "Too far, and farther all the time. They're rising still. Soon they'll be out of reach. They need a place where the earth touches the sky. Sky alone won't do. Kanora's sphere gave them the affinity they need."

His voice seemed to come from a great distance away. Araenè nodded absently, not really attending to him. She was trying to follow the barely seen glint of a dragon's curving neck, the long graceful coiling length of its body as it turned. It was made of pearl and air, foreign to anything of earth …

"You might want to tell the kajuraihi, since Kanora's not here to explain it to them," said Cassameirin.

"Tell them *what*? And why would Kanora Ireinamei have been able to explain –?" Then she blinked, looking up in startlement, but the mage was gone. The earth beside the pool still bore the imprints where he had knelt, but she had no sense of his presence. The shadows of the trees stretched out across the pool, and the air was much cooler. When she looked up in surprise, the sky was no longer blue and clear, but streaked with salmon and pink, dusky lavender and dove gray; the sun was nearly gone and the moon, visible above the trees, was visible as a translucent sliver in the sky.

Too far away, Cassameirin's voice echoed in her memory. And, *You'll know what to do*. But she didn't. She had no idea at all what she should do.

Except he had also said, *You might want to tell the kajuraihi*.

Tell them what? That the dragons were getting farther away, too far? That they needed a place where the earth touched the sky? She didn't even know what that *meant*. Araenè jumped to her feet. The mages might not need her in the hidden school … they might want all the other apprentices to help them, but not her … they might not trust her to do anything right, even though … was it possible she and Tichorei and Trei had actually protected the Islands? That Kotipa would have fallen anyway, and that little bit of magic they'd caught and brought back had stopped Milendri following? And even the other Islands?

It was hard to believe. But … if she trusted Cassameirin … she still didn't understand anything. Except she needed to tell the kajuraihi what he'd told her.

She thought of Trei. But no, her cousin wasn't the one she needed to talk to now. No, she knew *just* the kajurai who might know, or be able to find out, what all this meant and what to do.

10

Gohana was not in its place off Tisei's edge.

Three kajuraihi with flame-orange wings flew as an escort, leading them right through the empty sky where Gohana should have been before they all turned back toward the kajurai precincts on Tisei. Trei didn't understand why the kajuraihi insisted on flying through the sky where Gohana had once floated until they entered that area. Then he felt how wrong the air was there ... how thin, how attenuated, how truly empty. The winds had not looked that strange until they got there. Then ... the sky *felt* stranger than it looked.

Later, after they had finally landed in the kajuri hall of Tisei, the senior of the kajuraihi explained how it had happened. "The dragons lifted up into the heights, and Gohana ... just broke apart, cliff by cliff, and fell." He shook his head, unable to find words. Finally he went on, "It was terrible. You could hear the rock crack and sheer. It was the worst thing I've ever heard. And Tisei ... I thought Tisei would follow, the same. But a hard dragon wind came up right as Gohana fell. I think that saved us. But ... nothing could save Gohana." The man was old, with white hair and a seamed, experienced face, but his voice was not quite steady.

The room was big, but there weren't enough chairs for everyone. Tokabii and Trei, Kojran and Rekei and Nescana all stood because they were the youngest. The Tisein kajuraihi hadn't seemed to notice that Nescana was a girl—or they were still too overwhelmed by Gohana's fall to care. Trei could understand that.

One of the other kajuraihi handed around cups of watered wine and asked quietly if Master Anerii wished any other refreshment. Master Anerii waved this offer away impatiently. "Kotipa, the same," he said to the old man. "Have you word from the south?"

"No. No, not yet. I would have sent a man of mine to Canpra, only ..."

"I know. A thousand things to do after any disaster— there're only the few of you on Tisei? Right. Well, I'm going to ask you to send a man to Canpra after all. I know you can't easily spare anyone, but Wingmaster Taimenai needs to know."

The elderly kajurai nodded unhappily, clearly not liking this order but unable to object. "Your man had better go now, at once," Master Anerii told him. He glanced over his novices. "Get some rest, the lot of you. We'll leave Tisei at third bell. I want to go straight past Kansannè and raise Naransa before we break for the night. It's not much more than a hundred miles, but likely we won't make it till after dark. That'll give you all a chance to practice navigation by the stars. Some of you can use the practice."

Master Anerii didn't look at Nescana, but they all knew he meant her. Well, her and her brother and Tokabii. Kojran had picked up a decent amount of math, for a Third City boy.

"Third bell, on the balcony, wings on and ready to go," ordered Master Anerii. "Catch some rest while you can!" He waved a curt dismissal at the novices, then turned back to the Tisein kajuraihi. "Now, can you tell me—" he began, but that was all the novices heard, because the novice-master closed the door behind them.

"Food, and juice—you'd better not have much wine if you're flying," said the kajurai who had come out into the hall with them. He looked them over curiously. "You're all novices?" His eye had snagged on Genrai, who was certainly old enough to be a kajurai of rank, except he'd waited so long to audition. The Tisein kajurai wasn't much older, certainly. He went on without pausing, "If that's how you're stretched, well. Well, tell me what's happened on Milendri. I expect I'll be the one flying into whatever trouble it is, likely today."

Trei thought it was really too long a story to fit into three-quarters of a bell, but the others did their best to tell this part of it and that part, all in a chorus.

"Everyone ready?" snapped Master Anerii, arriving. He could see perfectly well, of course, that they weren't, and watched with a jaundiced eye as they scrambled. "Good," he said at last, looking them all over. "Nescana, I trust you can tell east from west. You can take point. You know where Kansannè is?"

"About half a point north of east," Trei muttered.

"What, are you Nescana all of a sudden?" the novice-master demanded. "When I want your navigation, Trei, I'll ask for it! You know how to set your flight path half a point north of east, girl?"

"Yes, sir!" declared Nescana, not looking at Trei. She had blushed bright red, but her voice was firm, even though they all knew she was stretching the truth.

"Then lead out, novice! Genrai and Kojran behind her, Rekei and Trei behind them, Tokabii and me at the back. Go!"

They flew with the sun at their backs, golden light streaming past them, gilding the sea beneath them. Clouds piled up in the south, brilliant white shading to dove gray and pewter: Trei could see by the winds that those clouds would stay off to the south. Heat beat down from above, but Nescana took them higher, and then higher, until they rose out of the warm air and into the cold heights. They flew in and out of wispy clouds, moisture beading on their faces and hair and on the feathers of their wings.

Nescana had set a course that wasn't quite right, Trei knew. She just wasn't good yet at judging the angle of their flight relative to true east. Trei thought if they were going to do a lot of training flights, they should develop secret ways of telling each other things.

The high winds were bright and hard, fun to ride but not nearly as easy as the warmer and more settled winds Trei could see far below. It was difficult to soar up this high because cold air had so much less lift. Trei was grateful when Master Anerii called out for Rekei to take the lead.

Rekei had clearly been waiting for that order, because the moment he had the point position, he altered their flight path to take them half a point west of south. Trei thought this might be an overcorrection, but maybe Rekei was right. And, since Rekei loved speed, he also led them in a sharp dive that leveled out four hundred feet closer to the sea and left them with almost half again the speed they'd held higher up. Plus, in this warmer air, they'd need to put forth less effort to maintain that speed, at least for a while.

They passed fishing boats bobbing on the waves, and half a dozen whales swimming in a formation a lot like their own, massive black backs rising and then sinking again with a lift of flukes. Trei had seen whales before, but not often and seldom so close. It occurred to him that his sister Marrè would have loved to see a formation of whales, that she would have loved to draw their rolling black backs and rising flukes, the plumes of steam they blew out and their small eyes and barnacle-encrusted jaws … but the thought came to him with a long slow swell of grief rather than the sharp, urgent pain he expected. Rather than flinch from the memory of his sister, he flew on thinking of the snow-covered mountains of northern Tolounn and of his lost home there, his parents and Marrè and his friends in Rounn, as they had all once been and not as he had seen them last, buried with the whole city beneath a deep covering of poisonous ashes.

"There it is!" cried Tokabii. "Look!"

It was unquestionably Kansannè: a verdant Island four or five miles across, not big but certainly not an insignificant pebble. The Island floated between blue sky and blue sea, casting a wide violet shadow on the waves beneath its bulk. A town occupied the eastern edge of Kansannè and stretched away into the interior of the Island, and Trei saw at least one other village as they passed over, but they stopped only long enough to stretch their legs and drink from a crystalline pool.

"Everyone all right? Nobody's struggling? It's just about that far again to Naransa, you know," the novice-master told them all. "No one's having trouble? Trei, you sure, boy? You get into trouble out there and I will remember you said you were fine. Tokabii? Nescana? You sure? Who's up for the lead from here to Naransa? Kojran, you want a turn in front?"

Plainly the novice-master was relentlessly giving every novice who was weak at navigation a chance to show that weakness to everyone. Kojran didn't groan out loud, but he darted Trei a piteous look. Tokabii grinned at the other boy's dismay, and Master Anerii said drily, "You think your turn's not coming along, Tokabii?" That got rid of the grin, and Kojran looked a little happier.

"Fifty miles or so, a fraction more than three points north of east," Master Anerii said to Kojran. "Trei, show Kojran the angle."

Trei put his back to the sun and held out his arms, showing Kojran true east with his right arm and three points north of east with his left.

"Yes, but you can't see where the sun lies if you're flying away from it," protested Kojran.

"Learn to," the novice-master said without sympathy. "Anyway, the first stars'll be out soon enough. What star do you use to find east? Anybody?"

"The tiger star's due east!" said Tokabii, who had a surprisingly good memory for stars considering he never studied. "You find the tiger star by lining down from the rim of the Bowl."

"Good, Tokabii. The rest of you know that? I should hope so. All right. Kojran's in the front, Genrai and me second, then Rekei and Nescana, Trei and Tokabii in the back. Keep us riding the dense air down low, Kojran, and let's keep a steady pace; this isn't a race! Ready? All right, boy, lead off."

Kojran held his direction pretty well for a while, but as the sky turned first pearl gray and then dusky violet and the stars came out, he drifted back toward due east. The tiger star was a bright one, and with it shining low over the horizon, it was just easier to set your course straight east. Trei was not unsympathetic, but on the other hand, Kojran always acted like he was so much better than Nescana, so it was only fair he should go off his course too. The moon might have given him his direction, but it was lost behind those huge clouds towering up to the south, violet and black against the luminescent sky. Lightning flashed in the midst of those clouds. Trei was glad they weren't flying south.

"Genrai!" called Master Anerii, startling Trei so that he momentarily and embarrassingly lost his place in the formation and had to work hard to get back into place.

"Sir!" Genrai shouted, sounding tense.

"You know where we are, boy?"

Genrai hesitated, but then shouted bravely, "Yes, sir!"

"Take the lead!" ordered Master Anerii. "Kojran, you take the second place!"

Genrai arched his wings to rise, and Kojran cupped his to drop out of the lead position. Neither of them looked very happy about it—not that Trei could see their faces in the dimming light, but he fancied Kojran's embarrassment and Genrai's nervousness showed in the angles of their wings.

Genrai took them four, almost four and a half points north of east, which seemed like a lot. Trei knew he was right when Master Anerii drove himself up Genrai's left, gently crowding him off a little more to the right until they were flying barely three points north of east. But the novice-master didn't say anything sharp, at least not yet.

"There it is!" called Nescana half a bell later, dipping out of formation to indicate the glimmering bulk where a big Island caught the very last light of the sun, looming black and violet in the sky, very much like the clouds to the south, only rougher-edged and not so high. Nescana came back to the formation with little looping skips, proud of her brother. She had a right to be proud of Genrai: Trei was almost sure they'd have found the Island even without Master Anerii giving

Genrai that last little hint. Or they would have if it wasn't so dark, anyway.

"Pace yourself, girl!" Master Anerii ordered gruffly. "I'll take the lead, Genrai! Unless you want to find the kajurai precincts in the dark!"

"No, sir! Yes, sir!" Genrai shouted back, relieved, and they all slanted down through the sky toward the half-seen bulk of the Island.

The novices saw almost nothing of Naransa. It was too dark to see anything when they arrived, and everyone was too tired to do more than eat the supper provided and go to bed. The supper was all right, although Trei suspected it wouldn't have impressed Araenè. The mutton stew had a distinct herbal taste he couldn't identify but didn't like—Araenè would have known what herb was responsible—and the cakes were too dry and flavored with something else he didn't like. Anise, he thought, and realized he would never have known that if not for Araenè. He missed her suddenly and fiercely, which made no sense because they didn't see each other very often anyway, but somehow it was worse when she was so far away, hundreds of miles. When he knew he couldn't just say her name and open a door and find her.

Though she might be able to open a door to find him. That thought made Trei feel a little less far away from Milendri after all.

But he still didn't think the cakes were very good. He gave Tokabii the rest of his. Tokabii liked any cake, whether it had anise in it or not.

Master Anerii did not have supper with them. He'd gone to talk to the senior kajuraihi of Naransa, and was probably having a much better supper with them.

"Master Anerii might have taken us with him," Kojran complained, startling Trei out of his own thoughts.

Nescana made the little flip of her hand which the Islanders used to indicate scorn. "So we could listen to a lot of old men worry about everything! We already know what's

142

happening—it's the kajuraihi here who don't know anything. You really want to have to tell everything all over again?"

"You think you—" began Kojran, but then caught Genrai's eye and subsided.

"Bed," Genrai said firmly. "We're all tired. No, Kojran, I don't want to hear it. Bed, now. It'll be an early morning tomorrow."

But to everyone's surprise, the novice-master didn't come to find them until close to second bell. That was plenty of time to first get bored and then start to worry.

"There's a situation here," Master Anerii told them disgustedly, when he finally arrived in the novice's hall to find them. He folded his arms, leaning his hip against the small stone table in the novice's common room and picking up a stale anise cake. He seemed more inclined to wave it around than take a bite out of it, which seemed reasonable to Trei.

"A situation, sir?" Genrai asked this cautiously, because the novice-master might be deciding what to tell them— probably was—and might not appreciate any attempt to prod him along.

This morning, however, Master Anerii didn't seem inclined to reprimand any impertinence. Most likely, Trei thought, because he didn't have anyone but them to complain to, and he clearly wanted to complain.

"Used to be a first-ranked kajurai in charge here," he said shortly. "Risenai Cersenra, no one you'd know. Well, seems he got his heart set on this girl over on Marisanai and just dumped everything here and moved right on over there to be with her. Where they were glad to have him, you can be sure, having no resident kajuraihi of their own. Well, a little pebble like that, they hardly need one, you'd have thought, but I guess Risenai decided otherwise. Wrote the transfer up as a proper request, but didn't bother sending it back to Milendri!" He snorted and finally took a bite of the cake, not seeming to notice that it wasn't very good. Though he did look around absently for something to drink, and took the cup of juice Nescana handed him with a nod of thanks.

Then he went on, "All kinds of business here's out of order now. These second-ranked kajuraihi let it get worse than it ever should have—let that be a lesson to you all: if you wind up in charge of an Island like this one and some irresponsible fool walks off and leaves you holding all his abandoned responsibilities, it'd be good to have some notion what to do with 'em! I expect Wingmaster Taimenai will have something to say to this lot! *And* to that fool Risenai, of course. But in the meantime, there's too Gods-cursed much to deal with right here, and all the time the Southern Chain waiting. And that won't wait long!" He took another bite of the cake, glowering.

"Easy flying along the Chain," Rekei said to no one in particular, leaning insouciantly back in his chair. He gave the novice-master a sideways look. "I mean, you can practically see one Island from the next all the way down the Chain, straight to Taraban. Nobody could possibly get lost along there, could they? And every Island along the way just a tiny little hop along, in case a storm blew up or somebody needed a rest or anything. Anybody could fly along the length of the chain, take a glance at Taraban and see if Fenaisa's still in the air, and come back the same way. Isn't that right, sir?" he ended, not quite innocently.

The novice-master transferred his glower to Rekei. "Aching to get off on your own for a day or two, boy? Easy flying and no lessons, is it? You think I should trust you to go off on your own? Maybe I'd be better advised to keep an impudent boy who's clever with figures right here with me so's he can learn all about paperwork, hey?"

"Oh, well—" Rekei said, startled and alarmed. "Master Anerii, sir—"

But the novice-master was grinning now. "No, no! It's a good idea, boy. Shouldn't be much trouble you *can* get into, out here. Out and back and no trouble, is that it? No playing games with wind and weather, no fool contests to see who can fly the highest or the lowest or the fastest—"

"No, sir!" Rekei exclaimed. Everyone was sitting up straight now, Tokabii all but vibrating with eagerness at the prospect of—exactly as the novice-master had said—getting away for a couple of days of easy flying and no lessons.

"You'll give me your word on that," Master Anerii said sternly. "Your word and no prevarication, boy, you hear me?" He glowered around the table, fixing a gimlet eye on Tokabii. "Any trouble, I tell you, we always need junior kajuraihi to handle the paperwork. Senneri sitting indoors with paper and ink ..."

"No, sir!" Rekei said. "We'll do just as you say, sir."

Tokabii echoed him, "Yes, sir! Really!"

"Then you should all take an extra cake," said the novice-master. "You'll have a long day flying if you mean to try to make Taraban by nightfall."

11

They didn't, quite. The Southern Chain stretched out farther than any of them had really realized, and Tokabii wanted to fly over every single Island they passed, at least every one with a town of any size. So did Trei. He liked looking at the towns: neat houses of red or yellow brick or mortared stone, with roofs of wooden shingles or expensive imported slate. Even thatch, sometimes, on the smallest Islands. There were farms and fields everywhere the land was flat enough. Quite a few of the very small Islands had nothing but pastures and maybe a temple.

All of them had people who looked up and waved when the kajuraihi flew by. Children ran and pointed and yelled, and then Tokabii and Kojran ... and then Nescana ... and Trei and Rekei ... and at last even Genrai did fast turns and loops and other tricks.

"Master Anerii wouldn't mind! It's not actually dangerous or anything!" Tokabii told Genrai, early on, when they stopped for travelers' rations at one small temple on a tiny Island. It was just bread and dried fish, but eaten out in the open in the shade of a single gnarled tree, with tawny goats grazing in the pastures and the land falling away on all sides and the sea stretching out limitless beyond, it tasted better than cakes with honey. Especially stale anise cakes.

"It's show-away nonsense," Genrai said sternly. "I'm sure you'd do far better grounded with paperwork than playing games with village children." But he couldn't quite keep his severe expression in place and nobody took him seriously.

Caanti and Anaranne, Botai and Horaii, Gitan and little Seirafenai ... one pleasant green Island after another. The sun crested in the sky and heat poured down, thick as honey, so they flew high where the air was cool and the winds cut sharply through the feathers of their wings. From that height, the Islands were glowing little dimples in the air, and the sea a deep and luminous green-blue. Clouds stood far away to the south, white at the edges, pearl gray shading to lavender and then pewter-gray where they were heaviest. The air there looked dark and heavy, but the storms didn't seem to be moving closer.

They were flying almost due west now, coming around the wide curve of the Southern Chain. The sun had slid slowly down the vault of the heavens and stood now almost directly before them, a handspan above the horizon. Kajurai eyes were not troubled by brilliance or easily confused by light shimmering off the water, but still, Trei was glad Taraban was a larger Island; it would be easy to see even against the light.

He knew the Dragon Island of Fenaisa would be a tiny little Island, like all the Islands of Dragons. Rugged and mountainous, with broken cliffs where small twisted trees clung to the red stone. And there would be dragons, of course. Dragons transparent as the winds, with their immense wings and graceful, elegant heads and long rippling bodes; transparent and yet glittering like ice where the light caught their feathers at just the right angle. Dragons, with their huge chatoyant eyes, and their voices like harp notes and silver chimes, and their riddles.

Only Fenaisa wasn't going to be there. Trei was sure of it. He was sure it had fallen into the sea at the same time as Kotipa and Gohanna. If it had just been Kotipa, that would have been different. But Kotipa *and* Gohanna? He knew all the Dragon Islands must have fallen. He didn't want to think about what that might mean. He didn't want to think about his own audition, about climbing Kotipa's heights, about the pool he had found there, and the white tree ... no one had to say out loud, *Without the Dragon Islands, there will be no way to make kajuraihi.* He knew that. He didn't want to think about it.

He knew Fenaisa was gone. But he supposed he understood why they had to go look.

Taraban seemed to emerge suddenly from the sky before them: an irregular broad shape dark against the light of the lowering sun, all green trees above and red stone below, for the Island was one of the few with real forests.

The Island grew larger and larger and still larger as they drew closer to it. There were ... Trei thought he remembered that there were two towns on Taraban, one in the hilly south and one in the easier lands of the north. But the people of both planted and nurtured and cut the trees, and traded the valuable timber for the grain they didn't grow. They didn't even have goats, because goats were bad for the woodlands. That was too bad, but Trei was hungry enough to look forward even to more fish. But he hoped the people of Taraban flavored their cakes with something other than anise ...

Then Genrai led them in a long sloping curve up and over the forested hills of the Island, on a path that took them around the western edge of Taraban from north to south, meaning to make sure once and for all that the little Dragon Island was not there. And it wasn't; there was only the wide sky and the long streaks of high clouds, amber and rose with the last of the sunlight, and the darkening sea below.

But eight ships rested on the sea, sails furled, riding the slow swell at anchor. And drawn up to Taraban, docked close against the red rock of the cliffs, with a narrow bridge of wood leading from its deck to the Island, rested a ninth ship.

It took Trei, not Island born, an instant to realize the impossibility of what he was seeing. Everyone else, of course, grasped it at once. Because Taraban floated hundreds of feet above the sea, and that meant that the ship, too, was floating in the air.

"That's impossible!" Rekei cried. Everyone else shouted at once.

What Trei shouted over the others, after the first moment of astonishment, when he understood that the others did not realize this, was, "That's not a Tolounnese ship! None of those are Tolounnese ships!"

"Then whose? They're not *ours*!" snapped Rekei, but Kojran had gone silent.

"Great generous Gods!" said Genrai. "They're Yngulin!"

These were indeed Yngulin ships. As the novices came closer, they could all see the eagle on its prow, the gold and black paint blazing in the sun. They could see men running across the deck and climbing the rigging, half naked in the evening heat, ebony-dark skin shining with sweat. The warriors who had crossed the plank bridge wore short linen kilts and long linen vests, and carried small round shields with metal spikes in the center, and broad-bladed short swords, and when they looked up at the novices overhead, they beat their swords against their shields and roared out words in their own language in a tone of scornful defiance.

Trei knew that fifty men like that could take Taraban. There were more men than that standing in those ranks right now. And that was only one ship.

Genrai started to shout something, but then crewmen threw down the plank bridge that had connected them to the Island, and cast off the anchor chains. The ship's sails unfurled, one wide triangular wing of linen after another, with the Yngulin carrion eagle on each, black with red talons and beak ... and the sails luffed and filled, and instead of oars, silver streamers poured out of the oarlocks, and the ship swung with ponderous grace away from Taraban and mounted slowly higher into the sky, turning as it rose, its prow swinging around to the south.

For one stunned moment, Trei thought the ship might actually be turning to flee. On his left, Rekei made an incredulous noise. Trei started to say something, he didn't know what, but then, as the ship turned its side toward them, a deep metallic *whuunng* rang through the quiet air, and the warriors below on the Island all shouted as one, and hundreds of small silvery bolts flashed through the air toward the novices, like deadly sharp-edged sleet driven before the wind.

The novices were too close to the ship to dodge properly, and too astonished, and there were too many of the wicked little darts. Trei closed his wings and dropped like a stone, and beside him Rekei followed only a heartbeat behind; Trei was dimly aware of Tokabii flinging himself one way and Nescana the other, and had no idea where Kojran had gone, or Genrai.

If the flight of bolts had been properly aimed, they would all have been struck down. But the Yngulin warriors had not taken time to aim carefully, and so the only novice struck was Nescana, whose desperate dodge took her the wrong way. She realized it, but not in time: Trei heard her scream, a high desperate sound like the cry of a bird, and twisted around in time to see her fall.

Nescana tumbled toward the sea, helpless to catch herself, but she fell the way a kajurai falls: slowly. Trei knew from that that she was alive. Everyone knew it. Genrai was already plunging after her, and Rekei. Trei let them go and stood on a wingtip, pivoting in the air, looking urgently for the Yngulin ship. It was turning, with that deceptive ponderousness that made it look slow, and he could see men aft working to re-arm and re-aim the small wide-mouthed catapults that had flung the bolts.

"Kojran!" Trei shouted, and, folding his wings, dove toward the ship. Below, he could see that Nescana had struck the surface of the sea. She did not sink, of course; her wings were too wide and too buoyant to let her sink, but they lay heavily on the surface of the water, holding her down as though they were chains. Soon they would be waterlogged and lose their buoyancy, and then she would drown—except that of course one of the other Yngulin ships down there would pick her up before that. He could see two of them moving now.

Genrai had come down so close to the sea that his wingtips sent up spray on every downbeat. He might be able to get his sister back into the air, if she didn't panic and if they had time.

Trei shouted to Kojran, who had come away from the disaster unfolding below to follow him toward the Yngulin ship, "You know any Yngulin?"

"Ylembai!" shouted Kojran. "The language is called Ylembai! I only know a little!"

"More than me!" Trei answered. There were *four* of those horrible bow-catapult things on the deck of the ship, with a crew at each to aim it, but he thought none of them could aim straight forward toward the bow of the ship. The ship could turn, of course, but nothing like so fast as a kajurai could fly. Trei ducked straight underneath the ship's keel ... and what *were* those silver ribbons below the ship? They weren't blowing straight away from the wind, Trei could see that, but at an angle to it. Something magical, of course, something to get the ship into the sky or steer it once it was up ... no time to think about it. He rose sharply, up and over the ship's prow, and dropped to the deck directly in front of the man in the fanciest feather cloak.

The man was very tall and extremely elegant. He had a narrow chin and wide cheekbones and black hair cropped close to a high, rounded skull. His cloak was of bronze feathers, and black, and tawny gold—eagle feathers, Trei guessed. He wore a longer kilt than the soldiers, and a vest edged with gold, and there was gold on the sandals that laced up his calves. He wore no weapons but a short black-hilted knife thrust through his belt, and he did not draw that. Instead, he put up a hand to halt the crewmen who had begun to rush toward Trei, then tilted his head and gazed down at Trei with aristocratic disdain.

"You shot a girl," Trei said quickly. "A girl no older than me, that's who you shot."

The man stared down at him in wordless scorn. But Trei could see that everyone was watching the two of them, crowding curiously forward and waiting to see what would happen. That meant no one was aiming those terrible bow-catapults at his friends. Trei stood as straight as he could, curving his wings around carefully, trying to keep the tips of the primaries from brushing the deck. As always, once he was down, the wings seemed to weigh ten times what they did in the air. He could feel their weight in his shoulders and all the way down his back, but he tried not to show it. He said, "Can you understand me?"

He heard the stiff rustle of wings above and behind him, and then Kojran backwinged into a perfect stall and came down at his side, taking two step to catch himself and then standing stiffly, staring up at the tall man in the feather cloak.

Here on this ship, standing next to Trei and before the ship's master, surrounded by the Yngulin crew, Kojran somehow looked both more and less Yngulin. He had the same narrow chin and wide cheekbones, but softened and rounded; and his black hair was curly but not the tight curls of Yngulin hair. And his skin was not nearly so dark, of course, but a softer, warmer color, like caramelized sugar.

But next to Trei, Kojran looked very Yngulin indeed.

The ship's master looked down his nose at Kojran, too, but his eyes had narrowed just a little. He said something filled with the strange consonants and difficult diphthongs of the Yngulin language. His tone was cutting, so Trei was afraid it was an insult or a threat, but he could see that Kojran didn't understand the man any more than he did himself.

The ship's master saw that, too. He said, in the speech of the Islands, his words slow and accented but clear, "One drop of blood from the Great King's own hound does not make a mongrel pup into a purebred."

Kojran paled, which on him was not as obvious as it would have been on a pure Islander boy. He stared up at the Yngulin man, speechless.

But Trei, now assured that the man could understand the speech of the Islands, said quickly, "We're couriers—you don't need to shoot us—you can tell us what you want. Don't you want to send your terms to Milendri, to the king in

Canpra? We can carry your terms there faster than even your ships can sail—"

The ship's master held up his hand again, and Trei fell silent, swallowing. He wanted very badly to look over the railing, see if Nescana had been picked up by one of the other Yngulin ships or whether she had by some miracle made it back into the air. But he didn't move. If he could buy Nescana time, it was by standing here and making this Yngulin lord pay attention to him and not to whatever drama was playing itself out in the sea or the sky. So he stood straight and stared into the Yngulin lord's face and waited to see what would happen. He more than half thought the man would command his men to leap forward and take Kojran and himself prisoner. He didn't know whether, if that happened, either of them would be able to get away. He planned what he would do if it happened—four or five steps to the railing, one foot up on the coil of rope there, up and over the side to catch the wind –

The Yngulin lord spoke, long choppy phrases in Ylembai. He half turned to address his own men, not Trei or Kojran, and his voice took on the cadences of a speech. Trei thought that was fine: the longer the lord took for his oration, the better. Then the Yngulin men all called out fiercely and beat their hands on their thighs, and Trei wasn't so sure the speech had been a good thing after all. Maybe it had been something like *Death to all foreigners* or *Rip the wings off all unnatural kajuraihi* or ... he couldn't even imagine.

"We should get out of here," Kojran muttered in his ear. "Trei, we really need to get out of here—"

Trei nodded and again measured the distance between them and the ship's railing.

Then the ship's master turned to face them again. He said, "You ask for terms, little flying boy. We have no terms. We do not need your little king to yield his Islands to the Great King as a gift: we will take them and do as we please with all we find here. You may take *that* word to your little king, if you wish." He glanced disdainfully at Kojran. "But we shall keep the mongrel, for it is not right that even one drop of Eshanki blood should be claimed by a lesser people."

He gestured, and two of his men started toward Kojran.

Trei made a throwing gesture toward the Yngulin lord's face. The man took a prudent step back, and for just an instant his men hesitated. Trei didn't, and Kojran didn't either: they bolted for opposite sides of the deck. Trei leaped up on the coil of heavy rope and flung himself over the railing and fell, snapping his wings open only when he'd gotten speed enough to dodge through the air like a falcon weaving through tree branches in a forest. He tried to see whether Nescana was still in the water, but he couldn't see anything but ships and the open sea; and he tried to look around for Kojran, but he couldn't find the other boy anywhere –

"Above you!" cried Kojran, his voice shrill and wild, and Trei looked up, and there he was, crimson wings burning in the last light of the sun. He *looked* wild, too: his eyes wide and his lips drawn back from his teeth. Trei didn't blame him. Kojran had loved his Yngulin grandfather, of course, and he'd always said someday he would go to Yngul and see his grandfather's people, and now that horrible Yngulin lord had tainted both the love and the dream. No wonder he was flinging himself through the air with such wild speed: that wasn't fear, not anymore. It was fury or grief, or something like both but more complicated than either.

Trei wanted to circle around and look for Nescana and the others, but the evening light was failing and he could see nothing but Yngulin ships maneuvering across the sea, and the one wheeling slowly back through the air toward the cliffs of Taraban.

They were both flying fast and straight now, because surely they were far outside the range of those bow-catapults. Taraban rushed past below them, all its forests lost in the gathering dusk. Soon, very soon, all those Yngulin warriors would be marching through those forests. They would come upon Taraban's town in the dark, like creatures right out of nightmares ... "We have to warn them!" Trei shouted. "We have to tell them!"

"We have to tell Master Anerii," Kojran yelled back. "We can't get all the way back to Naransa tonight!"

"You want to sleep *here* tonight?"

"Of course not!" Trei would have as soon bedded down in the middle of a room filled with spiders. Who knew how fast those Yngulin warriors would seize control of Taraban? Maybe that ship or another one would sail right around the Island and dock again right by one town and then the other. Maybe the other ships would sail right on around the Southern Chain. Or straight north toward Milendri ... kajuraihi never felt the chill of the air, but Trei felt cold all through. This was worse than the Tolounnese trying to conquer the Islands. This was a lot worse. The Tolounnese had tried to take Canpra, a swift move to subjugate all the Islands in one stroke. If they had succeeded, they'd have taken the king and all his family back to Tolounn and appointed a Tolounnese provincar to rule the Islands in the name of the Emperors. But once the fighting had been over, the Tolounnese soldiers wouldn't have killed anybody. Trei remembered the sneering expression of the Yngulin lord, the contempt in his voice when he said *We will do as we please with all we find here*, and had no idea what the Yngulin warriors would do.

He wished he knew what had happened to the others. He looked for them in the sky, he had been looking all the time since he and Kojran had gotten away from the Yngulin ship, but he couldn't see any other kajuraihi anywhere ... maybe Nescana had never made it up out of the water, maybe the Yngulin warriors had taken her, and if her, maybe Genrai, who might well surrender in the hope of protecting his sister. But then where were Rekei and Tokabii?

"There!" said Kojran, flying a quick dipping path through the sky to show Trei, and Trei looked that way, and there *was* a kajurai, wings something between crimson and black in the darkening sky, diving from the heights toward them.

"It's Tokabii!" said Kojran.

It was. It was Tokabii, alone, and Trei bit his lip, but then the younger boy curved around and dropped down and came into place just a handspan off Trei's left wingtip. "They're fixing Nescana's wing!" he shouted. "Genrai told me to go high and watch for you and tell you! I was scared I'd miss you in the dark!"

Half a bell later and they might well have missed one another, Trei thought, and what then? But mostly he was too relieved at Tokabii's news to worry about something which hadn't even happened. Fixing Nescana's wing! That sounded good, far better than he'd dared hope. He shouted, "Nescana?"

"She's all right! Down over this way, in the lee of that crooked rock!"

Trei could barely see the broken cliff Tokabii meant, but he fell in behind the other boy and let him lead the way down and down, rushing through the darkness ... there was a fire there in the lee of the cliff, no, three fires, built at the points of a triangle, the kind that people built to help kajuraihi come down in the dark. Trei was grateful Genrai had thought of that. He cupped his wings, slowing and slowing, and came awkwardly down on rough ground, staggering as the weight of his wings suddenly pulled him off balance.

Then Rekei was there on one side and Nescana—Nescana herself—on the other, and he sagged gratefully, letting them help him with his harness, aware of Kojran coming down nearby and of tall Genrai moving to help him.

"You're all right," he said to Nescana, a little stupidly, since he could see that she was.

"Not a scratch!" she said. "But my poor wing!"

"She broke *every* feather," said Tokabii.

"I didn't!" protested Nescana. "At least, it wasn't my fault! You try getting your wing shot up by a thousand little bolts and see how many feathers are left!"

"That's why I sent Tokabii to watch for you, since he's no good for featherwork anyway," Genrai said grimly, coming back. "But I was afraid he'd never see you coming, not if he watched all night. I was afraid we'd never see you again!" He took Trei's shoulders in a hard grip, looking him up and down. "But you're all right? I thank the Gods! You meant to distract them, of course? Of course. We'd never have got her up if you hadn't. But it was a great risk." His grip on Trei's shoulders tightened in unspoken gratitude.

Trei ducked his head. "How'd you get her back in the air?"

Genrai released his grip and said briskly, "Let her grab our ankles and worked like mad to drag her up into the air! I didn't think she'd manage it—if she wasn't so gifted she'd never have done it. Even then she barely made it! Stupid girl's proud as if she did it on purpose! You should see her wing." He sounded both proud and disgusted. "You never saw such a wreck."

"I've never pulled the winds so hard in my life!" Nescana said, and laughed. Her laugh contained all the relief and joy of someone who'd looked at her own death and then found herself, beyond all expectation, not only alive but well. Of someone coming out of a dark pit into the light.

Trei understood that perfectly. He looked into her face and thought of how she might have been lost or killed and instead was here, with them, and safe. She was luminous in her joy—she was beautiful in that moment, and Trei knew she always had been and he simply hadn't seen it until now. He said, as Genrai had, "I thank the Gods," and she looked at him and something changed in her face, but he couldn't tell exactly what.

"We're all working on her wing," said Genrai. "How many spare feathers do you have? It's the primaries and secondaries, mostly. We won't be able to get the wing back to what it should be, but we should get it to where it'll work. As long as she doesn't try any acrobatics, or fall into the sea again," he added sternly.

"Not unless I get shot again!" said Nescana, not in the least daunted by her brother's tone. "Featherwork by firelight; what fun we're all having! Come help, Trei." She touched his arm to draw him toward the largest of the fires. She was still smiling, and he couldn't tell whether there was something new in her face or not.

He followed her, slowly, the warm breeze coming against his face with the scents of woodsmoke and crushed leaves and the salt sea, and he was suddenly intensely aware that he was alive, and free, and well, and that he might not have been any of those things. Whatever might come, this moment was a gift, and he knew it suddenly, and told himself, *I will remember this forever*, but knew even as he thought this that the intensity of awareness was already fading. And Nescana, walking backward with her eyes on his face, knew what he was thinking because she was thinking it too. They both knew it. They smiled at one another with just a touch of sadness, and then Nescana turned and strode toward the fire and her damaged wing.

The wing was spread out, with threaded needles thrust into the feathers so they wouldn't get lost in the flickering light. Spools of extra thread and packets of feathers were scattered all around the wing. Trei stared down at it, dismayed. He could see they hadn't carried nearly enough feathers to repair the whole wing—especially not the long primaries.

"We'll take two or three primaries from everyone else's wings," Genrai said briskly.

He wasn't dismayed, Trei could see, relieved by the older boy's confidence. Genrai had had time to think about this, of course, and Trei saw at once that he was quite right, because that would work. Anybody could fly with one or two primaries missing. He said, "We'll need to donate some secondaries, too. I'll donate a Quei feather from each wing."

"Yes, good," said Genrai, nodding. "Thank you, Trei. So will I, of course." Everyone knelt down and reached for feathers and thread, except for Tokabii. And even he didn't wander away, but stayed ready to hand people things.

"But what I want to know," Rekei said, as though it was the continuation of some earlier argument, "is, what are we going to do next? Fly back up the Southern Chain and warn everybody? For what good it will do? Because that's all very well, but I think—"

"Yes, we know what you think," said Genrai, and said to Trei, "He thinks we should head straight north from here, right across the open sea, straight for Milendri. But look at this wing! I don't want Nescana trying to fly so far on this! And besides, we have to warn Master Anerii. And everybody else, of course."

Trei nodded. "You're both right. It's a long flight to Milendri from here, but not that long—we'd get there before dawn. That means whoever goes that way has to be good at navigating by the stars, because in the dark, anybody could fly right past even really big Islands like Tisei and Milendri and never know it. So that's me or Rekei, only one of us should go along the Southern Chain because flying at night, well, you know how easy it is to get off your flight path. I think it should be Rekei who goes with you, and me and Kojran who head for Milendri. Because we're the ones who landed on that ship."

"What did you learn?" Genrai asked. "Anything? Did they talk to you? Did they say what they wanted? Did they let you go, or did you have to escape?"

Trei thought of the Yngulin lord saying coldly, *We do not need your little king to yield his Islands to the Great King as a gift: we will take them all and do as we please with all we find here.* He muttered, "We didn't learn much, I guess. Just that they want to take the Islands, and we knew that anyway."

"We learned more than that," Kojran said quietly. His eyes were on the work of his hands, and he did not look up, but there was a note in his voice that drew all their attention. He said, "You didn't understand him, Trei. I didn't either, not everything. Except I did, some of it, that part when he made that speech to his men?"

Trei made an encouraging noise.

"What he said ... he said, *Feed the Islands to the eagle and make it strong to fight the lion.*" Kojran looked up at last, meeting Trei's eyes. "He said, *When the lion grows weak, the eagle tears the flesh from its bones.* He said it different ways, you know how you do in a speech, and he had this accent, but, Trei, I understood him after a while, and you know there's only one lion when a lord like that makes a speech like that. You know how Tolounn wants to take the Islands to use as a base to attack Cen Periven? Because I think—"

"Yes," said Trei, stunned. "Yngul wants to use the Islands as a forward base from which to attack *Tolounn.*"

There was a pause.

"They can't fight *Tolounn,*" Trei said at last. "Are they mad?"

"No," said Kojran. "They're the ones with *flying ships.*"

"Yes, and what kind of sorcery lets them do *that?*" said Tokabii. "And how come *we're* the only ones who don't have that kind of great, huge, immense magic? It isn't *fair!*"

Which was a babyish thing to say, except that Trei found himself inclined to agree with every word. He said fervently, "We *really* need to tell them in Canpra."

"We do," agreed Genrai. "So you're right, Trei. Are you up for that kind of flight tonight? Kojran, are you?"

Trei said firmly, "Of course," and Kojran echoed him.

"Then we'll divide as you suggested," said Genrai. "And the sooner we all get in the air, the better. How are we coming with these feathers? Tokabii, I've got some crackers in my pack—get them out and share them around, will you? Anybody else got something? How are we for clean water? There may be a pebble between here and Milendri with a pool, but then again there may not—anybody remember? Well, then, Tokabii, give my water skin to Trei and yours to Kojran. Shut up—every Island between here and Naransa's got water. Food, too. For half a Quei feather, I'd give them

all the food and let you wait—all right, then, that's better."
He turned back to Trei. "You're sure you know the way?"

"Yes," said Trei, who was at least fairly sure. He knew
they'd need to set a flight path some way west of north, but
he wasn't entirely certain how much. He said again, "Yes, I
know the way," and looked at Rekei. "It's seven points west
of north, isn't it?"

"Yes," said Rekei. ". . . I think so."

"Right," said Trei, pretending that Rekei had sounded
confident. "I can keep that flight path. North is easy. Your
job will be harder, actually—because you'll need to turn a
little more north of east all the time—"

"Teach your grandfather," Rekei said.

"We'll just get these few last feathers," Genrai said, his
firm tone shutting off the possibility of an argument before
one could start. "Then we're in the air and on our way, and
we won't be stopping for more than a moment here and
there, so I hope we're all ready for a long night! If an old man
like Master Anerii can do it, we can do it!"

"Oh, well! Glad we were loafing all day!" said Nescana.
"I've got some dried fruit in my pouch—everybody can have
a piece. Sugar limbers up your wings!"

Which was an axiom all novices firmly believed, and
lightened the tone besides. She'd done that deliberately, Trei
was sure, and grinned at her when she came to give him a
wide strip of sugared fruit. But she looked away, not meeting
his eyes, and only said in a far more sober tone, "Be careful!
And I think Milendri lies *eight* points west of north, not seven.
But I'm probably wrong."

12

When Araenè found Ceirfei, he was not alone.

Her disappointment surprised her. Araenè hadn't realized how much she wanted the reassurance of Ceirfei's company until she finally tracked him down, only to discover him in a crowd of servants and courtiers and ministers. She hung back out of the way, half behind a fall of lavender and orange flowers that tumbled down from a high window. She wouldn't have hesitated if Ceirfei had just been with his cousin Prince Imrei, because Imrei never minded anything. But Lord Minister Manasi Tierdana was definitely not someone she wanted to interrupt. Every time he saw her, something about the tilt of his eyebrow made Araenè know that he hadn't forgotten she was only Second City by birth and no fit friend for a prince. Especially a prince who was now heir to the throne.

Ceirfei looked ... well, he looked ... Araenè didn't like the way he looked. He was standing a little apart from everyone else. He was leaning against the windowsill, his face turned aside from the ongoing argument, gazing out over the city. Or, from his distant expression, out at the winds that he could see.

Kajuraihi liked windows no matter the wind or weather. Windows and rooftops. Araenè had learned that, among other things, over the past few months. Ordinary boys might escort a girl to the balcony of a public restaurant and buy her ices and cakes, but a kajurai wanted to go up on the rooftops of the city, find a place up high where only gulls and Quei flew.

Although a boy who was a prince as well as a kajurai would also make sure the rooftop was covered with soft cushions, and that sure-footed servants brought plenty of ices and cakes. Though, Araenè knew, the servants were also meant to be chaperones. Because Gods forbid a prince should be left alone for even a moment with a girl. Not that a girl who was also an apprentice mage couldn't make her own quiet way into the palace and out again, no matter the watchful eyes. But Ceirfei almost always followed the rules. He said it was all right for her, but he had to obey his mother, because he was a prince.

After this past summer, Araenè actually understood that. She wouldn't have, not so long ago. It was strange, remembering that once she would have thought a prince could just do as he pleased. That seemed ... so long ago.

Everything changed, and you could never go back. But Ceirfei was still a prince, and still had to follow the rules. That hadn't changed.

He didn't look happy. He didn't look sad, exactly, either. He was thinking about the sky, probably. The sky and the wind and spheres stuffed with dragon magic. Or about the Island of Kotipa, now shattered and gone. She wanted to cross the room, go to Ceirfei, take his hands in hers, say that she understood why he was afraid and that she was sorry and promise him that Master Tnegun would find a way to make everything better.

But she didn't move, because at that moment Lord Manasi exclaimed, his voice loud enough to carry easily to the doorway where Araenè stood, "May the Gods be merciful! The Tolounnese still own at least one of their accursed engines, do you recall it? At least one, more likely two! That we know of, and may the Gods preserve us if there are more!"

"Of course I recall it," Prince Imrei answered into the sudden hush created by Lord Manasi's outburst. His tone was perfectly reasonable. "That's why I think it would be best to reconsider Ambassador Ngewasi's offer. I know you don't like the man, Manasi, but he's been nothing but helpful in this crisis, you know."

"Helpful!" exclaimed Lord Manasi.

Prince Imrei was seated in a white stone chair with a white silk cushion, not a throne but the next thing to it. He sat up straight with his arms resting on the arms of the chair, like he was trying to look kingly, but Araenè thought he mostly looked worried—and she thought he was mostly worried because Lord Manasi was upset. If the Tolounnese still had working steam engines, that was *important*—but it was just like Prince Imrei to be more worried because Lord Manasi was shouting than because of whatever the lord minister was shouting *about*.

Lord Manasi said, not shouting but intense, "If we bring five thousand Yngulin mercenaries up onto Milendri, we'll be *paying them* to *conquer us!* And you think that would be *helpful?*"

Prince Imrei turned his head away slightly, wincing. "Now, Manasi, I do think that's a little harsh—"

"*A little harsh!*"

And at that moment, there was a quick but rising mutter of voices, and then the small crowd of servants and courtiers and ministers folded inward toward the walls and out of the way, and Trei came in. Araenè stared in astonishment.

Her cousin wasn't alone. Kojran was with him. Araenè looked in vain for the kajurai novice-master or any of the other novices, but saw only Wingmaster Taimenai himself. His presence instead of Master Anerii's seemed strange. And a little alarming. More so when she looked closely at Trei. He looked ... well, better than he had last time she'd seen him, but not a *lot* better. He was pale, and his face was drawn with tiredness, and he carried one arm tucked up next to his body as though it ached.

Kojran also seemed worn out and strained. In fact, he looked more tight-drawn and worried than even Trei. And Wingmaster Taimenai wouldn't have broken in so abruptly unless something was wrong. Everyone else knew that, too. A silence had fallen across the whole room. Even Lord Manasi ceased shouting at Prince Imrei.

"Wingmaster Taimenai," said Prince Imrei, rising to his feet with an alacrity that suggested he was glad of the interruption. "I see your novices are returned from the Southern Chain; that's good news! May we hope they have other good news to report?"

"One might have wished," the wingmaster said grimly, with a small, apologetic bow for Prince Imrei and Lord Manasi and a brief nod for Ceirfei. "I think you'll agree this is urgent news, if not good: not only have our novices brought word that all Dragon Islands in the Southern Chain are fallen, but they also report we have a small fleet of Yngulin warships out by Taraban. More than that: the Yngulin ships are able to pull themselves out of the water and into the air! They've landed men on Taraban, disembarked them straight onto the Island; we can assume we've lost Taraban, at least. And who knows how many others by now?"

"Flying ships," Lord Manasi said, his tone flat. "Ships that fly."

"Yes," snapped the wingmaster. "Armed to the waterline, and since they can fly, possibly below it as well! They're armed with some sort of new catapult that throws flights of bolts, wicked for kajuraihi to face in the air. No one can hit anything from the deck of a ship; we depend on that! But catapults that throw *flocks* of bolts all at once, that's something else again! It's a miracle of the Gods no one was killed."

"You haven't actually seen these ships—these flying ships—yourself, Master Taimenai?" inquired one of the ministers Araenè didn't know, raising a skeptical eyebrow.

Wingmaster Taimenai was not inclined to be patient. "Do you suggest anyone could mistake a cloudbank for a flying ship, Lord Safenasi? Or a school of flying fish for a flight of crossbow bolts? Or," he added, his voice taking on a warning edge, "do you mean to suggest *my novices* are *making it up?*"

"Enough," Lord Manasi said sharply. Wingmaster Taimenai checked whatever else he'd meant to say, and Lord Safenasi, who had begun what would undoubtedly have been a heated response, closed his mouth without a word.

"But you must admit it doesn't sound likely," Prince Imrei said reasonably. "Flying ships? Ships that fly? We've never heard of any such thing ..."

"Of course, if Yngul meant to attack us, they would hardly draw such a weapon to our notice," Ceirfei murmured. Somehow, although he did not speak loudly, everyone hushed to hear him. He looked straight at Trei, not at anyone else, not even at the wingmaster. "Trei?"

Trei took a visible breath, glanced at the wingmaster, and then said to Ceirfei and all of them, "It's true. It's all true. Yngulin ships, flying the carrion eagle, anchored out past Taraban. Where Fenaisa ought to be. Carrying lots of warriors—far more than crew. Shields and short swords, hundreds of men just from the one ship—"

Lord Manasi started to speak, but Ceirfei put up a hand and the lord minister stopped.

"They shot at you?" Ceirfei asked.

Trei nodded quickly. "Without even any warning! They hit Nescana. She was all right, but the bolts tore up her wing. She actually fell into the sea, but they got her out. Genrai and Rekei. But they needed time, so I—Kojran and I—" he hesitated. "Kojran and I went down to the ship. To make them not shoot anymore."

"Bravely done!" Prince Imrei said warmly. "Well done!"

"You actually spoke to the Yngulin captain?" Lord Manasi demanded.

"If you would permit my novices to answer—" Wingmaster Taimenai began.

Ceirfei cut them both off, his tone quietly decisive. "Please go on, Trei."

Trei cleared his throat. "I asked for his terms. The Yngulin lord's. Because I wanted him to stop long enough to give them, you know, not because I thought the Islands would take them! But he said they don't mean to offer terms, that they don't need our king to yield the Islands, that they will just take them and do whatever they want with them. And he said—" Trei glanced again at Kojran and then once more met Ceirfei's eyes. "To his own people, not to us, not even knowing Kojran could understand him, he said they would feed the Islands to their carrion eagle. He said the carrion eagle would tear the flesh from the bones of the lion. You know ... you know who the lion must be. So we thought ... that is, we think ..."

"It's clear enough!" said the wingmaster. "The carrion eagle, stripping the carcass of the lion? My novices showed great presence of mind to come straight back to Milendri. Straight across the open sea, at considerable risk to themselves, to bring us this news. Now that we have their news, I think we would surely be unwise to disregard it."

There was a little pause as everyone waited for Ceirfei to respond. Or really, Araenè reminded herself, Prince Imrei. Or *really* Lord Manasi.

Ceirfei said quietly, "Imrei? I think it is clear we have Tolounn on one side, but now Yngul on the other. And of the two, Yngul is likely the worse enemy."

"Um," said Araenè, edging forward a step. Everybody looked at her. She coughed and said nervously, "Um, the dragons? The sky dragons? They're, um. They're drawing away from us. From the Islands, I mean. So the Islands, I mean, Cassameirin seems to think, without Kanora's sphere to be a, a link between the sky and the earth? That maybe the dragons won't actually be able to stay close to the Islands. So I guess we might lose their magic? I mean, whatever's left, now that Kotipa's fallen."

Lord Manasi started to say something, but Ceirfei flicked a glance his way and he stopped. Ceirfei said quietly, "I believe any kajurai can confirm that our dragons have drawn away from us. Are still drawing away. The consequences of that are perhaps more difficult to estimate. So that, too, presents an unknown danger to us, now. Unknown, but most likely increasingly perilous." He paused, and then said again, "Imrei?"

Araenè felt sorry for Prince Imrei, who stared at his cousin and then at Lord Manasi, and then around at all the gathered ministers, and then at the wingmaster. He was so clearly overwhelmed. She didn't blame him, because anybody would feel overwhelmed, trapped between Tolounnese mages who could derive so much power from their steam engines and now this new and terrible Yngulin magic that could lift whole ships into the sky. And all this when the strength of the Islands had shattered and fallen into the sea and the dragons themselves fled! Poor Imrei! She *did* feel sorry for him. But she could also see perfectly plainly that he needed to do something, to do *anything*. Ceirfei wanted him to, too. He was leaning slightly forward, his eyes on his cousin's face, plainly willing him to speak, to act.

But Imrei didn't. He obviously couldn't. He looked a little like a fish, the way he opened and closed his mouth. Embarrassed for him, Araenè wanted to look away, but she couldn't. There was a terrible hush all through the room, everyone waiting. In just a moment, everyone would start to panic, and then rush out into the halls and spread the news of disaster, and then the whole *city* would panic –

Then Prince Imrei did something so unexpected and brave that it left her breathless. He stood up, held out a hand to his cousin, and said in a steady, clear voice, "Ceirfei. I don't know what to do. If you know what to do, please ..." he opened his hand in an unmistakable gesture of relinquishment. "Please do it."

There was another pause. This one stretched out, and out.

Then Ceirfei straightened his shoulders, turned to Wingmaster Taimenai, and said briskly, "Of course you have sent another team of your kajuraihi to attempt to destroy the remaining Tolounnese engines. Send your fastest kajuraihi after them, to recall them."

The wingmaster looked nonplused.

"And the team you have sent out to harass the approaching Tolounnese fleet—recall them as well," Ceirfei said, in the same brisk, cool tone.

"But—" began the wingmaster.

"Immediately. Your fastest kajuraihi. Please do that now."

After an infinitesimal hesitation, Wingmaster Taimenai bowed his head. "Yes, Prince Ceirfei." He turned on his heel and strode out.

Ceirfei turned to a hovering servant. "I will see Ambassador Ngewasi at once. In the formal throne room. And send for Lord Minister Horirei Taiben," he shouted after the man as he hurried out. "And Minister Saronasei Cenafansi! *And my mother!* I hope he heard me," he added in a mutter, as the servant was already out of sight.

"I'm sure he did," said Lord Manasi, his tone cool. "Or if not, I'm sure your lady mother will hear of your summons through other means."

Ceirfei turned and met the lord's gaze. He said, just a little stiffly, "I trust I will be able to count on your support, Lord Manasi."

"Of course you will," said Prince Imrei.

"Of course," said Lord Manasi, reluctantly, Araenè thought.

Ceirfei gave a little nod, accepting this, and turned to another servant. "Find Master Tnegun for me. And Master Kopapei. At once!"

That servant hurried out, too, not quite running, but nearly.

"Trei, come with me," Ceirfei said, quick and curt. "Everyone else, come along. Lord Safenasi, Lord Nacuanasei, if you please—" Frowning and distracted, he brought them all along with a gesture, toward the formal throne room. Araenè followed, since no one said she couldn't.

Araenè had never seen the formal throne room before. She surprised herself by falling in love with it at once. It was a plain but beautifully proportioned rectangular hall, with ranks of fluted columns rising straight and slim toward its gracefully vaulted ceiling. Everything was white marble, of course, because everything in First City was white stone and white plaster and white-glazed, all very glamorous but, Araenè thought, rather lacking in personality.

But the formal throne room had been rescued from the polished white sameness of First City, because despite all the white, white, white, the room was alive with color. The brilliant sunlight of late afternoon poured, rich as honey, through its wide windows, and vines cascaded beside every window, flowering red and orange and glorious purple. Quei, almost as large as mountain eagles, with their metallic-green wings and brilliant scarlet breasts and long trailing green tails, flew freely in and out of the windows.

"I like the throne," murmured Trei, beside her. She had edged over toward her cousin. Kojran, uncharacteristically quiet and subdued, stood on Trei's other side.

Araenè hadn't even noticed the throne itself in the midst of all the flowers and the flashing green and scarlet of the Quei, but now she followed Trei's gaze. Besides the flowers, the throne itself was the only ornament in the hall. It, too, was carved of marble. It was tall and slender, much taller than an ordinary chair, with a back that rose up and spread outward and curled backward right at the top. The longer one gazed at the carving, the more clearly you could make out the elegant neck of a dragon, the hint of a feathered wing. Then you would look again and not be quite sure if the carving really suggested a dragon after all. Only then you would blink and find that the tiny inlaid chips of opalescent shell suggested the glint of a nonhuman eye, the curve of a taloned foot.

Araenè decided that she, too, loved the throne. She was suddenly and fiercely glad that Ceirfei had sent for the Yngulin ambassador to be brought here and nowhere else; that the ambassador would be required to stand in this hall with the Quei flying overhead and that throne in front of him when Ceirfei asked him about those ships, and about what his country meant to do with them. She was sure it would be hard to lie with that half-glimpsed dragon gazing out at you from above Ceirfei's head, and Ceirfei staring at you with his crystalline kajurai eyes.

Ceirfei actually didn't take the throne, though. He stood to one side of it and turned to look at Imrei. For a moment the two princes stood facing each other in silence. Ceirfei said something, inaudible from where Araenè stood. Imrei answered. Ceirfei hesitated, then shook his head and said something else. Araenè wished she was close enough to hear, because this time when Imrei answered, she saw his words strike Ceirfei like a blow.

"He doesn't want it," Trei muttered, meaning Ceirfei, of course.

"He can't change his mind now!" said Kojran, sounding frightened.

Araenè gave a distracted nod, because of course they all knew that. "He knows he can't. He knows he can't let Imrei change his mind, either. Poor Ceirfei! But of course he had to do it. Look, you can see perfectly well how it is."

Everyone could, because Ceirfei finally stepped forward and sat down on the throne, and Prince Imrei moved away, putting himself back among the crowd of courtiers. Others were arriving all the time, courtiers and ministers, and Araenè was relieved to see Master Tnegun come in with Master Kopapei. And at last Ceirfei's mother, Calaspara Naterensei, entered the hall and moved to stand to the right of the throne, looking cool and regal in white and violet silk. Ceirfei got that cool poise from her, Araenè guessed. His sister had it too: Calassienè, her name was. She had come in with her mother and stood now to her mother's right hand, a grave young woman a few years older than Ceirfei. Lord Manasi, his mouth tight with displeasure, took his place on the other side, to Ceirfei's left.

And then at last Ambassador Ngewasi arrived.

Ambassador Ngewasi was the second full-blooded Yngulin man Araenè had ever seen. In some ways the ambassador did seem very like Master Tnegun. Araenè wanted to stare from one man to the other, comparing them, but of course that wouldn't be very dignified, since she would have to crane her neck around to look at her master.

Like Master Tnegun, Ambassador Ngewasi was a tall man, elegant rather than bull-powerful; and, of course, the ambassador's skin was also so dark a brown that it was nearly black. His eyes, an astonishingly light tawny color, were almost as striking as the eyes of a kajurai. He had high cheekbones and a broad nose; hooded, secretive eyes and an arrogant mouth. She thought his hooded gaze was not only secretive but sly, and the set of his mouth not only arrogant but cruel.

Though the impression of ferocity and furtiveness and cruelty might have arisen from Araenè's own distrust. She had not forgotten exactly who it was who had brought last summer's horrible plague to Milendri. Of course the Yngulin embassy had claimed that that was an accident, and the Yngulin ambassador—this very man—had officially apologized on behalf of his embassy and his country and his king. Even in her own furious grief, Araenè had not doubted that the plague was an accident. Now it was different. Now, probably everybody doubted those protestations and those apologies. But now, of course, it was too late.

Looking at Ambassador Ngewasi now, Araenè found it very easy to suspect him of anything. Unlike her master, the Yngulin ambassador made no concessions to the styles or expectations of the Floating Islands. Ambassador Ngewasi affected the most ostentatious Yngulin dress imaginable: sweeping wide trousers and a wide-sleeved shirt of cloth-of-gold, and over both a long garment like a very long vest, open in front, with a high, stiff collar. This outer garment was made of black silk and cloth-of-gold, patterned in sharply angled lines that interlocked in an aggressively abstract pattern that made Araenè think of thrown knives and slashing swords.

The ambassador wore three big teardrops of amber set in a heavy gold chain around his neck. Small round beads of amber ran down the front of his long outer vest. Trei leaned close to Araenè and muttered, "He's of royal blood. That's what the amber means. Three amber drops, see? He must be a cousin or nephew or bastard son of the Great King himself."

Araenè nodded, trying to look as though she'd known that all along. In a way, she had. To her, the ambassador looked like he was already considering taking Ceirfei's place on the Island throne. He made his bow to Ceirfei with perfect composure. He did not even glance at Imrei. Araenè was unwillingly impressed by his perceptiveness and his poise.

Once the ambassador had made his bow, Ceirfei set an elbow on the graceful, arching arm of the throne, leaned forward in grave, courteous inquiry, and said, "Ambassador Ngewasi." Ceirfei pronounced this difficult Yngulin name flawlessly, even carelessly, as though he'd said it a thousand times. Araenè wondered whether he had simply practiced carefully, or whether he was actually learning the principal language of the Yngulin Empire. Which was called Ylembai, she knew, and she couldn't even pronounce that, much less *Ngewasi.*

Ceirfei continued, "You have possibly heard of the arrival of your people's ships at the southernmost border of the Floating Islands. Perhaps you can enlighten us as to the reason for such outrageous behavior. No doubt these are pirates who, fearful of Yngulin justice, have sought safer waters and less perilous targets here in these waters, which do not belong to Yngul."

The ambassador smiled, a swift flash of white teeth in his dark face, an expression that somehow combined genuine humor with an arrogance that bordered on cruelty. "Of course you know these ships are not pirates." His voice was smooth; his tone grave. Nothing in his voice or manner showed even a hint of either the humor or the arrogance. "Indeed, Prince Ceirfei, I am astonished you might think those ships pirates. Did they show no banners? No colors? Did they give no evidence of their intentions? Have none of your people gone out to speak to them, and they sent no emissary to you?"

Clearly Ambassador Ngewasi knew everything. And clearly he was not making any attempt to conceal the fact. Araenè frowned, wondering how he'd found out what was happening. And so fast.

"Evidence of their intentions," murmured Ceirfei, raising his eyebrows and ignoring the rest of these questions. "Perhaps. Shooting at my kajuraihi ... shooting unprovoked at my novice kajuraihi. At children. One might take this as evidence of their intentions, perhaps."

"Alas!" said the ambassador, clearly amused. "In the sky, one kajurai looks much like any other. This was an accident, I feel certain. Why would my people wish to shoot at children? Of course they expected kajuraihi of rank and skill. No doubt they intended merely a warning and a demonstration, and found themselves dismayed when your inexperienced children failed to avoid the bolts from the scorpion—as such small shipboard catapults are known to my people. No doubt," he added delicately, "you, at least, are wise enough to take both the demonstration and the warning for what they were ... Prince Ceirfei." There was more than a hint of irony in the way the ambassador lingered on that title.

Ceirfei leaned back in his throne. He looked young, of course; he couldn't help that. But Araene was so proud of him, because he also looked just as regal and assured as the Yngulin ambassador. He said, "Perhaps the Islands should hire mercenaries, that we might be protected against the aggression of any who might seek to ... deliver to us a certain manner of demonstration, or a particular sort of warning."

Ambassador Ngewasi inclined his head, mockingly gracious. "A clever and long-sighted strategy."

"For you," Ceirfei said drily.

"Of course ... Prince Ceirfei."

"No doubt many clever and ambitious strategies are born in Tguw," said Ceirfei. "If the Great King for some reason harbored a desire to strike against Tolounn, for example, no doubt he might turn his thoughts toward the necessity of establishing a forward base. A place where his ships could re-supply, where his generals could linger to collect information and refine their plans. And develop new sources of information, no doubt, that might have previously been unavailable to Yngul. Someplace close to Tolounn, yet easy to defend against attack." Ceirfei paused. He didn't say anything about the Islands possibly sinking. Araenè wondered why not, since that would probably horrify the Yngulin ambassador: no Islands, no forward base for anybody. Maybe the mages hadn't actually told Ceirfei about that? She frowned, wondering if they hadn't and if she ought to. Not now, of course, but later ...

Ambassador Ngewasi listened to Ceirfei with grave attention. Then he turned his hands palm-upward, spreading his long fingers in a gesture not of denial, but perhaps of sympathy. "The Floating Islands are a tiny country posed between two great powers. You have done well, to be sure. You have no need to be ashamed. You have forced Tolounn to reveal its strength, and you have struck well against that strength, but your Floating Islands no longer have the means to hold aloof. Tolounn would take you, if we permitted it. But we shall not. You are too valuable to be permitted to fall into the possession of our ..." the ambassador paused to consider his words.

"Rival," murmured Ceirfei.

"Enemy," said the ambassador, and smiled. He looked straight into Ceirfei's eyes. "You have forced Tolounn to step back, and back again, and thus you have given my people their chance. The Little Emperor has missed his cast and come too late, and greatly will he regret it, for by that chance Tolounn has lost its chance to conquer all the world. We were not ready to act against Tolounn ... but you have gained us the time we required, and now we are prepared. We shall not be ungrateful. Yield your Islands into my hands, Prince Ceirfei."

"If I will not?" asked Ceirfei.

175

"Alas! You cannot prevent us from taking them, little prince." There was absolute assurance in that smooth voice. "But there is no need to feed the great fishes with the bodies of your people. You must merely look upon the ships of my people and know that you are lost, and thus yield your Islands into my hands."

Ceirfei leaned back in the throne. For a long moment, everyone waited. Lord Manasi glanced sidelong at Ceirfei. Ceirfei's mother gazed at the ambassador, lifting one eyebrow in cool scorn. Master Tnegun did not move, but Master Kopapei shifted his weight uncomfortably. Ceirfei's sister Calassienè stood as still as a marble statue. Imrei, standing to one side in the shadow of a column, took a breath as though he might speak, but then he didn't. Araenè knew they were all waiting for Ceirfei to think of something brilliant that would allow the Islands at one stroke to repulse both Tolounn and Yngul. She was waiting for that, too, even though she knew, as they all must, that it was impossible.

Ceirfei moved at last. He set his hands firmly on the arms of the throne and stood up. The throne stood on a low dais, and with these few inches of height added to his own, he was almost exactly as tall as Ambassador Ngewasi. He looked thoughtfully around the hall, and beckoned at last to one of men wearing the dragon badge of the palace guardsmen. "Tamasei. Ambassador Ngewasi will not need to return to the Yngulin embassy. He will prefer, for the moment, a room in the palace. Below ground, where it is cool and comfortable. One of the windowless interior chambers, perhaps, lest he should be discomforted by the view—foreigners so often dislike heights."

"Prince Ceirfei," the man acknowledged.

"All his staff, his servants ... everyone from the embassy may be offered such new quarters. Each by himself. We have a great deal of extra room in the palace, I believe, after last summer. So we will be able to offer our guests ample space. The palace staff extend such flawless service, I'm sure none of the Ambassador's people will want for anything, so they will not need to come and go."

"Yes, Prince Ceirfei!" agreed the man, starting to smile.

"Courteously, courteously," Ceirfei cautioned him. "Ambassador Ngewasi and his people are all my guests ... my personal guests, and I will attend to all their requests personally. No one else need do so. Is that clear?"

"Is this wise?" said the ambassador, no longer looking amused.

Ceirfei gave him a look of polite surprise. "Ambassador, we shall certainly discuss the matter at the earliest possible moment. Though I fear I shall be busy for some time. But I am quite confident you will find nothing to complain of in the service my people will offer." He glanced once more at the palace guardsman, who acknowledged with a nod, then turned to the ambassador and, with a bow, directed him firmly toward the door. No one moved or spoke while the ambassador reluctantly yielded to the guardsman's courteous, implacable direction.

"That was well done," Ceirfei's mother said after the ambassador had been escorted out. "That is an enemy. We can hardly mistake it now, when it is too late."

"It had better not be too late!" Lord Manasi growled. Various of the other ministers started to speak at once, but Lord Manasi, raising his voice, spoke forcefully over them all. "Bold words are very well, but if there's a way to *win*, I should like to know what it is—"

Ceirfei held up a hand, a sharp gesture that made the lord minister stop in mid-sentence. Ceirfei said, "Well, Master Tnegun, and perhaps you have advice to proffer, now that there's no way to win?"

"Of all men, *he's* got nothing to fear—" began Lord Manasi.

"Tnegun is an exile," Ceirfei said mildly. "From a small country called Mnewaaselika, which was conquered and no longer exists. The people of Mnewaaselika are scattered now. Their language is forbidden, their ways of worship forgotten.

Their children labor in the fields for Yngulin masters." He paused. There was dead silence. Master Tnegun stood quietly, his hands tucked in the sleeves of his black robe, his head slightly bowed.

Lord Manasi, difficult to quell, said at last, "Did he tell you that?"

"He told *me* that," Master Kopapei said drily. "Many years ago, when none of us had any reason to expect the matter to be of any but personal importance. You may, of course, doubt this tale—though the fate of Mnewaaselika is, I believe, a matter of common knowledge among those who concern themselves with the affairs of the Yngulin Empire. But it is hard for one mage to lie to another."

Lord Manasi started to answer Master Kopapei, but Ceirfei gave him a raised-eyebrow look, and the minister hesitated.

Into that small silence, Master Tnegun said in a soft, level voice, "The Great King has two palaces, you know. In Tguw."

Aracnè remembered after a second that Tguw was the capital city of Yngul, but she didn't know why it mattered how many palaces the Great King had there or anywhere.

"One is of stone and hard-baked clay ... not brick, for there is no need to fire clay in that country, where it never rains and men depend for water on the Great River. That is the most splendid palace in the world ... so men say, in Yngul. It has a thousand rooms, and a thousand slaves to care for the precious things therein. Trees of glass, with jewels for leaves; clockwork instruments of gold and pearl that play of themselves; tapestries woven of clouds and silk and the tears of women."

Lord Manasi started to speak, but Master Tnegun looked at him, his face perfectly still, and the other man stopped.

"The other palace stands near the first. Across the Great River it stands. A bridge rises between, so that the Great King of Yngul may walk freely from one palace to the other. But it does not descend to earth, that bridge. It ends in the air, supported by tall columns, so that one can stand there upon it and gaze down upon the other palace from above. It is of iron, that other palace. All of iron. Every wall and door, every couch and curtain. Cushions of iron on the chairs, carpets of iron on the floors, iron fountains in the courtyards, surrounded by iron trees with knives for leaves and flowers with razor-edged petals. The flowers do not rust, for the fountains are dry.

"There are no roofs atop that palace, and the walls are lattice through which the sun strikes. It is open to the unforgiving sky, there in that country where the sun blazes without surcease and rain never falls. At noon, when the sun stands at its height, one could bake bread within its walls. One could roast meat." The mage paused. This time, no one tried to interrupt. After a moment, Master Tnegun continued, "There the Great King sends the little kings of conquered countries. The little kings and their brothers, their wives, their children ... all those of their lineage and their blood. They cross the burning floor from the sparse shadow of one wall to that of another, those people, until at last they die of thirst and burning heat within the walls. The Great King's wives and courtiers wager on which will prove most stubborn, who will try hardest to find a way to climb a wall, escape the furnace of the palace ... no one escapes. There is no way out of that iron palace. They kill their own wives and children, those kings imprisoned there, and then they die. And that is the heart of Tguw," the mage concluded, speaking without emphasis. "That is the heart of Yngul. That is the heart of the Great King."

There was a long, fraught silence.

"That is Yngul Eshan," murmured Master Tnegun. "The Empire of Blood, the Empire of the Sun. Long ago the Eshanki subjugated all who might have stood against them, and they rule uncontested now. All the other peoples of Yngul are subjugated or destroyed." He lifted his head suddenly to meet Lord Manasi's eyes and finished softly, "I am a man of the Islands, but once I was of Mnewaaselika, and I tell you, it is better to die than to be conquered by the Great King of Yngul Eshan."

"In this day of peril," Ceirfei said quietly, "I think it is important that the Floating Islands—our tiny, fragmented country posed between two great powers—should be as little fragmented as possible."

"Imrei—" began Lord Manasi.

"No," said Prince Imrei, his tone brittle. "It has to be Ceirfei."

"He's too young! Gods! A boy! The Islands need an experienced man—a man used to governing—someone who knows how to rule, not a sky-mad youngster who's dreamed of nothing but the dragons and the heights of the sky from the time he was old enough to toddle—"

"Manasi! Have some sense!" snapped Ceirfei's mother. "The Islands won't unify behind you; you have far too many enemies—"

"I never thought *you* would be distracted by a mother's feeling for her son, Calaspara—"

Ceirfei said drily, "Lord Manasi, I'm certain you know better than to believe that my mother is ever distracted by anything."

Lord Manasi glared at him.

"You have done well during a difficult time," Ceirfei added, in a firm, polite tone. "We are all grateful for your dedicated service to my uncle and to the Islands."

Lord Manasi stared at Ceirfei. "You think you know what you're doing, boy?" he demanded at last. "Well?"

"When all options but one have been closed off for us, then the option that remains is the one we must take. It is then our task to be sure we drive that option to our will rather than allowing it to drive us where we will not go."

Lord Manasi didn't move for a long moment. Araenè imagined he was trying to decide what possible option Ceirfei saw. She knew she was. She couldn't think of anything at all they could do. But Ceirfei sounded so sure. He was looking at

Trei ... there was something between them, a moment of communication that left out everyone else.

Trei cleared his throat. "We have to surrender to Tolounn," he said.

The room hushed, stunned, and then exploded in a burst of whispers that rose rapidly toward shouts.

"Quiet!" snapped Ceirfei, and said into the shocked silence that resulted, "Trei Naseida is of course correct. When we stand between two enemies, sometimes the answer is to make one of them an ally—and we have no time to do that through some subtle diplomacy. So we will surrender to Tolounn. On terms, to be sure. We will have two terms. Neither will be negotiable." He paused, glancing at Lord Manasi. The minister glared back at him, but said nothing.

"First," said Ceirfei, "the Floating Islands must remain free to choose their own king. We will obey the Emperors and we will respect the law of the Empire, but within our own territory, we will continue to abide by our own laws, and we will in no case accept a foreign provincar set over us. Further, though the Empire may recruit among the young men of the Islands, there will be no forced conscription." He paused, looking at Trei, a little anxiously, Araenè thought. She knew why. She knew—of course everyone knew—that the Tolounnese armies always conscripted young men from conquered territories ... and she had never heard of a newly conquered province being permitted to live by its own laws or choose its own kings. That was why the Floating Islands had been willing to fight for its own independence.

Trei said earnestly, "The Floating Islands aren't some barbarian country. You were part of the Tolounnese Empire once. You're a civilized nation. If you pay taxes to the Empire ... if the armies of the Empire can come and go freely here ... if the artificers and mages of the Empire are allowed to study dragon magic and Island magecraft ... I suppose there's not much doubt that what Yngul *really* wants is to attack Tolounn. With their *flying ships* ... their mages must have learned how to harness some great power, at least as huge as the Tolounnese steam engines. If Yngul conquers us ..."

"Exactly," said Ceirfei.

"Well?" Lord Manasi demanded.

"Well, and so we see that the Little Emperor must agree. Our task is to persuade him of that necessity as quickly as possible." Ceirfei tapped the arm of the throne in an emphatic rhythm. "There is so little time in which to cause all the pieces to fall where they must. Tolounnese ships rush upon us; now Yngulin ships sail through the sky to join them. Time, time ... everything rushes forward! And we are caught in the wind of time as a leaf is caught in the currents of the wind, carried with it whether we will or no."

"Yes," said Trei, sounding suddenly sure of himself. "The Little Emperor will feel that, too. He'll agree, Ceirfei. He really will."

"The word of a boy!" said Lord Manasi.

"A boy who last year was Tolounnese," Ceirfei snapped, raising his voice for the first time. "And who has *met* the Little Emperor, as you and I have not! We are caught in the winds of time, I say, and we cannot compel them to stillness only because we wish it so. Well?" He stared at the lord minister.

Lord Manasi flinched just a little from that hard stare. He said at last, gruffly, "Very well. Very well! Perhaps you're right." He glared defiantly around at the ripple of response that went through the assembly and added, biting off each word, "We should have the coronation at once, and never mind the rest of the mourning period."

"Tomorrow," Ceirfei said quietly. "That will put it on Gods' Day. We could assuredly use the favor of the Gods." He glanced around, then added, "I am certain that you all have much to do. Lord Nacuanasei, if you will prepare an estimate of the time you think it might take for those Yngulin ships to reach Milendri, supposing they take the time to conquer each Island as they come to it. Minister Horirei, your best estimate of the time until the *Tolounnese* fleet reaches

Milendri, if you please. Minister Saronasei, if you would kindly prepare a speech to be read aloud to the people, explaining these events. Perhaps you can have that for me by fifth bell? Thank you. Lord Manasi, Imrei, Master Kopapei, if you would stay. And you, Mother, if you please."

Rising to his feet, Ceirfei made a little pushing motion with one hand, dismissing everyone else. He didn't glance at Araenè at all. She tried hard not to feel hurt—of course he was too busy for her now. Of course he was. She had meant to speak to him. Because he was a kajurai. Not for any other reason. But she'd already told him the important part, about the dragons going away, out of reach. He didn't need here. It was stupid for her to want to run to him, cling to his hands, ask if he was all right when she knew he wasn't, embarrass him in front of all those lords and ministers and his mother and everyone. She bit her lip.

When Master Tnegun's hand fell on her shoulder, though she flinched in surprise, she was almost grateful.

"I think you had better tell me everything you've been doing, lately," her master said quietly.

Araenè glanced once more toward Ceirfei, rubbed her face, and nodded. "*Oh*, yes," she said fervently. "Cassameirin said—" but then confusion tangled her tongue and she stopped. Master Tnegun raised one eyebrow. "Cassameirin, indeed? I see I must indeed have fallen far behind events, young Araenè."

13

Master Anerii and the rest of the novices arrived late in the morning the very next day, having pushed themselves hard. "Too dangerous for us to stay on Naransa," Genrai told Trei, throwing himself down in a chair by the table and waving away the mug of juice Kojran offered him. All of them were like that: too tired to even pick up a mug or a plate. Tokabii, youngest and smallest, looked paler and more exhausted than any of the others, even Nescana. He hadn't even stopped at the table, but had dragged right on past them and to his bed, with muttered threats against anyone who woke him up for anything less than the Island falling.

"Too dangerous for anyone to stay on any Island with that Gods-cursed Yngulin fleet moving up along the Southern Chain, and Gods know which way they'll turn from there," Genrai told Trei. "Everyone's either crowding onto fishing boats and running for Milendri, or else heading inland to hide." He ran a bony hand through sweaty hair and sighed. "Long flight, but better a high wind and an open sky than hiding in the inland farms and hoping the Yngulin soldiers take their time coming to look for you!" He hauled himself reluctantly to his feet. "Coronation this afternoon, I hear. I'm not missing it, but I've got to lie down for a little while. Nescana?"

"I'm not missing it, either," the girl said emphatically. "I get the baths first!" She jumped up with astonishing energy and darted for the bathing room before any of the boys could protest.

The coronation was supposed to take place a whole senneri after the death of the old king, which seemed strange

184

to Trei. In Tolounn, a new Emperor was always crowned the very same day an old one died, lest too many powerful men immediately tear the Empire apart trying to fill the vacant throne.

"They say the mourning period lets everyone get used to the new king," Rekei explained. They'd all gathered once more, clean and somewhat rested and starving—especially Tokabii, who ate half a dozen sweet pastries all by himself. Rekei, who also liked pastries but who hadn't been fast enough to get more than four, gave the younger boy a superior look and pretended that he had never wanted the others. He said to the rest of them, "My father said it's really to give the ministries time to sort out who's going to stand closest to the throne. The ministries have a lot of power, you know—more than the court lords. Sometimes more than the king himself."

"Ah," said Trei. That wasn't so different after all, perhaps.

"Anyway, the body of the old king is laid to rest under the earth and above the sea—there's a crypt below First City just for the kings and their royal relatives."

Trei hadn't known that. Neither had the Third City novices. "They're not buried in one of the cemeteries?" Nescana asked.

"Those are for ordinary people. They're not permanent enough for a king. I mean, you know cemeteries are put back into pasture after thirty years, don't you? And then into crops three years after that."

Nescana and the others nodded, but Trei, who had not known this, thought the custom was revolting.

"You've got *space* for permanent cemeteries, in Tolounn," Rekei pointed out. "They say on Cen Periven, they wrap up the bodies, take them out in special boats, and drop them into the sea. *That's* revolting."

"They burn them, in Yngul," said Kojran.

"They would," said Rekei, offensively.

185

After which Genrai had to physically restrain Kojran to prevent a fight. "Stop it!" he snapped, shaking the younger boy once, hard, to get his attention. "*You* aren't Yngulin! Would you want *your* body burned? And if you didn't want people saying things, why'd you bring up burning at all? And you!" He glared at Rekei. "If you want to start fights, you can start one with me! Or else sit down and be polite!"

Rekei, no match for the older and much more experienced Third City boy, sullenly picked up his chair, knocked over in the brief scuffle, and sat back down. He stretched out his legs, pointedly at ease, and pretended not to notice Kojran's glare.

Nescana, the only one of them who hadn't jumped up, lifted a mug of juice in a salute to her brother and said, her eyes bright, "I think we could use a lot more girl novices."

Despite everything, Trei grinned. "You should suggest that to Master Anerii."

"Sometimes I think the kajuraihi should stop auditioning boys entirely," snapped Genrai, picking up his own chair, which had also been knocked over, with a sharp, angry movement. "At least boys so young they haven't yet got the sense the Gods gave so many marmosets! Sit down, Tokabii!"

"I wasn't doing—"

"And shut your mouth! Gods weeping, we should dismiss any brats too young and stupid to keep their thoughts behind their teeth! I'll suggest *that* to Master Anerii! Or can we talk about the coronation? Well?"

Rekei shrugged, pretending indifference but actually, Trei thought, a little alarmed by Genrai's anger. He said, "All right! I didn't mean anything! It's not complicated, anyway. After the body of the old king is laid down in the crypt, the new king is asked to take up the crown of the Floating Islands. That's the public part. They do it right in front of the palace, in Quei Square. Anybody can come watch. People will have started gathering yesterday and waited all night to get a place in the square—"

"Mother did that for the last coronation," Nescana said unexpectedly. "Remember? We still have the coin she caught."

Genrai nodded. "It's brought us luck—I think it must have." He went on as his sister nodded in agreement, "I suppose the kajuraihi have a balcony, since the wingmaster said we're to attend, though I guess we won't be likely to catch a coin from up there."

"Coin?" Trei asked.

"They throw them out to the crowd," explained Nescana. "Mostly small ones, but some that are worth a lot. It's like a memory of the old king because they won't have started minting the new coins yet."

"That's after the coronation's over," Rekei said authoritatively. "They throw out the coins right at the end. Before that, they pass out oranges and melons and those little funeral pastries—"

Trei knew about that. In the Floating Islands, neighbors and friends always brought oranges and round cakes and tiny pastries glittering with pastel sugar to bereaved families— everything round and everything sweet, to remind the grieving both that life hadn't ended and could still be sweet. In his memory, the sugar tasted like bitter ash.

"And then the new king comes out on this low balcony where everyone can see him, and a priest brings out the crown on a cushion made of Quei feathers and asks the heir to accept it. And he does, of course—except this time, Gods, I don't even know who's supposed to be the heir anymore! I mean ... "

"It's not *really* like Ceirfei's deposing Imrei, if Imrei wasn't ever actually crowned," Nescana pointed out. "I mean ... I guess?" The girl sat down on the edge of the table, linking her hands around one drawn-up knee. Her tall gawkiness folded down into a surprisingly graceful pose. Trei tried not to look as though he was looking at her.

"Poor Ceirfei," Genrai said softly.

"Yes, poor Ceirfei, having to be king!" said Tokabii.

"Fool," snapped Kojran. "Would *you* give up the sky to be king?"

Genrai slapped his hand down on the table, and the younger boys immediately pretended they hadn't been arguing after all.

"Anyway," said Rekei after a moment, "after the new king's crowned, there's more cakes, and loaves of bread with salt to show that life still has savor and to bring good fortune, and *then* they throw out the coins with the old king's face on them, baskets of them, not just for memory but to show that the new king's reign will be prosperous. And then it's done and everyone goes home, and things get back to normal."

"Normal!" Trei muttered under his breath.

"Maybe not this time," Rekei conceded. "Gods! Who ever heard of such things!"

"Sixth bell, is it?" said Genrai, sternly shutting off this line of speculation. "We had better be ready by Fifth at least. And we'll need to change our black mourning pins for ordinary ones. Remember that, all of you. Nescana, put out the pins, would you? And you boys, you remember, if any one of you embarrasses us in front of everyone, whatever Master Anerii gives you, I'll give you double." His glance moved from Tokabii to Kojran to Rekei, so ominous that not even Rekei dared say a word.

"Novice Trei," Wingmaster Taimenai said sternly from the doorway.

Trei stiffened.

The wingmaster's manner was normally austere, but now, seeing Trei's expression, he added at once, "Nothing has happened to your cousin, Trei. I beg your pardon. I did not mean to frighten you."

If Araenè was all right ... Trei steadied himself. "Then it's Ceirfei?"

The wingmaster, looking closely at Trei, gave a little nod of apology. "He wishes to see you. I will escort you to the palace now." He cast a glance around at the other novices, then, and added, "And I shall wish to see you all, immediately upon my return. Have you recalled you must switch your black pins for colored ones? Good. Very well, then. Trei?"

He led the way out of the novitiate, down a short hall, up a long flight of stairs, and out of the kajuraihi precincts entirely. He walked with a firm quick stride, not often glancing either to the left or to the right as he took one street and then another.

Trei hurried to keep up. The royal palace was actually not very far from the kajuraihi towers, but the streets between were impressive. The slender white towers caught the late afternoon light and glowed gold. Here and there, high on the towers, Trei could just make out the suggestion of a slender carved neck or long feathered wing. None of the carving was really *meant* to be obvious, he decided. You were supposed to look and look and still not be sure whether there was really a carved dragon coiling around one tower or climbing another.

Aerial walkways linked one tower with the next. The walkways looked frighteningly narrow and the floating steps just plain frightening, but Islanders strode along them as though they were perfectly normal.

Quei flew between the towers and beneath the walkways, the sunlight flashing emerald fire off their wings and long trailing tails. They flew quite fearlessly right onto peoples' kitchen balconies to steal bread set out to cool, but no one would dream of chasing them away.

Though there were white towers and white-paved streets everywhere, Canpra's First City didn't lack color. Violet flowers cascading beside every window, with deep purple fruits half-hidden amid the flowers. Coppery-red marmosets no bigger than kittens, and larger fluffy brown ones with long white mustaches, clambered amid the vines, seeking the fruits. Marmosets might not bring luck like Quei, but even so, children put out pieces of sugared bread for them in the evening to tempt them to stay close by.

There were other flowers in wide planters along the streets: red and gold and orange and deep purple. Graceful fine-leaved flameberry trees lined the street that led to the palace. The trees had lost their red powderpuff flowers, but they were still beautiful because now they bore the clusters of the brilliant crimson and orange fruit that gave them their name.

The royal palace, set a little apart from the rest of the First City by wide avenue-gardens, included eleven tall white towers and three small slender ones. Slender balconies wove around each tower. And more of the cleverly carved dragons, too, twisted around some of the towers: here the hint of a fine-boned head and slender quilled neck seemed to overlook the rooftops of lower towers; there the ripple of a long feathered tail coiled underneath a balcony, half hidden by purple flowers tumbling from planters.

"It's a showpiece," Wingmaster Taimenai allowed, following Trei's upward stare. "They say Komaonn the Younger built it to impress ambassadors from Cen Periven and emissaries from Yngul. That's when they started carving the dragons all through First City—to remind foreigners that the Islands are defended by more than human strength." A slight irony entered the wingmaster's voice on this last.

Trei nodded, trying not to look awed by the size and scope and sheer arrogance of the Islander royal palace. He had flown above it, of course. That wasn't the same. It was a *lot* more impressive from ground-level.

And more impressive still once they were inside. They entered through great tall doors of some dark wood, intricately carved. Servants stood there to open the doors for them as they approached. Trei supposed that was what those men did all the time: stand there waiting for people to walk toward the doors so they could haul them open and then shut them again. It seemed ridiculous, until he thought of soldiers standing in an honor guard at the door of a provincar's palace in Tolounn. Then the custom seemed at once both more familiar and more understandable.

The tower's antechamber was vast, but somehow not overpowering. It was floored with white marble, but the marble was overlaid with rugs in bright colors, and there were tapestries hanging everywhere, and screens over the windows, so the interior of the tower was protected from the crashing heat and light of the southern afternoon. A quiet-footed servant came to guide them. He clearly recognized Wingmaster Taimenai and did not ask them where they wanted to go or whom they wanted to see.

The servant showed them to a much more modest room in which to wait, one with plain wooden furnishings and unadorned plaster walls. The tables were sturdy rather than pretty, and the chairs comfortable rather than elegant. The room's one window, open to the late breeze coming in off the sea, looked out over a sweep of white- and red-tiled roofs falling away below and then the endless blue sea beyond.

The wingmaster glanced around, looked at Trei, and drew breath to speak, but before he could say anything, the door opened again and Prince Ceirfei came in.

The prince was not alone. Lord Manasi was with him, which was not, Trei supposed, actually a surprise. Ceirfei waved all of them toward the various chairs and couches scattered through the room, though he himself moved, with a kajurai's reflex, toward one of the room's broad windows. He said briefly to Wingmaster Taimenai, "I believe we are resolved at least on the one issue."

"Ah," said the wingmaster. "Good." He glanced at Lord Manasi.

Lord Manasi shrugged. "Imrei is a good man. Pleasant. Cheerful. He likes to do nice things for people. He is also uncritical, accepting, unsuspicious, inclined to believe the best of people, and susceptible to flattery. If he were willing to be continually guided by experienced men, all this might be acceptable."

"My cousin is willing to be momentarily guided by anyone," said Ceirfei, his tone carefully neutral. "Including Ambassador Ngewasi. Thus we are, as I say, resolved on that issue. The coronation will take place this afternoon. It mustn't be delayed; the emissaries I send to Tolounn must be able to tell the Little Emperor that they speak for the king of the Floating Islands. I shall value Lord Manasi's support, both for that moment and later."

Lord Manasi frowned. But he said, his tone grim but resolute, "Well, it seems you will have it. If I may have your leave? There is still a great deal to do." He stalked out, barely waiting for Ceirfei's nod.

Ceirfei said crisply to Wingmaster Taimenai, "And there is a great deal for *you* to do, as well. Whom will you send? I think it must be Master Anerii, and I think Trei must go."

The wingmaster inclined his head. "I will send Master Anerii and all his novices."

"All of them?" Ceirfei asked sharply.

"Prince Ceirfei, I have no one else to send. All my kajuraihi ... *all* of them ... must be used to delay the Yngulin ships. Nothing else is more important, and that will be far too hazardous a duty for children. And if we fail, if everything we plan comes to nothing and those Yngulin ships reach Milendri before the Tolounnese, then my novices will be well out of it. If they must, if nothing else is possible, they can even appeal directly to the Tolounnese Emperor for protection, trusting that he will behave like a civilized man. Particularly because, if that should come to pass, Trei will be with them."

The wingmaster stopped just barely short of saying something that Trei was only now coming to understand: that if the worse really did come to the worst, then the kajurai novices might be among the few, the very few Islanders who escaped the terrible fate that would befall the Islands. If Yngul conquered the Islands, then they might be the *only* kajuraihi left in all the world—the *only ones*. They would have to figure out what to do, what would be *best* to do, what they should give away to the Tolounnese artificers and what they should keep secret.

He wanted to protest. He didn't want to be sent away, protected like a child—only it was too obvious that being sent to Tolounn was actually not at all the same as being protected. He said nothing.

"You are perfectly correct," Ceirfei said without hesitation. "If you will go arrange all these matters, Wingmaster. If you find your proper duty must be stretched to encompass things that normally fall without it, then by all means use my name."

The wingmaster gave Ceirfei a short nod that was almost a bow, touched Trei lightly on the shoulder, and went out. His boots rang down the hall until they were muffled by distance.

Trei didn't know what to say.

Ceirfei sighed and stretched. He gave Trei an ironic look. "Wingmaster Taimenai is important, but Lord Manasi is invaluable. Fortunately, Manasi does know the true stakes we're all facing, even if he sometimes gets distracted by trivial concerns, such as the desire to maintain his own power. But Yngul's flying ships have caught his attention."

Trei made a sound of acknowledgement.

"Now, you." Ceirfei tapped his fingers on the windowsill. Then he turned, leaning his palms on the windowsill, gazing out over the city. From somewhere out of sight came the distant echoes of human voices and, nearer at hand, the sharp twitters of marmosets darting through the flowering vines tumbling from someone's balcony. Far away and high above, a Quei cried in its distinctive high, wild voice.

Ceirfei tilted his head back, gazing up and up into the brilliant sky. Trei came and leaned on the wide sill beside him, following his gaze. The wind smelled of brine and hot tiles and flowers. The sun, invisible behind the rooftops of the palace, streaked the sky with carmine and saffron; it turned the tiled rooftops of lower towers to glowing jewels and struck gold out of the sea. Ceirfei stared out into the light with kajurai eyes that saw every layer and shift of the living winds that sang around and over and below the Floating Islands. If there were any dragons soaring in the crystalline heights, they were too far away for even kajurai eyes to find.

Ceirfei said without turning, "As you heard, I am sending Master Anerii as my official emissary. But I am

193

sending *you* with a separate command, Trei. You must make the Little Emperor of Tolounn agree to protect the Islands. Whatever bargain you must make, whatever terms you must offer or accept. You know what we want."

"Yes," said Trei, although that hadn't been a question.

"I have told Anerii that these terms are not subject to compromise. Everyone knows I told him that. I am telling *you* that, in utter necessity, everything is subject to compromise." He handed Trei a slim envelope. "Put this somewhere safe. In extremity ... in extremity, Trei, and I will not be surprised if you come to that ... everything is negotiable. And if you must negotiate *everything*, then the decision to give the Islands into the hands of the Little Emperor and the Great Emperor is yours. Not Anerii's. This makes that clear."

Trei took the envelope automatically, but then stood holding it and staring at Ceirfei. "You can't give this to me!"

"I have to. You are the only one who understands both Tolounn and the Floating Islands."

Trei looked at the envelope for a long moment. It was plain, stiff, slim, unmarked, sealed with violet wax. He put it away, carefully, in an inner pocket of his vest. Then he looked at Ceirfei. "I won't ... I won't let you down."

"Oh, I don't fear *that*."

Trei gave Ceirfei a long look. "You don't need to be afraid of being king," he said at last. "You'll be a good king. Everybody knows that. Even Lord Manasi. And maybe you could abdicate later. After, well," he spread his hands. "After all this with Tolounn is over."

Ceirfei only shook his head. "It will never be over. If both Tolounn and Yngul decided to leave us in peace forever, there would be something else."

Trei knew that was true. He said, "I'm sorry. I know you hate it. But I think the Floating Islands might do well to have a king who is also kajurai. Everyone says how the sky dragons have drawn farther from the Islands. How there are fewer kajuraihi than there used to be—fewer applicants for the auditions, fewer chosen. And now the dragon Islands have fallen, and who knows what that will do? So I think maybe a kajurai *should* be king. And you know ... once you *are* king, there won't be anybody to forbid you the sky. Although," he admitted, trying to be honest, "you'll probably be pretty busy, I guess."

Ceirfei was smiling a little, now. "Not so busy I ground myself, no." Then the smile slipped. "I did give my word, last summer, to pay any cost demanded of me. As a prince of the Floating Islands and before the Gods. I don't think ... I quite considered what that cost might be."

"You're thinking of the promise you gave the dragon last summer. You think you promised that you would be king? Even then, that long ago?"

"I promised I would serve the sky as well as the earth. I swore I would not protest to pay the cost. In my own name and in the name of the king my uncle, I gave my word." The corner of his mouth turned up in reluctant, wry humor. "One is hardly confident that a dragon may grasp such fine distinctions. I claimed the authority to bargain. How fitting that the Gods repay me now for my temerity by requiring me to take that authority in truth." He paused, then added in a slightly dry tone, "As you will inform the Little Emperor of Tolounn."

"I won't let him take the sovereignty of the Islands."

Ceirfei's mouth crooked. "Yes, well ... it would certainly be better if you avoided that. Fortunately, the Yngulin ships will help persuade him." He opened a hand. "You're our best chance. I believe that. The Gods love irony! Thus they brought you from Tolounn, and thus I send you back now in our need. May the wind bear you lightly on its back."

It was a dismissal. Trei nodded. He'd wanted to find his cousin—he'd wanted to ask her about Kotipa, about what the mages might be doing to make things right with the Islands. But he could see he wasn't going to have time. "If you see Araenè—"

Ceirfei looked strangely reserved at that, but he nodded. "Of course."

Trei nodded. He couldn't think of anything else—and he was sure Master Anerii would already have all their wings laid out and be waiting impatiently for Trei. Another long flight! Though at least he'd had a full night's rest, which was more than most of them. He thought briefly about the other kajuraihi, the men who would fly out tomorrow to find and harass the Yngulin ships. Then he flinched from that thought.

But returning to Tolounn ... finding the Little Emperor ... that thought was almost as alarming. Not because he was afraid of what the Little Emperor might do, but because he knew he would hear Ceirfei's voice behind him the whole time saying *You're our best chance.*

That was a terrifying thought.

14

It was all so familiar. Not only the rush of wind through his wings, not only the sparkling translucent blue of the sea below and the high milky blue of the sky above, but the nervous sense of urgency that grew as the dark bulk of the Tolounnese coast heaved up from the horizon before them. This flight was so different, yet the cost of failure hadn't changed at all.

Or it had, of course it had, but only for the worse.

How strange it was to make this flight again, this time not secretly or in enmity, but openly and hoping for alliance. How strange to fly straight inland and across the town, over the misshapen harbor edged by the remnants of broken wharfs and warehouses. Half-built structures stood everywhere, along roads newly laid out where the close-fitted stones of the old had been tumbled out of order. There had been a lot of rebuilding in Teraica since last summer. Trei was glad to see the town even looked prosperous.

At first Trei had been surprised that the Little Emperor was in Teraica, but this was as central a town as any, for a man who meant to oversee the subjugation of the Floating Islands. The Little Emperor was Dharoann enna Gaourr, a fiercely aggressive man who dreamed of adding far-flung lands to the Empire of Tolounn and so looked across the sea toward the Floating Islands and thence to distant, wealthy Cen Periven. The people of Tolounn loved war. And well they might, since they always expected to win. Trei hadn't seen anything wrong with that, either, until he had become an Islander and found out what it was like to expect to lose.

Only now, it seemed, the people of Yngul Eshan also expected to win. No one had seriously expected the two Empires, with so great an ocean between them, to ever

197

actually come to battle. Certainly Trei hadn't. But if Yngul and Tolounn intended to fight over the Floating Islands, he knew which he wanted to win.

The Little Emperor was staying, of course, in the provincar's palace, high up in the hills. The palace had been built back into the white chalk of the cliffs, with ornate colonnades and galleries along the front. A lot of those fancy colonnades had been cracked and broken, the last time Trei had glimpsed them. Artisans and artificers had repaired the plaster and replaced the stonework, and now the palace looked like it had never been touched by violence.

Master Anerii led the novices straight down into the central courtyard of the palace. A plain-spoken man to be ambassador, with an escort of children. This alone, Trei knew, showed how desperate the Islands had become.

Soldiers met them when they came down: a serious young teruann with his whole company, all of the soldiers standing stiffly in two rows with their spears grounded by their right feet and their eyes fixed straight ahead. Someone— the Little Emperor, Trei devoutly hoped—had realized or decided their open approach meant they wanted to negotiate. This certainly looked like the kind of reception an ambassador would meet. That was a huge relief. Of course the Little Emperor might have been expecting a diplomatic approach, after the Islanders had failed to destroy all his engines.

The teruann came forward and watched with interest while they helped one another with their wings and then laid the wings out carefully on the stones, since they didn't have proper frameworks. The kajurai were never happy to let ordinary men even look at their wings, far less touch them, and Master Anerii gave the teruann a hard look. "Careful with these! No one should lay a hand to them."

"No one shall, sir," the teruann answered gravely, and with a gesture detailed five of his men to see to it. The soldiers took stations around the courtyard without a word being spoken. While Master Anerii held ambassador's status,

Trei knew, no one would touch those wings—and if he lost that status, then they would probably have other things to worry about. But that would be the Emperor's decision. All the decisions would be his. And Ceirfei trusted *Trei* to make sure all those decisions would be the right ones. It was overwhelming, when Trei let himself think of it. He tried not to.

"You are kajurai Master Anerii Pencara, of course," said the teruann. "And ..." his gaze swept across the young faces of the novices. His expression did not change, but the corners of his eyes crinkled. He said, "And colleagues," without the hint of a smile, and went on at once, "I am Teruann Amarr enna Pohanann, by the Emperor's grace his voice to you. The Emperor has been made aware of your coming. He will see you at his earliest convenience. If you will accompany me, I will show you where you may wait."

The room to which the teruann conducted them was really an entire apartment, with heavy doors and thick bars on the windows, but generous appointments. Once they were alone, Master Anerii turned in a slow circle, taking all this in. He said to Trei, "We're prisoners, then? Is this honorable treatment?"

"Of course," said Trei, genuinely surprised. "I mean, we're at war, aren't we?"

"But it'll be all right," Kojran said anxiously. "Right, Trei?" He was anxious all the time now, inclined to gaze away to the south when he thought no one was looking.

"Hush!" Master Anerii said gruffly. He dropped a hand to rest briefly on Kojran's shoulder, then gave him a little shake. "You'll be all right, boy—one way or the other. Right, Trei?"

"Yes, sir," Trei said, surprised. He was confident of *that*. It was the larger problem he wasn't confident about.

A soldier rapped on the door and then opened it, and the teruann came in with a small bow and a deferential gesture toward the door. There was a broad curving stair and a short hall, and then a large, plain room with an expensive floor of inlaid wood and wide, silk-draped windows, and soldiers standing in ranks along its walls. And here, already seated and waiting for them, the focus and center of the room, was Dharoann enna Gaourr.

The Little Emperor of Tolounn was young for his position, not even as old as Master Anerii, but filled with the confidence of a man who knows himself to be standing at the apex of his career and has every intention of remaining there for years to come. The power that radiated out from him was exactly as Trei remembered. He wore the circlet of gold oak leaves, but he did not need any ornament to proclaim that he was the Emperor. His forceful gaze swept across them all, lingering on Trei for an instant before passing on to Master Anerii.

"Kajurai Master Anerii," he said. He did not smile.

Master Anerii bowed. "Emperor of Tolounn."

"And Trei enna Shiberren," said the Emperor, his dark gaze returning to Trei. "So we do meet again after all, not altogether to my astonishment. And is it with amicability between us? No—" He held up a hand when Master Anerii would have spoken. "Let the boy answer."

Trei bowed deeply. Then he straightened and said, as clearly and formally as he could, "I hope we will have amicability between us, O Emperor. The King of the Floating Islands asks for amicability and for peace, and for that is willing to yield himself and his Islands to your hand and the hand of the Great Emperor."

There was a little stir through the room, a surprise that was not quite invisible passing through the ranks of the soldiers.

The Little Emperor's eyebrows rose fractionally. He had not expected this, Trei could see. Turning to the novice-master, he said gravely, "Perhaps you had better tell me after all why you have come, Master Anerii."

Master Anerii nodded and answered in his customary straightforward manner, "O Emperor, we find ourselves beset from an unexpected direction: Yngul has found a way to power some great spell by which they are able to lift their ships into the sky." He stopped, letting the Little Emperor understand what he had said.

Dharoann enna Gaourr's eyebrows rose again, a little higher this time. He sat back in his chair, crooking a finger across his mouth.

"We are able to hinder them, but we can't stop them," Master Anerii said bluntly. "We looked only north and east when we should have been looking equally to the south. They'll conquer us, and we can't stop them. But the Floating Islands do not comprise Yngulin ambition. The Great King of Yngul intends—"

"I believe I can guess his intention."

Trei bowed, a swift gesture to draw attention. Though he frowned, the Emperor gave it with the lift of a finger. "We don't have to guess," Trei said. "Because we were there on the Yngulin ship. Kojran and I. We were *right there*. The ship's master wore gold and a cloak of eagle feathers." He saw the Emperor's eyes narrow at that detail, and went on more confidently, "He said Yngul would feed the Floating Islands to the carrion eagle so the eagle would be strong enough to tear the flesh from the bones of the lion. He *said* that. I was there, *we* were there."

He nodded toward Kojran, who nodded anxiously and put in, "We *heard* him say that, O Emperor, when he wasn't even speaking to us—he was speaking to his own people. So we brought that word to—to our king. And he sent us to you."

Dharoann enna Gaourr tapped his fingers thoughtfully upon the arm of his chair. He said to Master Anerii, "*You* met this Yngulin lord? *You* heard the man say this?"

"No," said Master Anerii, "But we know beyond doubt that the ships can sail off the sea and into the sky and we don't doubt the rest of it. Thus my king sent me here. With my novices, if you should wish to question them further."

The Little Emperor accepted this with a little nod. "Your king. Imrei Naterensei?"

"Ceirfei Feneirè, his cousin. The oldest living son of Calaspara Naterensei, who was sister to Terinai Naterensei."

The Emperor nodded again, frowning. "My condolences on your loss. Terinai Naterensei was a generous and wise lord for your Islands. One regrets his passing and prays that his successor may be worthy." He gazed at Master Anerii for some time in silence, then regarded Trei for an uncomfortable moment, and then turned finally to Kojran. "You are part-blooded Yngulin? You, too, witnessed these miraculous Yngulin ships mount into the sky? You are the one who heard this Yngulin lord speak of the carrion eagle and the lion?"

"Yes," whispered Kojran. Then he straightened his shoulders and repeated in a stronger voice, "Yes, O Emperor. I was there, and I heard those words. I don't—I don't claim fluency. But I heard the lord say those words."

The Little Emperor tapped his fingers on the arm of his chair again. No one said a word, not daring to interrupt his thoughts. At last, the Emperor said to Kojran, "From the beginning, young kajurai. Tell me everything. Discount nothing."

Kojran blinked, lifted his chin, and obeyed, stumbling slightly when he tried to describe that first sight of the Yngulin ships, the Yngulin warriors crowding on the high cliffs above the sea. The silver streamers that had poured down beneath the ship, and the catapult that shot flocks of bolts. "And after Nescana fell, Trei went down to the ship, to make them not shoot any more while Genrai tried to help her get back into the air. I went down after Trei—to help—I thought I might be able to help because ... " he hesitated.

"Yes," said the Emperor, seeming to understand everything Kojran had not said. "You did not find your part-blood useful?"

Kojran shook his head silently.

"No," said the Emperor, not unsympathetically. "One would not expect so." He gestured for Kojran to continue.

"Well ... that's all, I guess. The ... the Yngulin lord, he said he did not need to offer terms because his people would take what they wanted. And then he made this long speech to his men, about the eagle and the lion. And Trei and I thought we had better get away. And we did. So that's everything."

The Emperor inclined his head. He said to Trei, "And now I will hear it from *your* tongue, Trei enna Shiberren. Trei Naseida. Tell me everything. Leave out nothing."

Trei nodded. He said cautiously, glancing at Master Anerii, "I should start farther back. Before we flew out to look over the Southern Chain. *Why* we flew out ..."

"Trei—" Master Anerii said. He couldn't say out loud, *There are some things better left unsaid, boy! Show this foreign emperor all our weaknesses and maybe he'll wave us away and turn his attention to fortifying his own coast!*

Trei imagined he could hear all that anyway. *He* couldn't say out loud, *It's important to tell the truth, and if we leave out important things, that's the same as lying.*

"Trei Naseida?" said the Little Emperor, with the patience of a hunting lion.

Trei met his eyes. He could see the Emperor had missed nothing of that exchange. In a way that was a relief, because it made the decision for him. He said, "We flew down along the Southern Chain, from Naransa along the chain of Islands, you know, to Taraban—"

"Yes. I am familiar with the Islands of the Southern Chain."

Trei nodded. "We were looking for Fenaisa. Because dragons used to dwell there, it's one of those Islands, the little ones with the high mountains where the dragons fly—"

"Yes," said the Emperor again.

"Because those little Islands fell," Trei said simply. "When we—when we flew down upon your engines, the ones on the bank of the river. The magic we used then, it did things we didn't expect. We think maybe that's why our little Islands fell. The Dragon Islands."

"Ah," said the Emperor. He gave Master Anerii a thoughtful look.

Trei said hurriedly, "So we flew down along the Southern Chain to see what else might have fallen. And Fenaisa was gone, but those Yngulin ships were there. And then it was as Kojran said ..."

"Tell me the tale again."

Trei nodded. He tried to put everything in: the astonishment and terror of finding the Yngulin ships before them, the scorpion catapult, the arrogance of the Yngulin shipmaster, the long flight back to Milendri, just him and Kojran alone in the immensity of the sky.

"Yes," said the Emperor, once Trei had finished the whole tale. He rose, with a small gesture that kept everyone else in their places, and paced away down the length of the hall. He came back then, dropped again into his chair and looked carefully into Trei's face. "I think ..." he said at last. "I think you are a truthful boy, and I think you have told me the truth."

Trei felt himself flush. "I have!"

The Emperor's mouth crooked. "And I have said I thought so." Then he said to Master Anerii, "So your king believes, in this extremity, as his dragons draw away from his Islands and he finds himself beset from all sides, that it would be better for him to give his Islands into my hands than risk Yngul taking them."

Master Anerii, who had waited patiently through all this, inclined his head. "He offers terms, O Emperor, and hopes you will be generous—lest you find yourself battling Yngul's flying ships among Islands held by your enemies. And later, of course, along your own coasts. And inland. Ships that can mount the winds—"

"Enough," said the Emperor drily. "I understand Ceirfei Feneirè's position. What terms does he offer me?"

"The Islands to retain their sovereignty, though subject to Tolounnese law in dealings with the mainland of Tolounn. And to retain the perpetual right to be ruled by our own king

204

and no appointed provincar. And the levy of the Tolounnese armies to pass by the young men of the Islands."

Dharoann enna Gaourr smiled, a thin smile but not without humor. "This is a surrender?"

"A surrender on terms, O Emperor. You want a base from which you can reach out to conquer Cen Periven? We'll give you that, and willingly, as Cen Periven has declared it has no interest in the fate of the Floating Islands. You'll wish to own a base from which to guard against unexpected threats from the south. We'll give you that as well. Your fleet is very nearly in place at this very moment. When your ships come to the Islands, they will find themselves welcomed. All know of the discipline and honor of Tolounnese soldiers; we would welcome your men into our cities and support them against all our common enemies—"

"Indeed," said the Emperor.

"We Islanders think you are a honest man, never mind your ambition," Master Anerii answered without flinching. "We think you will deal honestly and truthfully with us. It's a loyal province you want, O Emperor. Are our terms so high a price to pay to gain one?"

"I will not recognize the sovereignty of the Floating Island, nor admit your right to choose your own king."

"O Emperor, I may negotiate, but not on those points."

Dharoann enna Gaourr opened a hand in a gesture of regret. "You do not negotiate from a position of strength. You are surrendering the Islands to my hand and to Tolounn. Do so, then."

"You don't speak from a position of strength either," Master Anerii said forcefully. "If you will prevent Yngul gaining the *only* strong position, you will deal generously with the Islands!"

For a long moment, no one in the room moved or spoke. Dharoann enna Gaourr and Master Anerii stared at one another, neither one looking likely to yield.

Trei felt the letter Ceirfei had given him weigh in his vest as though Ceirfei had carved his words in stone rather than writing them on fine paper and folding them into a waxed envelope. He shifted his weight, feeling the envelope press against his side. He blurted, "Time rushes forward, O Emperor, and we are caught in the winds of time as leaves are caught in the gathering storm—" he faltered as all eyes turned toward him and finished lamely, "We are *all* caught in this storm together. I hoped we would find amicability between us."

The Emperor tapped the arm of his chair twice, a sharp, decisive gesture rather than a nervous one. He said to Master Anerii, "Which will come to Milendri and Canpra and your king first: my word, or my ships, or the Yngulin fleet?"

Master Anerii hesitated. He said at last, "Your ships, O Emperor, or so we hope. Every kajuraihi we own will be harassing the Yngulin ships, or working to bring a fair wind around behind yours. So your ships should come there first."

"*Before* my word," said the Emperor.

"Inevitably so," admitted Master Anerii. He met the Emperor's shrewd gaze. "So, as the boy says, we hope for amicability between us. When we—when we met, last time, you reminded me that the Islands once belonged to Tolounn. So they did. They can again, if you are generous—and we will do all we can to support you against your true enemy—"

"Well, not *all*," said the Emperor, drily. "No, I understand you, Master Anerii. I understand you very well. I admire your new young king, who casts all he owns on this one throw of the dice: to welcome my ships *before* he has any hope of hearing my decision. When last we met, I believe I told you that Tolounn's generosity is not without limit. But that I was inclined to be generous."

Master Anerii inclined his head.

"I am so inclined," declared the Emperor. "To allow the conscription levy to pass by the Islands … yours is a peaceable people. So that is a small thing. Relatively. I grant it—though I may require a levy of artisans. A small levy." He paused, then said sternly, "I will not, however, recognize the sovereignty of the Floating Islands—no, Master Anerii, not for any argument! I hardly like to think what the Great Emperor would say to me if I permitted any province such a privilege! But I will give you *this* undertaking, which is generous enough: Your Islands may live according to your own laws save where those laws directly conflict with the greater laws of Tolounn. Where there is such a conflict, you may appeal to me, and I will decide whether your law may stand."

"O Emperor—"

Dharoann enna Gaourr lifted a hand and continued, "If my decisions displease you, you may appeal to the Great Emperor, which is of course the privilege of any Tolounnese province, though I do not necessarily recommend you exercise it. Further, I am willing to permit your Islands to select your own king in whatever way seems good to you, and I will either agree to your selection or bid you choose again, until I find your choice acceptable. But your king will not have greater authority than my provincar, whom I will appoint." He paused, considering, and then gave a decisive little nod. "It is not what you ask, or not all that you ask, but it is what I will give. Accept my offer, Master Kajurai, which, I assure you, *is* generous."

Master Anerii looked torn. "O Emperor, I may not negotiate—"

"I *will* not."

Trei coughed nervously. They could argue more ... but he was sure, almost sure, the Little Emperor wouldn't yield anything more. And passing time really did press hard against all their backs. He took the letter out and broke the wax seal with his thumbnail, then held it out to the novice-master. "You can negotiate, sir."

Master Anerii took the slip of paper without a word and glanced down it. There were only a few words. Trei couldn't read them from this angle, but he knew what they said. He knew they said, *Everything is negotiable.* And *Trei will decide.*

Master Anerii looked at Trei.

Trei said, "Dharoann enna Gaourr will deal honestly and truthfully with us, and offer no terms he will not keep. And," he added, "those *are* generous terms, sir. Truly. We should accept them."

Master Anerii scowled. He said reluctantly, "I know they are, boy. But—"

Trei said nothing.

Master Anerii glanced down at the paper he still held and snorted disgustedly. He refolded it with quick, curt gestures, slid it back into its stiff waxed envelope, and gave it back to Trei. "You'd better not be wrong, boy."

"I'm not wrong," Trei promised him, and prayed to the Gods this was true.

Master Anerii said to the Little Emperor, "The Floating Islands accept your terms, trusting you will hold to them and to your word, and that you will deal honorably and gently with the Islands and all their people."

"I will," Dharoann enna Gaourr said gravely.

Trei felt the whole world should tremble to mark that moment. Instead, the Little Emperor only went on, "And so it is done, and well done, we shall all hope. All this shall be set down plainly, exactly as we agreed, but we won't take time for that now, Master Anerii. *Now* we must assuredly work quickly to ensure that Tolounn's newest province does not fall to Yngul! I will consult with my mages and my artificers regarding this great magic Yngul has accomplished, and with my generals regarding our practical response. Briefly, I assure you." He glanced around the room and beckoned to the young teruann. "I will ask you to accept my hospitality while you wait ... I do have one last question, however, Master Anerii. I understand why you brought Trei enna Shiberren with you. But *only* children, in your retinue?"

Master Anerii said bluntly, "By now, a handful of the kajuraihi of the Islands are flying above your ships, to speed them on their way. Novices haven't the strength or skill for that. All the rest are flying against the Yngulin ships. Few are expected to survive. That's even less a task for children."

Trei had known this, of course. They had all known it. But it was something else to hear the novice-master say it like that, so flatly, as though all those men were already dead, their blood running out into the sea. Beside him, he heard Rekei draw in a breath, and he bit his own lip to stop himself making a sound.

"Yes," said the Emperor. "I thought that might be so. Go with my teruann, Master Anerii, you and your retinue of students. I will very likely summon you for consultation, so hold yourself in readiness; but I will give you a little time to rest if I can."

"You are gracious, O Emperor," Master Anerii said gruffly, and bowed. They all bowed, and the Little Emperor nodded and turned away, and there was suddenly a general and confusing movement as everyone went one way or another with very little ceremony.

The young teruann came over with a troubled expression. "Flying ships?" he said, and shook his head with sincere indignation. "Yngul is becoming far too powerful!"

"Of course we agree! Naturally Tolounn is the only Empire that should discover such power," Master Anerii said drily.

After a moment, the young officer laughed. "Indeed, sir—well, how should I disagree? But you've done well, coming to Tolounn and to the enna Gaourr! If the carrion eagle strikes at you, you may well fly to shelter by the lion! If Yngul has grown so ambitious, we shall have a war indeed!" He looked as though the prospect pleased him. Trei understood that, and at the same time had become enough an Islander that his own understanding troubled him. He remembered his Uncle Safei, Araenè's father, saying sternly, *Tolounn's only art is the art of war,* and how at the time he had not really understood what he meant.

The teruann led them not to the prison-apartment where they had waited earlier, but to a different apartment in a different part of the palace. There were no bars on the widows of this apartment, and only one guard on the door, a polite young soldier who assured them earnestly that he was at their service. Master Anerii immediately sent him, with Rekei and Genrai, to collect the wings from the courtyard.

"This hospitality doesn't surprise me, under the circumstances," Master Anerii said to Trei. "*You* surprised me, however."

"Ceirfei couldn't give anything like that to you openly," Trei said. He had worked this out during the long flight to Tolounn. "He had to give you the instructions he did give you. But anybody could see you—we—the Islands—needed to be able to give. Sometimes you have to let everything be negotiable."

The novice-master grunted and flung himself down on one of the apartment's scattered couches. "And now?" he demanded. "As you're the one who understands the Tolounnese, boy, you tell me." His tone was not as rough as his words, and he ended almost plaintively, "What will he do now?"

15

What Dharoann enna Gaourr did was cast his entourage, his soldiers, the palace staff, and the whole of Teraica into violent turmoil by declaring that he himself must clearly sail for the Floating Islands. Immediately.

Trei wondered whether all really important decisions were made that way, in the moment, on the wing, with the storm flinging you in wildly unexpected directions. So the Islanders decided to use a magical sphere they didn't understand against Tolounnese steam engines they couldn't otherwise hope to destroy, and so Ceirfei decided he had to be king, and so Dharoann enna Gaourr decided he needed to personally take possession of the Islands.

"I'm not going to claim a new province for Tolounn and then lose it to Yngul before the end of a single senneri," the Little Emperor declared. "This isn't the battle into which I meant to send my ships and my soldiers; shall I abandon them now that the shape of the war has changed completely? And become a hundred times more important? I hardly think so."

"He's good at war," Trei reminded Master Anerii, when the novice-master seemed inclined to blame him for this unexpected result of their negotiations. "You can't be surprised he wants to oversee this one himself!" But they were all surprised.

The Little Emperor would sail immediately, which meant in the morning—a very close approximation of *immediately* for an emperor. His ship, narrow-prowed and triple-decked and with tall purple sails that reached for the sky, was the finest and fastest in all the Tolounnese fleets, and Dharoann enna Gaourr was obviously pleased as a boy to have an excuse to let her race the wind. He would take few soldiers—"It's not numbers alone that will carry the day; what we need is speed and decisive action," he said, refusing every objection. But this didn't stop him from issuing orders for a lot more ships to follow him.

Though all the novices were to sail with the Emperor, Master Anerii was not to return to the Islands at all. "Not while I have many mages and artificers ready to my hand, but only one experienced kajurai," declared the Emperor. "My people will keep you so busy you will have little time to pine for your Islands, Master Anerii! And I will undertake to keep your novices safe. They will sail under *my* protection."

The novice-master had grunted in resignation, and told Genrai he was in charge of the other novices, and pinned the younger ones with a look so stern that even Tokabii was meek and quiet for the whole morning.

It was not Trei's first sea-voyage, but it was his first on a tall warship, with three ranks of oars ready to flash out when the morning breeze died. Though the novices might have called a breeze, Trei didn't suggest it. He liked seeing all the oars. The oarsmen were good, much better than on any other ship he'd ever been on. Even as the day wore on and the wind slackened almost to nothing, the ship hardly slowed— she might actually be moving faster than before. He wondered how long the oarsmen could keep that pace. Probably a long time. These would be picked men, on the Little Emperor's own ship.

The novices stayed up on the highest deck, out of the way, as the narrow warship raced across the sea, dipping and swooping as she met the waves. It wasn't like flying, but it wasn't entirely unlike, either.

It gave Trei a strange feeling to look up and see the Tolounnese lion black on the purple sails. He had been Tolounnese, once. And then Islander. He couldn't decide what he was now, if the Floating Islands were supposed to be a province of Tolounn. He didn't know what he felt, standing on the deck of this tall ship, which cut through the white-tipped waves almost as fast as a kajurai could fly, knowing that it carried the Little Emperor of Tolounn toward his newest province.

"The Little Emperor of the Floating Islands," said Nescana, coming up beside him. "It sounds strange."

Trei nodded.

"I wonder whether the dragons have come back down to the Islands? Now that Kotipa's gone, maybe they'll never come down from the heights ever again. Or maybe now that the Islands are just part of Tolounn, they might not like that, either."

Trei looked at her in surprise. "Why should they care?"

"I don't know. But what if they do? No one knows anything about the dragons, really."

Trei had to nod at that. It was true.

"And we don't know nearly as much about magic as we thought, either, or else how would the Tolounnese mages have come up with that way of using their steam engines?" Nescana tucked a strand of hair back behind her ear and added, "Or the Yngulin mages find a way to drag their ships right out of the sea and into the sky?"

"I know," said Trei. He wanted to say something comforting, only he couldn't think of anything, and anyway, Nescana didn't really look like she wanted comforting. But it seemed stupid to stand here in silence. He stared up at the infinitely layered sky, hoping for inspiration. If there were any dragons riding the high winds, he couldn't see them.

"Is it true you can see the winds?" asked the Little Emperor, unexpected, from behind them.

Nescana flinched and blushed. Trei hoped he didn't look so startled. He answered, hearing the awkwardness in his own voice, "Yes, O Emperor. All the different layers of winds, and the heaviness of the air, and how cool or warm it is."

The Emperor glanced from one of them to the other. He didn't comment about Nescana being a girl. He asked instead, "Do you find it distracting? To see so much?"

Trei thought about how to put it. He said finally, "You learn to see it all and past it all at the same time. It's very beautiful."

"It's good to see the beauty in the world," Dharoann enna Gaourr said, his tone a little wistful. He stepped past Trei to lean on the high railing. The morning breeze had died; the air this close to the surface of the sea was hushed and still. Below them, the three ranks of oars dipped and swung and rose again, flashing like the wings of gulls. "I think we generally learn to see past it and forget to look at it. Perhaps kajurai eyes—" he paused, gazing out across the sea. Then he said, in a different tone, "What do your kajurai eyes see out there? No, out away there, to the south and west."

Just then, a high-pitched voice cried out from far above, from the top of the highest mast, where a boy clung to the rigging. Trei could not make out what the boy shouted, but beside him the Emperor had gone very still. Beginning to be afraid, Trei stared again out across the sea.

"Oh!" Nescana exclaimed, gripping the railing. "*Oh! Ships!*"

As soon as she said so, Trei saw them too. Four of them. They ran long and low across the sea, sharp bronze prows glinting in the sun. Trei knew the jagged shape that slashed across the widespread sails: it was the black eagle.

"We'll heel away to the north," murmured the Emperor, not really to Trei, but only thinking out loud. "They've got the wind of us, but little good that will do them this time of day. And nothing can outrun my little *Tivoannè.*" He stroked the railing, as he might have touched the head of his favorite dog.

Trei nodded, sure he was right.

But the Little Emperor was wrong.

The winds strengthened, and strengthened again, favoring the Yngulin ships. That shouldn't have been true, but Yngulin mages somehow called up a furious hot wind out of the south, a storm that had nothing to do with the sea, a dry hurricane that tasted of sun-drenched sand and hot iron and that forced the ordinary sea breeze out of its way. No effort the novices made could turn that wind.

Still, they *should* be all right despite the efforts of the Yngulin mages. Those winds might not favor *Tivoannè*, but the ship ran so lightly before the hot foreign storm that didn't seem to matter. Most of her canvas had been taken in lest her masts should be torn down by the rage of the wind, but the three ranks of gleaming oars flashing in beautiful, disciplined order despite the torn and ragged waves. Dharoann enna Gaourr stood on his ship's highest deck, beside his shipmaster, one powerful hand closed on the railing, his face turned toward the sea. He was laughing in pride and delight at *Tivoannè's* speed and beauty, and Trei saw how he loved her and how his love for the ship put heart and pride into the sailors. Nescana stared at Tolounn's Little Emperor, looking almost awestruck. Trei didn't blame her. He thought, *This is how he leads men; they can't help but follow him when he's like that.* Then he thought, *Ceirfei will be like this someday. He's like that now.*

Then he thought that could be a problem. He hadn't thought of that before—that Ceirfei and Dharoann enna Gaourr might be too much alike to do well together.

He put that sudden worry away for later. With those ships out there, there were lots of other things to worry about.

The *Tivoannè* skimmed the waves as a gull skims the air, running before the burning winds of the Yngulin hurricane faster than any Yngulin ship could match. Anybody could see she would run far out to the north and then choose what direction she pleased, and no Yngulin ship would be able to touch her. So it was all right. It was better than all right: it was a great pleasure to watch the slower Yngulin ships fall behind despite their own hot wind. Trei found his gaze caught again by the Emperor, and found himself laughing as well.

Then the boy in the rigging cried out again, and they saw the other Yngulin ships.

It was immediately obvious that they could not possibly outrun these new ships. They had already crossed *Tivoannè's* new course, and the rushing Yngulin hurricane gave the Tolounnese ship far too little chance to maneuver.

"Eight ships," said Genrai, speaking loudly because of the wind. "Eight! Did they *know* we were coming?"

"They probably meant to stop any Tolounnese ships," Trei said. "They might not have planned to show what they can do, but they'll know this ship is special." They could hardly mistake the purple sails.

"Wings!" said Rekei, meaning they needed to get their wings and get into the air. "There's no use us going down with this ship!"

"They're not going to ram the *Tivoannè*," Kojran said, almost too quietly to hear. "They know it's an Emperor's ship. They won't ram—they'll want to throw him down at the feet of their Great King, and then send him to die in the iron palace in Tguw."

"Well, but he's not really *our* Emperor," said Rekei, but he sounded uneasy about it. "Not *really*—"

"He is," said Trei, tightly. "He'd better be. Do you think Ceirfei was just pretending?"

"Well, he's not going to be for long, then! And we won't have to figure out how to tell Ceirfei about it, if we don't get our wings!"

"Trei, he's right—" Genrai began.

"Rekei and Kojran can get the wings ready," Trei said, but he was looking at Genrai. He said, "One thing you can be sure of on a ship, there's plenty of rope. And that big chair in the Emperor's cabin, that's sturdy enough—though maybe something lighter would be better—"

"Great generous Gods, you've lost your mind!" said Rekei.

Trei felt like he might explode into a hurricane wind himself, he was suddenly so furious. Not even with Rekei, just with everything, but with Rekei too. "Get the wings!" he shouted, and then said to Genrai, not quite shouting, but still furious, "Get the chair! Or one that's not so heavy, but if it breaks—"

"Yes," said Genrai, looked strained, and gave Rekei a shove to get him moving. He delayed, though, to give Trei a speaking look.

"I know!" said Trei. "But what else can we do?"

But the Little Emperor, when Trei made him understand what they wanted to do, refused absolutely.

"Leave the *Tivoannè*!" he said. "For the carrion eagle to pick her bones? Of course you must all fly," he added more kindly. "I said I would protect you; I'm ashamed that I cannot. You can win free? You will be able to fly through this storm?"

"Of course!" said Trei. "But you—"

"It's true my *Tivoannè* may not win free, but I think we may yet contrive, Trei. I will set the *Tivoannè* against any ship in the world for agility in a battle."

He wouldn't let Trei speak again of flight, not even as the Yngulin ships drew closer. The hot desert wind roared without ceasing around the *Tivoannè*, so that the beautiful ship could not turn but had to run before the hurricane, while all the time the Yngulin ships before them rode a gentler swell. They were close enough now that Trei imagined he could see the shapes of the scorpion catapults amidships, that would let those ships stand away from the Tivoannè and throw slivers of steel across her decks. And those ships might have real catapults, too, that would throw fifty-pound stones to shatter her sides.

"You can't get away, and you can't fight, not so many!" Nescana said desperately, setting a hand on the Emperor's arm. That wasn't allowed—ordinary people weren't permitted to touch the Emperor—but he laid his hand kindly over hers and began a soothing response.

Then the decouan who led the personal guard that accompanied the Little Emperor cut across his words. The decouan, Sebionn, was an experienced man with a lined face and, even in this crisis, a bored expression in his pale eyes. He said, "Good thought, wouldn't work. Likely him and that chair together weigh more than the lot of you together, even with those wings thrown in on the scale."

To Trei, the decouan's skeptical tone said, *Persuade me.* He said quickly, "It's a recognized way to carry somebody! The weight matters less than you'd think—the wings hardly weigh anything, once we're in the air, and we ourselves don't weigh what you'd imagine—"

"And your burden? That weigh less than we'd imagine?" said the decouan, but the look he gave Genrai was assessing. "You look a strong young man."

The Emperor said sharply, "Sebionn, if I may trouble you to turn your attention to matters of more immediately importance? Allow me to suggest we consider instead methods by which we may get the *Tivoannè* and her entire complement past those ships in front of us. If we ram the closest and take the next with our catapults, we can get clear out away from the other two, and they'll not catch us then, whatever Gods-cursed storm—"

"Won't work," said the shipmaster, stepping up to join them, clinging to the railing against the pitching deck. "We'll ram the closest, sure enough, but those next two will rake us as we go by, make no mistake about it. Or if they don't, we'll have to dodge about to keep them off us, and then those behind us will run up our stern." He looked at the chair, which Genrai had brought up onto the deck; and the four long ropes that had each been fashioned into a rough harness. "Not that *I'd* ride in that. But I'd have to be blind not to see that the only man on this ship likely to live out the next bell or two would be a man with the nerve to sit down in that chair and get himself off this deck."

The Emperor began to refuse, his expression hard.

Trei said quickly, "Decouan Sebionn, if you want your Emperor to live through the next bell or two, you'll *put* him in that chair. And *tie* him in—it'll be hard flying in rough weather till we get out of this Yngulin storm!" He was shaking, he found; a fine tremor that he hoped wasn't visible.

He said furiously to the Emperor, "You're *our* Emperor now! Do you *know* what Ceirfei would say if we let you throw your life away?"

The Little Emperor stared at him, nonplused.

"I know what the Great Emperor would say to *me*, if *I* let you throw your life away," declared the decouan. "Though, not having wings, I suppose I wouldn't live to hear it, so that's some comfort. But not enough. So you will sit in that chair, Dharoann enna Gaourr, or my men and I will put you in it, just as the boy says." And he picked up a coil of light rope and stared at his Emperor, waiting.

Dharoann enna Gaourr gazed back at the decouan for a long moment while the hot wind roared around them, the black grit it carried scouring the decks and their skin alike. It had grown dark, not with clouds but with the rushing wind itself. Rekei and Kojran, already wearing their wings and harnessed to the chair, hunched down against the deck to stop themselves being carried up and away into the air. Nescana and Tokabii, the least suited to bearing a weight, spread their wings and let the winds take them, getting out of the way.

Genrai moved quietly, checking the knots in their makeshift harness. Two of the decouan's men held the two remaining sets of wings ready. They might not know how to handle the wings, but they had the sense to keep the feathers off the deck.

"Sit down in that chair," said the decouan in a flat voice, still staring at his Emperor. "Boy, get your wings on! Sit *down*, O Emperor! You, young man, tell me the best way to tie a man to keep him from falling."

Trei hurried to show the soldiers how to help him with the rope harness and his wings. Genrai had found a flatter kind of canvas strap to use for the actual harness—that was good. It was still far from the padded harness a kajurai would ordinarily have used. And so far as he knew, no kajuraihi would have dreamed of carrying a man so far. A mile or two, that was one thing, but forty miles or more? That was probably about how far they must be from the nearest waystation.

He turned as Genrai came up beside him. Dharoann enna Gaourr was in the chair, secured with ropes across his chest and hips and thighs. Trei didn't think the decouan had had to *actually* force the Emperor into the chair, but the Little Emperor's expression was so thunderous that he wasn't sure. But he dared not worry about the Emperor's temper, not now. He said quickly to Genrai, "Ahead or back? Ceirfei would want us to go on—don't you think?" The darkness and roaring made it hard to think. But if the Emperor had thought he'd needed to go to the Islands, probably he was right, and they'd come out so far already, ahead was no worse than back. He said, with hardly a pause, "We'll go on!"

"That's you and Rekei," Genrai said grimly. "Both of you work the math, and, Gods weeping! Your sums had better agree. How are your shoulders, Trei?"

"Fine," said Trei, hoping this was true. "I'm ready—everybody ready?" He looked from one to another of the other three. "We'll spread our wings and just let the wind take us up, don't worry about direction, we need to get up and clear! Right, Genrai?"

"Right!" Genrai agreed. Everyone nodded. No one hesitated or argued, not even Rekei. "Be ready to stroke all together!" Genrai added. "The ropes should be long enough we won't foul each other's wings, but we'll all need to get right out away from one another, understand? Once we start to stroke, we'll count off! And be ready for the weight!"

Trei nodded with the others, though none of them had ever tried to carry a burden before, so they couldn't really know what to expect. He prayed the weight of the man they carried would lighten in the air, as their own weight and that of their wings lightened.

Genrai shouted, "On the count of three! One—two—*three!*"

Trei snapped his wings open, and so did the others, and the driving hurricane picked them up and hurled them effortlessly into the sky.

The rope around Trei's torso instantly jerked tight, so forcefully he would have cried out except he had no breath. He had expected weight, but it wasn't like weight; he had no sense of carrying a burden; instead, it was like a violent sideways pull that crushed his ribs. He fought it instinctively, beating hard, and found that this was the right thing to do, which was lucky, because in those first instants he could not have done anything else. But they all fought the pull, and the struggle left them spaced well out away from one another. The chair with its burden did not so much dangle below them as occupy the center of a nearly flat square, with Trei or one of the others at each corner.

They could not actually fly, not really *fly*. They didn't know *how* to fly tethered like this, and the winds were too strong, and it was all very well to say they'd count off their wing-strokes; in those first moments it was impossible. They whirled blindly through the storm, pinwheeling around the chair that anchored and bound them; Trei cupped his wings, fighting to rise, and was pulled instead sideways through the air. He'd lost track of his direction—he couldn't tell what was sea and what was sky—if there were ships somewhere, he couldn't see them—Genrai was shouting something, but Trei couldn't understand him.

But Genrai tipped his wings and fought to pull them all one way, and as soon as Trei realized that, he tried to help. He could tell the moment they all began to strive together in a single direction, because suddenly the pull across his ribs seemed less. Genrai was shouting. The count, he was calling the count. At first Trei couldn't tell where in the count the downbeat was supposed to come, and then he stopped thinking and held back one downstroke and came into the rhythm by feel. The pull lessened again, and the world straightened itself out at last, and they were climbing. The sea below was the color of lead, the sky above a roil of dark cloud, but they were riding the Yngulin wind now, climbing fast. The weight of the Emperor dragged heavily at them, but, Trei thought, not *too* heavily He looked down, angling his neck awkwardly, but could not see the Emperor's face.

"Trei!" shouted Genrai. "Straighten out!

Trei flinched, embarrassed. He turned his gaze forward and concentrated on height ... the scouring winds hissed passed his ears ... they climbed steeply, by unspoken common accord, and broke at last up out of the Yngulin storm and into a clear and gentle sky.

Below them the rushing wind was still pewter-dark; but above them now the sky was a pale and delicate blue. Wisps of cloud trailed above them, almost close enough to touch; the sun stood above at the apex of the sky, at the very top of the vault of the heavens, above every storm and every struggle of men. Nescana and Tokabii swept past them, shouting, their voices thin with distance but relief vivid in their steep, swooping circles.

For the first moment, Trei found the quiet air welcome. Then, without the desperation and struggle of the storm, the weight of their burden began to impress itself on his awareness. He looked quickly to see how well the Emperor had come through the storm.

Dharoann enna Gaourr was sitting very still. His face was turned upward toward the sun and the fair sky. His expression was calm, but Trei, with the acuity of his kajurai sight, could see how quickly his breath came and how he gripped the arms of his chair until his knuckles were white. Trei looked away. It had not occurred to him until that moment that fear of heights, of the open sky, might have been the greatest cause of the Emperor's reluctance to leave his ship. If he had guessed—but he couldn't think of anything any of them could have done differently.

The ropes of the harness cut into his back and ribs with a pressure that made it hard to breathe. He hadn't realized how important deep breaths were for a kajurai until he could take only shallow ones. His shoulders hurt. They hadn't really hurt for days, but now he seemed to feel every muscle and ligament stretching to its limit. He tried to guess how much the Emperor weighed—the Emperor and chair together—he was becoming sure now that nothing about kajurai magic prevented a burden from weighing exactly what it should.

"Trei!" called Genrai, before Trei's thoughts could scatter into true absurdity. "Where are we? Do you know?"

And Trei, looking around, and then up at the noontime sun that stood directly above, realized he had no idea.

16

It didn't occur to Araenè that Imrei might not actually keep his word and pass the crown to Ceirfei until she was actually on the balcony above Quei Square, staring downward as the palace servants passed out oranges to the crowd, and melons, and round cakes and pastries dusted with sugar dyed pink or blue or yellow. Araenè didn't like to look at all those pastries. They were too much like the offerings people brought to a family after a death. She stared instead up at the carved dragons on the face of the palace. But that wasn't actually better. The dragons made her think of Trei. She wondered where he was now, and what he was doing, and whether he was safe—whether they were all safe, his friends and Master Anerii and everyone.

The balcony where Prince Imrei and Ceirfei and everyone stood was so low it was like the stage for a play more than an actual balcony. Prince Imrei stood right at the edge, where everyone could see him. How many people knew it was really going to be Ceirfei who took the crown? She couldn't see Imrei's expression from this distance. She flinched away from trying to imagine how he probably felt. Angry and ashamed and hurt ... poor Imrei. But what if he changed his mind?

She looked anxiously for Ceirfei. He was standing with the rest of his family right at the back of the low balcony, as in the wings of a stage. As though he was an actor waiting for his cue. That was actually very close to the truth, she supposed. She couldn't see his expression, she was too far away, but she knew his face would be calm. Only if she looked carefully, she would see fear and resolution in his eyes. She knew the exact expression. She wondered if everybody did, if maybe his mother and sister did, or if it was just her.

She wished she was down there with him. But even if Ceirfei had wanted her there, his mother probably wouldn't have allowed it. Her own mother had known so little about Araenè's life ... or Araenè had believed she knew nothing, and only wondered too late whether she had really needed to hide so much ...

"Must be nice for a *girl* who's *such good friends* with the new king," Kepai muttered behind her. Araenè stiffened, but didn't turn. Kepai's snide comments seemed ... small and powerless, somehow. Especially because everyone knew, now, that Cassameirin had said her idea about catching some of Kanora's dragon magic had been good, that it might even have saved Milendri. Which she wasn't sure was true, maybe she hadn't understood what Master Cassameirin meant, that seemed all too possible. But she did find it easier to ignore Kepai now. And anyway, she could hear the little shuffle and hiss that meant somebody, probably Kanii, had shoved Kepai and made him shut up.

Only the apprentices had come to see the coronation; the mages were busy, of course. And of course they needed the adjuvants, because the Tolounnese might have their steam engines and the Yngulin whatever amazing new thing *they* had, but Island mages still depended on adjuvants for strength. That was why Kepai was being so unpleasant: all the apprentices were on edge. The Islands needed the mages and the mages needed the adjuvants, but the apprentices were useless. Except Tichorei. Tichorei was with the mages, or he'd have made sure neither Kepai nor Kebei said anything. Even if no one had made the formal declaration, Tichorei *was* a mage now—everyone knew it—he was far more use than any of the rest of them.

Even if she'd been right about Kanora's sphere ... even if she had actually been right about trying to capture the dragon winds in a different sphere ... Araenè was still the newest and most ignorant apprentice, and about as far from being a mage as anybody could be.

A priest stood behind the triple altar. The altar was draped in white, of course. White altar, white stone towers and balconies and flagstones ... white was the color of grief, Araenè decided. A blankness that lay over everything and robbed color from the world. She thought she might never be able to face going into First City again. And there was all this pageantry to get through, and couldn't they just get *through* it. . . and then they must have, because one of the priests was bringing out the crown.

It wasn't really a crown. It was a simple circlet made of gold wire, with a single long Quei tailfeather braided into it. The priest held it up and said, in a strong voice that was clearly audible over the low murmur of the gathered throng, "The joys and griefs of men are transitory, our intentions blow away on the wind, but the designs of the Gods are constant and trustworthy. Trusting in the beauty and perfection of the Gods' designs, we surrender our mortal ambition. Humble in the face of our ignorance, we surrender our pride."

Then the priest mounted the balcony, stopped in front of Prince Imrei, and said gravely, still in that clear, carrying voice, "Prince Imrei Naterensei. Are you prepared, before the Gods, to set aside both ambition and pride, and take up this crown, and with it sovereignty of the Floating Islands?"

There was a long pause, which started out anticipatory and then became tense. The priest did not move, but continued to stand in front of Prince Imrei, holding out the delicate crown. Imrei didn't move either, but Araenè barely noticed because she was staring at Ceirfei. He was standing perfectly still, his head slightly bowed, as though listening to something only he could hear. Beyond him, his mother turned her head to stare at him, a sharp movement, and Araenè wondered, suddenly and for the first time, what Ceirfei's mother actually thought of her son. She looked at him now like she didn't recognize him at all.

"What's he *waiting* for?" muttered Kanii, and Araenè who had always liked cheerful, easy-going Kanii, especially after he'd shown he didn't mind her being a girl, found she wanted to shove him. She said angrily, "He hates this! Don't you know how much he hates it?"

"Because being king is just so terrible!" said Kebei.

"*You* don't know anything about it—you don't know what you're talking about—"

"Be quiet, both of you!" said Jeneki, who was older than either of them and who had a temper, and Araenè flushed. It was too stupid to argue about anyway. Especially with the twins. But they made her want to scream ... so did Imrei's hesitation ... just when Araenè thought she couldn't bear the tension another moment, Prince Imrei stepped back. He said, his voice hoarse but clear, "It's not for me. I—it's not for me." He turned, stumbling a little as a murmur rose up in the assembly. Ceirfei, standing beside his mother, lifted his head, his expression still.

"There!" said Jeneki, but Araenè didn't know him well and couldn't tell whether his tone held satisfaction or disapproval or something else entirely.

But Ceirfei didn't seem to hear any of the muttering, even from those much closer than the mage's balcony. He didn't look either to the left or to the right. He simply walked forward, touched Imrei on the arm—he might have said something, Araenè wasn't sure—and turned toward the priest. The man still hadn't moved. He didn't move now. He simply waited, as though he was prepared to stand there in exactly that pose all evening and then all night, until the rising sun came up to strike gold and green sparks once more from the circlet.

Ceirfei said, in a voice that came out steady and almost hard, "I am prepared."

"Then take it," said the priest gently. "And may the Gods grant you wisdom in place of ambition, humility in place of pride, and a steady heart that sustains faith in even the darkest hour. May good fortune and prosperity attend your reign, O King, and may the Gods grant you wise, strong sons to follow in the path you lay down." He proffered the circlet.

Ceirfei took it. The gold sparked like flame in the late sunlight, and the Quei feather blazed as though it had been spun out of emeralds. Ceirfei placed the circlet on his own head and turned to face the gathering, and the crowd called out—the first acclamation a little hesitant, but the second louder. On the balcony, Prince Imrei started to step away, but Ceirfei seized his arm and stopped him, and embraced him, and the crowd, reassured, shouted a third time. This third acclamation rang off the white stone of the towers and filled the whole city, until Araenè thought they must hear it in the farthest streets of Third City. It must echo farther than that; she was sure that sheep farmers would hear it ring through their pastures all the way on the other side of the Island.

Bells were ringing somewhere close at hand ... of course there were bell towers rising up above the palace, but she had forgotten, or had never known, that they rang the bells for a coronation. Araenè found herself smiling as the great brazen voices rolled through the air. She thought she could feel its echo ringing through her bones. The first bell was joined by another. And then by another, this one with a lighter, sweeter tone; and then another and another, each higher-pitched than the last, all ringing against the others so that all the bells together formed a harmony.

Another bell rang out, its voice deeper and heavier, an iron bell rather than bronze; dissonant against the others as though someone had dropped roasted garlic into sweet cream. Araenè flinched. Beside her, Kanii frowned and shook his head. Little Cesei said impatiently, "They're doing it wrong!", but Taobai, who had been born in the First City and knew things the rest of them didn't, said suddenly, "No one could ring the iron bells by mistake; they're in a separate tower!"

Araenè realized at once that Taobai was right. Below, the gathered people in Quei Square mostly still cheered and chattered, making their way slowly toward the avenues that led away from the square and back into the city; they didn't know anything was wrong. But everyone on the low balcony was standing so still. Listening to the bells. Ceirfei had his hand on his cousin's arm; but as Araenè watched, Lord Manasi pressed urgently past the priests to come to him, and Ceirfei dropped his hand and straightened his shoulders and took one step forward, away from his family, meeting him alone while the iron bells tolled out alarm across all the city.

Because Ceirfei *was* alone, now. Alone in the midst of his family, alone even though he was surrounded by the whole palace and city and by the whole Island of Milendri, and all the other Islands beyond. Araenè suddenly couldn't bear it, or couldn't bear that Ceirfei had to bear it, and shoved past a startled Kanii and Cesei, and past frowning Jeneki and quiet Taobai, jostled past Kebei and Kepai, who gave her identical hostile glares, reached blindly out, opened the door she found under her hand, and stepped down from the mage's balcony and straight into the noise and brilliant light that filled Quei Square.

For a moment, she could only blink, half-blinded by the pouring sunlight. People pressed past her on both sides, their voices raised cheerfully as they called back and forth; even now, they mostly hadn't realized about the bells. The mellow notes of the bronze bells that rang for celebration and joy and to mark the hours of the day had all died away, but the iron bells continued to toll: heavy, leaden notes that reverberated in the mind and heart like grief. In the thrumming semi-quiet between tolling strokes of the bells, Araenè could hear Lord Manasi's voice, raised in furious expostulation.

"Without any kind of understanding, without any kind of agreement, and I can't imagine what you—"

"Let them come," Ceirfei answered, with an air that suggested he had said this before. His light, calm voice slipped right through the noise and confusion, somehow carrying far better than Manasi's shouting. "I will go down to speak to their commander; I will be sure we *do* have an agreement, lord minister, and I assure you I don't intend to give away anything we've a chance of holding. Now, of your kindness, please go silence those bells, and shall we agree that they should not ring forth again until the Yngulin ships are glimpsed?" Lord Manasi began to say something else, and Ceirfei repeated, his voice no louder but substantially more intense: "I hope we shall indeed *agree in every detail*, lord minister."

Araenè stopped, wanting to laugh and strangling the impulse back to a cough. She'd heard Ceirfei do that before—but not often and not to Lord Manasi. But he had stopped the older man in his tracks. Now he said, his tone not exactly conciliatory but no longer so sharp, "I shall depend upon your support, Lord Manasi, in this and every crisis."

The lord minister stared at him. At the circlet with its Quei feather braided around and through it; at the violet pin that held his white cloak; at Prince Imrei, who stood behind him and wouldn't meet Lord Manasi's eyes. He cleared his throat. "Yes," he said, just a little too loudly. "Of course." Ceirfei lifted an eyebrow at him, waiting, and after a moment he added, "My lord king."

Ceirfei gave him a nod and a brief smile and turned to speak to Araenè. "How good of you to come, lady mage," he said, courteously and very formally. "I think your skills will again prove invaluable, if you will be so kind as to provide a door for me to the deck of the foremost Tolounnese ship? An unwavering door," he added prudently, with a glance at his mother. "A door through which one may *reliably* come and go."

His mother did not exactly relax, but she nodded.

Araenè prevented herself, with an effort, from exclaiming, *A Tolounnese ship?* Instead, she smiled, nodded, and said, carefully formal to match Ceirfei, "If I may possibly look at the Tolounnese ships, um, my lord king, I think that would help. Um. I hadn't ... I don't seem to ... the Tolounnese mages don't seem to be pushing the dragon magic out of the way, this time ..."

"A reassuring sign that the messages of peace and parley my kajuraihi have been showing the Tolounnese have been received," Ceirfei agreed gravely, and offered Araenè his arm. She laid her hand on the crook of his elbow, thinking *Peace and parley?* But she didn't ask any questions, or ask Ceirfei what he meant to say to the Tolounnese shipmaster, or to the soldiers those ships undoubtedly carried. Either everybody else knew and she didn't, which she would hardly want to point out, or else *nobody* knew anything because Ceirfei was making all this up as he went along and in that case she didn't want to press him for explanations in front of everybody. And she thought that was more likely.

"You could fly down," she pointed out, as they strolled along. She wanted to rush forward to one of the seaward balconies and see what was below, but Ceirfei held her back to a dignified pace.

"I need to speak to them as a king, not a kajurai," Ceirfei murmured in return. "How do I look? Is the Gods-blessed circlet straight? How's my vest, can you see any stains on it? All this white, it does get tiresome ..."

"You look fine," Araenè assured him. "You look like a king."

Ceirfei grimaced. He lowered his voice even further. "Is my mother following us? Lord Manasi?"

Araenè glanced back. "No, Manasi's gone away somewhere, to tell them about the bells, I guess, and it looks like your mother's taking your sisters back into the palace. And Imrei's with her, and his little sister ..."

"Good," said Ceirfei. A little of the tension went out of his shoulders. He said apologetically, "My mother wanted to be the one to speak to the Tolounnese ships, once we knew they were coming in without bringing in that dead air. Which might be because we damaged and destroyed enough of their engines to stop them pushing the living winds out of their way—but then they should have turned back. So we think it's the messages we've sent."

Araenè thought about this. "Your mother helped write those messages, didn't she? Peace and parley, is it? I can see why she'd want to be the one to go down to those ships. That might even work. After all, she is your royal uncle's sister ..."

Ceirfei grimaced again. "She is. She never forgets it. She'll press me harder than Lord Manasi, if I let her. But I can't have her negotiate with the Tolounnese."

"Because she's a woman?"

"Because she's too aggressive." Ceirfei glanced sidelong at Araenè and grinned at her expression. "Araenè, if my mother had won a war and was going to lay down terms for her enemy's surrender, she'd be fine. But we haven't won this war, and she doesn't know how to give way gracefully. Or I'd have suggested Imrei step back for her and not for me."

Araenè thought about this. "Besides, she and Manasi, well." The dislike between the lord minister and Calaspara Naterensei was famous.

"And without Manasi, the ministries would never accept a ruling queen," agreed Ceirfei. He sounded ... resigned, Araenè decided. "So here I am. And here we are! Don't be afraid; I won't let you fall." And he stepped right up to the very edge of the balcony he'd brought her to, one that extended way out over the sea, and offered her his hand.

"I never worry about falling when I'm with you," Araenè said truthfully, and took his hand. His fingers closed around hers, strong and warm and sure, and she stepped up beside him to the edge of the balcony. She thought she could feel the warm pressure of the air before them, denser than air should be, ready to catch them if they started to overbalance. She had never been sure whether that sense of building pressure was her imagination or not.

"Look," said Ceirfei. He nodded downward at the tall many-oared ship riding at anchor below Canpra.

"They're trusting," commented Araenè. "Anybody with good aim could drop boulders on them. Or pour down burning pitch."

"That's only the one ship. You see those five others standing away out of range? Even if we had good catapults, which we don't." Ceirfei didn't say, though Araenè knew it was true, that he'd had been arguing for months that the Islands needed to build catapults, but hadn't gotten his cousin or the ministries to agree. Araenè wondered whether Ambassador Ngewasi had been the one to persuade Imrei that figuring out how to build catapults wasn't worth the trouble.

"They're testing our intentions," Ceirfei said aloud.

"You sent kajuraihi to them?"

Ceirfei nodded. "They dropped olive twigs and the feathers of white doves. Then a man went down to speak to them in my name, asking them to come in quietly for parley and pledging the honor of the Islands that we'd make no attack."

"You did all that before you even knew for sure Manasi would support you! How did you have the nerve?"

Ceirfei smiled, not a very humorous smile. "I didn't have any choice. Neither did he, so I knew he would support me in the end. Can you give us a door that will let us step right down onto the deck of that ship?"

"Yes. I mean … yes, I suppose. You don't want to send for a real mage?"

"Our mages are otherwise occupied. As who should know better than you?" Ceirfei quirked an eyebrow at her. "And I trust you, Araenè. You have a gift for doors. Who should know that better than I?"

Araenè met his confident eyes and put her hand out to thin air, pushing open the door that stood there, set solidly on nothing, a step away from the balcony.

It opened to the deck of the Tolounnese ship. The ship rocked slowly underfoot, not quite steady, a strange feeling. Araenè had never gone out in one of the little fishing boats; had never thought of setting foot in a boat in her life. She had not expected a big ship to feel so uncertain underfoot, and gripped the heavy carved frame of her door for balance and security as well as to help keep the door in place. It might vanish anyway, but if she didn't think about it too hard, she could probably hold it.

High masts swayed above, tower-tall, slender for their height but much bigger than she had imagined. The sails had been taken in, lashed down; the ship surged gently and rhythmically, either with the motion of the sea or in response to oarwork. Ceirfei and she stood high up, out in the open on the highest deck of the ship. There were Tolounnese men here, but not as many as Araenè had expected. No crowds of soldiers. She counted seven men in undyed linen, barefoot and weaponless, who must be sailors; they had stopped what they were doing to stare at her and Ceirfei. One of them caught a rope and swooped away and down to a lower deck, but the others all stayed where they were, caught motionless by surprise and uncertainty.

"We want the ship's master," murmured Ceirfei. "Or perhaps the commander of the soldiers. Though I would prefer to speak to the general in command of the whole military operation—ah, here we are, let's see who this is."

Half a dozen men had come up a ladder to the high deck. No undyed linen here: two wore the black and gray and red of Tolounnese soldiers, and three gray and blue, and the other one a black robe that, though plain, was belted with a gold cord—that one must be a Tolounnese mage, Araenè knew, and tried not to stare at him. She couldn't tell if he could stop her holding the door open on the deck of the ship, or if he tried, if she could do anything to keep it open. Of course she should have realized there would be Tolounnese mages on these ships, she would have if she'd thought for a second, but she hadn't had time to think about it and she felt shocked and frightened. She glanced at Ceirfei, but his calm expression hadn't changed. She tried to look that calm, but didn't know if she succeeded.

Trei would have known everything about all of these Tolounnese men from their clothing: rank and position and everything. Araenè didn't know anything. She risked a quick sidelong glance at Ceirfei, but couldn't tell whether he knew more about such things than she did. But he was focusing on one of the men, one of the soldiers. This wasn't the oldest, nor the most richly dressed. But nevertheless, this was the man Ceirfei faced when he stepped forward.

The Tolounnese all stopped. So did Ceirfei. Araenè waited nervously, her hand still on the door. But Ceirfei didn't seem worried. He stood quite still, his chin up and his shoulders straight, facing the man he had picked out.

The man gazed back at him. He was a lot older than Ceirfei, but then everybody was. His hair was grizzled but still dark; his beard, neat and tight against the line of his jaw, was gray. He had deep-set eyes placed wide apart in a broad, weathered face. He wore a sword, and his hand rested on its black hilt, but he didn't seem inclined to draw it; he stood that way as though it was the way he habitually stood, not as though he was making a threat. He took a step forward, facing Ceirfei directly.

Ceirfei, in white and violet and with the gold circlet crossing his brow, looked every bit a king. At least to Araenè. She wondered what the Tolounnese saw when they looked at him.

"General ..." Ceirfei hazarded.

The man inclined his head slightly. "I am General Paolarr enna Entarrann." He opened one hand slightly. "If it is I you seek, then I am here."

"General Paolarr enna Entarrann," repeated Ceirfei. "I am Ceirfei Feneirè, nephew of Terinai Naterensei, who was King of the Floating Islands and who has passed into the hands of the Gods. I am now King of the Floating Islands." He paused.

The general nodded gravely, his expression unchanging. He said, "We received your messages, Ceirfei Feneirè."

He gave Ceirfei no title at all, Araenè noticed, and tried to decide whether she was offended by that, but he was going on and she had no time to think about it.

"You have claimed you wish parley, pledging your name and your word. Both of which I recognize. So I am here, Ceirfei Feneirè. I will hear your words. But," the general said grimly, "I fear there is little likelihood of peace between us unless you are prepared to surrender your Islands to the authority of Tolounn, without conditions as well as without battle. But I will hear you, taking your word that this ship may withdraw from the shadow of your Island without harm whatever the outcome of this parley."

It was perfectly plain the general did not expect any useful outcome from this encounter. And yet, Araenè thought, here he was.

"Of course I guarantee your ship may withdraw, though I think you will not find it necessary. Nor will I offer you the Islands without conditions," Ceirfei said, his tone only a little dry. "But those conditions are not for you to debate, General Paolarr enna Entarrann; I am certain you will both yield to and uphold the will of your Emperor."

That was stretching the truth a little, Araenè thought. Maybe more than a little. She admired Ceirfei's ability to say something like that so smoothly, like no one could possibly argue.

The Tolounnese officer looked taken aback. Whatever he had expected, it had not been an appeal to the authority of his own Emperor. He began to speak, but hesitated.

"With whom I am currently negotiating," Ceirfei said, still with that extraordinary smoothness. "He and I both count on you to maintain Tolounn's options in this area. You have not, perhaps, yet heard of the Yngulin ships that have moved to forestall Tolounn ambition?" His gaze shifted to the Tolounnese mage. "The ships that sail up from the waves and into the sky," he said, gently barbed. "So efficient, compared to your Tolounnese methods."

The mage blinked, drew himself up, and declared, "Impossible!"

"Evidently not," Ceirfei said, now very dry. "Indeed, we should be pleased to hear that Tolounn's mages have strength

236

to match the strength the Yngulin mages have shown to us. How many engines do you now have to draw upon? Two, I believe? Well, that must suffice."

The Tolounnese general held up a hand to forestall the mage's intemperate response. "Ships that fly," he said, expressionless.

"Would you own Milendri? Would you defend her city and towns and pastures and farms from the Yngulin warriors who wish to take them? If you will," said Ceirfei, "then surely better from the streets and stone of the Island than from the waves. I will show you where and how your men may mount to the Island ... if you will permit me, General Paolarr enna Entarrann."

"You would give your city into my hands?" said the general, not quite disbelievingly. It was hard to disbelieve Ceirfei when he looked like that: absolutely assured and perfectly confident.

"Certainly," Ceirfei said without hesitation. "And you will give your men into my hands; I am still the King of the Floating Islands. The battle is yours. My people will support yours with our utmost effort. You will respect my people as your allies and you will take your strategic orders from me, though not, of course, your tactical decisions. As your Emperor will confirm," he added, when the Tolounnese general drew breath to object. "But, alas, not immediately; we expect the Yngulin fleet to arrive well in advance of that confirmation." He paused for a breath, and then said gently, "So the decision is yours, General Paolarr enna Entarrann. Everything I have said to you is true—"

For a generous enough conception of the truth, Araenè thought.

"So now it is for you to say what you will do," Ceirfei said, still gently.

The silence drew itself out.

"I think—" began the general.

Above them, the sound rolling like lead through the quiet air, the iron bells began to toll.

"Yes. *Those* Yngulin ships," Ceirfei said, with no appearance of surprise, turning to the south, where indeed, tiny dark shapes were barely visible against the horizon. "They are before even our expectation. You may, of course, cede those ships possession of Milendri. Certainly *we* cannot prevent them taking the Island. Or you might attempt to battle them here upon the surface of the sea, though ships that ride the waves, well, one cannot quite see how they may challenge those that mount into the air—"

"We will press them down," snapped the Tolounnese mage. "Down where ships belong, where they may be rammed and broken like any ships—"

"Perhaps," said Ceirfei. "But it is dragon magic you are accustomed to battle, and whatever power those Yngulin mages draw upon, it isn't dragon magic. Who should know," he said gently, gazing at the Tolounnese mage with his crystalline kajurai eyes, "better than I?"

"You—" said the mage.

"I think you will find the Yngulin mages outmatch you. But who knows? Perhaps not."

"Enough," said General Paolarr enna Entarrann abruptly. He did not speak loudly, but with a sharp intensity that stopped his mage in mid-retort. He had shaded his eyes with one hand and stared out toward the Yngulin ships. Araenè thought they already looked closer. And she thought one of them—no, two of them at least—were already rising into the air. By the time they came to Milendri, she thought they would be far above the reach of any Tolounnese ships.

"Without the dense currents of dragon magic that should support and surround Milendri, our options are severely limited," murmured Ceirfei, his attention on the Tolounnese general. "Can you feel the Islands losing their magic? I assure you, it's happening. Our options are few, but if you will not ally with us, General Paolarr enna Entarrann, then your options will rapidly become even more limited than ours. All the choices here are yours—now. But that will not last. Your delay will give Yngul all the power to make choices here. What will you do?"

The Tolounnese general turned to him, a sharp decisive movement. "You have spoken to Dharoann enna Gaourr? To our Little Emperor? You maintain that he himself recognizes that you are king here? That he himself cedes strategic command to you, Ceirfei Feneirè?"

"He and I will negotiate these matters," Ceirfei said coolly. "But I give you my word that my firm intention is to surrender these Islands into the Emperor's hands. They are his, if he can keep them. I don't see how you yourself can possibly do ill by preventing Yngul from seizing them now from our Emperor's grip."

"I think ..." said the general, and paused. Then he said in a firm tone, "I think, Ceirfei Feneirè, that you had better show me how my men may best climb to your Island." And he turned to one of the ship's officer and said, "Signal the rest of this detachment to come in. Pass the signal on, warning every ship of the Yngulin threat. We shall have some few moments to discuss these matters—let us see what we may do—"

"Araenè," Ceirfei said quietly. "I'll need to stay with these men, but you had better go. I need you to make sure Master Kopapei knows what's happening. I'll show these people the sea-stair—"

"I'm not leaving you," Araenè said, shocked that he would ask her to. "No! Don't say it! I don't care! You don't know what might happen, and neither do I."

"Araenè. I would like for the Islands to be something better than a helpless client state of Tolounn. The moment in which we may make that happen is already upon us, and the chance will be fleeting. We *need* to work *with* the Tolounnese. I depend on Master Kopapei and Master Tnegun—I have to have their support."

Araenè tried to interrupt, but he kept on, ignoring her, "You can come and go. I can't; if I left this ship now, the Tolounnese general would quite reasonably suspect perfidy.

I'll stay here; I'll go up the sea-stair with these people; I'll be perfectly fine. All right?"

"You'd *better* be perfectly fine," Araenè told him fiercely. She turned to glare at the Tolounnese general. "You promise me you'll act in good faith! I know you'll keep your word if you give it! You haven't said you recognize Ceirfei's really the King of the Floating Islands! Say so out loud, so we all know, all of us on the Islands, that we can trust you!"

General Paolarr enna Entarrann, his attention pulled abruptly away from his urgent discussion with the ship's officers and his mage, stared at her, taken aback. But not, she thought, actually offended. He said after the barest pause, "That's for my Emperor to decide and declare, lady mage. But I will wait for that decision and that declaration, and while I wait, I judge it would suit no good purpose to fight one another. For this moment, we will be allies. So it will be as your king has said." He glanced sharply at Ceirfei. "But all the tactical decisions of the battle will be mine."

Ceirfei made a little gesture of agreement.

"Then all the strategic decisions may be yours," conceded the Tolounnese general. "For this moment! But for the moment, you are king here, and I do not dispute your authority."

Ceirfei inclined his head. "So you see you may safely go. Araenè, you have to go, it's important. I need you to do this—and I don't need you to stay here. Tolounnese honor, remember?"

Araenè glared at him. "I'll go because you're king! But you better be right! About everything!" She started to turn back toward her door, but said over her shoulder, "And you better not let any Yngulin ship catch you still on the sea!" One more step and she would be through the door. She said fiercely, "And we'll figure it out! About the dragons and the magic! You do the rest of it, and we'll figure that out!"

"I know you will," Ceirfei said, not as though he was trying to pacify her, but as though he really believed it.

And if he did, Araenè thought maybe she could, too. She gave him an abrupt little nod and stepped through her door, and it swung shut behind her, closing against the salt spray and the rolling waves, and she stood again high above the sea, on the broad white balcony of the palace. Below her she could see the ship, but not Ceirfei. Off to the south, she could see the Yngulin ships far too clearly.

Everything was horrible. It might get better, or at least not worse, but Ceirfei was right: nothing could really be right until the dragons came back down to the Floating Islands.

Burning with anger and fear, Araenè turned, snatched open a door she found ready to her hand, and strode through it without even looking.

It took some time after she left Ceirfei, but at last Araenè found Master Tnegun, along with Master Kopapei and Master Akhai, in one of the workrooms. She hated the delay, resented every confusing hallway the hidden school took her through to find her master, because all the time she could hear in her mind the urgency in Ceirfei's voice. But she found the right workroom at last, and was relieved to find all the mages together, so at least she could tell her master and Master Kopapei at the same time.

From the clutter of wooden scraps and stone chips and the fire blazing in the glassblower's hearth, the mages had been working to make more than one kind of sphere, but she couldn't guess what kind of spells they'd wanted to invest in those spheres. Candles and bits of string littered one table; another was strewn with feathers of metallic blue and scarlet, black and pearlescent gray.

Then she was distracted by a sharp, cold wind that whipped through the room, carrying with it the crystal-pure air of the heights. Araenè stopped dead still, staring as the feathers scattered across the room and every candle flame leapt up and then blew out. Across the room, the glassblower's furnace blazed up, and the mage who had been working there—it was Master Akhai—stumbled backward with a cry and the smell of singed cloth.

The wind, confined by the walls, spun in a tight gyre around the room, ripped through chinks in the plaster and gaps in the shutters, tore tiles off the roof, and was gone out into open sky. It left behind a shocked stillness and the smell of hot wax and candle smoke and burned cloth. Master Kopapei subsided into a plain wooden chair and mopped his face. Master Akhai shook out a smoldering flame that was trying to climb the sleeve of his robe. Master Tnegun put something that appeared to be a glass timer strung with half a dozen slender filaments of crystal down on a table, very gently. Araenè pressed her hand over her mouth, trying not to laugh. It wasn't funny.

"Well," said Master Kopapei after a moment, "that didn't work."

"Really?" said Master Akhai, rather savagely. He had a vivid red mark across his hand and up his wrist, and his sleeve was only half the length it should have been.

"Araenè," said Master Tnegun, sounding both kind and distracted. "This isn't the best time."

"I ..." she began, meaning to explain about Ceirfei and the Tolounnese general and the Yngulin ships. But Master Akhai snapped, "I rather think you've done enough already, girl!"

"Akhai!" Master Kopapei said. The younger mage threw up his hands and stalked away to the far end of the room, where he started doing something mysterious with a complex object made of gold beads and silver wire. "Araenè," said Master Kopapei. "None of this was your fault."

Araenè nodded because he clearly expected her to. She tried not to think about it. She started again, "I came to say—"

Master Tnegun came over to lay a dark hand on her shoulder. The strength of his grip was comforting. Araenè looked up at his hawk-fierce face and thought that surely he would know what to do, and how to do it. That her master surely knew what to do about everything, and how to do anything.

Only she knew at the same time that it wasn't true.

"Araenè," Master Tnegun said quietly. "If we cannot recapture the living winds, we will do something else. Soon the monsoons will come down upon the Islands; perhaps we will bring them early. Whatever art and strength the Yngulin mages use to lift their ships, they will not likely be able to withstand the great storms. That would gain us time to create an alliance with Tolounn—"

"Alliance!" Master Akhai said from the far end of the workroom, his voice loud and tight with scorn. "Is that what you call it?"

Master Tnegun turned his dark, hooded gaze to the younger mage. "Yes," he said. "That is what I call it. Unequal it may be, but make no mistake: it is an alliance the young king will build and not a submission."

"Oh, he means well, to be sure!" snapped Master Akhai, and would have gone on, but Araenè found herself suddenly, blazingly angry. She squared her stance, facing the young mage. He wasn't so much older than Tichorei; he wasn't *so* intimidating.

She said furiously, "You don't know anything about it! You think you could do better? If you want an alliance with Tolounn, you'd better be glad it's Ceirfei who's king, because *he* can do that! He already *is,* that's what I came to tell you: he's already got the Tolounnese general to agree to defend the Islands! *You* didn't do that!"

"Araenè," Master Tnegun said quietly.

"Nobody needs to say that Ceirfei *means* well! He knows what he's doing. The Tolounnese ships are here, they've come, and Ceirfei's already got the general agreeing to do what he wants, and that's a good thing, because the Yngulin ships have been sighted, too. *That's* what I came to tell you!"

Master Akhai was staring at her. He looked offended, but also thoughtful, not as though he was thinking about what she'd said, but more as though, after he had long

243

dismissed the possibility, he thought she had finally said something interesting.

"Araenè," began Master Tnegun again, but Master Akhai moved a hand to forestall him and said, much more temperately, "I meant no offense, girl. I'm sure we are all relieved to hear this news you bring. The news about the Tolounnese general, of course, not about the Yngulin fleet." He glanced around the workroom and let his breath out in a deep sigh. "I was upset," he admitted, sounding almost sheepish. He glanced at Master Tnegun. "If we're to support the Tolounnese forces ... maybe we had better begin thinking about weather working?"

"If we are to bring the monsoons, we'd best also consider the energy they'll bring with them," put in Master Kopapei. He came over to pat Araenè absently on the shoulder. "You're a good child, Araenè, and is there anything else we should know? Very well, then you might find the other apprentices and tell everyone we won't have lessons for a few days; we shall call on them—on you all—to do what you can for the Islands while we are distracted." Master Kopapei gave her a shrewd look from below bristly eyebrows.

Araenè flushed and nodded. And retreated. She supposed she should find her way to the other apprentices. She'd delivered Ceirfei's message, and what else was there to do, now, except find out from Tichorei what they would all be expected to do?

But she didn't want to. The thought of dealing with Kebei's barbed little comments and Jeneki's snippy attitude ... it was all more than she could bear. And it wasn't as though it mattered where she went. They didn't need her, anyway. She found her way to the kitchens instead.

The chef, a big man with a booming voice who approved wholeheartedly of Araenè, passed her a pastry with a filling of chicken in a cream sauce. "Tell me what you think of the nutmeg!" he ordered her. "I put in just a touch. You should not be able to taste it, but it should deepen all the flavors. You tell me if it works!"

Everyone was busy, thought Araenè. Everyone but her, and what was she supposed to do? Decide whether there was too much nutmeg in the creamed chicken! Which there was, actually. She suggested it might be cut by a pinch next time. "And maybe we could add some sweet potatoes, diced small? That would even out the flavors, wouldn't it?"

"A clever palate!" boomed the chef. "Excellent! Do so, young Araenè, and then taste the dessert sauce. Is it too sharp? It should accent the cakes, not overwhelm them ..."

It was good to lose herself in pleasant tasks she understood, among people who didn't know anything about magic, who didn't worry about the Yngulin fleet or the Tolounnese or anything except whether the dessert sauce was too sharp for the cakes. Araenè almost wished she could be one of them for real.

17

Trei flew with his eyes closed. No one was keeping the count now. They were all keeping the rhythm without thinking about it. This was good, because Trei, at least, couldn't think about anything. His awareness had narrowed to the dragging weight across his back and shoulders. Carrying weight required constant work. It was hard—too hard. They had been sinking gradually all afternoon. He knew that if he opened his eyes, the sea would be markedly nearer than the last time he had looked. So he did not look.

They flew fifteen points west of south. Trei imagined that was still their course. He had set it for them a long time ago, after the sun had finally slid down enough in the sky to show them where true west lay. The fifteen points were a guess. The Islands were spread out over a lot of area. They would eventually sight one Island or another: Talabri or Candara or one of the little Islands, or a nameless floating pebble. Unless they drowned first. This was much easier to imagine now than it had been when they had flung themselves away from the Emperor's ship. Especially if they were all flying with their eyes closed, and flew right past some Island that might have saved them all.

Genrai would be watching, though. Trei was sure of it. Nescana and Tokabii, free of the burdon the others carried, would be watching. And of course the Emperor himself would be watching, though he'd have to get close enough to see the Island itself; he wouldn't see the way the winds flowed around stone.

Trei found himself wishing *he* could sit in that chair just a little while, just long enough for his back to stop hurting so much. Though maybe it would be worse, to know you might drown through no fault of your own and not even be able to

246

try to save yourself ... Trei opened his eyes. His eyelashes stuck together and his eyes stung. That might be sweat. He refused to think it might be tears. He couldn't wipe his eyes, blinking hard instead.

Below, the Emperor sat quietly in his chair. He had undone most of the ropes, which now lay coiled in his lap. Trei understood that. Of course Dharoann enna Gaourr was not the kind of man who would let himself fall bound and helpless into the sea. If they fell, he would free himself and swim. He would swim long after the rest of them had drowned, pulled down by waterlogged feathers and exhaustion. He would swim until he, too, was too exhausted to keep afloat, or until one of the great fishes came up underneath him, or until by some miracle of the Gods' favor he was rescued by some fishing boat. That would be something for the crew to talk about all their lives: how they picked the Little Emperor of Tolounn out of the sea ... Trei wanted to laugh, but didn't have the breath. And his back hurt too much to laugh. Even though it *was* funny.

There were no Islands in sight anywhere, no telltale swirl in the air where the winds curled around a pebble too small to see. Only the white-capped waves, sparkling with sunlight. A long dark shadow below the waves suggested the presence of a great fish, and a lone gull winged past, unburdened, white wings flashing in the sun. It curved past them and then tilted its narrow wings and came back again, no doubt amazed at the sight.

"Height!" Genrai called. "Work for it! A quarter of a bell and then you can rest again!"

This wasn't the first time he had made them all work to regain some of their lost height. At first they had been able to drag themselves upward quite a long way. Later, a quarter of a bell had proven well beyond their ability, and they had hardly gained any height at all.

"Kojran!" shouted Genrai. "Help me pull the winds! Downbeat on my count: one, two, three! Trei, put some muscle into it! Tokabii could do better than that! *Nescana* could do better!"

Trei would gladly have let Nescana try, except there was no way to trade places. She was flying unburdened and would be perfectly all right, which meant she would get to watch the rest of them drown. That was nearly the worst thing Trei could imagine. Though she could at least tell everybody else what had happened. She could tell Araenè –

"Trei!" shouted Nescana. "Don't be a baby! Count!"

Trei wanted to laugh, but he also found himself really fighting to keep the count, to haul himself upward in the sky with the others.

"Better!" shouted Genrai. "Good, Trei! A little longer! Call the count with the downbeat! One! Two!"

Trei joined the others, choking out, "Three! Four! One!" with every laborious downstroke. It did seem to help, a little. He was sure they were higher now.

"Look!" cried Nescana. "A pebble! A little one, do you see! Straight ahead! You can reach it! We can get there!"

Trei could see nothing, either straight ahead or anywhere in the empty sky. He was sure Nescana was making it up.

"Yes! There it is!" shouted Genrai. "Will you give up *now? I* won't drown! For a bunch of lazy slugs! Who ought to be dragging their tails in the mud! Since they won't fly! *Put your backs into it!*"

Trei would never have thought of lying like that ... he *hadn't* thought of it ... maybe there really *was* a pebble in the sky. Genrai truly sounded furious. Trei closed his eyes again so he wouldn't see the empty sky and put everything he had into flying. If there *was* a pebble, they would surely reach it soon ...

"There's a *ship! Two* ships! No, *three!*" shouted Tokabii, his voice high and excited, and Trei's eyes flew open.

There *were* ships, approaching rapidly. Very soon Trei could make out the long narrow shape of those ships, the sharp bronze prows for ramming, the gaunt shapes of catapults amidships and the jagged black eagles slashing across the largest of their golden sails. He could see the Yngulin sailors who swarmed up the rigging and cried out in gleeful excitement when they saw the laboring kajurai above them.

"*Gods!*" Genrai cried. "Gods *weeping!* We can't come down *now!* Height, height!"

For a moment, terror and fury broke through the grinding hopeless exhaustion, and they curved a steep path up through the sky. It wouldn't last, Trei knew. They all knew it. He could already feel himself failing. He could not maintain the pace, and across from him, he could see Kojran trying to take up the weight he couldn't hold, and failing. Below them, the Yngulin ships had heeled sharply around to follow them

"Where's that ... Gods-cursed ... pebble of yours ... now, Nescana?" Rekei got out, his breath heaving. "Liar!"

"I'm Third City! We don't fuss about lies like you stuck up Second City brats! You can complain to the wingmaster when we get back!"

"The ship! It was going *somewhere!*" Trei got out, before Rekei could answer. "We could be close!" Close to *something.* But though he strained his eyes staring into the empty sky, he could see noting. Nothing anywhere. Only the layered winds and the Yngulin ships with their golden sails pacing them across the infinite reaches of the sea.

Then the kajuraihi came. They had been following the Yngulin ships, harassing them or just keeping track of them; Trei understood that later. But in that first instant, their coming seemed utterly miraculous, like the direct intervention of the Gods. Even later, he thought the Gods must have had a hand in them all coming together there, them and the Yngulin ships and the kajuraihi who pursued them.

The kajuraihi slid down from above, from the cold heights, their wings flaming with sunlight, golden-winged Candaran kajuraihi and one crimson-winged kajurai from Milendri, men with vastly more strength and experience than any first-year novice. The winds followed them and came up hard and dense below Trei, below them all: not enough, but it helped. Just having the kajuraihi *there* helped, but that wouldn't last, Trei knew, and he realized with despair that they might very well fall even yet, because what could these Candaran kajuraihi possibly do to really help?

"Fly, boy!" urged one man, coming up alongside Trei. "Never mind you can't, you must! We've got clips, by the grace of the Gods, but that's a lot of weight you've got there! It's a trick and a half to do an exchange on a heavy load! But we'll get it done! Can you hear me?"

"Yes," Trei thought he shouted, but the word came out hardly loud enough for him to hear himself. They were sinking again, and he knew it was his fault; he was the one failing, unable to take his share of the burden. His shoulders and back were on fire, but he could have worked through the pain, he thought he could, he was sure of it, only his muscles just would not answer.

"Just about got it!" shouted the man, very close. "Can you hear me, boy? When I tell you! Lock your wings and be still! Let yourself lose height! It's all right! I'll turn upside down, I'll be right below you, face to face! You'll need to match my angle or you'll foul the rope! I need to clip your line to my harness, and cut you loose! You need to get slack in the line to let me make the exchange! Do you understand? Can you hear me?"

"Yes," Trei tried to say.

"When the weight comes off you, the winds will throw you away and up! Don't fight that! You need to get out of the way! Keep your wings locked and ride the winds! You'll be fine if you just keep your wings locked!"

Trei tried to nod.

The kajurai abruptly dropped away from Trei, who immediately lost sight of him. Trei could see other kajuraihi maneuvering near Kojran and Rekei—not Genrai, at least not yet. He could see the Emperor, his chair swinging unevenly in circles, turning his face alertly back and forth to watch the intricate choreography of the kajuraihi.

Then Trei's vision was blocked as the kajurai rose sharply from below him. As the man had said, he was flying upside down. His wings were locked, and he had actually got his hands free of the wing-harness so he could work with the carrying-harness. A knife was stuck through the harness at his hip.

"Lock your wings!" he shouted at Trei. "Let yourself sink! Plenty of room to fall, don't worry over it! Hear me? Lock your wings, boy!"

Trei closed his eyes and locked his wings, and immediately dropped—he thought he was actually going to land right *on* the other kajurai, but the other man adjusted his own height with breathtaking precision, sinking away just fast enough to keep pace with him. It seemed unbelievable. If Trei beat his wings at all, he'd foul the other man's wings— but they were falling—they were actually *below* the Emperor's chair, now –

The other kajurai jerked at the rope harness binding Trei's chest, jerked again, harder, and said sharply, "Ready? Clear!" He grabbed the knife and slashed once, dropping the knife immediately to resume proper control of his own wings.

The weight fell away from Trei with the cut rope and he whirled up and away, flung into the high reaches of the sky by the fierce updraft. Below him, he caught spinning glimpses of the man swinging right side up in the air, and the rope going sharply taut on that side, so that the Emperor's chair heeled steeply and swung. But they were climbing again, not falling, and another Candaran kajurai was maneuvering into place to do the same exchange with Kojran. Below, far below, the Yngulin ships still followed. But the high-pitched cries from the Yngulin crew now carried thwarted fury, not triumph. And far ahead, at the edge of his sight, Trei could see the great dark dimple in the air that was the bulk of one of the big Islands.

This time it was not despair that made him close his eyes. It was the sure knowledge that he didn't have to look, because everything was over, and it was all well. Everything was well. His back still felt as though red-hot knives had been shoved up under his shoulder blades, but it didn't even matter. Yngulin ships might sail in Island waters, yes, and no Tolounnese ships were in sight, and later he might worry about that, but right now he shut his eyes and lay quietly on the rushing wind, wings locked, and knew everything would be fine.

He woke in a dim, unfamiliar room that smelled of soap and of something sharp and astringent. A great lassitude held him, so that he did not immediately open his eyes. He felt safe; his breaths came slowly and quietly. The air moved gently against his face, a light breeze that carried the ever-present scent of the sea. The room was cool, so he knew, without having to think about it, that he was in one of the underground rooms carved out of the stone of a Floating Island. But not the novitiate; he knew that, too. The smells were wrong, and the quiet. He did not know where else he could be, but he found himself incurious about that, as he was incurious about everything ... he could not remember how he had come to this place. But that was all right. Eventually he would remember. He thought maybe he would just go back to sleep ... but something niggled at the back of his mind, some thought or memory, and he moved, suddenly frightened without remembering why he should be afraid.

"Trei," said a quiet, familiar voice.

Trei blinked. His eyes felt gritty. He blinked again, and drew a deeper breath. The room *was* dim. Even with his eyes open, he could see very little. The light that came in through a window high in the opposite wall was the pearl-gray of very early morning. It was morning. He remembered ... he wasn't sure what he remembered.

"Trei," said the voice again, no more loudly than before. A hand touched his shoulder. "You're awake."

Trei tried to answer, but his mouth was too dry to speak. He shifted, meaning to sit up, and found his arms too weak to push himself up. He didn't understand this weakness, and tried harder, but his arms quivered with the strain and he couldn't lift himself more than an inch before falling back, his breath catching.

"Yes, I know," said Ceirfei. It was Ceirfei of course. Trei found he was not surprised.

"You tore every muscle and ligament you own, nearly," said Ceirfei. "Again. One does hope you will find a different hobby. Still, the healers here put you back together. Don't worry about the weakness. That will pass. I'm assured you'll be all right." The hand shifted, supporting him so that he could sit. "You're thirsty. I have a glass of water ... just here. Can you hold it?"

Trei could. His arm trembled at even that weight, and his fingers felt thick and numb, but he could hold the glass. He could sip the water, which was clean and cool and faintly flavored with lemon. It cut through the sticky feeling in his mouth. He remembered, suddenly and all at once, that last flight, the Little Emperor, the failing struggle for height ... the Yngulin ships.

The water spilled.

Ceirfei took the glass out of his hand. "That's all right," he said gently. "You're all right. You're safe. Everyone's safe. The Little Emperor is perfectly well. Or so I presume. I haven't seen him yet, as he hasn't sent for me."

Trei remembered the Little Emperor. He remembered everything all at once. His heartbeat thudded, and he caught his breath sharply—but he was safe. Ceirfei said he was safe. Everyone was safe. Everything was all right. He asked, huskily, "Where –?"

"Candara," said Ceirfei. "You're on Candara. You made it nearly all the way."

He didn't say that they would probably have drowned actually in sight of the Island, but Trei guessed it. Or maybe they would have been picked up by the Yngulin ships. That might have been worse than drowning.

"You did very well," Ceirfei said warmly, ignoring all the things which might have happened. "I've had the tale from

Genrai and the others. You all did *extremely* well." He tipped his head to the side inquiringly, his mouth curving. "Did you truly persuade a Tolounnese decouan to *force* the Emperor into that chair?"

"It was the only thing I could think of," Trei said. He thought of the decouan, of his flat declaration: *You will sit in that chair, Dharoann enna Gaourr, or my men and I will put you in it.* The decouan must be dead now. The *Tivoannè* must have been destroyed. He looked away, out the window. The curtains rippled in the breeze. Even in these few moments, the light had brightened from pearl and rose to a pale translucent gold.

"You were all very brave," said Ceirfei. "I know! Also very desperate. But all's well. I flew in last night. But I think both Dharoann enna Gaourr and I would prefer you be there when we meet at last." His mouth twisted slightly. "He has inquired after you twice, but he has been most careful to have his people imply that he does not want to see me. That will change shortly, I'm sure."

Trei didn't understand.

"He'll want to wait for full day before he summons me," Ceirfei explained. "So that there are plenty of witnesses. Both his own people and mine. He needs to be seen to summon me, and I need to be seen obeying that summons. It's perfectly reasonable." There was only the faintest trace of distaste in his tone. "And, as I say, I think we both prefer that you be there also. Can you stand?" There was an infinitesimal pause. "How are your shoulders?"

Trei stopped, responding to that pause and to something unidentifiable in Ceirfei's tone. "What about my shoulders?"

Ceirfei had been steadying him with a hand under his elbow, but now he stepped back and folded his hands, taking on a more formal stance. "Trei—"

"Tell me the truth!"

Ceirfei met his eyes. "There's no pain now, isn't that right? Your shoulders are fine. They *will* be fine."

Trei didn't believe him.

254

". . . if you stay on the ground for a few *senneri*," Ceirfei conceded.

"A few *senneri!*"

"Perhaps until spring. I'm sorry, Trei. You're very thoroughly grounded until everything knits properly. Trei, look at me."

Trei, who had been about to protest, swallowed the words.

"If you try to fly before you're fully healed," Ceirfei said quietly, "then there's every chance that even if you make it down alive, you'll tear yourself up so badly no healer-mage in the world will be able to put you back together. If that happens, you won't be grounded until spring. You'll be grounded permanently."

Trei said nothing. The silence stretched out between them, filled with the shared knowledge of just what that would mean to a kajurai.

"But it won't happen. Because you'll obey the physicians."

"Yes," muttered Trei. The word tasted sour in his mouth. But it was the only thing he could say.

"Of course you will. Now," and Ceirfei's tone became light and brisk, "it's early, but I took the liberty of collecting some pastries from the kitchens. You'll feel better after you eat something. I believe someone found clothing for you. Gray and black, very appropriate for a novice kajurai, and a red feather for your hair. Yes, here we are. Can you –?"

Trei couldn't, without help. Raising his arms so he could put on his shirt was hard; reaching around to catch the end of his sash was impossible. Ceirfei helped with both, without comment. He pinned Trei's sash with a red pin and looked him up and down. "You'll do. Not fancy, but anyone can see you're a kajurai. Can you walk? Never mind, just sit down again and have a pastry."

Trei obediently sat down on the cot. "What—" he began, and had to stop and clear his throat. "What's been happening? Are things ... is everything ..."

Ceirfei had been rummaging in a linen bag, but paused. "Everything is ... fraught," he said at last. "The Tolounnese secured the heights of Milendri and Bodonè and Candara, all three, before the Yngulin ships could bring warriors up to contest their ... occupation of our cities. We have therefore fallen into an impasse which I believe none of us fully anticipated. Tolounnese and Yngulin ships skirmish below, the Yngulin ships having the advantage. Of course our kajuraihi support the Tolounnese, but we are still outmatched. Upon the Islands, the Tolounnese hold fast. You were quite right to say that Tolounnese soldiers are the best in the world. For which I thank the Gods! But the Tolounnese can move only defensively, while the Yngulin warriors strike where they will." He glanced sidelong at Trei. "Perhaps Dharoann enna Gaourr will find a way to break the deadlock, now that you have delivered him to us. For which I thank *you*, Trei, as well as the Gods. If the Little Emperor of Tolounn cannot find a way for us all to victory, then he too will fall in defeat here. I imagine he will therefore be highly motivated."

Trei grinned at Ceirfei's tone. "He would be anyway, you know. He hates to lose. He's not used to it—and we beat him last summer. He won't want to lose again now!"

"Good," said Ceirfei, and handed Trei a pastry.

Trei found it impossible to lift his arm to take the pastry. Was it supposed to be like that? Maybe the damage was worse than the physicians had told Ceirfei. Maybe they just hadn't wanted anybody telling Trei the truth—maybe there was already no hope, even if he didn't try to fly again until spring. Maybe the truth was he would *never fly again* ...

"Trei?" said Ceirfei.

"I'm fine," Trei said. His voice sounded surprisingly normal. He took a deep breath and used both hands to lift the pastry. His shoulders didn't actually *hurt*. That had to be a good sign. He believed that, determinedly. He asked suddenly, thinking of pastries, "Araenè?"

"She was well when I last saw her. Anxious for you, but she knows you are well."

"She—"

"Eat," Ceirfei said firmly. "I'm perfectly sure Master Tnegun would have informed me if your cousin had found a dragon's egg or a mysterious sphere made by some long-vanished mage or any such peculiar and dangerous object."

Trei grinned, a little unwillingly. The pastry wasn't bad. Not as flaky as it would have been if Araenè had made it, but not bad. Outside, the first bird calls broke the stillness of the early morning, and somewhere a marmoset chattered. Closer at hand, a door opened and closed, and the pattering steps of women, light-footed in soft slippers, hurried by in the hallway, unseen.

"I'm sure—" murmured Ceirfei. But then a man's boots rang across the stone tiles, approaching, and Ceirfei stopped, shrugged, and said, "Or perhaps not."

The man who came in was clad in white, with a violet sash pinned with a gold pin and the dragon badge at shoulder and breast. He had a long knife at his belt, and a leather-clad truncheon; weapons that a Tolounnese soldier would laugh to scorn, but traditional in the peaceful Islands where there were few guardsmen and no real soldiers at all.

"My lord king," said the man, faintly reproving. "I did not know where you'd gone."

"Well, you seem to have found me, Tamasei."

"Yes," said the man, still reproving. "And just as well, my lord king." He straightened and said formally, "Dharoann enna Gaourr, the Little Emperor of Tolounn, bids you come to him. At second bell, my lord king, he bids you come to him; to the Hall of Dragons, without fail." There was an edge of stiff disapproval to that message. The guardsman might as well have said aloud, *How dare he!*

"He *is* the Emperor," Ceirfei said gently. "In fact, he is *my* Emperor. Or we shall certainly hope he is. Thank you, Tamasei. I will need my circlet. I did remember to bring it, didn't I?"

"You did, my lord king."

"Good. I was starting to worry." Ceirfei did not look worried, though in fact Trei thought he was actually more worried than he looked. But he said easily, "Then I shall certainly answer that summons precisely at the appointed time. I imagine quite a lot of people will be present in the Hall of Dragons by second bell. You might make sure of it, Tamasei, if you would be so kind. Slip the word here and there ..." Ceirfei waved a vague hand. "You know where it should go. And you," he added to Trei, "have plenty of time for another pastry, if you don't dawdle."

Trei had no appetite. He took a second pastry to please Ceirfei, but it was like dust in his mouth and he put it down again. He wished he knew what Dharoann enna Gaourr was thinking. He wished he knew what *Ceirfei* was thinking. He wanted to say something, reassure Ceirfei, but the whole situation was impossibly awkward. He said nothing.

The Hall of the Dragons was the petitioner's hall, where people could bring a dispute or contract or other public business before a minister of justice. It wasn't really a hall. It was a pavilion, carved of the native red stone rather than the beautiful imported white stone of Canpra's First City. At first Trei couldn't see why it was called the Hall of the Dragons, and then between one blink and the next he suddenly perceived that the decorative edge that ran right around the scalloped edge of the roof was actually subtly carved with the abstract suggestion of a dragon.

"The sculptor was kajurai," said Ceirfei, watching him.

Trei nodded. He had known that already.

"I fear we must go on."

Trei nodded again, took a deep breath of warm air, and walked forward. His arms and shoulders didn't seem as tired, suddenly, and he was starting to feel that his hands really did belong to him. Trei thought it was the dragon, but it might have been the gathering warmth of the day. He asked, "What are you going to say to the Emperor?"

Ceirfei shrugged. "It depends on what he says to me. If it starts to go wrong, try to advise me, if you can." He led the way up the wide shallow curving stairs, each stair just a little too broad for comfort, and into the Hall of Dragons.

There were a lot of other people present. Ceirfei had sent for them, of course. Or at least arranged for them to be there. Trei remembered that, after a moment. But it seemed like a lot. Important people: ministers and well-born men and a lot of Tolounnese soldiers. Yes, Ceirfei had said he'd brought the Tolounnese soldiers up from the fleet. That they'd already defended Candara against the Yngulin warriors. They looked like they could defend Candara against anything: broad-shouldered men in the black and gray and red of Tolounnese soldiers, like a wall between the world and the center of the pavilion. But they recognized Ceirfei, or possibly Trei, or maybe both of them, and stepped aside with respectful nods.

Dharoann enna Gaourr, the Little Emperor of Tolounn, waited for them in the center of the pavilion. There was a chair there, just the one. It reminded Trei of the one in the throne room in the palace in Canpra: a heavy thing of stone, with a high, flaring back and wide arms. Like the outside of the pavilion, the chair was subtly carved. The flaring back suggested the curves of a dragon's wings, feathers implied with a repeated abstract motif in the carving. Something in the way the vaulted ceiling twisted above the chair suggested the long curving neck of the dragon, and though they had not been explicitly carved into the ceiling, Trei could almost make out the quills behind the faint suggestions of the dragon's long head, and see the deep-set eye. Though so abstract it was nearly invisible, somehow the carved dragon seemed to look right at them. Trei doubted the Emperor could possibly find that a comfortable chair to sit in, or this a comfortable hall to occupy. Even if he had been invited to occupy it.

He stood up when they came in.

The Little Emperor looked every bit an Emperor. He wore the plain black and gray and red of a Tolounnese soldier, but no one could have mistaken him for an ordinary soldier. He looked unmistakably royal.

Ceirfei walked forward. Young as he was, he looked every bit as royal as the Little Emperor. This moment was so clearly for the two of them that Trei stopped without waiting for Ceirfei to signal him.

For what seemed a long time, Ceirfei stood facing the Emperor, not moving. Neither he nor the Emperor spoke. Their eyes met, and held. The Emperor was expressionless, remote as the sky. Trei could not see Ceirfei's face, but knew from the set of his shoulders how he would look: reserved. Immovably calm. In that moment, they looked somehow very much alike, the young man who wanted to be kajurai and had become king, and the ambitious Tolounnese Emperor who stood at the pinnacle of his power. Trei wondered whether Dharoann enna Gaourr had given up anything to achieve that ambition, and if so, whether he remembered that sacrifice now.

Ceirfei knelt. He made it a formal gesture, a gesture of fealty but somehow not of surrender. He said, in a clear, carrying voice, "Dharoann enna Gaourr, Emperor of Tolounn. Will you take the Floating Islands into your hands, from the greatest to the least, in your name and in the name of the Great Emperor and in the sight of the Gods, to hold and to rule? Will you take the people of the Floating Islands into your hands, to rule and to protect against their enemies?"

Dharoann enna Gaourr answered formally, "In the sight of men and of the Gods, I claim the Floating Islands, from the greatest to the least, and declare that they once more belong to Tolounn as they did long ago. I swear that I and the Great Emperor above me will rule them generously and honorably, in accordance with the will and dictates of the Gods Who are above us all, and guard the Islands closely against whatsoever enemies may threaten to do harm to their people."

"Then the Floating Islands are yours," said Ceirfei. He lifted the circlet from his head with both hands and held it out.

The Emperor did not smile. He gave a very slight nod, and then leaned forward and lifted the offered circlet, in both hands as Ceirfei had offered it. Then he glanced up and around the pavilion. His gaze was stern and powerful; when the Emperor's gaze crossed his, Trei felt that contact almost as a physical touch. He bowed, not even thinking about the gesture. He could feel the same kind of reaction go through the gathering, as though a sharp wind had bent down the stalks in the field.

Ceirfei stayed where he was, kneeling before the Emperor. But, though he did not move, Trei could see that he had flushed, and he could see the tightness in his shoulders and back, so he knew Ceirfei wasn't as calm as he looked. The Emperor had not given him permission to rise. Trei wasn't sure what that meant. He waited. Everyone waited, not presuming to move or speak.

Finally, the Emperor asked, his voice level, "Ceirfei Feneirè, who rules here?"

After the barest hesitation, Ceirfei answered, "You do, O Emperor. No one could mistake it."

"You have set the Floating Islands and all their people into my hands. I have taken them. Do you yield yourself as well into my hands?"

This time, there was no hesitation at all. "Yes, O Emperor. I await your will."

The Emperor leaned forward, offering the circlet back to Ceirfei. "As you yield to me, I raise you up. Take back your crown from my hands, Ceirfei Feneirè, king of the Floating Islands. You may stand."

Ceirfei took the circlet, set it back on his head, and got to his feet without a word. His color was still high, but he stood straight and looked the Emperor in the face.

"We shall converse," the Emperor said to him. He glanced around the pavilion once more. "You may all go."

But he kept Trei in place with the crook of one finger. A handful of his own people stayed as well: officers of rank and one decouan with his men, probably as an honor guard. After the crowded gathering, it seemed very few. Once everyone else had gone, there was a slight pause. Then the Emperor said, "A bold and brave move, Ceirfei Feneirè, to bring my men up to your heights before ever you spoke to me; before ever the emissaries you sent to me could return to you."

Ceirfei inclined his head. "Gods grant I was wise to do so, O Emperor, and wise to set my Islands and my people into your hands, since it is certainly impossible to take them back now. But I believed you would protect my people when I know I cannot, and indeed, so you have sworn to do. Of course I trust the word and the honor of the Little Emperor of Tolounn. I think you will find that the people of the Floating Islands are worth defending."

"I'm certain I shall," said the Emperor, and paused again, regarding Ceirfei. Who did not bow his head. Trei wanted to nudge him, but wasn't sure he dared. After a moment, the Emperor's mouth tightened. But he went on, "I have not ceded the right to appoint a provincar over the Floating Islands. You know this?"

Ceirfei nodded. "I am aware of that, of course. I ask you to appoint no one above me, O Emperor. That would cause unnecessary consternation among my people, and thus possibly difficulties for you."

The Emperor answered, his tone flat, "You need not explain this to me. I declare the feather crown is also the mark of the provincar of the Floating Islands. This is the precedent I set, which I will set into law: that the king of the Floating Islands is also their provincar, and responsible to Tolounn in that capacity. Though I warn you," he added scrupulously, "that any provincar who seriously offends the Emperors of Tolounn will be removed from his office, and the Floating Islands will not prove an exception. But this I grant you for perpetuity: that the people of the Floating Islands may select their king according to their customs, and the Emperors of Tolounn will strive to find their choice acceptable as provincar."

"A most generous gesture," said Ceirfei, slowly. "Thank you, O Emperor." He did not bow his head, but looked steadily into the Emperor's face.

The Emperor's fingers tightened on the arms of his chair. Ceirfei must have seen that—yes, Trei could tell he *did* see it, but he didn't seem to understand. It hadn't occurred to Trei that Ceirfei might not understand what the Emperor meant, but now he saw that he didn't, or at least not all of it—and Ceirfei didn't realize that the Emperor was taking his manner for deliberate insolence. Trei cleared his throat and came forward one small step.

They both looked at him, with surprisingly similar expressions. Behind the composure, Ceirfei had to be nervous and Dharoann enna Gaourr was probably—certainly—irritated. Maybe even angry. *Probably* angry.

Trei said, "Forgive me, my Emperor. I don't mean to speak out of turn, but Ceirfei doesn't mean to offend you, truly." Then he said to Ceirfei, "Our Emperor wants everyone, all the Islanders, to be *glad* to be part of Tolounn and wonder why they were ever afraid of being made a Tolounnese province, and he wants that to happen right away, immediately, so that everyone on the Islands will be glad to support his men in everything. That's why he made you provincar as well as king, but now he thinks you're taking advantage of the danger we're all in. He thinks you're being deliberately insolent because you know he has no choice but to tolerate it, unless he wants to cause trouble between his people and yours. You should say *my* Emperor now, and you should bow when our Emperor extends a gracious gesture."

Ceirfei and the Little Emperor still had similar expressions, but now they were both surprised and amused. Trei said, as diffidently as he could, "I beg your pardon, if I spoke out of turn."

"Not at all," Ceirfei said at once. "Thank you, Trei." He turned back to the Emperor and bowed. "Forgive me, my

Emperor, and please believe I would never be so stupid as to offend you deliberately. I am indeed very grateful for your generous gesture, which I hope neither of us will ever have cause to regret. I will do everything in my power to ensure that my people—that the people of the Islands support your soldiers in every possible way."

"Our people. Our soldiers," said the Emperor. His tone was still a little dry, but his manner had eased.

Ceirfei bowed again, making the gesture almost look natural. "If you will have it so. Thank you. After the Yngulin threat is gone and we are all safe—"

"Even then, I hope you will not find my generosity begrudging or my honor doubtful, Ceirfei Feneirè."

"I assure you, my Emperor, I have no reservations about either," said Ceirfei.

"Good. Now. Trei Naseida," said the Emperor, and paused.

Trei bowed low. "I'm sorry if I was impudent. I was afraid you might misunderstand each other."

The Emperor made a dismissive gesture. "You are often usefully impudent. I have frequently made note of this. You were extraordinarily impudent when you saved my life. It was a most memorable flight. I understand you in particular took harm of it."

Trei knew he was blushing. "I—"

Dharoann enna Gaourr rose to his feet, came forward one step, and said formally, "I acknowledge I am in your debt, Trei Naseida. You may call upon me, and I will hear you."

Trei could think of nothing to say. He nodded silently.

"And I am grateful for all you have done to make us understand one another," said the Emperor. "But I think now I must speak to your king alone, if he will grant me the favor."

Which was an extremely polite way of phrasing the command for both Trei and Ceirfei. But it was, of course, unmistakably a command. Trei bowed again and stammered

264

something; he did not really know what, and backed away. And only then remembered to look at Ceirfei, who nodded that he should go. So he went, though, once alone, he was not sure where he should go or what he should do.

He wanted to find Araenè. But he couldn't guess where she might be, or whether he might find her all the way from Candara.

18

The next few days made it obvious that the Yngulin lords hadn't expected to find the Tolounnese fleet in the Islands before them, or at least they hadn't expected to find the Tolounnese soldiers already established and defending the Islands. They drew off to consider what they would do. And so everything that had seemed to move so fast now seemed to drag and drag, until Araenè wanted to scream with frustration. She stayed to her apartment, mostly, and gave herself pounding headaches wondering what Master Tnegun and the other mages were doing, and whether they'd found a way to make another sphere like Kanora's, or if they'd thought of anything really effective to use against the Yngulin mages, and tried not to worry. Which was impossible, though the anxiety was as bad as the headaches. Worse.

Two days after she'd hidden in her rooms, Tichorei found her by her pool while she struggled, not very successfully, to once again build the structure in her mind that would summon the right kind of vision into the pool. He leaned out her window, glanced around, and called, "Araenè?"

She glared at him, and he raised a defensive hand. "I know you'd rather have Kanii. But you put such a strong don't-bother-me spell across your door, he couldn't open it."

"That meant I wanted to be left *alone*. What do you *want?*" Araenè demanded, exasperated.

Tichorei swung one long leg and then the other across her windowsill, stepped down into her garden, and came to join her by the pool. He crouched down, folding up his knees awkwardly, and picked up a handful of pebbles, letting them fall through his fingers one at a time, into the pool, little miniature splashes, watching the spreading ripples rather than her face.

"*What?*" Araenè asked again, beginning to be frightened.

"They say he's going to be fine," Tichorei said, glancing up into her face. "All right? They say—"

Cold dread ran through her. "Ceirfei? Trei? Gods weeping! Just *tell* me!"

"Sorry, sorry ... no, look, it's Trei, but he's fine, I swear by the Gods. There was this thing with storms or Yngulin mages or something, we just heard, and he and the other novices wound up actually carrying the Little Emperor almost all the way from Tolounn—"

"They can't have! Not really?"

"They did, though. Everyone's talking about it. They made it to Candara, Araenè, everyone's fine! I guess there are sprains and things—do kajuraihi sprain their arms or their wings? *Can* they sprain their wings? Anyway, they're supposed to rest on Candara for a few days, but Prince Ceirfei's gone to meet them. He'll take care of everything, you know."

If Ceirfei had gone to meet them, he really *would* take care of everything. Araenè sat back, slowly. "You're sure he's all right?" But she knew her cousin must be fine; if they'd made it to Candara, then what could be wrong? She whispered, "I wasn't even watching ..."

Tichorei clicked his tongue impatiently. "You're halfway to overextension. I'm not *blind*, Araenè! You've been working too many spells for vision, and you know that's really too advanced for you anyway! You've been having headaches, haven't you? Well, then!" He got to his feet and shoved his hands in his pockets, staring down at her. "You don't have to stay all penned up here! We've all been watching, and taking turns is a whole lot easier than trying to do it all by yourself."

"I ..."

"You can't hide from everybody forever." Tichorei paused. "Everyone thinks probably we weren't stupid, trying to recapture some of the freed magic from Kanora's sphere.

They think now maybe that releasing that magic here might have protected Milendri. You know that, don't you?"

Araenè snapped, "No one knows anything, because no one's ever really tried to understand dragon magic! All we really *know* is the Islands are still sinking, which will be a joke on the Yngulin king, won't it, if he wins?"

Tichorei flung up his hands. "Fine! Cesei misses you, Kanii worries about you, and I—anyway, we're all in the common workroom if you want to join us! And you'd better, if you want to keep pouring spells for vision into water! Or you *will* overextend, and I don't think Master Tnegun would be pleased to be pulled away from whatever he's doing just to tend to an overextended apprentice!"

Araenè knew that part was definitely true. She fixed her eyes on the ripples in the pool, refusing to look up.

"All right!" Tichorei said, and stalked away, vanishing back through her window.

Once he was gone, Araenè looked up after all. She half wanted to jump up, run after Tichorei, assure him and Kanii and Cesei that she wasn't upset with *them*. But she needed Trei. She had to see him herself, make *sure* he was all right. Even if she wasn't supposed to.

She knew why Master Tnegun had kept her at the hidden school even though she couldn't do anything useful. He'd told her to stay because he thought if she went anywhere, she'd get into *more* trouble. But she didn't see why staying in the hidden school would help, when she'd never had to leave it to get into trouble *before*. So that was just ridiculous.

She needed to talk to Trei. Tichorei had said he was still on Candara and was supposed to rest for a few days, so that meant he'd need another way to come back to Milendri anyway, and after all just stepping through a door to Candara and right back again, that would be perfectly safe. As long as she just made *sure* not to step through any door unless she was positive where it led. Which she *would*.

She jumped to her feet. But not to follow Tichorei or find the other apprentices.

Araenè found Trei sitting in the shade under a puff flower tree, studying a huge pavilion of red stone that loomed across the other side of a wide, cobbled town square. The pavilion wasn't much like anything on Milendri, but she barely spared it a glance. There were lots of people around, mostly standing and muttering to each other in low voices, but Araenè wasn't interested in them either and didn't listen. Trei was alone, though one Islander guardsman stood nearby, scowling alternately at Trei and the pavilion, apparently equally impatient with both. Araenè ignored the guardsman too, studying her cousin. Trei looked all right to her. It was a huge relief.

"Trei," she said, leaning against the heavy, ornate frame of the door she'd called: Akhan Bhotounn—'the friendly one', which was normally cooperative, though sometimes whimsical. She didn't step through to Candara; as long as she didn't, she technically hadn't left the hidden school. Besides, she didn't want to go to Candara; she wanted Trei to come through to Milendri. "How are you?" she asked, a little tentatively, ignoring the guardsman's frown.

"Araenè!" Trei exclaimed. He started to get to his feet, but sank back again. "I'm fine, really!"

Araenè scowled at him. "How *fine* can you be if you can't even stand up?" She transferred her glower to the guardsman. "Tamasei, isn't it? How's my cousin really? What did he do to himself?"

"Araenè!" Trei protested.

The guardsman gave her a professional nod. "Lady mage. Your cousin is well enough; only worn from injury and hard healing, or so it was reported to my lord king."

"I *told* you," said Trei.

"I'm *still* not sure I believe it," Araenè declared. "What did you do to yourself? Tichorei told me you and the others carried the Little Emperor of Tolounn all the way across the sea, but he said you weren't hurt. I didn't know, didn't help, I wasn't watching—I'm so sorry—"

Trei looked embarrassed. "You can't look after me every minute, Araenè! Anyway, it doesn't matter, does it? I'm fine." This time, he made it to his feet, one hand pressed against the tree for balance or support.

Araenè looked her cousin up and down. Now that he was up, he looked all right. Just tired. He'd overextended himself, she guessed—some kajuraihi version of overextension, not the mage kind. Flying too far, carrying too much weight ... though she'd have thought the dragon magic imbued in kajuraihi would protect them better than that ...

She blinked, struck suddenly by a powerful realization that of course kajuraihi magic *was* dragon magic. And that the kajuraihi still had their magic, even though the dragons might have withdrawn. She'd *known* this, of course. Only the realization suddenly seemed important ... the Islands still had kajuraihi, the kajuraihi were almost like dragons ... well, no, but they were a *link* to the dragons. They sort of *contained* dragon magic, didn't they? The same way Kanora's sphere had contained ordinary magic and dragon magic.

Well, not the *same* way, maybe. But still ... She closed her eyes, catching after an idea that unfolded like a magical spell in her mind.

"Araenè?" her cousin asked, sounding worried.

Araenè opened her eyes again. "Look, I want—I need to talk to you. Can you come here, or shall I come there?" Another idea struck her and she asked, "Is Ceirfei there with you?"

"Ceirfei's with the Emperor." Trei glanced across at the pavilion, then gave the guardsman a doubtful look.

"I don't think the king would welcome interruption from anyone, lady mage," the guardsman said with smooth authority, and then continued less smoothly, "It would assuredly be more appropriate to wait until he or the, um, our Emperor signals that their, ah, audience is concluded."

"Yes," Araenè said, thinking about it. "Yes, that's all right. That might even be better, for now." She patted the smooth whorls of the carving on the doorframe and stepped forward, firmly ignoring her suspicion that Master Tnegun would be furious if he found out. She glanced around, but none of the people in the wide, cobbled street turned to stare. They hadn't noticed her stepping out of the door in the air; they were all too busy with their own worries. Well, everyone had plenty to worry about. Only if Araenè's idea worked, then soon maybe there would be one thing fewer, and that would be ... well, that would be worth a lot. Probably it wouldn't work, probably she was all wrong, but Trei ... maybe Trei would know.

She gestured her cousin to sit back down, dropped down to join him, and looked at the guardsman. "Do you mind, Tamasei?"

The guardsman gave her an ironic look, but strolled away to lean against a different tree.

Araenè looked searchingly at Trei. "I just had this idea," she said. "Maybe it's a stupid idea, though. It depends. On kajurai magic and dragon magic and Island magic and everything."

Trei nodded with flatteringly close attention. "All right ... ?"

"Well," Araenè said rapidly, "Kanora's sphere was stuffed full of dragon magic, right? It wasn't made of anything normal, stone or crystal or wood or anything, it was made of the wind—what you kajuraihi call the living wind, which means the kind of wind that holds dragon magic, right? Kanora Ireinamei made that sphere, or that's what everyone says, but that wasn't the kind of thing a mage would make, you know? Mages don't have anything to do with dragon magic, do they? They don't *know* anything about dragon magic. They've never wanted to, I guess, except maybe Cassameirin. And Kanora. The last time I saw him, Cassameirin said something about air and fire, which are aspects of dragon magic, aren't they?"

"I guess ..."

"Well, that makes sense if you think about it, because you know about the fire dragon that lives at the heart of the hidden school? It's all about the balance between earth and fire and the living winds, they're all allied, right?"

"Maybe ..."

She could see he didn't get it, not yet. "Look, they say the labyrinth is the foundation of the hidden school, and that's where I found Kanora's sphere; and it's important for a fire dragon to live at the heart of the school, and there you go, fire and air, Island stone containing dragon-magic. I mean, everything about the Floating Islands depends on dragon magic, not on ordinary spellwork. We *know* that. And Kanora Ireinamei made her sphere out of dragon magic, which definitely wasn't ordinary spellwork. So it's not surprising that Master Tnegun and the others can't figure out how she did it, or how to do it again, because they're mages, and I think ..."

Trei nodded for her to keep going.

"Well," said Araenè, "I think maybe Kanora Ireinamei wasn't just a mage. I think she might also have been a kajurai. There was plenty of human spellwork in that sphere. But that wasn't what it was *for*. That was just to show the dragon magic the shape it should take." Araenè hesitated. "I think."

"Then we can't make another sphere like that," said Trei. "I mean ... you're not kajurai. There aren't any mages who are kajurai." But he was looking at her with his eyebrows raised, obviously waiting for her to go on.

"Well, maybe she wasn't a kajurai herself. Maybe she just worked closely with a kajurai. And," she opened her hands. "Here you are, a kajurai. And I'm a mage—well, not really, but at least I have the mage gift. But Cassameirin said something about the alliance between fire and air and between fire and earth. And about how fire and earth were both allied to glass. So I think ... I wonder ... I think maybe the two of us can put *two* spheres together—I mean, one of Island stone and one of the living winds, one for human magic and one for dragon magic, stone and air, with fire to bind them together so they'd do the same thing as Kanora's sphere—"

"Can you *do* that?" asked Trei.

"I don't know. But if we can prove the idea, if we can show it's possible, don't you think maybe my Master Tnegun and your Wingmaster Taimenai could do it right? Because I bet they could." She looked at her cousin anxiously. "You don't think it's a stupid idea?"

"I think it's an idea," Trei said decisively. "And I don't think we have enough of those to throw one away. It doesn't sound stupid at all. It sounds like it might work. I think Ceirfei needs to know about it, first." He looked around. "I guess we should tell Tamasei and then go find Ceirfei—"

A great rushing wind roared down across them, across the square, across the whole Island: not the ordinary sea wind nor the rolling rain-heavy winds of the winter monsoons, but a hard and terrible wind, gritty and hot and dry, smelling of stone and iron. Trei yelped, staggering, and Araenè screamed, more startled than frightened. The wind parched the moisture from her mouth and sucked the breath from her lungs so that she gasped for air. Her eyes stung; she squeezed them shut and caught Trei's hand in hers, steadying them both. The abrasive storm winds slashed against her cheeks and arms. She tried to scream again, but couldn't catch her breath. Trei dragged at her, but she was too disoriented to even know which direction he wanted them to run. She reached out with her other hand, snatching desperately after quiet and calm air, and found intricately carved wood under her hand, and a familiar knob, and jerked the door open, and pulled Trei after her, away from the storm and Candara and into the quiet depths of the hidden school.

Tichorei caught her, and steadied Trei. "Great generous Gods, Araenè!" he exclaimed. "Tell me you didn't find any more ancient spheres or dragons or anything!"

Araenè pulled away, shaking. She had grit in her hair and her teeth, and all her exposed skin felt abraded and tender. She glared at Tichorei, then around the workroom, crowded with startled and alarmed apprentices and cluttered with cracked glass spheres and basins of water and one heavy

273

obsidian sphere that teetered on the edge of a table and even as she put a hand out toward it, fell. The shattering crash and flying shards of volcanic glass sent everyone ducking and left behind an echoing, fraught silence.

"It's the Yngulin mages, of course," Trei said, breaking that pause. He looked at Araenè. "I think it was a really good idea, but it might be too late."

"It's *not* too late!" Araenè declared. "It can't be! Even if—anyway, there's still me and there's still you, only I guess now we have to do more than just prove the idea. I mean, if nobody else can do it, we have to. We have to at least *try!*"

"Araenè ..."

"It's true we don't know enough! But you know who might?" Araenè gripped Trei's arms hard, not just for balance, but in sheer excitement. "You know who must know *all about* working with dragon magic? *Dragons.* Don't you think?"

"*What* are you talking about?" Tichorei said warily. Araenè ignored him.

Trei didn't say anything. She couldn't tell whether her cousin was stunned beyond speech, or thinking about what she'd said. She said quickly, "If it turns out that a dragon *does* know how to put the right kind of magic into a sphere, then it doesn't matter that *we* don't know how. I mean, we need to put a spell into a sphere, but Tichorei could do that part, we know that, because he did it before. Maybe that's all we need to do, make one ordinary sphere, if a dragon made the other kind of sphere. You could fly our sphere up to ask them—" She hesitated, uncertain. Trei was shaking his head.

Araenè said, hurt, "Maybe it wouldn't work, but don't you think it's at least worth trying? I mean, I think I should *try* this, I think everyone should try everything, since otherwise Yngul—"

"I can't do it. I can't, Araenè."

Araenè didn't understand why he was so hesitant. She *knew* he was brave. "You can fly up and find a dragon, I know you can, you've done it before. The dragon spoke to you, all that about glass and fire and calling the winds, I think this is what it meant. Don't you think it's a least worth *trying* to find out if this is what it meant?"

"It's not that." Trei was gazing at her. He said at last, "Araenè, I'm not supposed to fly. For a long time. I mean, maybe not until spring, even. I guess I tore up my shoulders. And I'd already strained—" he made a small, vague gesture. "Everything, I guess. So I'm not supposed to fly."

Araenè opened her mouth, but closed it again without speaking. "Oh," she said at last. "Oh. Then I don't know."

"Araenè ..." Tichorei said, speaking slowly and deliberately. "Maybe you'd better explain your brilliant new idea to us all?"

"Her *brilliant new idea*," said Kepai, rolling his eyes, and his twin added, "The hope of the Islands!"

"Shut up!" snapped Kanii. "Do you have any ideas at all? Then shut up!"

Araenè ignored them all, though she was surprised and happy that Kanii had defended her. She said to Tichorei, "It doesn't matter, if Trei can't fly. Or maybe ... maybe we can find another kajurai ..." but Araenè knew that there was no chance of getting anyone important to listen to her. Any kajuraihi left would be out in the sky right now, in the Yngulin storm, trying their best to bring down the Yngulin ships. She looked at Trei. "Another novice, maybe? Nescana was with you, that time, wasn't she?"

"But—" began Tichorei.

The hidden school jolted beneath and around them, swung sideways, cracked open, shuddered, and closed up again. Everyone clung to whatever they could reach: the heavy tables, or shelves that tilted and spilled papers and feathers in all directions; the light-lit spheres swinging from their chains or each other. Kanii flung an arm around Cesei and kept the much smaller boy from sprawling; Tichorei and Trei both caught at Araenè. She let them steady her, caught her breath, and tried to figure out what had happened.

"It's the dragon at the heart of the school," Cesei's young voice said shakily. He had shaken free from Kanii's hold and crawled across the floor to crouch over a spilled pool of hot melted wax. He'd drawn a symbol in the wax, something mathematical and abstruse that Araenè didn't recognize. He raised a young, woebegone face to look up at the rest of them. "It's gone. It's *gone*. We lost the sky dragons, and now the Yngulin mages have driven off our fire dragon and we don't have anything left."

"That can't be right," said Kepai, uneasily.

"Cesei knows more math than any of us," Kanii began.

"I don't care!" shouted Kebei, balling up his fists and stepping up beside his twin.

"Hush!" commanded Tichorei. "Cesei *is* right. You can *feel* it's gone. Just like last summer, when the other dragon—" he hesitated, glancing at Araenè, and finished lamely, "Anyway, it's gone."

"I'm going to find Master Akhai," Jeneki said, firmly, not looking at Tichorei. "Taobai?" He darted a meaningful look at Araenè and walked out. Taobai shrugged at her, half scared and half apologetic, and followed Jeneki. The twins didn't say anything at all, just darted out the door after the others.

"I bet they don't," murmured Kanii. When everyone looked at him, he shrugged. "I called Master Kopapei just now, you know. I mean, when it, uh, happened." He looked faintly embarrassed. "Of course he didn't answer. I mean, we're all fine, aren't we? And they've got more important things to do."

Araenè shrugged, feeling lost and ignorant and young and helpless. She looked at Trei. "That wind –?"

"Nothing like a dragon wind," Trei said. "Nothing like. That's the kind of storm they brought against the Emperor's ship—"

"The Yngulin mages brought it," declared Araenè. "And now they've got rid of the fire dragon at the heart of the school!" *Her* dragon. She was startled by the hot, possessive anger that welled up in her. She glared at Trei. "Fire and air, both gone! We need them *back*!"

"I know," Trei agreed. "All right! You're right. We have to do something, right now."

"Araenè?" demanded Tichorei, looking from one of them to the other.

"It's something good, I bet!" said Cesei, bouncing, his eyes sparkling, already recovered from his recent fright. "You've figured out how to get another fire dragon?"

"Don't be stupid!" said Kanii, but he almost looked like he, too, thought Araenè might have a fire dragon hidden in her pocket.

So then she had to explain her idea about Kanora Ireinamei being both a mage and a kajurai at the same time, and about replacing Kanora's sphere with one each of earth and air. *And* her idea that maybe Kanora hadn't made her sphere alone. That maybe a dragon had helped her make it. That maybe a dragon would know how to make another sphere out of the living winds.

There was a respectful silence.

"Maybe this, maybe that! We need to ask Master Kopapei," Kanii said at last. He pushed his hair, always disorderly, out of his eyes with a worried gesture.

Araenè glared at him, trying not to show her own anxiety. "Oh, we need to ask Master Kopapei! I'm sure I'd like to! I'd like to ask Master Tnegun, too, or even Master Akhai, but how likely are they to answer? You call your master right now. Go on, call him!"

Kanii sighed, but he didn't answer. They both knew perfectly well none of the mages would answer. Not now.

"Master Kopapei!" Tichorei said aloud, in a clear, sharp tone. He turned his head from side to side as though he was listening, or as though he was peering through the walls of the school after something small and far away. They all stood still, waiting.

Nothing happened. Araenè didn't know whether she was disappointed or not. Well, now, of course she *was*

277

disappointed, but on the other hand, what if Master Kopapei had said her idea was a stupid one? What would they do then, when there wasn't anything at all left to do? She looked at Tichorei, wondering if *he* thought her idea was stupid; or whether he might even have thought of something else useful to do, something that didn't involve dragons or making things out of dragon magic, or anybody flying up to find dragons in the hope the dragons would talk to them and know what to do.

Tichorei said, his tone reluctant but resolved, "If we made a sphere out of the red stone of the Island. Say we did. If we put human magic in it ... say we did that, too. And got the dragons to put their magic in a glass sphere, make it into a sphere of the winds." He glanced around the room, at Kanii and young Cesei and Trei and finally met Araenè's eyes. "Fusing the magic of two spheres together, that's not something we know anything about."

"Except we know Kanora Ireinamei did something even harder, making her one sphere," Araenè pointed out. "This ought to be easier than that!"

"Maybe a dragon did it for her. Maybe she was kajuraihi and figured out how to do it herself. That's not to say *we* can do anything of the same kind—"

Araenè started to protest.

"*But*," said Tichorei, raising his voice, "I can't think of anything else better to try, and I'm afraid we don't have a lot of time to think about it. Kanii? Cesei?"

"I don't know," said Kanii, looked worriedly at Araenè, just as Cesei exclaimed, "Oh, but it'll work, it's a great idea! Wouldn't you like to work with dragon magic? If it works we'll learn all kinds of things about how magic works! Anyway, everyone's right, we have to try something!"

Araenè looked at Trei. Her cousin didn't say anything, so she said herself, "We can make the spheres, and Nescana can carry the one up to the dragons—"

Trei said, "I'm the one who's held fire in my hands. I'm the one who's supposed to summon both winds and fire."

278

Araenè bit her lip. "Are you *sure?*"

Trei quoted, "'You have held fire in your hands. Fire attends the birth of glass. Fire burns at the heart of glass.' What glass, except glass you'll make, Araenè? 'Call the winds. Summon fire. Set the sea alight with the living winds.' That's what it said. Nescana's got a gift for pulling the winds, but what about the fire? Do you think we dare ignore that part? Just because it *might* hurt me to fly?"

"Might?" Araenè said hopefully. "They only said it *might* hurt you?" She looked her cousin up and down. He looked perfectly fine. But she was suspicious anyway. "If Nescana's got a gift with pulling the winds, she might at least help you. Isn't that true?"

"Of course it's true!" Cesei said instantly, with a child's insouciant disregard for danger, and especially for other people's danger. "Of course we should do this! We can make a glass sphere for the dragons, that's no trouble—at least, it's easy enough to clear all the magic out of a sphere, we can do that—"

"Get one then," ordered Tichorei, in a brisk tone. "A good glass sphere, fetch one here, and mind it doesn't have any cracks or flaws. Now," he went on, turning to the others once the little boy had obediently run off to find such a sphere, "I agree we might as well do something as nothing, Araenè, but I admit, I don't know exactly how to do something like this. Kanii, have you ever heard of anything that might help?"

Kanii shook his head. Fair and stocky and usually comfortable to be around, he looked worried and tense now. "But we could make a glass sphere right now, and figure out the stone one, um, I mean—"

"You mean, while my cousin risks his life flying the glass one up to the heights," Araenè said hotly, though she wasn't even sure why she was angry; of course Kanii meant exactly that, but they all knew it anyway. *That* was why she was angry, of course: because she knew Trei would risk everything on a plan none of them was sure would work. He had before, and she'd let him, and he'd almost died. And now he would do it again and she couldn't stop him because what other choice did any of them have?

Kanii and Tichorei had been muttering together, and now Tichorei put a hand on her shoulder. Araenè almost pulled away, but it was actually oddly comforting. He said, his tone almost gentle, "Araenè, why don't you go with Trei to talk to Nescana? And we'll bring your glass sphere to the novitiate when we have it. All right?"

Araenè stared at him. He was giving her an excuse to spend time privately with her cousin, she knew. In case ... well, just in case.

It was a kindness that surprised her, in Tichorei. And then somehow she found she wasn't surprised after all. Kanii had suggested it, of course, it was just like Kanii to do something like that, that wasn't surprising at all, but somehow she wasn't surprised that Tichorei would be kind, either. She couldn't smile, but she nodded at them both and took Trei's hand, and turned to find a door that would take them both to the kajurai novitiate.

19

Araenè was really upset. Trei didn't blame her, but it made it hard to hide his own growing fear. Fear of failure, mostly. Fear of what failure would cost them all. But there was also fear of what Araenè's idea might cost him personally, even if it succeeded and everything worked exactly as they hoped. If they failed, they'd all have other things to worry about. But what if they succeeded? He tried not to think of what it would be like, to be grounded for the rest of his life. To live in Canpra and watch kajuraihi fly every day and know he couldn't. He *did* think of it, of course. He couldn't help it.

He knew he wouldn't be able to bear it, if that happened. Even if everything else worked out perfectly. He'd leave the Islands. He would have to. Except Araenè was here, his only cousin, his only family in the world, and so how could he leave the Islands?

He tried not to think about how Araenè would feel if her idea worked, but left him grounded. That was almost worse than imagining how he would feel himself. He thought if that happened, if he left the Islands, she would come with him. Somewhere. He had no idea where. But how could he ask her to leave the Islands, the place she'd started to make for herself in the hidden school? Could he pretend to be contented hard enough to fool his cousin? He was fairly sure he couldn't.

"It won't happen," Araenè said fiercely. She'd opened a door to the novitiate dining hall and they'd stepped through, but now she stopped where she was, holding it open, refusing to let go and look for Nescana. She stared at Trei, her eyes wide and worried, belying her fierce tone. "It'll be fine. They fixed you up last time, didn't they? Everything will be fine."

Trei nodded.

"And Master Camatii! He's good at healing magic, you know. That's what he *does*, healing magic. He's the best in the Islands, or he wouldn't be at the hidden school, right?"

"Right," said Trei.

"Oh, Trei! You'd better not try after all! Nescana can do it herself—she was there when the dragon spoke to you last time, maybe it *was* really speaking to her after all! *She* can carry up the glass sphere and talk to the dragons and everything!"

"You know we can't risk it," Trei said, and bit his lip, knowing he sounded far too angry.

"Can't risk what?" Nescana asked, coming in from the hall that led to the balcony. "I can do what? Did you say something about talking to dragons? I don't know, Araenè, I don't think it *was* talking to me that other time. I've thought and thought about it, and I think it was talking to Trei." She looked from one of them to the other. "What?"

Araenè crossed her arms and Trei could see she was going to be stubborn. He explained himself, while his cousin glared off the other way, refusing to look at either of them.

"I'll help. I'll do anything I can to help, Trei. Of course I will," Nescana said earnestly, once she understood Araenè's idea. She looked from Trei to Araenè. "Maybe the dragon was talking to me after all. Maybe it was. But I don't know if we can take that chance. I'm sorry, but I don't. It's awful out there."

Nescana's hands were actually trembling. Trei didn't blame her: she'd been watching the dark Yngulin storm from the novitiate balcony, she said; the Yngulin ships riding those storm winds while the Tolounnese ships were battered aside. If there hadn't already been Tolounnese soldiers in Canpra, the Islands would have been lost. Nescana hadn't said that, but Trei was Tolounnese enough to know which way the battle was going. He thought he could *feel* it, the way he felt the hot Yngulin wind against his face.

"But I can help Trei pull the winds," Nescana went on. She looked anxiously at Araenè, as though afraid she wouldn't believe her. "I can do that better than anybody. I really can. The rest of them don't like to think there's anything I can do better than they can." She rolled her eyes. "Boys!"

Araenè nodded, clearly agreeing. Trei hadn't really thought how alike they were, Nescana surrounded by boy novices exactly the way his cousin was surrounded by boy apprentices. Though Nescana had never lied to anybody about who she was, so maybe it was easier for her. And everybody knew the dragons chose who to make into a kajurai, anyway, so Trei didn't have a lot of patience with Rekei or Kojran resenting Nescana.

Araenè said firmly, "The boys at Cesera's, the ones trying to get noticed by a master chef, they're like that, too."

"They're *all* like that," declared Nescana, tossing her head. "Except Trei." She glanced his way, not smiling, but questioningly.

"Anybody can see you're both gifted," Trei said, a little impatiently. "But—"

"It's because he's from Tolounn," Araenè said to Nescana, interrupting her cousin. Both girls nodded wisely, though Trei suspected neither of them had much idea what Tolounn was like compared to the Islands.

"But it's good Nescana's gifted," Araenè added, now speaking just to Trei and very seriously. "Because if you can't fly, you can't, and we'll just have to hope this works anyway—"

"And if it doesn't?" Trei looked her steadily in the face.

"It will—" Araenè began.

Trei said bluntly, "If we do this wrong, then even if your idea is a good one, we're going to lose. We won't have time to do it over. Then those of us who are left can watch Yngul and Tolounn fight it out. Only it won't actually be *us*. Because the Yngulin mages would never leave even an apprentice mage free on Milendri would they? Nor a novice kajurai. They'll take us back to Yngul, if they don't kill us. Think,

Araenè! Staying here won't keep me safe. It'll just be a different kind of danger—a worse kind."

Araenè shivered, but she didn't argue. "*Can* you do this? Tell me the truth!"

"I can. I will." Trei looked at Nescana. "If you'll help me. I'll do it. I can do it. I don't know what the dragons will do, but I *can* carry Araenè's sphere up to the vault of heaven."

"All right," said Nescana, very quietly. She looked at Araenè. "You've got this sphere? This glass one?"

"Tichorei and the others are going to bring one," explained Araenè. "Then while you and Trei fly up to the heights, we'll make the other sphere, the one of stone. Native Island stone. We think that's right. We're almost sure." She glanced quickly at Trei and away again, and he knew she was thinking about being wrong and about how he might ground himself permanently for nothing.

"If you're wrong, we really will have other things to worry about," he pointed out.

Araenè rolled her eyes. "Oh, that's comforting. I feel so much better now." She turned before Trei could answer, looking expectantly at the door.

Tichorei stepped through, looking grave and solemn and rather frightened. He held a delicate bubble of glass in one hand. He nodded quickly to Trei, glanced curiously at Nescana, and said to Araenè, "We put in light and summoning and finding your way, silence and breath when there is no breath. The spell for turning air into glass, that's one we don't know ..."

"Dragon magic," said Araenè, not sounded very sure.

"We hope so, certainly." Tichorei stepped forward and held the sphere out to Trei with a formal gesture, as though he was presenting some kind of ceremonial weapon. In a sense, Trei supposed he was. He took it carefully. It didn't feel as fragile and light in his hands as he'd expected.

"We don't need to know how to make it work," Araenè said nervously. "Right? Because the dragon will. Or if it doesn't—but it *will*. It must."

"It will," Trei said, with all the surety he could manage. "Of course it will." He looked at Nescana.

"I'll help you with your wings," she said, very quietly.

They climbed in a narrow spiral, riding the warm air that pressed upward from Milendri, turn and turn and turn again, each circle higher than the one before. Trei's wings were barely moving; the rising air did most of the work. Nescana flew just below and behind him, pulling the winds upward so they could rise easily and smoothly. Her pull was steady and constant, much better than Trei could have done. He hardly had to do anything at all, just tilt a feather now and then to turn.

His shoulders didn't hurt at all. Well, there was a kind of ache, but it was nothing. He could fly forever if it didn't get worse than that. Those healers, they just hadn't known how easy flying could be. It wasn't even really flying. It was really just resting on the wind. You could lock your wings and just relax into the gentle grip of the wind. How dangerous could that possibly be?

He refused to think about getting high enough to rise above the warm thermals. Up there the air would be cold and thin and they would need to work much harder to gain height. Harder than usual, even, because the dragon magic was so terribly weak now.

The dragons were so high, much higher than kajuraihi normally flew. Trei looked up occasionally, though it was awkward and strained his neck. He thought he caught a glint of light now and then, from something tremendously high that could only be a dragon. Maybe the highest winds would still be filled with their magic. That might make flying easier.

He never looked down. He was too aware of what he would see below: the thinning crystalline breezes that still surrounded Milendri in an ever-shrinking circle, and beyond that, the too-close waves, driven into chaotic frenzy by the fierce dark storm winds of the Yngulin mages. The Yngulin ships climbing slowly upon those winds and docking against the white towers of Canpra. The kajuraihi, their wings ashen-red and burnt-orange and gray-gold in that dark storm, fighting to get at the Yngulin ships before they could draw their lines fast to the Milendri. So many kajuraihi, flying hard and fast, dodging the sheeting flights of scorpion bolts from the Yngulin ships. Or failing to dodge, and falling, pierced and screaming. He tried not to listen, but he couldn't stop hearing those cries, faint with distance.

Trei tilted the feathers at the tip of one wing and swept around in a long, slow turn. The wind that whipped past his face carried a noticeable chill. He could feel the lack of lift. Cold, thin air made for hard flying, no matter how gifted a kajurai might be. Glancing down, Trei could see the rippling strata of density and warmth below them, but above were only the still, crystalline heights.

"No dragons!" Nescana shouted up at him.

"They'll be there!" Trei shouted back. "We need to get higher!" He began a more active kind of flight, long smooth strokes, not too fast. He could feel the cold winds come up hard from below, which was Nescana's work, of course. He couldn't tell whether they were as high yet as the other time. When he looked down, Milendri seemed so small; he could have covered the whole Island with the palm of one hand. He couldn't see the ships at all, but the dark Yngulin storms covered a huge area. He stroked harder, the tips of his primary feathers whistling through the wind.

"You're all right?" called Nescana.

"Not much higher now!" Trei answered, hoping it was true. He could feel the effort now, not pain yet, but an uncomfortable tightness all through his shoulders and back that promised pain to come. Nescana called again, but he couldn't make out what she said and didn't try, not wanting to hear any suggestion they turn back. They couldn't turn back; he knew that. And if there weren't any dragons after all ... he didn't want to think of that. He was silent, putting his effort into flying.

He tried to look up, but it *was* awkward. He wanted to roll, turn over on his back, fly upside down for a moment, look for dragons that way. But he was afraid to try turning over—flying upside down would let him rest his arms and shoulders, but he was afraid of what twisting in the air might do to his shoulders.

Nescana suddenly came around beside him, her wingtip nearly brushing his. Then she beat her wings hard, rising and slanting off to the side. Then she twisted abruptly, turning completely over, dropping sharply because she didn't know how to keep her height when she flew upside down. Trei couldn't explain it—he could have shown her, but of course not now—he would teach her that later, he resolved. Or if he couldn't—he stumbled over that thought, half thinking that Genrai could teach her that maneuver and half trying not to think at all. Without her helping, his wings seemed suddenly almost heavy; he had to work much harder just to keep from sliding downward after her. The thought of having to climb up the same column of air twice made him grit his teeth and use his wings hard, ignoring the warning ache in his back.

"There!" screamed Nescana. "Right above us! But so high! So high! I didn't know the sky went up that high!"

"The sky goes up forever!" called Trei. He wanted to laugh. A dragon! Above them, so it could only be waiting for them. He knew it was, he was sure of it—almost sure—he *was* sure. He wouldn't let himself doubt it.

Nescana twisted about again, falling well below Trei, but then flying hard to catch up. Which she did really fast, so that Trei realized he hadn't been climbing fast himself. But the certainty that there *was* a dragon above them sent strength pouring though him, and then a sharp, clean wind came up hard under his wings—that was Nescana again—and the pain eased. So he knew it was all right; he couldn't have torn anything yet or it would surely hurt more, and they were almost high enough—and anyway, the sky went up forever, right to the vault of heaven, so of course they would be able to fly up that high.

He didn't let himself think about the long, long flight back down. Or least of all about the possibility that the dragon couldn't or wouldn't help them after all, so the whole effort would have been wasted.

The dragon stayed above them. Nescana turned now and then to look. Trei couldn't turn and had given up even trying to tip his head back far enough to see. He flew grimly, steadily. Nescana helped. She flew behind Trei, mostly. He knew it was because she was afraid to let him out of her sight in case he faltered and she didn't see. Not that there would be a lot she could do that she wasn't already doing. He wanted to tell her that he knew he'd never have made it up so high without her help, but he couldn't spare the breath to shout.

And the dragon was still above them. It never seemed to get closer. It was as though it constantly drifted higher, maintaining its distance as they worked to get closer. Trei hoped that was his imagination. Araenè had seemed so sure that the dragons would *want* to help, that they would want another sphere like Kanora's to be made. She couldn't have been wrong. She wasn't wrong. She was right, and he'd been right to insist on making this flight, and it would work, everything would work –

"Above you!" Nescana shouted, her voice high and urgent. "Trei! Above you!"

Trei backwinged before he even looked. He felt the effort in every muscle he owned, but he hardly noticed. From Nescana's tone, he already knew what he'd see. And he saw it. The dragon was there. It must have dropped suddenly straight down from the vault of heaven, because it was *right there*, close enough that Trei could almost have brushed its pearlescent feathers with his own wing.

This dragon was almost completely visible, so that Trei thought even a normal person might be able to see it. It was white, white as ice in the far north where Trei had grown up. Not pure white. An opalescent white filled with soft flowing blues and golds and apricots. The dragon glittered as though every feather and quill and talon had been coated with glass. Sunlight refracting off its feathers filled the air with dazzles of color, blue and green, gold and deeper gold, apricot and pink, as though they flew surrounded by and within a gathering of rainbows.

Trei couldn't tell whether this was a different dragon than the one he and Nescana had seen the first time. Maybe it was the same one, and they changed according to their mood or the weather or what kind of magic filled the air below them: he didn't know and couldn't guess. No one knew anything about dragons.

But the awareness that the sky dragons really give kajuraihi a small part of their magic gave Trei the courage to lock his wings, slide one arm out of the harness, take out Araenè's glass sphere and hold it up. Though the sphere weighed almost nothing, his arms trembled with the strain of even that movement. He was terrified he'd drop it, terrified he'd grip too hard and crush it, but he made himself hold it steady.

The dragon's long body undulated, rippling all around them, moving with them, curving around them, stunningly close but always exactly the same distance away. It seemed to fill the whole sky. Its great feathered wings stretched right across the vault of heaven. Its elegant, fine-boned head turned from side to side as it regarded them from one chatoyant eye and then the other.

The dragon spoke. Its voice was like the wind passing across harp strings, only every humming note was deeper and more resonant than any ordinary harp. It said, "Glass is born in fire and of the living wind. Summon the fire, kajurai. Summon the fire and the wind and forge a link to the earth. "

This sounded promising. Trei called up at the dragon, "We're trying! But we don't know how to make it work! All we know how to make is ordinary glass! We need your magic to make ours work!"

The dragon's vast body coiled and uncoiled around them, the feathers at the tips of its wings shifting delicately. A great cold radiated from it. Every feather of its wings and its vast body seemed made of ice and veined with crystal. A bitter wind had followed it down from the farthest heights, a wind that cut through its sharp-edged feathers to create a fine, thin-voiced music, harmony and counterpoint to the coiling of the dragon's body and the thrumming harp-notes of its voice. The cold burned against Trei's face and throat and hands.

The dragon turned its head, its lambent eye glimmering with light. It reached out with one taloned foot and lifted the glass sphere from Trei's hands, so delicately he had no fear it would break the fragile sphere—he thought there was probably less chance of than that that he would break it himself. His fingers had grown numb, even though kajuraihi never felt the cold.

"Call the winds and the fire," said the dragon. "Kajuraihi. Use human magic to bind the winds of the sky to the earth. Use the magic of the earth and the magic of the sky, kajurai, and call us down."

"Yes!" Trei shouted. "But we can't do it unless you start!" He wanted to weep with frustration. The sheer slogging weariness of the long flight down seemed to drag at him already, and worse than all the rest of it was the knowledge that he hadn't made the dragon understand, that he had failed, that he still had no idea how to summon fire or *anything* –

"Look!" cried Nescana. "It's gone white!"

Trei stared at the sphere balanced delicately between the tips of the dragon's delicate talons. It still looked like it was made of glass, but now the glass was white as milk. No. White as clouds. White as the pearlescent feathers of the dragon. White as condensed air.

"Summon the winds," said the dragon. "Now. Kajurai. Summon fire."

"Nescana!" said Trei. "Can you summon the winds? Call them as hard as you can!" And then he shut his eyes and let himself remember fire. Fire sleeting across the sky; fire bubbling molten out of the earth. He had touched fire. He had held fire, and carried fire. Fire had burned his whole life to ash, until he'd thought he'd turned to ash as well.

He knew fire. He had held it in his hands.

The winds came up hard and fast; not the thin cold winds of these brittle heights, but a warn dense wind redolent of salt and red earth and growing things, and behind that a faint fragrance of—he was sure of it—baking bread and hot sugar. Somehow the sugar made him think of fire.

And fire came: a sharp hot spark that leaped through the sky, scorched through the feathers of the dragon's vast wings, and buried itself in the heart of Araenè's sphere. Trei stared, holding his breath: he thought the sphere would explode and send molten shards scattering through the sky, but instead it only came alight, like a porcelain lamp that had just been lit.

"Kajurai," said the dragon. Its voice was still not at all like an ordinary human voice, it was still like the thrumming of huge harpstrings and a harmony of chimes, but somehow this time Trei thought it sounded weary. It said, "Use your human magic to bind the winds of the sky. Bind the sky to the earth, kajurai. Use the magic of the earth and the magic of the sky, and call us down." And it put Araenè's sphere back into Trei's hand, and the whole great length of it rippled and drew away, coiling outward and upward, rising up beyond the heights, to the black sky where the stars lived. It dwindled as it rose, smaller and smaller, a creature of opal and pearl and diamond against the clarity of the sky.

"Did it work?" Nescana called. "Trei! Did it work?"

Trei had no idea. He fumbled the sphere into its pouch. Its lambent glow shone right through the leather. Then he worked his cold-stiff hand and arm back into the harness, and tilted his wings to begin the long, long fall back toward the sea and the Islands and the world of men.

By the time they were halfway down, Trei knew he wasn't going to be able to make it all the way back to Milendri and to the novice's balcony. He knew he was going to just tumble over like an arrow-shot bird and fall. From this height, the waves might as well be stone—he didn't have to fear capture by the Yngulin warriors; he would be killed just by the fall. He was almost looking forward to it. At least after he gave up and fell, he wouldn't have to keep *flying*.

On and on and on, in what ought to have been a perfectly straightforward descent but was actually a nightmare of pain and exhaustion and dragging weight, with the sea spread out below, half-hidden by the dark rushing storm. Sometimes he thought the darkness was black smoke. Sometimes he thought the city below them was Rounn, choking in smoke and poison air, buried under ash, dying. Sometimes he knew it was Canpra. Sometimes he thought he heard his sister call out to him, her voice high and despairing, and sometimes he thought it was his cousin Araenè, and sometimes the voice seemed to belong to Nescana. Only it couldn't be Nescana. Nescana didn't belong in Rounn, where the mountains shattered into fire and the very winds turned to poison ... nothing could fly in air like that ... *he* shouldn't be asked to fly in poisoned air, it wasn't fair ...

"Trei!" Nescana screamed. "Trei! Can you hear me? Your angle's too steep, Trei! You have to level off! I've got the winds around to the east, but I can't fix your angle! Trei! *There's nothing wrong with your Gods-cursed fingertips, get your primaries angled at a backwards slant, right now!*"

That *was* Nescana. Trei opened his eyes, only then realizing he had been flying with them closed. There was no mountain, no fire. He was immensely relieved. Which said something right there, when *this* was better than the nightmares in his head.

He was suddenly terrified that he'd lost Araenè's sphere, dropped it somehow, and he ducked his head to look at the pouch. Pain speared through his shoulders from even that movement, taking him by surprise so that he choked, breathless. For a long moment he couldn't see anything but blackness and glittering spots, neither of which, he was almost certain, were real.

"Trei!" shrieked Nescana.

She was so near to him that he flinched. That hurt too, worse, leaving him breathless with pain and exhaustion. He remembered she had said something. Something about flight angles and tilting his wings. He couldn't tilt his wings—she should know that—he resented Nescana suddenly and fiercely. How dare she tell him to tilt his wings?

"Your primaries! Level *off!*" Nescana screamed at him, her high, piercing voice drilling right through Trei's head.

But this time he heard her, and realized she was right. His angle *was* too steep, and it really *was* hard and dangerous to come down like that. He flexed his fingers, correcting the slant of the primaries at the tips of his wings, curving gradually into a much more shallow flight path. He could feel Nescana's dense eastern wind against his face, rushing past and beneath him, shoving him upward, offering lift. The strain across his shoulders immediately eased. He wanted to shout something reassuring back to Nescana, but couldn't catch his breath.

He was not exactly flying but neither was he falling, yet. Or at least, it was a *controlled* kind of fall. So far. He couldn't really downstroke anymore—and he couldn't backstroke at all; he had no idea how he was going to land. If he got close enough to Milendri to even try to land.

If he got down alive and Araenè hadn't got her part done, he was never going to speak to her again.

"The Yngulin storm's just ahead!" Nescana shouted, swooping past him. "We have to go through it to get down! It's hard even to see Milendri through all that dark air! I'm going to try to bring a high, clear wind down, cut a path for us right through the storm!"

She wasn't having any trouble with her descent. *She* was fine. It hadn't been so very long ago that Trei had been the one to help *her* down from the heights, and now he couldn't even ride storm winds. He resented the reversal, a feeble resentment because he no longer had the strength for anything fiercer. He nurtured it because, stupid though he knew it was, he could cling to it when all he really wanted was just to *stop*.

But there was a problem, some other problem, something Nescana hadn't thought of. He fumbled for it, as clumsy with his thoughts as he was with his hands and his wings, and finally realized—he shouted back, "You can't! Because we can't let the Yngulin mages notice us! We can't interfere with their storm! Or they'll come looking for us!"

"No *choice!*" Nescana screamed. "You can't ride those storm winds! *Don't argue with me!* Just get ready to ride the wind I'm going to call! Lock your wings and hold that angle and I'll cut right through the storm! And throw us both right onto the novitiate balcony! Get ready!"

Trei wanted to argue, but he couldn't seem to catch his breath.

"Ready!" cried Nescana. "Steady! *Now!*" And she called down the high winds, which was something novices never did, they always wanted dense air from low down, the warm rising winds that offered support and lift, not the thin frozen winds of the heights. But those were the winds Nescana called now, with a force and surety that even Trei hadn't suspected, even though he'd known—he thought he'd known—how gifted she was with windworking.

Rushing winds, these were; winds that slashed like knives through the dark storm and whipped the sea into a white frenzy below, sending Tolounnese and Yngulin ships alike heeling suddenly far over. Trei and Nescana screamed down side by side along those cold winds, all their remaining height transformed into blazing speed.

Trei rode the wind, his wings drawn in tight, using just tiny movements of the tips of his wings to guide his flight path, his eyes slitted against the rushing air, knowing that if he tried to really use his wings properly at this huge speed, he would tear every shoulder muscle he had left. He really, really hoped Nescana knew how to use the wind to break their landing.

He could make out Canpra's white towers at the edge of the cliffs; he could see the balconies of white stone above and red stone below; he looked for but could not find the balcony of the novitiate—there were Quei riding the winds beside them suddenly, dozens of them, the clean sunlight pouring along Nescana's wind striking emerald fire from their wings—they were flying out of the dark Yngulin storm and into the brilliant light that pierced down from the heights— Trei wanted to whistle to them, as Island children did, but his mouth was too dry. But they cried anyway, their sharp, wild voices all around him.

20

There was no point in looking up from the novitiate balcony. Trei and Nescana were just little black specks in the sky. They might as well have been fish eagles as kajuraihi. Araenè had given up worrying that Trei would fall—well, she was trying to give up that worry, since it was far too late now and anyway there was nothing she could do about it if he did. Except call up a vision and be ready to summon a door, but she doubted that trick would work twice, it had practically killed Trei the first time, and anyway, she couldn't spare the time, she had other things she needed to do.

Like help Tichorei make a sphere out of stone carved out of the heart of the Island.

Tichorei knew, at least, all about making spheres and putting spells into them, each one solid and stable and ready to be used by any mage who needed it. He didn't know about putting the heart of human magic into a stone sphere, but at least he wasn't afraid to *try*. She was starting to think that was the most important thing for a mage, or an apprentice—not being afraid to *try*. She looked at him, waiting for him to explain what they had to do.

"Making a sphere—" he began. But before he could explain anything, a door opened up in the wall behind him, all thin woven slats of black wood inset with jet and obsidian beads, and Master Camatii—Tichorei's own master—put his head out, looked around, snapped, "Boy, I need you! Right now!", caught Tichorei by the wrist, and pulled him, staggering, through the door and away. The door vanished while Araenè was still staring at it, open-mouthed and horrified.

She tried to get the door to come back. When that didn't work, she tried to summon a door that would take her to

Master Tnegun. When that didn't work either, she called out to her master, as loudly and urgently as she could. Then she tried shouting and stomping in a circle. *That* didn't help, either, but it made her feel a little better.

Araenè was years away from making even simple spheres, and she knew it. That was why she'd depended on Tichorei. Whoever had been injured, whoever Master Camatii had been working to save, couldn't possibly be important enough to snatch Tichorei away just when she needed him most! He would know that—he would tell his master—Master Camatii would send him back. No, better, he would summon Master Tnegun and everybody, and Araenè wouldn't have to figure out how to do all these things by herself after all. Which would be a huge relief. Any moment now. Araenè clenched her teeth and glared at the wall where the door had appeared.

Any moment now. Any moment.

Nothing.

Araenè was too furious even to curse or stomp in circles. She *had* to make a sphere. A sphere of Island stone, with fire in its heart, the way the Island had fire at its heart. Or was supposed to, except the Yngulin mages had driven it away—or killed it, even—*her* fire dragon! And now she couldn't even make a stone sphere and Trei would half kill himself getting a sky dragon to put its magic in the glass sphere and she wouldn't even have the right kind of sphere to balance his and it would all be for *nothing*.

Screaming wouldn't help. Araenè paced in a small circle, looking at nothing, trying to think. She hadn't felt this helpless since ... she shied away from thinking about the last time she'd felt this helpless. She hadn't been able to save her mother or father, she hadn't been able to do *anything*, they had died and she hadn't been able to do *anything*. It was like that again now. She wanted to strike out, batter her hands against the walls.

Then she stopped, and stood very still.

She said out loud, "The harp. *Cassameirin's* harp. The dragon." A stone dragon, an earth dragon, a dragon made of polished hematite, with chalcopyrite eyes. Would a dragon of stone and earth work?

Hematite was good for spells involving fire. Chalcopyrite was even better.

And the dragon had been right by the labyrinth. Or at least, she'd found it right before she'd found the labyrinth. Which in the hidden school might mean anything. But she suspected now that it meant *something*.

She wasn't sure what. She didn't know what exactly she could do with the stringless harp or the dragon. But maybe if she found some kind of dragon magic, any kind of dragon magic, maybe she could figure out a way to help Trei, even if she couldn't make a sphere. She glanced upward despite herself, but could see nothing but streaks of high cloud in all the empty sky. The Yngulin storm winds did not reach high enough to drive those clouds away, but Trei and Nescana were nowhere in sight.

Araenè found the door almost right away, once she started to look for it. She was grateful for this. She felt a huge pressure, time behind her, time rushing past her like the winds, unstoppable and far too fast. She had a terrible and compelling feeling at the back of her mind that she would figure all this out, the harp and the spheres and the dragons and everything, and it would be *too late*.

But she found the door right away. That seemed like a good sign. It seemed that maybe the hidden school itself was on her side. It made her feel a little less alone. She didn't tell herself that this was ridiculous, because she was very glad to feel less alone.

The door was still made of ebony and crystal, and it still opened to the dusty, plain little room, and the room was still occupied only by the single harp standing on its stool. It was a harp, at the moment, and not a dragon. While harps were less frightening, Araenè felt that under the circumstances the dragon might have been more helpful.

Dust motes drifted in the slight breeze created by the opening of the door, glinting in the light that poured past them into the room. Glinting more than ordinary dust, Araenè thought. Like finely powdered gold or pearls or something like that, something special. Something infused with magic.

The harp was definitely the one she remembered: red wood inlaid with swirls of ebony, elegant in its simple lines, with pegs of ebony and silver, but without any strings at all. Except she suspected it was really strung with magic. The whole room, every floating dust mote, felt heavy with magic. It prickled on her skin, coriander and bitter orange and the strange musky, minty flavor of dragon magic. But hot. Much hotter than Kanora's sphere.

She took a step forward. Another. The tight feeling in the air intensified.

There was something familiar about the harp. Something she hadn't noticed before. Something like the musky, minty taste of dragon magic. But the harp wasn't strung with the living winds. It was strung, she was suddenly sure, with fire. No. With the memory of fire. With the magic behind fire. With the magic of fire dragons. She thought she could feel that magic now, burning with contained power.

"But I don't know how to play even an ordinary harp," she whispered, reaching out to touch the ebony-inlaid face of the harp. But maybe it played itself. Or maybe *playing* it wasn't exactly what she needed to do.

She wasn't Kanora Ireinamei. She wasn't kajurai, she didn't know anything about dragon magic. But she had a gift for working with fire. Master Tnegun said so. She wasn't even really a mage, but she thought this harp was exactly what she needed. If she could figure out what to do with it.

What one did with a harp was play it. But if she played this one, she would free the magic in it, and she didn't know how to capture that magic. The fire would burn out of the harp and into the air and be lost. She knew that, she felt it. She needed ... she needed a sphere, of course. A sphere to catch the fire. A sphere in which to invest the magic. She turned her head, not really looking at the room. Looking at the red stone out of which the room had been carved. Red stone that contained fire and the memory of fire and the magic of fire; red stone at the heart of the hidden school, which was the heart of the Island. They had intended to make a sphere out of this very stone. Maybe ... maybe she still could.

She needed Master Tnegun. Or at least Tichorei. Or even precocious little Cesei, or the annoying twins, or *anybody*. But nobody was here. Nobody was going to come; no one could. They were all desperately working on other things and didn't have any idea that what she needed was more important. Maybe it wasn't. Maybe they were all saving the Islands, one way or another, and if anybody came to help her, the Islands would fall.

But she was sure that if the Islands were to be saved, they had to bring back the dragons. And Araenè was going to make the right kind of sphere to help with that, because somebody had to and nobody else was here to do it. Maybe no one else even could; *she* was the one who was supposed to be sensitive to dragon magic. Maybe that was why she was here, now, and no one else.

Anyway, she knew how. She *did* know. She'd *watched* Tichorei do it. Surely that would be enough. At least, she knew what she had to make her sphere out of: magic and fire, and the living winds, and stone from the heart of the Island ... that was a start. That was enough to go on with. She laid her hand flat on the gritty red stone of the wall. And, as she sought for the structure of spellwork that would carve a smooth sphere out of that stone and drop it into her hand, the half-remembered pattern unfolded inside her mind.

She had remembered that this kind of spellwork was almost like watching a flower unfold, or unfolding it yourself with your fingertips. But she hadn't realized it was like a flower that was made of slivers of glass and razor-edged steel, or that she would have to fold out each petal herself, in its own right time and direction. She hadn't realized how hard it would be to hold each petal of the spell in place while she folded out the next petal, and the next after that.

Tichorei had said this kind of spellwork was too advanced for her. He'd been right. But she *could* do it, following the structure he'd shown her. It hurt. Working advanced spells always hurt. But if you could hold the pattern in your mind, you *could* work them, sometimes. But she couldn't let go even for a second because if she did the spell would fold back up on itself and she'd have to start over. She hadn't known it would be like that. She bit her lip till she tasted blood, but she didn't let go; she didn't; she *wouldn't*. She *was* doing it right. She knew that, at least. There wasn't even any *way* to do it wrong: if she did it wrong, the whole structure of the spell would collapse, like a glass flower shattering, and that would be extremely hard to miss.

She blinked, and blinked again, and the structure of the spell glittered suddenly in her mind and hands, beautiful and complete. Her vision blurred with tears, or maybe with magic, and a perfectly smooth sphere of red stone fell neatly out of the wall and into her palms.

It was about the size of her two fists together, and heavy. She nearly dropped it, but dropped to her knees instead, feeling that her legs might fold up underneath her at any moment anyway, and let the sphere roll carefully out of her hands and onto the dusty floor. The dust rose up around her, glittering. It tasted like dust. Like ashes. Like the memory of fire.

She wanted very badly to close her eyes and do nothing at all for a little while. Or maybe cry. Her eyes felt hot, but then everything felt hot. Reaching out, Araenè ran one hand across the harp strings that weren't there, and fire bloomed in the air and within the stone and kindled in the dust and leapt up behind her eyes and in her mind, and she poured it through her mind and hands and into the sphere she'd made without even worrying about whether she knew how.

*

The balcony was there before them; Trei saw it suddenly, lit as though by the deliberate hand of a God, Nescana's wind drawing a dazzling line straight to it from the very vault of the heavens. He rushed toward the balcony's edge—the cold winds suddenly swirled sharply around and surged back violently against his face, and he called them as hard as he could, trying to help. He had no idea if his efforts added anything to Nescana's, but there was no more time, and he caught his breath, shut his eyes and spread his wings to catch the winds because he had to, he *had* to, or he would smash into the stones of the balcony faster than a horse could gallop. Every muscle and ligament in his shoulders tore; he felt them go; he thought he could feel each one separately stretch and then rip, just like a rope asked to take up too great a burden. He screamed with pain, but his wings also caught Nescana's violent winds, the air piling up between him and the stone, cushioning him so that when he struck, it was with only two or three times the force of an ordinary landing. He staggered and went to his knees, the immense weight of his wings dragging him down, pain stabbing through his back as though thin-bladed knives had sliced suddenly up under his shoulder blades.

He was dimly aware that Araenè was there, running forward; of her frightened, wordless cry. "Careful!" he gasped. "Careful of the sphere—"

"Never *mind* the sphere!" cried his cousin, but even before she began to help him, clumsily, with the wing harness, she was careful to take the pouch where the sphere nestled and put it gently aside.

Beside him, Trei was aware of Nescana coming down in a clumsy but perfectly adequate landing. The force of the landing drove her, too, to her knees, but she almost managed to keep her wings clear of the stone. The winds she had called rushed once around the balcony and then away. Trei said, gasping, "They'll know—they'll have seen—nobody could have missed that—"

"Nobody for miles around!" Araenè agreed. Even at this moment, he noticed that her face was white and drawn, her cheekbones stark under her fine skin. Her fingers were shaking on the straps of the harness. "It was like watching a lightning bolt cut through the storm straight for us! Oh, Trei, you can't move your arms at all?"

He couldn't. He could twitch his fingers, but he couldn't lift either arm even an inch. He could barely sit up. He said, his own voice thin and strange in his ears, "But it worked! It worked, Araenè! The dragon put the living winds in your sphere, fire and the living winds, and I called fire, and the dragon changed your sphere so it could hold dragon magic—"

"Thank the generous Gods!" said Araenè. "And mine holds fire and earth—I think! If I did it right! I—Tichorei—but it doesn't matter now! Your poor shoulders!" She put a careful hand under Trei's arm.

"I'm all right. I'm all right." Trei couldn't quite keep his voice steady. Nescana had left her wings discarded on the floor and come to help him with his, wordless and worried. The relief when the weight came off was huge. Trei refused to think about maybe never being able to take that weight again. He tried, carefully, to get to his feet. It shouldn't be hard; there was nothing wrong with his *legs*. He might have twisted his knee, landing, but that wasn't anything. He said to Araenè, mostly to hear himself say it out loud, "We still need to bind the two spheres together—earth and fire, with the living winds to bind them. What's going on out there? Is Yngul—?"

"I don't know, I don't know! I'm sure Yngul is winning, can't you feel that? All the magic in the air is Yngulin. Can you walk?" She put out a hand without even looking and opened a door that had never been there before. "We'll go to my apartment—no, my garden, that'll be better—binding earth and fire and air, I've been thinking about that, I'm pretty sure it'll be easier to bind everything together with the living winds if we're outside—"

Trei nodded. This sounded right. He took a tentative step. Another. It wasn't actually impossible to walk. The door was only right over there. He could glimpse Araenè's pool, the graceful smooth-barked tree leaning over it, trailing its long leaves in the water. It looked very peaceful and serene. He wanted very badly to sit down by that pool and stop moving.

Nescana had put a hand out to help him but stopped, helplessly, afraid to touch him. He wanted to put his hands in his pockets so the weight of his arms wouldn't drag at his shoulders, but he couldn't lift his arms enough even for that. He thought of asking Nescana to do it for him, but that seemed impossibly awkward. He said instead, "Maybe you can help me make a sling? Two slings. I'm going to look ridiculous ..."

"Nobody's going to laugh," Nescana said tersely, and ducked away, through the door and quickly up over Araenè's windowsill and into her apartment. And back again, very quickly, with two lengths of gauzy blue cloth.

Trei stepped through the door after Nescana. His foot came down on the soft earth of Araenè's garden. The air was quiet here within the walled garden, heavy with the scents of damp earth and growing things and the herbs they crushed underfoot. And yet the living winds were here, too. Trei had never been so aware of dragon magic, attenuated as it had become. There was no Yngulin magic here, he realized. Araenè's garden was heavy with Island magic untainted by the darker power the Yngulin mages had brought with them, as though the garden's high brick walls kept out everything inimical. Even Trei's shoulders seemed to hurt less, here. He let his breath out, slowly.

"Can you sit down?" asked Nescana. "Look, right here, this is a nice spot under this tree. You probably don't want to lean back. Let me measure this. Just a moment ..."

Trei closed his eyes, letting Nescana fuss over him. "Araenè?" he asked.

"Doing things! She doesn't need us for this part! I'll tell you when she's ready. Here, I'm going to try to settle your right arm, then we'll do the left." Nescana slipped the first improvised sling over his head and gently maneuvered his first arm into place. Trei bit his lip again, hard enough to taste blood this time, and tried not to make a sound.

"Those mages! Never around when it matters!" Nescana said. "Good thing you don't need your arms to help your cousin. Or if you do, I'll hold things for you. Just a moment, I'll have the other sling ready in just—"

"Ready?" called Araenè, from the other side of the pool. She sounded rather breathless.

Trei opened his eyes and looked at her. His cousin was kneeling by the water with one sphere in each hand, the one of red stone filled with human magic and fire—he almost thought he could see the fire, if not the magic—and the one of glass filled with fire and also with the living winds. She looked intense and absorbed and almost exalted, her attention turned almost entirely inward. She also looked strangely thin, almost translucent, as though she'd been burned down to nothing by terror and determination, and for the first time Trei wondered where Tichorei was and why he wasn't here helping and just who had made that sphere of red stone, and if his cousin had, what it had cost her.

"He can't hold anything—" Nescana began, her tone almost hostile.

"He doesn't have to! At least not yet. This part is almost normal spellwork! I think I know how to do it."

Above them, the sky suddenly began to darken, Yngulin storm clouds piling up and thickening. Trei felt those clouds as a pressure, as though the Yngulin storm was forcing the living winds of dragon magic down upon the surface of

305

Milendri. He was sure the Islands were going to sink and crack under that weight. Araenè didn't seem to notice, but Nescana flinched and glanced up and then looked worriedly at Trei. He returned her gaze, knowing what she was thinking—that the Yngulin mages had found them, that they were out of time.

"Do it!" said Trei. "Do it, Araenè! Hurry!"

*

Araenè was aware of the Yngulin magic above them, but tangentially, as she was aware of the warm stillness of the air and the scent of the crushed herbs and dragon magic. She was much more aware of the sphere she held in her hands. It tasted of a complex blend of spices: cardamom and rosewater, jasmine and vanilla, pepper and oranges, mint and ginger; and behind and between everything else, very strong and pressing hard against the rest, the musky scent of dragon magic. The Yngulin magic above her was dry and dusty, nothing that she recognized—not exactly *hostile* to dragon magic, but somehow unsympathetic. It was a magic of earth, but not like the magic that filled the stone of the Floating Islands. She would have liked to figure out what it *was* like, but knew there was no time—in just a moment, that heavy, dry Yngulin magic would crush the magic she held—it *was* crushing her, there *was* no time, she dropped to her knees to get away from it, but she hadn't moved fast enough and now it was *too late* –

Half a dozen Quei slanted suddenly through the sky above them, the sun striking brilliant green fire from their wings, riding the storm winds with consummate ease, their wild cries piercing the sky like threads of lightning. The Yngulin magic seemed to hesitate and draw back, and Araenè cried out in warning and slammed her two spheres together.

The two spheres clicked together, and all at once Araenè was holding just one sphere.

It seemed to be made of rose quartz. That was the closest Araenè could come to a description, but it wasn't accurate, because really the sphere didn't look like it was made of any kind of mineral, or anything solid. It glimmered delicately, as though she'd blown a bubble out of soapy rose-colored water and then caught it in her hands. It was big, but light, almost weightless. It didn't exactly feel fragile, but somehow insubstantial. It tasted very strongly of dragon magic, and of something else, something new, something sweet and bright, but with a bitter edge beneath the sweetness, a little like burnt sugar, unfamiliar but not unpleasant.

"Trei!" said Araenè, and remembered, belatedly, that of course her cousin couldn't easily get up and come around the pool to join her. But really he didn't need to move. Neither did she. She felt breathless and frightened and blazingly happy, and when she met Trei's eyes across the pool, she knew he felt the same way. It was the magic, of course. He felt it, the dragon part of it. She said, on a quick half-breath, before she forgot words, "Nescana! You should get out, get away—get away, into the school—" Nescana was shaking her head, but Trei knew better, and gave her a look that made her go, where nothing Araenè said had made a difference.

Araenè was grateful Trei had managed to send Nescana away. She thought something big was going to happen, she felt the heavy power of magic gathering around them, a lot of magic, far more than she knew how to use. She said to Trei, her voice shaking with power. "On three!" But then there was a huge twisting silent blow as the magic broke out of her hold, and she cried, "Now!"

She had no idea what it felt like to Trei, but to her it felt like trying to fold the air itself into a new shape, like trying to teach the wind to blow in an entirely new direction; like trying to carve a gemstone into an intricate filigree using only the tips of her fingers. It hurt, but the sensation wasn't really pain and actually wasn't really unpleasant—well, it was, but not *exactly*. Araenè heard her own voice screaming, and Trei's. All around them, the earth and then the very stone of the Island cracked and shattered; above them, it felt exactly as though the air was doing the same.

Araenè could *see* the air. It was beautiful and terrifying, layers and masses of crystal that moved, rushing past and over one another, mingling and sliding apart again. She could *see* the winds, the dark storm winds the Yngulin mages had brought from the south and the brilliant, blazing crystalline winds that the dragons created and called and rode and *became*. She'd never guessed that, that wind-dragons were really wind—or the other way around—she didn't know what she even meant by that, but it was strange and beautiful—the fiery winds rushed past, whipping through the leaves of the trees in her garden, lashing the surface of her pool into white wavelets—there was a fragrance to it, a dazzling fragrance that wasn't anything she knew.

She could see the stone below her: gritty red stone veined with quartz and flecked with chalcedony and pyrophyllite. The stone was breaking, the wind prying it apart, shattering its orderly structure—she would have screamed out loud just to give the breaking stone voice, but she had no breath, and anyway she was not frightened. She could hear Trei screaming, but she knew he felt the same magic she did and she could hear no fear in his voice; he was crying out with the stone's voice, with the wind's voice. The wind was invading the stone—but it was supposed to, it was all right; the stone was breaking, but that was all right, that was supposed to happen, too. The rose-pink sphere she'd made of stone and fire and the living winds condensed in her hands, hardening, burning with magic. It burned her hands, and with a feeling that this, too, was supposed to happen, she loosened her grip and dropped it into the pool.

The Yngulin magic fell down upon them, a brutal hammer-blow, but they fell out from underneath it and into the empty air, so that they were flung first one way and then another. Araenè screamed in earnest, but then found herself laughing, a sound almost like her scream. She clung to the grasses by the pool. *Trei* couldn't hold onto anything, but he didn't seem to need to. The winds that slashed around *him* flung themselves into a tight, savage spiral that left him unmoved. They were dragon winds. She could *see* them, as though she was a kajurai. She wondered whether Trei had her mage's awareness as she had his kajurai sight, whether he could see and feel the stone below them and the sphere burning in the pool and the light that blazed around them all. The new little Island they rode hurtled with them through the sky.

"It's a Dragon Island!" shouted Trei over the wind.

"I know!" Araenè cried. "It's a binding!"

"I know!" Trei answered, and then, "Here they come!"

The dragons were coming. Down from the frozen heights where the thin air shone with brilliant cold, down from the vaults of heaven, riding their violent winds straight down to the new Island, their storm driving against the dark, hot, dry storm winds of Yngul, driving the Yngulin storm aside and away and back to the south, raking across the Yngulin ships and forcing them down. Araenè felt the Yngulin mages break, all their heavy, grounded strength shattering beneath the savage force of the crystalline winds. Trei caught the magic of those winds and gave it to Araenè, and Araenè took it and flung it away again, into the stone, into all the Floating Islands, and the fire that had gone out of the heart of the Islands suddenly caught and blazed up. She was aware, distantly, of Master Tnegun. Of the sudden power that flooded him, flooded all the Island mages, of their shock at it—not that they were slow to take the power she gave them—she was aware of all the Islands flooding with magic, flinging themselves into the sky.

The sphere blazed up and then, sinking to the bottom of the pool, quieted. The winds gentled. The water gradually became still. But Araenè was only faintly aware of any of this. The dragon magic had burned through her and left her floating in a passive stillness. She was lying on the ground ... she was faintly aware of that, too. She wanted to look up, look at Trei, make sure he was all right, but that worry, too, was a pallid thing that gave her no real anchor ... the winds had died and she fell, slowly, as a leaf falls, drifting, carried by any breath or breeze ... down and down, sinking ... she was gone.

21

Trei never quite fell into the stillness that had come in the wake of the storm. He was too worried about Araenè, and too aware of the dragons. There were a lot of dragons—five, six, nine—he tried to count them, but they shifted in and out of his sight, transparent as clear glass, glittering with light. Translucent shimmers of blue and green and gold and apricot refracted from their feathers and the quills that spilled down around their delicately-boned heads, until Trei couldn't see where dragon feathers stopped and wind started.

The dragons wound among and between the jagged new mountains of the new Island, here and there coming down to cling to the sharp-edged red peaks. Trei had no idea where those mountains had come from. If a piece of Milendri had broken free of the main Island and hurled itself into the sky, then it seemed to him it should have been a piece of the city that surrounded Araenè's garden. But these rugged mountains that slashed upward toward the heights were nothing like the gentler lands in and around Canpra. There were mountains like those at the western edge of Milendri, but that was *miles* away from the city. It didn't make sense. Araenè might be able to explain it. She might even have expected a chunk of Milendri to rip itself free and fling itself into the sky; he had no idea.

Araenè hadn't moved even yet. She lay on her face by the pool, her chestnut hair spread out, half on the gravel and half floating in the water. The pool and the garden looked the same, but the wall of the hidden school was nowhere to be seen. And the pool itself was different. It threw back light differently, or light had gone into the water, or something. It glimmered, faintly. The luminescence was visible even in the hot afternoon light that stretched out, heavy and golden, through the garden.

The tree had changed, too. He saw that as he got, slowly and painfully, to his feet. The bark of its slender bole and graceful limbs had peeled in little strips of gray and tan and salmon-pink, but now the tree's bark was smooth and white. And its leaves were no longer long and trailing, but smaller, fluttering in the wind, silvery-green above and silvery-pale below. Fruits now hung in clusters here and there. The fruits were small, translucent, golden. He knew that they would bear seeds that were white and faceted as jewels. He didn't reach for the fruit. Even if he could have lifted an arm, he wouldn't have picked it. He knew somehow that one of those fruits was all anyone should ever taste.

Instead, he picked his way slowly around the pool and knelt down awkwardly at Araenè's side. His cousin was breathing slowly but steadily. Her face, smoothed out by sleep or unconsciousness, seemed the face of a girl both younger and more trusting. She looked more like Trei's mother now, her aunt. He hadn't seen that before, but she looked more like Trei's mother than her own. Trei wanted to pick her up, lift her away from the pool. He could not even brush her hair out of her face. He only knelt and watched her breathe, while above them dragons frayed into and out of the wind. He felt very peaceful, and strangely empty.

Behind him, a heavy foot gritted across the crushed gravel. Trei turned his head, looking up without surprise into the dark hawk-fierce face of his cousin's master. He said, "Master Tnegun."

The tall mage bowed his head. "Trei Naseida. Don't worry for your cousin. She is well enough, I think. Only ... emptied out, by the working of a great magic." He knelt down beside Trei and plunged his hand and arm into the pool with a complete disregard for the icy water that soaked the sleeve of his robe. Then he held Araenè's sphere up to the light. It looked small and surprisingly heavy balanced on the tips of his long, elegant fingers. "A great magic," he repeated.

His gaze caught Trei's, quizzical and sardonic. "For both of you, I surmise."

With an effort, Trei refrained from saying, *And where were you?* He knew perfectly well the Island mages had done everything they could, within the limitations of ordinary magecraft. Master Tnegun looked weary, worn to bone and nerve. It wasn't his fault he had never guessed there might be a way for a mage and a kajurai to share their magic, and by the time Araenè had figured it out, there had been no way to explain.

Trei did blame him a little, anyway, though. He looked down again at Araenè.

Master Tnegun followed his gaze. He reached down and did what Trei had wanted to do: lifted Araenè gently from the gravel, brushed the wet hair away from her face, and settled her across his knee. "She's well enough," he repeated, and met Trei's eyes. "And you, young kajurai?"

Trei began to shrug and stopped, wincing.

"We may be able to do something about that," murmured the mage. He rose to his feet, effortlessly lifting Araenè in his arms as though she were a much smaller child.

He made no effort to help Trei up, for which Trei was grateful, as there would have been no way the mage could have helped without hurting him. He got up on his own, painfully awkward and slow. The slings Nescana had made for him did help. He asked suddenly, "Nescana? The hidden school—"

"Perfectly undamaged," murmured the mage, meaning both Nescana and the school, Trei understood. Master Tnegun gave a sharp glance to the air, and a door appeared there, a simple door of plain wood with a lintel of red stone. "We'll take her back to her own apartment, which is, I believe, precisely where it has always been, though it now lacks a private garden." He stepped toward the door, but paused and added, "Evidently the hidden school relocated itself twice, very quickly. Or the magic you and Araenè made relocated it." He glance up and around at the high, jagged mountains that surrounded them and said approvingly, "Far more satisfactory than giving the sky-dragons half of Canpra. Though we would have been willing to do even that, by the end. Did you and Araenè find suitable mountains on purpose?"

"No," said Trei, and then wondered whether possibly his cousin *had* deliberately moved her garden to a place of wild mountains and vivid sky. Perhaps prompted by the kajurai magic he had given her—he couldn't guess. He looked around. The dragons were still there, twisting slowly around and among the sharp-edged stone of the highest mountains, their transparent wings cutting through the streaming clouds.

"Everything is over," said Master Tnegun. "Everything is securely where it must belong. The Islands in the sky, the dragons bound between earth and the vault of heaven, the Tolounnese ... well. One imagines we shall become accustomed to one another, in time. Many of the Yngulin ships rolled and broke under the wind your dragons brought down from the cold heights. The rest have fled."

"I know," said Trei.

"Do you?" The mage didn't sound surprised. He opened the door by looking at it and nodded for Trei to step through.

The healer-mage, Master Camatii, did what he could to fix Trei's shoulders. That was late the next day, for the mage had come very close to overextending himself during the brutal aftermath of battle. Trei gathered the Little Emperor himself had been badly injured doing something important and heroic—Trei didn't have the details straight—but whatever exactly had happened, Master Camatii had saved him. Or Tichorei, actually, since Camatii had exhausted his own strength and summoned his apprentice. So he supposed he had to be grateful to Tichorei, even if he had abandoned Araenè at the very end. Trei was glad that he'd only heard about this from Tichorei later, who'd come to see Trei mostly because he was embarrassed he couldn't tell Araenè he was sorry he'd left her. Trei was just as glad he hadn't known at the time how impossible a task had been forced on his cousin.

Though it hadn't actually proved impossible. Which, in retrospect, thinking of Araenè's fierce determination, he actually didn't find that surprising.

There had been fighting in Canpra itself. And people had drowned, too. Mostly Tolounnese ships' crews had drowned, and mostly Tolounnese soldiers had been injured and killed in the battles, with all the mages and even their apprentices pouring out their strength and the strength of the adjuvants to help them. Of all the Islanders, only the mages and the kajuraihi had really suffered in the fighting, this time. Trei wondered what the rest of the Islanders thought of the Tolounnese now. What they thought of being part of Tolounn.

"We think the Tolounnese are the best soldiers in the world," Wingmaster Taimenai said gravely, when Trei, greatly daring, asked him. "Of course, we knew that already. You told us so, after all. But now we're grateful for it. This won't soon be forgotten."

The wingmaster had come to the healer's hall to see not only Trei, but all the kajuraihi injured. Their losses had been terrible, Trei guessed. He had not asked. He did not want to know how many kajuraihi had been lost, or injured. Mostly the ones who had survived were elsewhere in the healing hall, being tended by skilled hands as well as by magic. Their injuries were not the same as Trei's. They had been injured by bolts from the Yngulin scorpions, mostly, those that had survived. Those that had been cast into the sea by the Yngulin storms had almost all drowned, though a very few had been rescued from that fate by Tolounnese sailors.

He wasn't going to die. *He* was going to heal—at least mostly. He tried to be glad of that. He tried not to think what it would be like to spend the rest of his life grounded.

"We'll just have to give it time, Trei. Try to rest," the wingmaster said, and touched Trei's shoulder—vey lightly— and went away, leaving Trei to the dim quiet of his private room. Trei shut his eyes and tried not to weep. He was so tired. And his shoulders and back ached, with a lingering pain. The pain was different this time. His shoulders felt all wrong. He knew he would never fly again.

"Well, now," said a light, cool, interested voice, and Trei opened his eyes again, tried to sit up, gasped, winced, gritted his teeth against the piercing pain, and held very still.

"Yes," said the voice, amused. "I wouldn't try that if I were you. Quite a mess you've made of your shoulders. I wouldn't have thought it possible to do quite this sort of damage. I really must see one of your people fly. Very slowly, so I can watch properly. How slowly can you fly?"

It was an accented voice, a familiar voice—not one Trei had expected or thought of, but very welcome. It belonged to a slender, elegant man with long spidery hands and angular features and sharp gray eyes. Not Tolounnese, not Islander: Master Patan was from Toipakom, originally. The Little Emperor himself was his patron, but Trei had not guessed he had come to the Floating Islands. He said, in the calmest tone he could manage, "Slowly enough to stall. I'll show you—if you can fix my shoulders. They say the damage can't be— can't be fixed—"

"Oh, I imagine it won't be so very difficult," said Master Patan dismissively. "And a good thing, too, as the Emperor made his preferences on the subject quite clear." He strolled forward, looking Trei up and down with an amused, curious gaze.

He was not exactly a healer and not exactly a mage. He was an artificer, his business to put mechanisms together and take them apart. Trei suspected he didn't precisely care about people, but he enjoyed difficult problems, and he was fascinated by kajuraihi wings and flight. He wanted to make wings that would let ordinary people fly. Trei thought if anybody could do it, Master Patan would be the one.

"Let's turn you over, boy, and take a good look at what you've done to yourself," Master Patan commanded. His voice was light and calm and remote as a northern winter, his touch perfectly impersonal. "Yes. Yes. Hmm. Fascinating. You use your own muscles to fly, clearly. Precisely as though your wings were your own, while you wear them. Yes. Fascinating." He touched Trei's back lightly, ran a hand firmly across the skin. The pressure hurt ... but not really. Heat passed across Trei's back and shoulders, deepened until it nearly burned, and eased. "Like splicing rope," murmured the master artificer. "Except more difficult, and with an annoying degree of scarring in the way. That's your mage's work there: altogether too hasty. Healers don't understand mechanics. Pity your folk didn't call me in immediately."

Trei wanted to ask whether it was all right, whether Master Patan could still fix all the damage, but the artificer said, "Hush! Take a deep breath and hold it. Good. Again. This will hurt: try not to flinch." The heat went through his back again, and a sharp, vivid pain, like a knife. Trei bit his pillow and tried not to move.

"There," said Master Patan, his voice cool and satisfied, and the pain eased. "Sit up, boy. Stand up. Reach up. No, higher, as though you meant to touch the ceiling with your fingertips. Bend over and touch your toes. Yes, there we go; a little residual scarring, but nothing to signify."

Trei straightened up and looked at the artificer, who looked decidedly pleased with himself. He said after a moment, "I'll show you how kajurai fly. Any time you want. I mean," he added, belatedly, "as long as it's all right with Wingmaster Taimenai."

"I'm sure your wingmaster will have no objection," Master Patan said smugly, "since you kajurai Islanders are Tolounnese citizens now. I shall hold you to that. I believe I know how your body is put together better than your own mother, now. Quite a lot better, actually. You might want to find your clothing, novice. I'm quite sure you'll have another visitor as soon as I've made my report."

He sketched a coolly ironic bow and withdrew, leaving Trei staring after him, trying to catch his breath and adjust to the idea that he would—soon—tomorrow, even—be back in the sky where he belonged.

But not this instant. Because right now he needed to find his clothing. Because, from Master Patan's tone, he knew exactly who his next visitor would be.

He was mostly right. And he was mostly dressed. Someone had put novice's clothing in the chest at the foot of the bed: a sleeveless gray shirt, black trousers, a red sash. A gold pin for the sash, not the black they'd all worn after the old king's death; a red feather for his hair, which was at last getting to be about the right length for a kajurai. Trei had everything arranged except the feather when the heavy knock fell on the door. The door was flung open at once: Emperors, when they did you the great honor of coming to you instead of summoning you to them, didn't wait for permission to enter your room.

Trei dropped the feather on the bed and turned hastily to face the door, bowing. He *could* bow. Bending and straightening didn't hurt at all. Or there *was* very slight residual ache, but compared to before, that was nothing at all.

The decouan who had opened the door glanced in and back out, ignoring Trei completely. The Emperor came in alone—the room suddenly seemed much smaller—and hooked his hands in his belt, regarding Trei narrowly. "A great improvement," he observed. "I'm told you will indeed fly again, Trei Naseida. That's welcome news, as I fully expect to require your services myself. If, of course, your king will release you to me."

"Eventually," said Ceirfei. He had appeared in the doorway, and leaned there now, against the doorframe, smiling at Trei. He wasn't *actually* smiling, but his eyes were smiling.

Trei grinned back at him, a flood of relief and joy rising through him. "You're all right. The Islands are all right?"

Ceirfei bent his head, a grave gesture, but his eyes still glinted with humor. "All is well, and all will be well! For which we thank you, and, of course, your cousin. Who is also perfectly well, Trei, if you had any doubt of it." He glanced sidelong at the Little Emperor. "Our sovereign Emperor has seen fit to send his soldiers to clear any remaining Yngulin warriors from our Islands. We anticipate little difficulty, all things considered."

Trei looked at the Emperor, who had a deeply ironic look in his eyes, probably, Trei realized, at being ignored. It probably wasn't something the Emperor was used to. He said hastily, "I beg your pardon, O Emperor—I was surprised and, and—"

"And no doubt so much relieved as to forget yourself," said the Emperor gravely. "I forgive it, of course, Trei Naseida. I doubt you are capable of any impudence I would not forgive. I look forward to seeing you fly. You will demonstrate your kajurai magic for me tomorrow, I hope. A delegation of sorts has arrived from Tolounn; I look forward to showing them a kajurai in flight. I wish to show them you in particular."

"Yes, O Emperor," said Trei, slightly stunned by his instant guess about this delegation. He looked at Ceirfei.

"Yes, I know," said Ceirfei, his tone rather dry. "My Emperor has learned to explain things to me in very clear terms."

"We understand one another quite well, these days," said the Little Emperor. He clapped Ceirfei on the shoulder, gave Trei an approving nod, and went out. His boots and the boots of his soldiers rang like drumbeats down the stone of the hall.

Trei stared at Ceirfei. "The Great Emperor's sent his own people?"

Ceirfei shrugged. "I suppose we shouldn't be surprised. I think we can trust the Little Emperor to protect us, if necessary." He caught Trei's look and laughed. "Don't worry, Trei! I think we have indeed learned to understand one another, he and I. You won't be surprised if I confess I had my doubts. But I think he can be trusted. Tolounnese honor! It's a great reassurance, to those of us who must depend on

Tolounnese strength." He gave Trei a searching look. "And, of course, on the strength of dragons. I believe I understand what happened, more or less. Walk with me and tell me about it, if you would. You are well enough, now?"

"I'm fine," Trei said sincerely, and laughed, beginning to believe that this was true.

"Walk with me, then," Ceirfei repeated, and led Trei out of the healer's hall and down a wide flight of red brick steps and into the broad avenues of Second City. Flameberry trees cast their delicate shade across the streets. Marmosets leaped from branch to branch, competing with sapphire-winged birds for the heavy clusters of fruit. To the east, the high white towers of First City blazed in the sun. A quartet of Tolounnese soldiers went past, off-duty, probably heading for Third City, not noticing a couple of Island boys standing in the shade of the healer's hall, not knowing Islander customs enough to recognize Ceirfei's white clothing and violet ribbons.

"They only have one ruler," said Ceirfei, following Trei's glance. "Well, two, I suppose, but one's the Little Emperor and the other isn't me, either. That's all right. Their officers will recognize me as provincar, and the men will, and that will do. That's a rank they understand."

Trei made a noncommittal sound.

"We'll be fine." Ceirfei sounded amused and assured. He clapped Trei on the shoulder. "You're fine, I'm fine, the winds are sharp and clean, the day is brilliant with promise, the dragon flies above the lion. Everything will be fine."

22

Araenè opened her eyes and gazed blankly, for some time, at the ceiling of her own bedroom. It *was* her own bedroom. She recognized the pale blue plaster and dark wooden trim of the ceiling. She recognized the feel of the mattress on which she lay and the whisper of the breeze through the open window.

She felt ... she felt very strange. Hollow. As though she'd been like a pitcher, filled up with water and then emptied out again. That was an odd image. She puzzled over it for some time, gradually realizing it was sort of true. She had been filled up with dragon magic and had poured it out again. She remembered that, in a strange vague way, as though it had happened to someone else. It occurred to her that it *had* happened to someone else, in a way—that it had happened to *Trei*. Fear twisted through her, sharp and sudden, and she sat up abruptly. Then she squeezed her eyes shut, dropped her head into her hands and held perfectly still, wondering whether the top of her head was actually going to come off.

A long, cool hand touched the back of her neck, and another laid itself firmly against her forehead. "You are well enough," murmured Master Tnegun. "You merely overextended yourself a little."

His deep, smoky voice was very quiet, as though he knew exactly what Araenè was feeling. She supposed he did. She wanted to say, *A little?* but she was afraid that if she said anything at all, the sound of her own voice might be enough to shatter her skull.

Then Master Tnegun's mind brushed hers, an insubstantial touch like feathers against the inside of her head, and the pain eased.

"Better?"

Araenè risked a tiny nod. When that didn't bring the pain back, she nodded again, more firmly. That was all right, too. She blinked, cautiously. "Yes," she said, not entirely certain. "Maybe. I think so. Yes."

"Good." Master Tnegun lifted his hands. "How is your sight? Are there blotches floating in your vision? Halos around lights? How many shadows does my hand seem to cast?" He held his hand up, his fingers black as ebony against the light.

Araenè rubbed her forehead. "Everything looks normal. Well, maybe there are halos. But only faint ones. I don't know." She rubbed her head again. "You're casting only one shadow."

"Good. You were only a little overextended, after all. But with a quite unusual sort of magic, of course. A most unusual experience." Her master folded himself down to sit on the edge of her bed and looked searchingly into her eyes. "But you seem to have taken no harm from it. Though I suspect you have stretched your magic into a somewhat unusual shape. We shall be curious to see how that develops over time."

Araenè was ridiculously relieved. She hadn't actually expected Master Tnegun to be angry—anyway, maybe she had done all kinds of things that weren't approved or allowed, but she hadn't *meant* to. Or she had meant to, of course, but only because there wasn't any choice. And because—she said accusingly, "I *tried* to find you, you know."

"I know," Master Tnegun said smiling. "Be easy, young Araenè. You took quite amazingly wide actions, but you were, after all, right. You may not follow the rules, but you do, somehow, tend to be correct in your decisions." His mouth crooked in the faintest suggestion of a smile, and he glanced across the room, toward the window.

Araenè followed that glance, and stared. The window no longer showed a glimpse of her private walled garden. It now opened to the vast and empty sky. Clouds wisped past, carried by a cool breeze that wandered in and swirled gently

322

around her apartment and wandered out again. A Quei swept by, its wings and long trailing tail flashing metallic green as it flew in and out of the sunlight.

"Yes," said Master Tnegun. "I fear your garden has taken on a new and quite different purpose."

Her master didn't *sound* angry. "Master Kopapei's not ..." Araenè began, and hesitated.

"I believe you will find everyone fascinated rather than angry. I believe Kopapei in particular will be most interested in the new shape of your magic. As I am. But you may certainly take a day or three to recover yourself. Particularly since we must wait for your magic to settle into whatever new channel it has found. In the meantime," and Master Tnegun touched her forehead again, lightly, just with the tips of his fingers, and then smiled and rose. "In the meantime, perhaps I should instruct the kitchens to send up a tray? I imagine you would not care, just yet, to join everyone in the dining hall for supper."

"Everyone?" Araenè rubbed her eyes gingerly with the tips of her fingers. She couldn't face the idea of joining everyone for anything. "No, please!" And besides that ... "Is it suppertime? How long ... what time is it? What *day* is it?"

"Moon's Day," said Master Tnegun, gently. "It is Moon's Day, and it is indeed nearly suppertime. You lost two and a half days, Araenè. You're fortunate you only extended a touch too far beyond your strength. Young as you are, you'll recover quickly. Don't be concerned. We are all very interested in what you did and how you did it, but I think you will find we are all willing to wait until you are recovered before we demand your tale. And I think you will find that everyone is now perfectly satisfied that you are a proper apprentice—well, an apprentice, at least, if perhaps not entirely proper—and one who will, Gods willing, make a mage."

A mage with her magic stretched into a strange shape. Araenè might have worried about that, but she still felt too hollow and headachy to concentrate on anything. She wondered, vaguely, what the shape of dragon magic might be, if you were the sort of mage who perceived magic as geometric shapes.

"Rest, then," Master Tnegun said gently above her. He touched her cheek gently and went out, quietly, closing the door softly behind him.

Araenè leaned back against the pillows, closed her eyes and drifted.

After an unmeasured interval, a different voice said, tentatively, "Araenè?"

Opening her eyes again, Araenè blinked. Her vision was a little blurred at first, but after a moment she made out Tichorei's face. She blinked again, her vision slowly clearing.

Tichorei was holding a tray in both hands. He looked worried and a little apprehensive. "How are you?" he asked. "Are you ... all right? I brought you rice and broth. And vanilla custard."

Araenè wasn't hungry, but custard sounded good. Soothing. "Thank you."

Tichorei set the tray on a table near the bed. "Everyone's all right," he told her. "The school's all right. Milendri's fine, mostly. All kinds of people have wanted to visit you, but you were ... you know. Overextended. Recovering from overextension. You're fine now," he assured her, as though she might doubt it. "Your friend Hanaiki came. I thought you'd like to know."

Araenè sat up, not quite cautiously enough. She held very still, waiting for the dizziness to pass. But she also said, her voice sounding quick and strange to her own ears, "Hanaiki came? Here?"

Tichorei nodded. "Twice. I'll—I hope you'll allow me to escort you to that tavern, later, when you're better? Your friend—I think he'd like to know he didn't—I think he'd like to see you back there."

"Yes ..." Araenè tried to adjust to the idea that Hanaiki might still want to be friends.

"Here, do you want this custard? Your friend must have an important family," Tichorei added. "I think he got Prince Ceirfei to bring him to the school—I mean the king, of course! Or maybe your cousin—"

"Trei!" said Araenè, amazed she had forgotten her cousin. "He's not—he's—"

"He's fine," Tichorei assured her. "He came to see you, too."

Araenè got to her feet, catching at a bed post for balance. Glancing down, she found she was wearing a plain linen dress. It wasn't fancy, but it would do, if she added a belt. She looked around for one. And a comb. And earrings ... where were her earrings?

"Are you sure you should be up?" Tichorei asked, in a tone that made it clear he didn't think so. "Araenè, you should lie down. You need to be careful—"

"What?" said Araenè, distracted. "Would you hand me that belt? The green one?"

Tichorei sighed, handed her the belt, and said sternly, "You're more tired than you think! When you realize you need help getting back to your bed, call me, all right? I'll be listening, I promise. I won't tell Master Tnegun about this unless you actually collapse on your face, so don't do that!"

"Yes, of course," agreed Araenè, not really listening. "Call you. I can do that." She put out a hand and opened a door that hadn't been there a moment before.

The door opened to a wide, white room hung with violet and blue, with blue and purple flowers tumbling out the wide windows, with sapphire rugs on the gleaming marble floor and couches with cushions of amethyst and rose-pink velvet pushed back against the walls and, on the other side of the room, graceful arched doors made of thin strips of bleached and braided wood standing open to show the wide curve of a generous balcony.

Trei was there, of course. That was what Araenè had intended when she'd opened her door. And Ceirfei. She'd known *he* would be there, too, the moment she'd seen all that white and violet, those sapphire rugs and amethyst cushions. A table filled with platters of pastries and breads stood between them; the fragrance of sugar and toasted nuts filled the air.

Araenè hadn't realized she'd wanted to find Ceirfei, too, maybe almost as much as she'd wanted to find Trei, until she opened her door and found them both there, turning with pleased surprise to greet her.

"Well," said Tichorei behind her, sounding resigned, "All right, go on, then."

Araenè barely heard him. She glanced apologetically over her shoulder, but she was already stepping forward, into Ceirfei's airy palace apartment, toward the open air of the balcony. The door swung shut behind her, but she was barely aware of that, either. "You're all right," she said to Trei. There was a relaxed ease in his expression that was immediately reassuring. "You *are* all right. Your shoulders?"

Trei got to his feet and came to take her hands, moving his arms and shoulders without any sign of difficulty. "They think I'll be able to fly again. They're sure of it! There's this Tolounnese artificer—your Master Tnegun's met him. I don't think they'll like each other, exactly, but, well, I don't think that's going to matter. They're both, I don't know, I think they might be too much alike. In some ways. Anyway, *you're* all right, of course. They swore you would be, even if you wouldn't wake up. I sat with you; I really did. But Master Tnegun said he should be there when you woke up. You look tired! Here, sit down—have a pastry—have two—they're probably not as good as yours—" He made her sit in his own chair and pressed a pastry into her hands.

It was filled with rose-scented cream and decorated with crystallized rose petals, and it was every bit as good as Araenè could have made. Better, even. She bit into it contentedly, watching Trei move and gesture and fuss around, reaching for bread and spreading it with fig jam for her, with no sign that he'd ever been hurt. She didn't look at Ceirfei, not yet.

She was filled with a quiet patience that was part of the contentment, and she was happy to wait.

Trei told her about the Tolounnese soldiers, who had taken over nearly a fifth of Third City and a bit of Second, and who were showing every sign of settling in with astonishing ease.

"They're good neighbors, everyone says so; they drink but they don't brawl, and they're polite to shopkeepers and girls, and they *love* Island food. The Little Emperor says we're planning to seduce them all with pastries and those spicy little meat things on skewers, turn them all into Islanders—"

"And of course he's right," Ceirfei put in cheerfully.

"– and of course he's perfectly right," agreed Trei, just as cheerfully. "Not that they'll ever be *real* Islanders." His tone was faintly smug, exactly as though he'd been born on Milendri himself. "But they're a permanent garrison. They'll marry Island girls and their children will be much closer to Islanders—"

"They'll make particularly honorable pastries," Ceirfei said, very dry.

"And skewer those little meat things on the points of their swords," said Trei. "The Islands will have to change, too! But in some ways, that's good!" He glanced at Araenè and went on quickly, "Plus we'll never be as vulnerable again, even if Yngul stays ambitious." Then he looked across at the sun and jumped to his feet. "I'm supposed to go see Master Patan," he told Araenè apologetically. "The Tolounnese artificer. Just to make sure everything's healing the way it should. It will be! He's amazing. Come find me later, all right?" And he gave Araenè a quick hug and Ceirfei a nod that was almost a bow and darted away, taking the floating stairs that led down from the balcony to the street far below, almost running but not quite, perfectly secure in the midst of the open air. He looked, Araenè thought again, gazing after him, as though he'd been born an Islander.

"Yes," said Ceirfei, knowing exactly what she was thinking. "We'll have more like him eventually: Tolounnese-born, but Islanders at the heart. Not the soldiers themselves; they're Tolounnese to the core, and too old to change. But their children will be almost Islanders—and some of their children will be kajuraihi, and Islanders at the heart. Daughters as well as sons."

He would make sure of it, if he had to personally select some of those children to audition and order the kajuraihi to make room for them. Araenè could hear it in his tone. She smiled.

"And some of their daughters will be chefs, perhaps," Ceirfei added. "Or mages."

"Both," said Araenè. "But probably not at the same time."

"We all have to make choices," Ceirfei agreed. "No one can have everything. But, if we're fortunate, sometimes all our choices can be good ones." He rose and held out a hand to her. "You're well? I know you overextended yourself, Araenè."

"Only a little," Araenè said defensively, and laughed. She felt very calm and sure of herself and happy. "So did you!" she said.

"Not the same way," he said drily. "And it's not something I'll recover from, I fear. But that's all right. Will you come? I want to show you something." And he led her around the curving length of the balcony and stood with her at the railing, facing outward.

Away in the distance, a tiny Island floated. Araenè was almost sure it was new, and almost sure she knew exactly how it had come to be there.

"Our new Dragon Island," Ceirfei told her, confirming her guess. "The Island Araenei—we all agreed on the name. The dragons love it, evidently. There are always some there, amid the high peaks. Can you see them?"

Araenè stared out through the crystalline air and almost thought she could.

ENDNOTES

Thank you for reading The Sphere of the Winds—I hope you enjoyed it! I am sorry it took so long to bring it out. I do have an idea for where a third book could go. If I write another book set in this world, I hope it will not take ten years!

The story in which Nescana becomes a kajurai is "Audition" in the collection *Beyond the Dreams We Know*.

For a look at an entirely different world and story, turn the page.

TUYO

Raised a warrior in the harsh winter country, Ryo inGara has always been willing to die for his family and his tribe.

When war erupts against the summer country, the prospect of death in battle seems imminent. But when his warleader leaves Ryo as a sacrifice—a tuyo—to die at the hands of their enemies, he faces a fate he never imagined.

Ryo's captor, a lord of the summer country, may be an enemy ... but far worse enemies are moving, with the current war nothing but the opening moves in a hidden game Ryo barely glimses, a game in which all his people may be merely pawns. Suddenly Ryo finds his convictions overturned and his loyalties uncertain.

Should he support the man who holds him prisoner, the only man who may be able to defeat their greater enemy? And even if he does, can he persuade his people to do the same?

Turn the page to read the opening scene of TUYO.

1

Beside the coals of the dying fire, within the trampled borders of our abandoned camp, surrounded by the great forest of the winter country, I waited for a terrible death.

I had been waiting since midday. Before long, dusk would fold itself across the land. The Lau must surely come soon. I faced south, so that my death would not ride up behind me on his tall horse and see my back and think that I was afraid to face him. Also, I did not want to look north because I did not want to see that trodden snow and remember my brother leaving me behind. That might have been a different kind of cowardice. But I could only face one direction. So I faced south.

The fire burned low. My brother had built it up with his own hands before he led our defeated warriors away. Now it was only embers, and the cold pressed against my back. I wished I could build the fire up again. Mostly that was what I thought about. That was as close to thinking about nothing as I could come. It was better than thinking about the Lau. I hoped they came before the fire burned out, or I might freeze to death before they found me. Even an Ugaro will die of the cold eventually, without fire or shelter.

I tried not to hope that I would die before they found me.

Then I heard them, the hoofbeats of their horses, and there was no more time for hope. I held very still, though stillness would not protect me now. Nothing would protect me. I was not here to be protected.

They came riding between the great spruces and firs, tall dark men on tall dark horses, with the Sun device of their banner snapping overhead in the wind. Ten, twenty. Twice twenty. And even this was only the vanguard. I stood up to meet them, raising my hands to show that I was bound to a stake driven into the frozen earth—to show that I was tuyo, left here for them. They looked at me, but they rode past, down the trail my brother and our warriors had left. They rode through the remnants of our camp, around the fire and around me, and a little distance more. At first I thought they meant to leave me to die alone in this place while they went on to pursue a broader vengeance against my people. That would have been a death even more terrible than the one a tuyo should face. But then they came back and circled around me, not many paces away, looking down at me. My relief was so great that for the time it pushed away fear.

I knew immediately which must be their warleader. My people prefer silver, which is the metal that belongs to the Moon. The Lau decorate their warleaders with gold, as befits the people of the Sun. This man had gold thread worked into the collar of his coat and the backs of his gloves and the tops of his boots. He did not carry a sword or any weapon, only a polished black stick as long as a man's arm, with gold wire spiraling around its length. I had seen illustrations, so after a moment of puzzlement I recognized this as a scepter. This man was not only a warleader, but a scepter-holder, carrying the authority of the summer king. I had not known any such had come to the borderlands. At least my death would come at the hands of a worthy enemy.

The scepter-holder's horse was the color the Lau call fire bay and we call blood bay, which is common for their animals and very rare for ours. It was a fine animal. The Lau breed beautiful horses, but they belong to the summer country.

They are too long-legged and too thin-skinned for the cold of Ugaro lands.

Like their horses, the Lau are long-legged and thin-skinned, and they like the cold no better. They are a graceful people, with elegant features and smooth brown skin. Lau men often grow beards, rare for Ugaro men, but they shave them short, just to outline the jaw and mouth. The warleader had a beard like that. He had cut his hair short to match. No Ugaro man would do such a thing; for us, cropped hair is a mark of shame. We tie our hair back or leave it loose, but we do not cut it.

For a moment, while the warleader gazed down at me, the silence was almost complete. A horse picked up one foot and set it down again, and the wind blew across the snow, and leather creaked as a man shifted his weight in the saddle. Other than that, there was no sound. At last the warleader dismounted. He was far taller than I; even taller than most of his own people. He looked cruel to me, with a hard set to his mouth. I knelt and bowed my head to show the proper respect the one defeated owes to the victor.

He looked at me and then at one of his people who had come up beside him. He said to that man, "We must have pressed them even harder than we knew, if they've left a tuyo for us. I suppose this must be the son of an important Ugaro lord, but he seems merely a boy."

I must have jerked in outrage, for he turned quickly to look at me again. I said, speaking carefully in darau, "Lord, I have nineteen winters, so I am not a boy either by your law or ours. You should accept me as tuyo. No one could set any fault against you for it."

He tilted his head in surprise, perhaps at my words, or perhaps because I spoke darau at all. He asked, "What is your name? What is your father's name?"

I answered, "Lord, it is a son of Sinowa, lord of the inGara, who kneels before you in defeat. It is a brother of Garoyo, warleader of the inGara, whom you hold in your hand. My name, if you wish to know it, is Ryo. In leaving me for you, my brother acknowledges defeat. Accept me as tuyo, permit my brother and our warriors to withdraw, and my people will not challenge you again."

He nodded. But he said, "I understand that giving you to me constitutes a promise to cease hostilities. I might have trusted the efficacy of that custom when your people raided mine more rarely. Today, I don't believe I can expect much of a check in your people's aggression."

I could not protest. He was right. The war was too important for the inGara to step away from it. But I said, "Yet my people will not wish to face *you* a second time, lord, for to do so would be an offense against the gods. My father and my brother will take care to stay out of *your* way. Is that not enough?" I took a breath, making sure I could speak steadily. Then I said, "Please, lord. Let that be enough. Whatever vengeance you desire for every blow my people have struck against yours, take that vengeance on me and be satisfied."

Again a pause stretched out. The warleader looked into the forest, the way my brother had gone. Then he looked around at the long shadows and the deep forest that spread out all around that place. At last he turned back to me. He said, "Well, this is the first time anyone has ever offered me a tuyo. No doubt it will be a novelty."

"My lord, surely—" began the soldier beside him, but the warleader lifted his hand and the man fell silent.

The warleader tucked the scepter under his arm, drew a knife, and stepped toward me. I set my mind at a distance so that I would not disgrace myself or my people by flinching at the first touch of the blade. But he did not begin my death.

Instead, he cut the thong that bound me to the stake. So I understood he would take me back into the summer lands and kill me there. It meant he intended to take his vengeance at greater leisure than was possible here in the winter country, but even though I knew I should wish to have my death over and not waiting ahead of me, I could not help but be relieved at any delay.

He put the knife away and said to the man beside him, "Take him to my tent and hold him there." Then he walked away.

***

TUYO is available now.

ALSO BY RACHEL NEUMEIER

Young Adult High Fantasy

The City in the Lake, Knopf

The Floating Islands series
  The Floating Islands, Knopf
  The Sphere of the Winds

The Keeper of the Mist, Knopf

The White Road of the Moon, Knopf

Adult High Fantasy

The Griffin Mage trilogy:
  The Lord of the Changing Winds, Orbit
  The Land of Burning Sands, Orbit
  The Law of the Broken Earth, Orbit

The House of Shadows duology
  House of Shadows, Orbit
  Door into Light

The Mountain of Kept Memory, Simon and Schuster

Winter of Ice and Iron, Simon and Schuster

The Tuyo series
  Tuyo
  Nikoles

Tarashana, forthcoming spring 2021
Karanauni, forthcoming 2022
Untitled 5th book, forthcoming

Urban Fantasy

The Black Dog series
  Black Dog
  Black Dog Short Stories
  Pure Magic
  Black Dog Short Stories II
  Shadow Twin
  Black Dog Short Stories III
  Copper Mountain
  Black Dog Short Stories IV, forthcoming
  Untitled fifth book, forthcoming

Collections

Beyond the Dreams We Know

.

Manufactured by Amazon.ca
Bolton, ON

30463690R00192